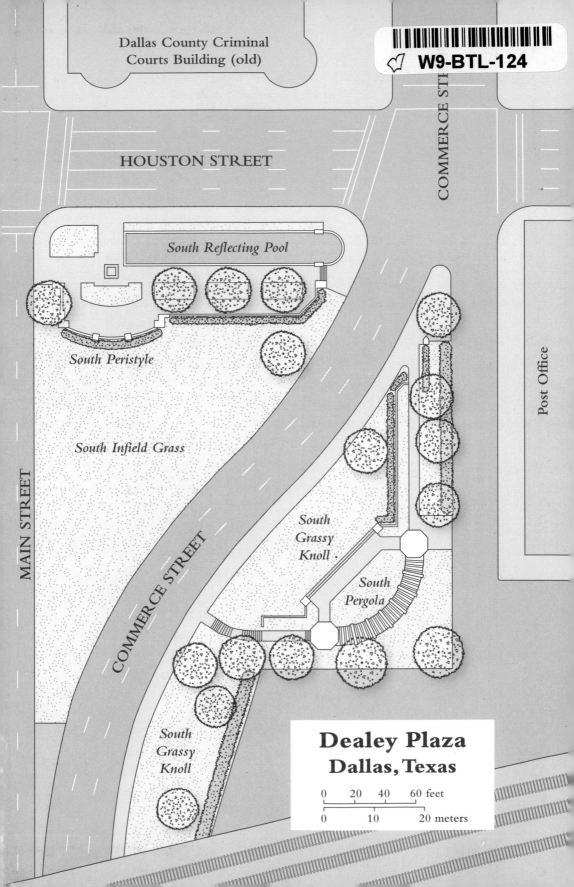

Dallas County Criminal
Courts Building (old)

HOUSTON STREET

COMMERCE STREET

South Reflecting Pool

South Peristyle

South Infield Grass

COMMERCE STREET

MAIN STREET

Post Office

*South
Grassy
Knoll*

*South
Pergola*

*South
Grassy
Knoll*

Dealey Plaza
Dallas, Texas

0	20	40	60 feet

0	10	20 meters

The Third Bullet

A BOB LEE SWAGGER NOVEL

Stephen Hunter

Simon & Schuster

NEW YORK   LONDON   TORONTO   SYDNEY   NEW DELHI

Simon & Schuster
1230 Avenue of the Americas
New York, NY 10020

First Simon & Schuster hardcover edition January 2013

SIMON & SCHUSTER and colophon are registered
trademarks of Simon & Schuster, Inc.

For information about special discounts for bulk purchases,
please contact Simon & Schuster Special Sales at
1-866-506-1949 or business@simonandschuster.com.

The Simon & Schuster Speakers Bureau can bring authors to
your live event. For more information or to book an event,
contact the Simon & Schuster Speakers Bureau at
1-866-248-3049 or visit our website at www.simonspeakers.com.

Text designed by Paul Dippolito

Endpaper map by Paul Pugliese

Manufactured in the United States of America

1   3   5   7   9   10   8   6   4   2

Library of Congress Cataloging-in-Publication Data

Hunter, Stephen.
The third bullet : a Bob Lee Swagger novel / Stephen Hunter.
—1st Simon & Schuster hardcover ed.
p. cm.
1. Swagger, Bob Lee (Fictitious character)—Fiction. 2. Marines—Fiction. 3. Snipers—Fiction.
4. Kennedy, John F. (John Fitzgerald), 1917–1963—Assassination—Fiction. I. Title.
PS3558.U494T47 2013
813'.54—dc22
2012014575

ISBN 978-1-4516-4020-5
ISBN 978-1-4516-4025-0 (ebook)

For late-in-life friends who've made it so much better:

Gary Goldberg
Jay Carr
Ed DeCarlo
Frank Starr
Roger Troup

I think it's time we stop, children, what's that sound?
Everybody look what's going down.

—"FOR WHAT IT'S WORTH,"
BUFFALO SPRINGFIELD

PART I

U.S.A.

"There's something happening here"

CHAPTER 1

Baltimore

The sidewalk before him bucked and heaved, blown askew by high winds howling through the night.

Oh, wait. No. Let's edit that. There was no bucking and heaving. Ditto with the "blown askew" and the "high winds howling through the night."

It just seemed so to Aptapton, because the winds that toyed with the stability of the sidewalk blew—"howled"—only through his own mind. They were zephyrs of vodka, and they'd substantially loosened his grip on the solidity of the little chunk of earth that lay between the bar he'd just exited and the house where he lived, a few hundred yards ahead.

Aptapton: alcoholic, writer, success, melancholiac, and gun guy, was in a zone that might be called greater than a buzz but less than a full staggering drunk. He was one sheet to the wind, you might say, happyhappyhappyhappy, as three vodka martinis will do to a fellow with only moderate capacity for drink, and what lay ahead, although slightly challenging, didn't really seem insurmountable. After all, he had to walk only another few feet, cross the street, and then—

Digression. Pause for autobiographical interlude. It's allowed when under the influence. One thing suggests another, and in this case the suggestion is appropriate.

The street was called Light, and that suggested a kind of hopeful conclusion to the evening. Light as in light of heart, light of spirit, light at end of tunnel, light as in amusing, fey, witty, light as symbol of hope and life. But also: Light as in Light for All, as a famous newspaper, located a mile or so up the very same Light Street, had proclaimed on a daily basis for 175 years or so, twenty-six of which he'd spent in its employ and where his wife to this day toiled.

Yes, he was *that* James Aptapton, minor local journo celeb who'd gone on to minor fame as a writer for money of hardcover books about gunfights and the stoic heroes who won them, and now he found himself at sixty-five improbably successful (in a small way) and awkwardly pleased to be himself. He had it all: beautiful wife, a couple of mil, a nice house in a fabulous part of town, a minor reputation (enough to take some pleasure in), a grand future, a munificent multibook contract, a really cool project ahead, and a lot of guns.

The reason for the three vodka martinis was liberation, not celebration. His wife was absent, ha ha ha, too bad for her. She was at some newsroom woman thing, birthday party, maybe—why did women take birthdays so *seriously*, by the way?—and so he'd wandered on his own to the nearby bistro, had a burger with a Bud and then V.1, which weakened his resolve to resist V.2, which shattered his resolve to resist V.3. Fortunately, there'd been no V.4, or he'd be asleep in the men's room.

Now.

Where was I before digression?

What place is this?

Where am I now?

Ha ha ha ha.

Oh yes: home is the hunter. He. Was. Walking. Home.

The street slanted, then rolled. Ahead, it humped up, then dipped down to permit a view of the valley. It rocked. It rolled. It shook, it rattled, it coiled, it double-bubbled, boiled, and troubled.

He laughed.

Do you find yourself amusing? his wife always asked, and the truth was, yes, he did find himself amusing.

The mood, like the geography, chemically amplified by red potato crushed by kulak descendants, was quite good. *That* James Aptapton had been recognized. It happened. Rare, but not without precedent for your minor-league non-qual-lit celeb.

"Mr. Aptapton?"

Halfway through V.3, he'd looked up to see an earnest young fellow, possibly the assistant manager.

"I just wanted to say, I've read all your books. My dad turned me on to them. I really, really love them."

"Well," said Aptapton, "say, thanks so much."

The young man sat and gushed Aptapton love for a bit, and Aptapton tried to give him a meaningful Aptapton experience. The transaction worked out well for both of them, in fact, and at the bottom of V.3, a pause in the praise gave Aptapton the time to gracefully excuse himself, bid Tom? maybe Jack? possibly Sam? good-bye and make his exit. So his mood was mellow and radiant. He'd cross Light Street here, and only the narrow alley called Churchill lay between himself and horizontality in bed, his destination.

The Russian watched from the stolen black Camaro parked on Light. This looked to be the night. He'd been stalking for three days now, in his patient, professional way, and part of his talent lay in understanding exactly when the arrangements favored him and when they did not.

Thus, a police scanner played out its truncated cop-speak ten-code and laconic locality identifiers, and it suggested no police presence here in the immediate Federal Hill area. Thus, it was late enough that the action in this night-town district had played itself out and the streets, though glistening with dew, were largely empty, and only periodic parties of drunken twentysomethings rolled this way and that. Thus, finally, the target had emerged, functionally reduced by alcohol intake and self-love, and bobbed his way along the street.

The Russian saw a man in jeans and a tweed coat with a pair of writer-like glasses, Trotsky out of Orwell by way of Armani or some such. You saw glasses like that in New York. The man had a round, pleased face, bearded after Hemingway and to disguise jowls, narcissism blasting out of him more powerfully than any other human attribute. Expensive shoes. Nice shoes. A well-turned-out fellow.

Barring the unforeseen arrival of some whimsical force that favors thriller writers above all others in the world, it was probably going to happen tonight. The Russian did not believe in whimsical forces: he believed only in the power of a fast car to break the spine of a poor unsuspecting fool like this one a hundred times out of a hundred times. He had seen it, he had done it, he had the nerve and the cool and the coldness of heart to do such damage without a lot of emotional involvement. He was a professional and well paid.

The target for tonight, joints loosened by the alcohol, managed to get himself across Light Street without falling. He navigated with that overcontrol typical of the drunk. Great forward movement, momentum building, but without the capacity of adaptation; he arrived at where he tended, not at where he aimed, and at the last, lurching moment, he bumbled through a sideways correction, a sort of exaggerated funny-walk bit.

All of this meant nothing to the Russian, who found nothing funny. He noted distances, angles, and surfaces as a way of computing acceleration rates into speed on impact. The Russian prosaically jacked two wires together in the torn-out key unit of the dashboard, and the beast of a car stirred to life. He was not showy or stylized, so there was no gunning of the engine to allow the horses under the hood to roar and the exhaust pipes to bellow steamy toxins. He eased into first, nudged his way into the empty street, and waited just a bit, because he needed at least three seconds of acceleration time in the alley to get to fifty miles per hour, which was the killing impact.

On either side, there was nothing but Baltimore. At the mouth of Churchill, a church to one side and a typical Baltimore row house meant for the miniature people of the 1840s to the other, Aptapton re-aimed himself and pressed onward down the concourse. It was listed as a street in city records but had been constructed as an alley many years ago, its tiny brick dwellings serving as servants' quarters or backyard administrative units for the larger houses that faced outward to prouder, wider streets. For a hundred years this back way had probably been the province of pig and horse shit commingled with blood and Negro or immigrant sweat, where the invisible servers lived to sustain the opulent ease of those in the big houses. Then it became the inevitable slum, but that condition never quite went terminal, as the dwellings were too cute for demolition. Now, of course, gentrification had come in the form of museum-quaint cobblestones, which gleamed moistly as if at an art director's bidding, little mock-gaslight streetlamps, lots of gardening and painting and each tiny building essentially remanufactured from the inside out, so that they had become nesting sites for the young urban hip. Aptapton, *that* Aptapton, began to amuse himself by inventing sexual perversions he imagined were ongoing on either side of Churchill. Then he heard the sound of a car engine.

Agh. This meant he'd have to re-adjust his somewhat sloppily functioning internal gyro and get himself off the cobblestones and onto the little shelf of sidewalk. He heard basso profundo, deep-chest utters, and turned.

He made out the streamlined form of the Camaro one hundred feet away and felt himself seized in its illumination. A friendly type always, he raised a hand and smiled, and indicated that he yielded to superior power and would manfully attempt to arrive upon the threshold of the curb. At the same time the whole thing reminded him of something, and it froze him in place as his mind examined its files.

Finally, it came to him: an image from one of his own books.

Didn't he do one where the bad guy, some kind of car genius, used Camaros and Chargers and Trans-Ams to take people out? He'd thought he ought to get away from guns for a bit, and so he'd moved on to the high-pro muscle car as weapon of choice. Nobody seemed to like it very much, however. He'd also tried swords in one, to much chagrin. He was a gun guy, so he did best when he stuck to his guns.

Anyway, this was setting up sort of like a scene in *Thunder's Evening,* as the one had been called, and he had to laugh ("Are you amused by yourself?") at the thing at the end of the alley, hazy in the glare of its headlights but sleek and black and damp, the odd refraction of street- and houselights playing magically off its shiny skin, film noir to the very end.

It's from my id! he thought.

In the next second it accelerated.

It came at a speed he'd never imagined possible, as if it had gone into warp drive, blurring the stars, and well before this information could be processed, he was airborne.

He was airborne.

There was no pain, though the blow he'd been delivered must have been a mighty thud. Again, when he rejoined Earth in a heap of breakage and ruin, there was no pain. He lay askew on the cobblestones, thinking, Oh, she's going to be so mad at me, because he knew he was in big trouble with his wife.

CHAPTER 2
Idaho

I n Cascade, everybody goes to Rick's. Even Swagger.

He showed up every once in a while, maybe three, four times a month, preceded by myth, isolated by reputation, and cloaked in diffidence. He sat alone, if he came, at the counter, and had a couple of cups of coffee, black. Jeans, old boots, some kind of jacket, and a faded red Razorbacks ball cap. He could have been a drifter or a trucker or a rancher or a gunfighter. The body was rangy, without fat, slightly tense, also radiating signals of damage. He always arrived, if he was to arrive at all, at 5 a.m. with the ranchers. It was said he had trouble sleeping—said, that is, by Swagger watchers, since the man himself spoke hardly a word—and if he was still awake when the sun cracked the edge of the world, he'd drive from his place out on 144 to Rick's, not so much to join in the community but to reassure himself that community was there.

That was pretty much Rick's purpose in the general scheme of things. The food wasn't much—it was primarily a breakfast place whose short-order cook knew every way to wreck an egg and had the gift for the right fusion of crunch, grease, and chew to pan-fried potatoes—and the early risers—who drove the Cascade economy, paid the taxes, hired the Mexicans, guided hunters for a week or so in the fall, and plowed the roads—always stopped there to fuel up for whatever the long day of honest labor held in store. Swagger, though no glad-hander, seemed to like the company, to enjoy the ranch badinage and the talk of Boise State football and the weather complaints, because he knew no fool would come up to him with questions or requests or offers, and that these sinewy gentlemen, themselves joshers but not speech givers, always played by the rules.

As for them, they knew only what they'd heard, though they weren't sure where they heard it. War hero. Retired marine. Lots of deep-grass stuff in a war that we lost. Supposedly the best shot in the West, or at any rate, a hell of a shot. Gun guy, got a lot of stuff from Midway USA and Brownells. A late-arriving daughter, Japanese by birth, who was the twelve-and-under girls roping champ and seemed born to horseback. Beautiful wife, kept to self, running the barns the family owned in three or was it four states. Business success. Knew of the big world and chose to live in this one. Out of a movie, someone said, and someone else said, Except they don't make them kinds of movies no more, and everybody laughed and agreed.

That was the easy truce that reigned at Rick's, and even Rick and his two gals, Shelly and Sam, seemed okay with it. That is, until the Chinese woman showed up.

Well, possibly she wasn't Chinese. She was Asian, of an indefinite age somewhere between young and not young, with a strong nose and dark, smart eyes that could pierce steel if she so desired. Though she seldom showed it, she had a smile that could break hearts and change minds. She was short, rather busty, and looked pretty damned tough for someone who was probably soft in all the right places.

She showed at 5, took a seat at the counter, ordered coffee, and read something on her Kindle for two hours. At 7, she left. Nice tipper. Pleasant, distant, not an outreacher, but at the same time completely unfazed by the masculine brio of the 5 a.m. ranch crowd at Rick's.

She came every day for two weeks, never missing, never reaching out, maintaining her silence and her secrecy. It didn't take the fellows long to figure out that none of them was of interest to a crafty, contained beauty, so she had to be there for Swagger. She was stalking him. A reporter, a book writer, a Hollywood agent, somebody who saw a way to make some bucks from whatever secrets Swagger's war mask of a face concealed without murmur or tremor. Yet when he came in, she made no move toward him, nor he—he noticed her instantly, as he noticed everything instantly—toward her. They sat with an empty stool between them at the counter, each drinking black coffee, while she read and he ruminated or remembered or whatever it was he did when he came in.

This ritual continued for another week or two, and it consumed the Cascade gossip circuits, such as they were. Finally, almost as if to satisfy the town gabbers instead of any genuine impulse of his own, he walked over to her. "Ma'am?"

"Yes?" she said, looking up. In the light, he saw that she was quite beautiful.

"Ma'am, it seems the fellows here believe you're in town to have a chat with a man named Swagger. I'm Swagger."

"Hello, Mr. Swagger."

"I wanted to spare you any more trouble, because I imagine you've got better places than Rick's in Cascade, Idaho, to spend your time. I have essentially retired from the world, and if you're here to see me, I have to disappoint you. I don't see anyone. My wife, my daughters, and my son, that's about it. I just sit on a rocking chair and watch the sun move across the sky. I don't do a thing no more. My wife does the work. So whatever it is you want, I'm sparing you the time by telling you it's probably not going to happen. And this is more than I've said in a year, so I better stop while I'm ahead."

"That's fine, Mr. Swagger," she said. "Time isn't the issue. I'll stay years if I have to. I'm in this for the long haul."

He didn't know what to say in response. He just knew he had no need whatsoever to go back to what he called, in the argot of that war so many years ago, The World. Each time he went, it seemed to cost him. The last time it had cost him a woman he'd allowed himself to care about, and he did not relish a revisit to that grief, at least during waking hours. He had enough to worry about with two daughters and a son, and at sixty-six, with a steel ball for a hip, enough scar tissue across his raggedy old body to show up on satellites, and so many memories of men dying, he needed no more adventures, no more losses, no more grief. He was afraid of them.

Then she said, "I know about you and what you did in the war. It seems to be a profession that prizes patience. You sit, you wait. You wait, you wait, you wait. Isn't that right?"

"Waiting is a part of it, yes ma'am."

"Well, I can do nothing to impress you. I can't shoot, ride, climb, or fight. No book I've read would amaze you, no accomplishment I've achieved would register on your radar screen. But I will show you patience. I will wait you out. This week, the next, this month, the next, on and on. I will wait you out, Mr. Swagger. I will impress you with my patience."

It was a terrific answer, one he'd never counted on. He let no emotion cross the Iron Age shield that was his face. Possibly he blinked those lizard eyes, or ran tongue over dried lips, as he was a dry old coot, wary and contained, who made noise when he moved because one adventure or another had left him with a limp, and even if the wind and the sun had turned his face the color of Navajo pottery, his eyes had somehow bled themselves of color and were reptilian irises, untainted by empathy.

"Yes ma'am," he said. "So we'll wait each other out."

It took over three weeks. Each time he showed, he thought she'd be gone. But there she was, tucked away in the corner, not looking up, her face illuminated by the glow of the reading machine or whatever it was. He skipped for ten days straight and assumed that would surely drive her away. It did not.

Finally, halfway into the fourth week, she went to her rented car in the general cloud of pickups pulling out for the day's first duty station and found his truck, a black Ford F-150, next to hers. He lounged against its fender, ropy and lean in his baseball cap, a high-plains drifter, a Shane, a truck driver off the interstate.

"All right," he said. "If you were in this for money, you'd be long gone. If you're crazy, the jabbering of those old men in this joint would have sent you off to the nut bin. What I'm getting is some kind of stubborn in you that usually equals high purpose. You win. I'll give you what you want, as much as I can and stay my own man."

"It's not much," she said. "No, no money, no contracts, no angles. I'm not from a big flashy city, just a blue-collar rust bucket called Baltimore. I want your judgment, that's all. You know things I don't. I want to put something before you, and then I want you to tell me if it's anything or if it's craziness, coincidence, whatever. That's all, except I forgot the best part: it's very dull and boring."

"All right," he said, "you have earned the right to bore me. I can be bored, it's not a problem. Can you meet me at the T.G.I.F.'s off the interstate in Iron Springs tomorrow at two? It's a craphole, but it's crowded and loud and nobody'll notice a thing. We'll drink coffee and talk. I chose that place because I don't want the old goats in this place all giddy over seeing us."

"Fair enough, Mr. Swagger. I'll see you there."

She was punctual and found him sitting in a booth in the rear of the gaudy place, whose cheesy cheerfulness seemed in counterpoint to his grave countenance and all the hollows and planes of his tight old face, with its deltas of fissure extending from each eye like the broken cataracts of an ancient river of kings. Or maybe, sans the warrior romance, he was just a beat-to-hell old guy. Meanwhile, the kind of citizen who defines the interstate as freedom and paradise swirled and bobbed through the busy place, raising clamor, eating ice cream, yelling at children, and exhibiting all the discontents of motorized civilization that one can manage.

"Ma'am? Say, I don't even have a name for you."

She sat across from him. "My name is Jean Marquez. I'm Filipino by heritage, born and raised here. I am a journalist by profession, though this is not about a story, and I'm not working for my newspaper. I'm the daughter of two doctors, fifty-five years old, and a widow."

"I'm sorry to hear of your loss, Ms. Marquez. I've lost some very close people and understand the hurting."

"I thought you might. Anyhow, you should call me Jean. Everybody does. My husband was named James Aptapton. Does that name mean anything?"

"Hmm," he said, and somehow, yes, it did. His mind and face fogged in search, and finally, he said, "I'm coming up with some kind of writer. Wrote about snipers? Knew guns, is that right? Don't believe I ever met the fellow or read his books, but I'd run into the name here and there. I'd get asked, now that I remember, if *I* was some hero he wrote about, Billy Don Trueheart, something like that?"

"Something like that. Yes, Jim was a gun guy. He was one of those men who loved guns, and if you lived with him for twenty years, as I did, you got used to guns everywhere. He eventually got wealthy enough to spend seventeen thousand dollars on a Thompson machine gun. If you want to rent a Thompson machine gun, let me know. I can let you have one at an affordable daily rate."

"I'll bear that in mind, but I hope my Thompson days are long over."

"Anyhow, the guns everywhere, the gun magazines, the biographics of people like Elmer Keith and John M. Browning, the dead animal heads, all that, that was who he was, and I knew that going in and accepted it. His politics, never, but the gun thing, it was okay because he was also funny about it, as he was funny about everything. He was also kind, and even when he became successful, he never turned into an asshole and stayed true and decent to his kids and my family and his mother and the people he knew. It was never about getting to the table where the cool kids sat. It was about buying guns, drinking vodka, and making people laugh. Everyone who knew him is missing him and will for a long time."

"Is this about his death?"

"Yes. The idiot went to a bar one night and had three instead of the allowed one martini. He walked home, reflexes all messed up, and managed to get himself killed by a hit-and-run driver. It was merciful, they say, he went fast."

"I'm sorry. Did they catch the driver?"

"No. That's part of the issue. It seems that over two thousand people a year are killed by hit-and-runs, and about ninety-eight percent of those cases are solved. There are those that aren't, and it is remotely possible that he was murdered. I know, I know, it was probably some kid high on meth in a hopped-up car who saw an old guy staggering down the street and stomped on the pedal. For kicks, for laughs, for the warm and fuzzy memories, I don't know. But . . . maybe not."

"I have had experience with a man who killed by car. It's more than possible. Driven by a professional, it can be a lethal instrument. I suppose you're going to tell me why this could be a murder."

"I am. We are at the boring part. Maybe you'd better pour yourself a cup of coffee."

"I like your husband. I like you. It's fine. Go on, try to bore me."

"As I say, it's a story in which almost nothing happens. It has no vivid characters, no sudden turns of fate, no dramatic reversals, no humor, no drama. It's about something that happened in a workplace a long time ago."

"So far, so good."

"It can't be verified. It's hazy in parts. It might be a hoax, though it's so dreary, I can't imagine how anyone could gain anything off it. I don't have the exact dates. It was first told in a letter, then years later in another letter, then years after that in a third letter. I've read none of the letters, and the passage of time between each installment suggests the erosion of failing memory. On top of that, my only experience with it was as told to me by my husband, and I must confess I didn't pay much attention, so my own memory is questionable as well. All in all, as evidence of a crime, it's a pretty pathetic deal."

"It must linger?"

"It does indeed linger. People can't quite put it aside. They think they have, and go about their lives, and then it comes back in the middle of the night and pokes them awake. It did that to the three letter writers and to my late husband. It did it to me enough times that I found out about a Mr. Bob Lee Swagger and tracked him to a flyspeck diner in a dying wide-spot in the road called Cascade, Idaho, and invested close to two months in earning an audience with him."

"The lingering part is very interesting. So far, you've got me hooked."

"We start with a young man, a recent graduate of an engineering school in Dallas, Texas. The time is unknown, but I'm guessing mid-seventies. He's smart, ambitious, hardworking, decent. He wants to join a construction firm and engineer giant buildings. The first job he gets is entry-level, for an elevator contractor."

"Elevators?"

"Right. Not exactly the glamour trade. But elevators, which we all take for granted, are heavily engineered. That is, they are overdesigned, overmaintained, overregulated, and no one involved with them takes them for granted. His firm installs them and maintains them on contract so they can pass their yearly examinations and don't drop ten people fifty stories."

"Sounds reasonable."

"It's hard, crummy work. The shafts and 'engine' rooms, as they call the motor and pulley devices that make them run, are dark, poorly ventilated, and not air-conditioned. Even more so back then. The space is cramped, and it involves a lot of twisting and bending to get access. The work is intensive and highly pressurized, because the building managers hate it when they have to shut down the elevators and the tenants hate it and everybody hates it. Are you getting a picture?"

"I am."

"This young man and his crew are in the engine room on the roof of a particular building, and they've set up lights, and they're measuring cable wear, gear wear, electrical motor wear, lubricating, trying to work fast so they can get the box, as they call it, back in service. It's hot, crowded, and except for the light beams, dark. Not pleasant, not happy, and suddenly—kaboom."

"Kaboom?"

"One of the workers, maybe resting, maybe backing away to make room for someone else, maybe doing whatever you do in an elevator engine room, bumps into something on the wall, and there's a loud crash and the sound of stuff falling to the ground, a big cloud of acrid dust, everybody's coughing and wheezing. All the flashlights go onto it, and they discover that he's bumped into a shelf on the wall, and for whatever reason—the screws rusted or came out, the brick or stucco or whatever gave way, the metal itself sheared—when he jostled it, it collapsed, dumping its pile of whatever was stored there to the ground. That's the action scene, by the way. The shelf falling, that's as exciting as it gets."

"My heart's beating so fast, I can hardly stand it."

"Here's the really boring part. They figure out what's wrong with the shelf, and somehow get it remounted, and start restacking the stuff on it. The stuff is carpet remnants. That is, the lobby of the building has a big carpet, and they ended up with remnants that they had to keep around for patching or whatever, so they had a shelf in the engine room and someone decided that would be a good out-of-the-way place to store the remnants."

"Sounds pretty top-secret to me."

"And someone says, 'Hey, look at this.' Be cool if it was a rifle, huh? Or a box of ammo, a telescopic sight, a spy radio, something really James Bond?"

"That would be very interesting."

"Sorry. It's just a coat. I told you it was a boring story."

"It ain't without interest. Please go on."

"It turns out to be a man's overcoat, XL, tan gabardine, fairly high-quality, in extremely good condition. Maybe almost new. It had been methodically folded and slid into the pile of carpet remnants in the engine room sometime in the past. Again, no dates, no specifics, nothing."

"I've got it," said Swagger.

"They unfold it and immediately make a discovery. It stinks. Unfolding it puts out some kind of chemical stench, very unpleasant. Flashlights go onto it. It seems that the left breast wears a rather gaudy petro or chemical stain, and even now, who knows how many years later, the odor of that stain is powerful. It hasn't gone away. Instead of finding a free coat, they've found a fixer-upper, which would involve dry cleaning, which might or might not get the stain and the smell out, and no one is interested, and so it goes into the trash. It is thrown out. It disappears. It is gone forever. End of story. Not much of a story, is it?"

"No, but I give you it's got some moments," Bob said. Somewhere in his rat-pointed tactical brain, he was beginning to play with them. Something had been subtly provoked. Dallas. Abandoned overcoat. Strange smell and stain.

"Okay," she said. "The Engineer is promoted, and he leaves the firm and goes to that big construction outfit. Again, he is promoted, because he's very intelligent and hardworking. He's the type that built America. He becomes a partner. He marries his high school girlfriend, they have three beautiful daughters and move to the suburb where partners live. He joins a country club. He becomes venerable. His daughters marry wonderful men. I'm actually making up the details, but you get the picture. One of the daughters becomes engaged to the son of a rancher, another prosperous fellow. The Rancher and his wife invite the Engineer and the wife out for a get-to-know-you weekend and barbecue. They're sitting there in the big paneled living room looking out the picture window to the swimming pool and the white horse fences and the green meadows, and the Engineer notices something: dead animals all over the place.

Turns out the Rancher is a hunter. He's been all over the world. Lions and tigers and bears. Ibexes and sables and kudus. They're all drinking highballs and having a good old time and the Rancher says, 'Say, Don, care to see the shop?'

"Don nods and off they go. They walk into a big gun place. Guns, heads, safes, benches, targets, photos of men with dead animals, maybe an old Marilyn calendar, tools, all that, the sort of thing my husband had, although I'm guessing this Rancher kept his a lot neater than my husband did. And whammo, the Engineer is hit by an odor. It's an old, old odor. I don't know if you know it, but psychologists consider olfactory cues the strongest reminders. A smell can take you back to a time and place and re-create cues to all the other senses. So suddenly, you're back where you were when you first hit that smell, and of course, Don is back in the engine room of the elevator in that building in Dallas thirty-odd years ago."

"GI or Hoppe's 9?" Bob asked.

"Hoppe's," she said. "Yes. Barrel solvent. Chemical cleaning fluid especially for guns. Been around since the twenties. That's what Don smells in his new pal's shop, and he realizes that's what he smelled all those years ago in the building that I of course didn't name."

"You're going to tell me it was the Texas Book Depository?"

"If only. No, it's the building across Houston Street from the Texas Book Depository. It's called the Dal-Tex Building. It was there in 1963 too. Dal-Tex doesn't mean Dallas, Texas, but Dallas Textiles, as it was the headquarters of the Dallas wholesale garment industry. Actually, Abraham Zapruder's office was there, along with a hundred other offices. Nothing particularly special except that it did offer close to the same angle and elevation down Elm Street next to Dealey Plaza that our friend Lee Harvey Oswald used. You can see why it lingers."

"I can," said Bob, trying to conjure the structure from a rush of image memories of Dealey Plaza, that triangle of grass at the heart of American darkness. He got nothing, no vision, no sense of place.

"It's figured in a few of the thousand conspiracy theories. I checked into them; none of them are that interesting or convincing. Someone claims that a photo shows a rifle on a tripod on the fireplace, but it's just shadows. There were some 'arrests' after the building was closed down a few minutes after the shooting, but nothing came of them. Some people claim without evidence that it was one of the nine or is it twelve shooting sites that the CIA, Sears, Roebuck, the Canadian Air Force, and Proctor and Gamble used in their conspiracy. All in all, it's not much."

Bob nodded.

"But it lingers," she continued. "For the Engineer, particularly. He can't get it out of his mind. You see why, don't you?"

"The Hoppe's suggests that someone had need to clean a rifle, which suggests the presence of a rifle. And you can assume the juice was somehow spilled or leaked onto the coat during the cleaning process. But the coat was carefully hidden, as if whoever had spilled the Hoppe's, with its chemical smell, didn't want it exposed to the public eye or nose. Lots of folks in Texas would recognize it right away, including most policemen. It was the universal gun cleaner then. All this could have happened on or around November 22, 1963. There's your lingering. It puts a rifle where there ain't been one. But it is thin. It's real thin."

"It gets thinner. A few more years pass. The Engineer doesn't know what to do about it. He's no dummy; he gets how thin it is too, way too thin to take to law enforcement. Then he reads a book. The book is called *Shootout on Pennsylvania*. It was written by my husband and a friend. It's the story of an assassination attempt on Harry Truman in 1950 that ended up in a gunfight in the middle of the street in the middle of the day in the middle of downtown Washington, right across from the White House. Two men dead, three wounded. Almost totally forgotten. Anyhow, the Engineer reads the book. He reads in particular about a Secret Service agent named Floyd Barring, who was in command of the watch at Blair House, where the fight happened, and was considered the hero. He shot one of the bad guys in the head and took him down and maybe saved Harry Truman's life. The Engineer finds from the book that Floyd is still alive and that, thirteen years after being a hero in Washington, he was the agent in charge of the Secret Service advance party for the Dallas trip, and was in Dallas for the assassination and testified before the Warren Commission and all that. The Engineer takes a shine to Floyd, who seems upright, decent, hardworking, committed. Since Floyd is retired yet invested in the assassination, he seems like a candidate to hear the Engineer's tale. So here's the first letter: the Engineer writes to Floyd and details everything I have laid out to you."

"You never read the letter, however."

"Not even close. I'm telling you more or less what I later heard from Jim when I wasn't listening hard."

Swagger nodded, seeing the old agent getting the thick packet from an unknown person in Dallas and slowly considering its contents. "What did this Secret Service guy do?"

"For whatever reason, nothing. In fact, he probably threw it out. Crazy Kennedy bullshit, you know the drill. He was sick of it, as he'd figured in some theories too, and he didn't like it. He was also in ill health, living in a geriatric apartment in Silver Spring, mourning the death of his wife, and knew he didn't have much time."

"I see."

"Yet it lingered. He couldn't put it out of his mind. A few years after that, he writes a letter—half a letter—to my husband. He never finishes it. He never sends it. Maybe he thinks better of it. Who knows? Anyway, he dies. And that would seem to be that. No more lingering. The lingering is over. But then: his daughter finds the letter a few years later. So she sends it on to Jim. So years after the coat was found, years after the identity of the smell was discovered, years after it was communicated to a retired Secret Service agent, years after he died, courtesy of his daughter, it was sent to my husband."

"And he sees the possibilities?"

"More than most. He's looking for a project. He has a contract that calls for a book a year, he's just finished one, but there's no rest for the wicked, and when he gets the half-written letter that Floyd almost sent him concerning the lost letter the Engineer sent to Floyd, he sees something. He spends a few days researching, looking at maps, reading books or at least examining them, and then he has some kind of eureka moment. He claims he's solved the JFK assassination. I suspect vodka played a part. It turns out he means he has an idea no one else has had. And he has to go to Dallas. And so he goes to Dallas."

"Was he successful?"

"He talked to a bunch of people, I think he got into Dal-Tex, he came back very excited. He started working like a madman. One day a week later, he goes off to a bar for a drink and ends up with a broken back and pelvis in an alley."

"You think he was killed because he was looking into a certain idea about JFK's death?"

"I haven't said that. I've spoken only in facts, and the fact is that now *I'm* the world's sole possessor of the story. And it lingers. I can't get it out of my head, and the connection between it and Jim's immediate death by possible homicide won't let me sleep at night. I have to do every last thing to make sure that the story is properly processed. Someone has to deal with it, judge it, assess it, contextualize it, someone who knows this stuff and has worked in this world. I have nominated you for that high honor. So now I ask the question I came all this way for. *Is it anything?*"

He let out a large breath.

"What does that signify?" she asked. "You think I'm an idiot? The whole thing is nonsense? What a colossal waste of time?"

"No. I can see how it provokes. I ain't denying that. And I'm not saying I'm a hundred percent Warren Commission lone-gunman guy. I haven't looked at it hard enough, but I do think, like you, that a lot of the 'theories' are stuff people dreamed up to make a buck. I also think that the thing has been looked at so much by so many people for so long that it's highly unlikely there's anything left unfound."

"Fair enough."

"Let me put it before you in a different way, all right? I think you're missing something, and I think your husband missed it and Floyd missed it, all the way back to the Engineer. That thing you all missed is Texas. Texas is gun country. You may have to explain why you have a gun in Baltimore, but you sure don't in Texas. *Everyone* has a gun in Texas. They have 'em to wear to barbecues or the opera or the swim meet. Nobody blinks an eye, and that was especially true down there then, before JFK. Nobody thought a thing about a gun. It just was, that's all. The presence of a gun in that building isn't remarkable. In fact, it's nothing. I can think of a hundred reasons for a gun in that building other than killing a president. Maybe some boys were heading out for deer season straight from work. Save time, get there opening-day morning. They brought their rifles in, and one of them knew his needed cleaning, so he does the job. Nobody says a thing because it ain't remarkable. He leans the gun in a corner and it rubs up against somebody's coat. When that guy gets his coat, he sees it's ruined, it goes into the wastebasket, and later that night the janitor finds it and decides to scavenge it. He hangs it up to dry out, but Hoppe's being powerful, the stink never does go away. So he stuffs it somewhere, meaning to check it out later, and forgets about it. Years later, the elevator people discover it. That could have happened not just for deer season but in pheasant season too, as they kill a lot of them birds down there, and doves and pigeons and anything that flies. So you have found the suggestion of a gun in a building in Texas, and it surprises you only because you don't know guns or Texas."

"I see," she said.

"Ma'am—Jean, if I may—you've got what the Marine Corps would call intelligence that doesn't rise to the actionable level. It doesn't carry enough meaning to be acted on. There are too many other possibilities here for anyone to do anything about it. My best advice is to congratulate yourself for following up on your duty to your husband and then go back to your life. I think your husband would have found that out in time too. Maybe he could do something with his discovery if it were a fiction book, but I don't see it as having any real meaning in the world, and it sure didn't have anything to do with his death. Sorry to be so blunt, but you didn't come all this way and invest all this time for sugarcoating."

"No, I didn't, Mr. Swagger. I believe you've set me straight."

"I hope I helped, ma'am. And I'm very sorry about your husband. Maybe by the time you get back, they will have caught the boy."

"Maybe so."

"Let me walk you to your car, and we'll get you out of this godforsaken place."

"Thank you."

They both rose as he peeled off a few bills for the waitress and headed out to her Fusion.

"I guess we'll never know," she said as she got to her car, "who ran over the mystery man with a bicycle."

He was only half listening at this time, trying to sneak a look at his watch to see what time it was and how soon he could get back, because he'd promised to help Miko on her low-roping skills and—

"I'm sorry," he said. "What did you say?"

"Oh, the back of the coat, it had a smear on it that appeared to represent a tread. The Engineer thought it could have been from an English bike, you know, thin-wheeled. It was an impression, about an inch long, where it looked like a tread mark had been printed. That's all. A minor point, I forgot to—"

"Do you have a list of the people your husband visited?"

"I have his notebook. It's hard to read, but it does have some names and addresses there. Why, what is—"

"I have to set some things up. It'll take me a week. I want you to go home and find that notebook and FedEx it to me. If he had computer files on the Dallas trip or notepapers, get me that stuff too. I'll get down there as soon as I'm set up."

"Do you want to borrow the tommy gun?"

"No, not yet."

"You're not joking, are you?"

"No ma'am."

"Do you want me to help defray the expenses? I mean, I seem to be wealthy now, and I—"

"No ma'am," said Swagger. "This one's on me."

CHAPTER 3

A man sat on a park bench at the corner of Houston and Elm, under a spread of aged oak trees, before some kind of odd rectangular white cement ceremonial pool that appeared to be full of Scope. Around him, *la vie touristique* occurred, a subspecies of human behavior mandating that small knots of oddly dressed people congregated here and there, with cameras inadequate to the scale of the urban space, called Dealey, which they commanded. It was all very strange. Sometimes a particularly brave one would dash onto Elm Street to stand, during a brief traffic interruptus, at one of two X's that marked the spots on which a man had been shot to death. Meanwhile, homeless men roamed, some to beg, some to sell for five bucks a rag called *The Conspiracy Chronicles* that promised the latest dish on 11-22-63.

Directly across Elm from the man stood a box of bricks seven stories tall, undistinguished but famous, called the Texas Book Depository. Despite its banality, it had one of the most recognizable facades in the world, especially a corner of the sixth floor where the ambusher had lurked fifty years ago. The sky was bold Texas blue, and a slight wind blew east to west across the territory, which was surrounded by the churn of cars and trucks as they cascaded down Houston and made the tricky turn to the left down Elm for the access to the Stemmons Freeway just beyond the triple underpass. People had things to do, places to go, and for most Dallasites, the tragedy of Dealey Plaza had long since faded. Swagger sat alone, but in his mind, it was 1963, 24/7.

He looked this way and that, up and down, around, down streets, at his shoes, at his fingertips, and he tried to remember. It had been a day like this one, cloudless after a threat of early rain, the sky as blue as a movie star's eyes. At least that's what the papers said. He himself had been asleep at the time, half a world away on an island called Okinawa where, as a seventeen-year-old lance corporal, he'd just made the battalion rifle team and would spend the next three weeks cradling a ton of Garand on a flat, dry firing range, trying to put holes in black circles six hundred yards or so off. He didn't know a goddamn thing about anything and wouldn't for years.

But at 12:29 p.m., back in Dallas, the president's motorcade turned right off of Main Street and proceeded one block up Houston, at the northern boundary of the triangular open park that was Dealey Plaza. Now he saw it. Lincoln limo, long black boat of a car. Two up front, driver and agent, two lower, Governor Connally and his wife, then the regal couple, the blessed, the charismatic, John F. Kennedy in his suit and his wife, Jackie, in pink, both waving at the close-by crowds.

The car reached Elm and cranked left. It had to access the Stemmons Freeway, which could only be entered from Elm. It was a 120-degree turn, not a 90-degree turn, so the driver, a Secret Service agent named Greer, had to slow down considerably as he maneuvered the heavy vehicle around the corner. Speeding up, he passed by some trees and continued on a slight downward angle along Elm Street. Immediately to his right was the seven-story building known as the Texas Book Depository, the undistinguished pile of plain brickwork that now loomed over Swagger. He ran his eyes up its edge and halted them at the corner of the sixth floor and saw . . . only a window.

On that day, at 12:30 p.m., as the car passed by the trees, a sound that virtually everyone agreed was a gunshot was heard. It appeared to have struck nobody directly, but at least one witness, a man named Tague, reported being stung by what can reasonably be assumed was a fragment, as the bullet broke apart when it hit the curbstone behind the car or a branch in the trees. Bullets do this; it is not strange or remarkable. Within six or so seconds, a second bullet was fired, and most people there assumed it came from the looming depository. That bullet hit the president in the back, near the neck, tumbled through his body, emerged from his throat, nicking his tie, and flew on to hit John Connally horizontally. It penetrated his body entirely too, hit and broke his wrist, and thudded into but did not penetrate his thigh. It was found later that afternoon on a gurney at the hospital. This was the "magic bullet" that many claimed could not have done what this one did.

The third bullet was the head shot, a few seconds later (how many would be legendarily unclear) delivered at a distance of 263 feet from the sixth floor of the Texas Book Depository. It hit the president high in the back of the head on a downward angle. It appears to have disintegrated or detonated, as the few traces of its existence are controversial at best. It blew a large chunk of brain out of the skull, exiting in a burst of vaporized material that jetted or exploded from the right side of the head.

Chaos ensued. The limousine raced off to the hospital, with its cargo of two gravely wounded men and their women. Police moved, perhaps not quickly enough, to cordon off the building from which the shots seemed to have been fired. In time, after a roll was taken, police learned that an employee named Lee Harvey Oswald was missing, though he had been seen there that day and was even confronted by a police officer in the lunchroom right after the shooting.

A description of Oswald was broadcast, and some miles away, in Dallas's Oak Cliff section, an officer named J. D. Tippit spotted a man who matched that description. Tippit stopped and called him over. He got out of his car and was shot four times by the suspect and died on the spot.

The suspect walked away, but concerned citizens followed him; others noted his odd behavior and knew that suspicions were flying around Dallas about the Kennedy assassin. They noted that he sneaked into a movie theater, and the police were called. Thus was Lee Harvey Oswald arrested.

Meanwhile, at the Book Depository, officers found a "sniper's nest" of book cartons arranged at the site of the sixth-floor (NE) corner window, three ejected 6.5 mm Mannlicher-Carcano casings, and a hundred feet away, at the site of the sole stairway off the floor, a surplus Mannlicher-Carcano Model 38 carbine with a cheap and poorly attached Japanese-made scope. The rifle had been cocked and carried a live cartridge in its chamber.

It soon proved that Oswald's fingerprints were on the rifle and on the boxes in the sniper's nest, that he had carried a suspicious bag of "curtain rods" into the depository that morning, that he had ordered, under pseudonyms, both the Carcano rifle and the .38 Special S & W revolver used in the Tippit slaying. Moreover, he was a notorious malcontent with "revolutionary tendencies," a self-proclaimed Communist, a former defector, a mediocre marine (accounting for his shooting skill), a wife beater, and an all-around creep.

He never stood trial because he was murdered by Jack Ruby on the morning of November 24, 1963, as he was being led to an armored car for transfer to a more secure holding area.

Those seemed to be the facts which, after much haggling, all had come to believe and accept. Swagger believed them and accepted them—that is, until his chat with Jean Marquez.

Her words touched one of his own memories, not a public memory at all but a private, long-buried one. He had been stalked once by a certain team of men in his long and turbulent past, and the smudge she had reported on the back of a coat had a meaning for him that it would have for no other man on earth. Amazing that it had, in some form and after all these years, reached him.

"I can't believe I'm here," said someone, and Swagger was pulled from his time travels to see a friend, younger, better dressed, a kind of Dallas up-and-coming executive type in a worsted Hickey Freeman suit, approaching on a beeline to sit next to him.

"We put the dumbest intern on the JFK squad," the man said as he shook Swagger's hand and dispensed with the how-are-you bullshit. "He fields the ten or twenty calls we get each day from people who've solved the case and now know for sure the Gypsies were involved with the Vatican and Japanese imperial intelligence."

Nick Memphis was now the special agent in charge of the Dallas field office of the FBI. In most instances it would have been a plum assignment, but for him it was a last stop on the way out. His career had topped out when a new director took over the Bureau, heard he was intimately involved with the tragic incident at a huge mall in Minnesota, and wanted him far from headquarters. An assistant, some acid-blooded corpse named Mr. Renfro, had handled the delicate task of prying Nick from his deputy directorship and reassigning him to fieldwork in an office that was big and produced more than its share of cases closed but didn't need radical shaking up or bold new leadership, just a dozing caretaker to sign the requisitions, approve the budget, and make sure the squads were adequately staffed until he retired.

Swagger didn't say a thing. He knew he'd shaken up his pal with a strange request a few days ago and that Nick had to vent. He let the younger man flail away, unburden himself, get it all out.

It was typical Swagger, laconic and detached and seemingly camouflaged even if he wore a suit, an off-the-rack khaki rag that resembled a grocery bag on a scarecrow. He had one leg cranked awkwardly over the knee of the other, showing a beat-to-hell Nocona, and looked younger sitting than walking, because when he walked, the vibrations of several competing wound-deficient parts of him turned his progress into a slow and uncertain shuffle. You winced for the pain that hip had to cause him and wondered why the old coot was too stubborn to take painkillers. At least he wasn't wearing that goddamn faded Razorbacks cap.

"I can't believe I wasted a Justice Department witness protection identity on you," Nick fumed. "Who do you think you are, Mark

Lane? It's over. Oswald did it. Nobody else. That's what all the sensible research shows, that's what the latest computer re-creations show, that's what all the House panels concluded. Only fruitcakes and vegetarians believe in a conspiracy. Man, if it gets out that I bought in to this kind of scheme, Renfro will have my ass on a clothesline by Wednesday."

"I appreciate your kindness," Swagger finally said. "And no, I ain't gone insane. I think my mind is working normally. Slow, as usual, but normal."

Nick made a sound that expressed frustration. "Man," he said, "I should never try to outguess you. JFK! Never in a million years would I guess you'd tumble into that slime pit."

"If it helps, and you have to justify it"—the secret identity didn't require formal computer paperwork and headquarters approval, which could be penetrated by hackers, only the okay of the senior bureau field officer, that is, Nick himself—"you can tell them you took a flier on a murder investigation. Fellow came to Dallas, your neck of the woods, went home to Baltimore, and got himself killed under circumstances that look very much like a professional hit."

"Murder isn't in our jurisdiction," Nick said grumpily. "That's a local issue."

"True, but the wheelman traveled from somewhere to Baltimore to do the job. Maybe from Dallas. We know that because there can't be but two or three professional car killers in the world at any one time, and they ain't known to hang out in Baltimore."

"You don't even know it was a pro. It could have been a kid on meth."

"I saw the Baltimore report. There was a witness, a girl walking a dog. She was observant. He accelerated clean through the hit and kept on a line afterward, without a waver or a wobble, then took a hard left at speed and was out of the neighborhood in about three seconds flat, without one squeal of brakes, one skid mark, one spinout or dent. That's professional driving, even if nobody in Baltimore figured it out. If he went from anywhere to Baltimore, he's your baby, and when you're done with him on interstate violations, crossing state lines to commit a crime, five to eight, you hand him to the Baltimore prosecutor and he goes down for the long one and rots out in their pen."

It was hardly enough, Nick knew. Murders were a dime a dozen. He tried to spin it enough to make friends with it. He came up with: contract killings were rare, and a good bust on some flashy mechanic from the Dark Side might be a good career feather, even if Mr. Renfro had knocked the cap off his head. Nice to go out taking down some pro kill jockey with a flashy résumé. Maybe if the guy was hard-core enough and the evidence was strong enough—Swagger was good at digging up evidence—they might get an HRT team to go in hard and cap his ass and save everybody the hassle of a trial. The press loved it when HRT whacked genuine bad guys. It was so commando-chic.

"If you have any interaction with local or fed LE, don't you mention the JFK angle. Not a word. It's straight interstate to commit a crime. I didn't want a local player, so I got an undercover who'd worked with the bureau before and that I knew and trusted. That's the game. Who are you this time, by the way?"

"I seem to be one John 'Jack' Brophy, a retired mining engineer from Boise. I did some counterchecking against myself, and those boys did this one real good. You don't find good work like that just anywhere these days."

"The program was designed to keep Mafia snitches alive long enough to testify, then incentivize the possibility of a new life away from the Mob, although they usually revert. Putting one together is expensive and time-consuming work, and it requires a big payoff to make it worth the time and effort. That's why I hate to waste it on somebody who isn't named Vito."

"Well, if it makes you happy, call me Vito."

"Give me your plan, Vito."

"I have the victim's notebook. It ain't much, because his handwriting is so awful that I can't read most of it. It's got his schedule and his appointments. I know exactly where he went and who he talked to and the issues he raised. I'll follow that same path. Maybe someone will try to smoke me. Then we'll know we have something."

"Jesus, that's it? You, sixty-six years old with a hip that hasn't worked in ten years, are going to play the tethered goat? What on earth makes you think you can match it up with a pro forty years younger and walk away?"

"If it comes to guns, I'll put ninety-nine out of a hundred in a hole in the ground to this day."

"Are you packing?"

"Not yet. If I pick up cues that I'm in someone's crosshairs, I have a .38 Super and three mags of straight hardball stashed in my room at the Adolphus. I figure if I'm shooting, I'm shooting through windshield glass or door panels, so I need speed and strength, not expansion."

"That stuff ricochets like crazy."

"I know. I'll be careful."

"All right. This is how it has to work. You call the number I give you every morning and report your sked and plans for that day. If I can, I'll put a backup team on you to make certain no one else is on your tail. If someone is, I'll call you on the cell I'm going to give you, and we'll set up our own ambush. I don't have to tell you this as a friend, but as the federal officer who's running you, I am obligated to do so: No cowboy shit. Shoot only when shot at or your life is in danger. I would so much prefer if there was no shooting, not because I think you'll miss, but because one of them might, and with my luck, he'll hit the orphaned violin prodigy on his way to accept the Nobel Peace Prize. You keep me informed, Brother Brophy, or I'll have to pull you in."

"I always play by the rules."

"No, you never play by the rules, and my career has benefited from it to no end. If you say this ultimately might have to do with something we nearly unraveled twenty years ago but which slipped through our hands, that's fine. I'll buy in to that, cautiously, like the pension-scared bureaucrat I've become. But I remember. Everything I got since then, I got because of that wild ride we went on out of New Orleans that made me a Bureau star back in '93. And I don't forget you saved my life on that ride. I will always owe you, and I will stand by you on this last wild ride, even if it goes straight into craziness. Just . . . be careful."

"Thanks, Nick. Stick with me, and we'll get you back to Washington."

"Yeah," said Nick, "maybe in a casket or a pair of handcuffs. So what's the first stop?"

"Up there," Bob said, suggesting by shoulder twitch the sixth-floor corner window. The sniper's nest.

He paid his $13.50 and received some kind of tape recorder to wear around his neck. The instructions were to push a certain button when the elevator dumped him off at floor six, and thereby launch the recorded narrative that would guide him across the floor at a certain pace and direction. He saw that the point of the tape recorder wasn't to inform people, most of whom, if they self-selected themselves for the trip, knew where they were going and what they would see, but to isolate them, to keep them moving at a steady pace and to cut down on the chatter, as if it were a reliquary.

And it was, holding not the bones of a saint but the bones of the past. Now the empty, box-filled space of nothingness that had been the sixth floor fifty years ago had been turned into a generic JFK museum, a polite narrative of the themes of that day expressed neutrally, without outrage or snark, in the old journalism tradition of the five Ws. Swagger knew the five Ws of this one already and didn't need a refresher, so he left the tape recorder silent and slid through the thin crowd of tourists who clustered in smallish groups at each of the signboards and photo displays that followed the strands. It all led to one spot.

Swagger looked at it. The good fathers of Dallas had decided to cut down on the vicarious teenage thrill of being Lee Harvey and lining up the head shot from exactly his place and posture; they had erected a cubicle of Plexiglas to seal off the corner but also as if to preserve it in amber, a frozen ghost of a lost bad time.

Swagger stared at the array of Scott Foresman boxes, arranged just as the screwball from New Orleans had done, building a childish little fort that would block him from the view of anyone else on the sixth floor and also give him a solid supported position for the shot. The guy had been a marine, after all; the importance of the sound position had been drilled into him, and on his day of days, he had not forgotten it.

Swagger looked, unsure what he was supposed to feel. Too many people were drifting by or resting on benches for it to have any ceremonial dignity; it was just a crummy corner of a crummy building looking through a crummy window. He went to the window—not Oswald's, which was unreachable behind the Plexiglas, but the next one over, and saw how close the two crosses in the street were. The longest was 265 feet away, if he remembered correctly. The head shot. Under a hundred yards. The range wasn't as important as the angle: he was here for the angles. This one was an outgoer, about three or four degrees to the left, diminishing slightly as the distance increased, moving laterally right to left but just as slowly. With any modern hunting rig and a hundred bucks' worth of Walmart optics from low-end Chinese glassworks like BSA or Tasco, it would be an easy enough shot. Given the angle and the speed, it was hardly a mover at all; given the stability offered by the carefully arranged boxes, it was like shooting bull's-eye at the bench.

There were other things that leaped out at him. The first was that when the big limo had pivoted around that 120-degree turn, it must have been almost still, or at least moving so slowly that the movement would have no play in the shooting. Moreover, it was so close. It was seventy-five feet away, almost straight down, and JFK's chest and head were in total exposure and the windshield between the passenger compartment and the driver's compartment was overcome by the vertical angle of the downward trajectory. That was the shot. He tried to figure out why Lee Harvey hadn't taken it.

Maybe he would have had to lean out too far. Maybe if he'd had a better shot, they also would've had a better shot, and even a good pistol guy with a four-inch Smith .357 or a Colt .45 ACP, as both feds and Dallas cops carried in those days, could draw, fire, and hit in a second's worth of move. Maybe Harvey would be the one with the brain shot from some Secret Servicer's Smith four; he'd be the one with cerebellum shredded and blown raggedly everywhere. Or maybe he'd fogged the scope. Maybe he'd had a qualm, a regret, a bolt of fear, and lost his killer's determination, a brief crisis of confidence. All of those could explain it, but which one did?

Swagger looked to the right. Lee Harvey doesn't take that shot. Instead, he lets the car crank around the corner and disappear behind the line of oak trees at the side of the road, and shoots through them. Duh. How stupid is that? Why would he do something so stupid? Was he an idiot, in the grip of panic, a hopeless loser? And of course: he missed.

Swagger then looked at the first X on Elm Street, which would have been Lee Harvey's second shot fired, after the miss. That was probably his best opportunity after passing on the turner below him and after recovering too quickly and missing the first shot, but he'd blown that one too, at least in the sense of missing the head shot and landing a few inches low, in the back under the neck. Yes, he was coming off a swift bolt throw, but the target was under two hundred feet away, and from the target angle (always the angles!), it did not present an image moving harshly or radically. By his standards, he missed, and given the president's lack of visible reaction, Oswald might have counted it as a clean miss. You'd think, still, if he were going to hit a head shot, *that* was the one he would have hit, not the third, even farther out, the target even smaller, coming off another fast bolt throw. It was the third he'd hit. And he had hit it. No doubt, no regret, no pain, no nothing, no force on Earth could change the fact that a 6.5 mm bullet had hit Jack Kennedy in the head at 12:30 p.m. November 22, 1963, and shocked the world with the visceral reality of the shattered skull, the vaporized brain tissue, the animal vibration of catastrophic trauma.

Could Oswald have made that shot? Bob considered. The question wasn't abstract; he might have had the skill, but that skill had to be expressed through the system he used, and it had to be forced through the prism of the actual. He was a punk nobody shooting at the president of the United States in a hurry, working a bolt that had to be at some level unfamiliar to him—he'd trained on the old semi-auto M1 Garand, as had Bob—so the adrenaline must have been coursing through his veins like lighter fluid. All the buck-fever things must have been happening; eyes wide to f/1, auditory exclusion, loss of fine motor control, vision impingement, the sensation of oxygen debt. Yet he made the shot.

It was an easy shot. Bob probably could have made it offhand, as any of the dozens of snipers he'd known could have. So what? The issue was, could this little monkey from all our dark furious dreams, with his hatred and bitterness and political crackpottiness, his incompetence and long history of failure, could *he* have made that shot on that day at that time?

It was stupid to ask, even if thousands had done so publicly. That's because to answer, you had to be familiar with the capacities of the rifle at its maximum and at its minimum. He turned, and as if by magic, there it was: a full-size silhouette of C2766, the Mannlicher-Carcano Model 1938 carbine made in Terni, Italy, in 1941 and scoped by an anonymous mechanic—"gunsmith" was far too grand a word—with a cheesy 4X tube out of a Japan that hadn't yet discovered its postwar optical engineering genius and was attached to the receiver by a machined piece of pot metal in the form of a scope mount, all of it held together by two screws when there should have been four. The image floated at Bob off a signboard a few feet away. He walked over and confronted the thing as reproduced in the full-size photo.

The FBI forensic ballisticians had done a number on the weapon as soon as they received it, but Bob had looked through the testimony and found it somewhat spotty. Frazier, the agent, was revered in the Bureau as a gun expert, but Bob noted that he was a high-power shooter by choice (and a champion at that), which meant he specialized in the discipline of shooting large, stable targets at long range (out to six hundred yards) with service rifles through open sights. His skill set would have included stamina, sophisticated wind doping, trigger control, and long-term nervous system control. By experience, he was not particularly knowledgeable about or comfortable with the telescopic sight or precision shooting. The one shot/one kill mantra of the sniper would have been lost on him. Though his testimony in certain areas seemed problematic, Swagger knew he'd have to look more carefully at it on another day.

Here, in 2-D glory, the rifle looked like something an eight-year-old tin soldier in a red papier-mâché tunic might carry in a junior high version of *The Nutcracker.* He'd been dragged to a production when Nikki was in her ballet phase and remembered the stiff-legged little boys with the red circles painted on their cheeks under the tall cardboard faux-hussar hats. That was how miniaturized and quaint it seemed. It was small, hardly a weapon of war. Like many of the rifles of the Mediterranean, it seemed somehow to lack seriousness of purpose; it wasn't a heavily machined vault that could shoot a bullet a mile with accuracy or provide a platform to drive a bayonet into a man's guts, like a Mauser, a Springfield, a Lee-Enfield. You might use it to pot rabbits, as it was of light caliber: roughly .264 in an age before high-velocity powders, not a .30 with its tons of muzzle energy. The ballistics were unimpressive. He looked at the stamped pot-metal scope mount, well resolved in the photo blowup, and noted that it boasted enough detail to depict the two empty screw holes on the plate that held rifle to scope. What influence would that have had on events? How long would the two screws hold the scope tight, if they'd been tightened at all? Through one shot or two or, most important, three? What would the consequences be of a loose scope, which would reset itself whimsically after each shot, screwing up accuracy? All good shooters tightened their scope screws before they fired; had Oswald? Would he have known that? He wasn't trained on scopes in the Corps, just the knurl-index click system of the M1 peep sight, a brilliant mechanical device in its day. Did Oswald understand the concept of zeroing a scope? Was this scope zeroed? Was it altered after recovery? All these questions would have to be answered in re: this particular rifle, not any other, before one could issue a comment on its capabilities.

If that was the thing that did it, he'd have to know more about it. He resolved to acquire and study such a piece—they were available dirt cheap, usually under three hundred or so. Could he learn the bolt throw, could he find a target fast through that little four-power, not particularly clean scope, could the rifle sustain its accuracy over a string of shots, could that improvised sling improve the accuracy, if indeed Oswald, who knew of slings from the Marine Corps, applied it during his shooting? All yet to be discovered.

Swagger tired of the place. No big deal, no emotional reaction to the foreign visitors, the running kids, the goofball Ohio tourists; it was just enough, and was time to go.

Now, the grassy knoll. It was a kind of absurd conceit, a mock Greek temple etched into a grass hillside along a busy commercial road in the heart of the city. Someone's long-ago idea of class, when the Greek model was beloved and appreciated in America. But it looked like something out of an ancient Rome movie, and you half expected to see people lounging around in togas.

Swagger stood to the side of the circle of columns at the height of the crest and tried not to think of togas; he considered the angles. Below him, maybe fifty feet, cars rushed down Elm toward the triple underpass. The slope of grass ran down to the curbside, the road itself fed the commuters onto the Stemmons Freeway, and beyond that stretched the field, also pool-table green, of Dealey Plaza.

Here, the shooting was *so* close. Some kind of professional hard-core hit team without access to the TBD, which loomed to the left through some thin trees, almost certainly would have chosen this spot. They could yank subguns—grease guns, Thompsons, Schmeissers, all the common war bring-backs plentiful in the America of 1963—and lay down a fusillade that no man could survive. Then they could race off and try to gunfight their way to freedom, but they'd fail, enough police would arrive eventually, and they'd die of extreme ventilation of the twelve-gauge variety at some roadblock a few miles away.

But one shooter, knowing he had to hit cold-bore on his first shot to syncopate with the patsy Oswald's sure misses? He couldn't make any sense of it. I came here for answers, Swagger thought. All I am getting is more questions.

Still, like all the other rubes, he moseyed down the hill and stood at the curb not seven feet from the X that marked the position of the car when the third bullet hit head. He'd seen it enough to view it with dispassion, but unbidden, a sound cue came to him. He had been near men hit in the head, and he knew that it was a sound like no other on the planet. He didn't want to, but from some forgotten atrocity in his long and violent past, that noise abruptly reproduced itself. It sounded like a baseball bat hitting a grapefruit, as it held both the thud of power and the squirt of liquefaction. Vapor was left in the air, a cloud of atomized brain particles thick enough to register on Zapruder's film before it dissipated in the rush of the car accelerating away.

Swagger shook his head. He hadn't expected that moment of horror. He tried to clear his brain. He turned, looked up Elm to the cube of the depository with its front of mismatched windows, arc and square and arc and square, now lacking the gaudy Hertz sign that had commanded the heights in 1963, and he saw Lee Harvey's window 288 feet away and 66 feet off the ground. But he saw another thing. He waited until a traffic light at the corner halted the stream so he was able to walk the seven feet to the X and turn and look back.

The other thing he saw was a building. It was also a brick box, and it was just across Houston from the depository. From this angle, its seventh-story window was but a few feet to the right of Oswald's nest. Any fair computerized trajectory cone, imprecise to begin with, would have included it too.

It was the Dal-Tex Building.

Because the writer had spent an afternoon there, Swagger next found himself in the local history room of the Dallas Public Library on Young Street a few blocks from his hotel on Commerce. The library itself, which seemed to match City Hall across the street, appeared to resemble a spaceship crashed into the earth. It was a kind of inverted or upside-down pyramid thing, and each floor addressed the world through a line of wide, deep windows. It was so old-fashioned modern.

The room on the fifth floor was any other library room, in fact nicer than most, and the young woman behind the counter couldn't have been nicer herself. Swagger was following James Aptapton's notebook and explained that he'd like to see the Dallas Yellow Pages from 1963, and in seconds, literally under a minute, he was sitting at a table with a copy of the Dallas Yellow pages, not merely from 1963 but from November 1963.

As serious research, it was probably pointless. But he saw that the writer would use it as a source by which to re-create the city of 1963. It probably helped him if he knew what the cab companies called themselves, where you took your dry cleaning or went to meet your refrigeration or photography needs, where you'd go to get a nice tan overcoat, what the phone number of the Texas Book Depository was (RI7-3521) or that there were eight pages of churches but only one strip club—Jack Ruby's Carousel, "across from the Adolphus." He learned that you could eat Mex at El Fenix or buy liquor from a Mr. Sigel, who had stores everywhere, or stay at the Statler Hilton or the Mayfair or the Cabana as well as the Adolphus; buy a straight-up drink at the Tabu Room or the Star Bar or the Lazy Horse Lounge; buy ammo for your gun at Ketchum and Killum on Kleist, in Oak Cliff, or Wald's; buy a book at the North Dallas Book Center, hear a song on KBOX or KJET or KNOK. Yes, a storyteller might find all this interesting, but it quickly drained Swagger of interest and his eyes glazed over in a bit. He hung around on sheer willpower, so that he traced exactly the writer's footsteps.

Leaving, he hailed a cab. African cabdriver with a little magic box for getting directions, so the fellow had him on his way to 1026 North Beckley, in Oak Cliff, in seconds. That destination was noted in Aptapton's little book, and Swagger knew it to be the location of Oswald's roominghouse in the six weeks before the assassination. A writer would have to see such a thing and know for sure, as Swagger soon learned, that it was a wooden box under trees with a scruffy yard off the main drag of Zang Boulevard, that it had a mansard roof concealing what had to be a small upper story, that it was deep, probably much bigger than it seemed from North Beckley Street, containing many small rooms, one of which had housed the creepy young killer. Nothing marked its place in history. It sat among other decaying wooden houses on a block that seemed to be slipping into disrepair and possibly into something he had never heard of until he started reading—that is, existential despair. It held no mysteries for Swagger.

He directed Mr. Ruranga to drive farther down Beckley to Tenth, for that was the route of Oswald's last walk as a free man. Oswald had thundered down Beckley with seemingly no direction in mind, then turned on a street called Crowley, which led him to another turn down Tenth. Swagger had forgotten Crowley and settled for Tenth. When they reached it, it turned out not to go through, so the driver had to mull around until he found a way around the church parking lot that now barricaded it. That route led to the bleak street where Oswald had been confronted by the police officer, right before the corner of Tenth and Patton, and Oswald had hit three of his four shots, all fatal. No plaque marked J. D. Tippit's falling place among the rotting bungalows and uncut lawns, just a whisper as dry leaves caught in the persistent Texas wind rushing over the earth. It seemed so wrong.

Then it was a brief shot up Oak Cliff's main drag, called Jefferson, to the low strip of commercial buildings that held the Texas Theatre. The theater was still there and still called Texas and recognizable from a million reproductions of photos taken at 2:30 p.m., November 22, 1963, when the surly young man with the snub-nosed .38 Special was taken down by Dallas Homicide, getting a shiner in the process. In retrospect, he was damned lucky he didn't get a .357 in the thoracic cavity, as the Dallas cops in those days weren't particularly merciful to cop killers.

Again, the theater held no fascination for Swagger. It was just an old building, and its deco stylings spoke thirties, not sixties, and its marquee in Spanish suggested that a new wave of inheritors had moved in.

Swagger ordered the cab back to the Adolphus, because it was, happily, nap time.

The nap never arrived. Not even with lights out and shades down would sleep approach. Too much danced in his brain.

Conspiracy theory. Second shooter. Third shooter. Triangulation of fire. All that Oliver Stone stuff. How could you think about this thing at all with all the crap around it? You couldn't see the target, there was so much camouflage, some of it deceitful, some of it well meant, some of it earnest, some of it crazy. CIA. Castro. From deep within the government. The trilateral commission.

He told himself: Think hard. Think straight. Concentrate.

Could there have been a second gunman elsewhere in Dealey? How do you attack that proposition? There was no reason why there couldn't have been one, from a gunman with a rifle in his umbrella to a guy on top of the TBD to someone on one of the other buildings that ringed the square, Dal-Tex or the Records Building or even the Criminal Courts Building.

But . . . What am I missing?

What am I missing?

He had nothing. Then he had something.

Most if not all of the multiple shooter/grassy knoll theorists proceeded from a fundamental lack of rigor, under false assumptions. Most assumed, sloppily, that what became known on November 22, 1963, was known before that. It was not. You have to discipline yourself, when thinking about this shit, to limit your thoughts to what was known on November 22 and not after. Most of them had not been able to do that.

There was one unassailable fact: only one bullet was found that could be associated with the murder of John F. Kennedy. That is what is called an anomaly. Swagger knew from too much experience that many shootings feature anomalies: things that could not be predicted, that could not be expected, that were seemingly impossible. Yet they happened, because reality does not care what people think or expect.

No sane planner could have assumed that only one bullet would be found, WC399, the later-to-be-famous "magic bullet." Any planner utilizing multiple shooters (i.e., personnel on the grassy knoll) would have to assume that bullets from their firearms would be recovered as well. The odds certainly favored that outcome. If that was the fact, why bother to use Lee Harvey Oswald as a "patsy"? Why not do the job straight out, like a Mob hit, and make a break for it after the last shot? Why not use an automatic or a semi-automatic weapon and put a burst on target instead of three shots separated by several seconds each? A good man with a Thompson at the grassy knoll could have killed everyone in that car in two seconds. The only reason to have a single shot fired from the knoll was the false-flag operation, to set up a chump. Why would you do that if your own assumed-to-be-recovered bullet would give that away quickly? The deceit that Oswald was the only shooter would last, it had to be assumed, until an autopsy surgeon removed a bullet from JFK's brain, or Mrs. Kennedy's left shoulder, or John Connally's lung, or the upholstery of the limo.

Any "other-shooter scenario" without some kind of ballistic deceit, meant to link whatever really happened with Oswald's Mannlicher-Carcano 38, was utterly dismissible on its face. It was even surprising that such craziness wasn't laughed off the face of the earth when it was first theorized, though nobody in the press knew enough about rifle ballistics to catch on.

He sat back. That seemed solid. He looked at it a thousand ways and couldn't see through it or around it. It was okay.

Progress? Maybe a little.

And tomorrow. To make sure it was there, he picked up the Aptapton notebook and noted what the writer had inscribed in a careful hand: "National Institute of Assassination Research, 2805 N. Crenshaw."

CHAPTER 4

As is true of many grandly named enterprises, the National Institute of Assassination Research was located in somebody's basement. The house was shabby, with shedding shingles, in another decaying Dallas prewar bungalow neighborhood, a one-story wreck that hadn't seen paint or putty in too many years. The glass-and-steel spires of New Dallas seemed a long way away from this broken-down zone. As Swagger walked through the gate in the cyclone fence on a sidewalk smeared with wet leaves, he noted a sign that said "Bookstore in Back." He followed that around and found a stairway down to another sign that instructed him to "Ring Bell," which he did.

"Come on in, it's open," came a shout.

He walked into a room jammed to bulging with bookshelves, all of them ominously creaky and distended from load-bearing responsibility as their fibers struggled with the tonnage of pages they were asked to contain, the whole thing musty and basement-smelling. The shelves were indexed by handwritten-on-tape topic labels: CIA, RUSSIA, RIFLE, LHO EARLY, LHO LATE, WARREN COMMISSION PRO, WARREN COMMISSION CON, DOCUMENTS, WITNESS ACCOUNTS, FBI, JACK RUBY, and so on and so forth. Bob looked for one called DAL-TEX, but didn't see it. He moseyed, unmonitored for a good deal of time, pulling this or that tattered paperback from a shelf, tracking the conspiracy theories from Mafia to KGB to Castro to MI-Complex to Big Oil to Far Right, none of them particularly motivating.

The stuff felt like an undertow; it could suck you in and in minutes you were annealed into the gel of conspiracy, your clarity gone, your logic-gyro hopelessly out of whack, your ability to distinguish this from that eroded into nothingness. Too much information; which of it was trustworthy, which dubious? Too many claims and assertions, too much speculation, some out-and-out lies for profit. In all, as if some madhouse virus of paranoia had been set loose, infecting all who breathed it.

"Hi, there," a voice said. "Sorry, I was trying to catch up on shipping. Can I help you?"

The man was tall and gangly, a kind of seedy academic with a matting of thick blondish hair and glasses held to his head by an elastic strap, now pushed back into his hair. He wore a tatty green crewneck sweater under a tweed jacket that had some mothholes flagrantly displayed on the lapel. Mid-forties, no commando type, his hollow, pale cheeks bristly with day-old beard. He smiled, introducing the fact that he hadn't discovered tooth-whitening strips, and extended a long-fingered hand. Bob shook it, discovering as he'd anticipated that it was slightly squishy and moist, and smiled back.

"Well," Bob said, "I seem to have a bug in my head that's saying 'Dal-Tex' over and over again. If there was a second rifle, it had to be there, given a bunch of other factors. I thought you might have books on it. I thought you might have a file."

"Ah," said the proprietor of NIAR, "very interesting."

"I stood at the Elm Street X, and I couldn't help but notice how close its trajectory is to the Sniper's Nest."

"Agreed. Many, many folks have found that fascinating."

"I'm sort of late to this game, so forgive me for my ignorance. I'm guessing that a lot has been thrashed over, gone through, shaken out, and I don't want to waste my time doing what someone already did in 1979."

"I don't blame you, friend," said the man, settling easily into a conversational posture by resting his rear on the counter and crossing his arms. "Especially now. You know, with the fiftieth coming up, we're anticipating a big surge in interest and attention. It seems like Stephen King isn't the only guy working on an assassination book. I'm aware of a great deal of activity."

"I'm no writer," said Bob. "Lord knows, I couldn't string two words together if my life depended on it. It's the puzzle aspect of the thing, the pure solution, that is so damned fascinating."

"I hear you," said the man. "I'm Richard Monk, and I guess I'm CEO and janitor of NIAR. Also shipping clerk, accountant, and lightbulb replacer. It's pretty damn glamorous."

Bob got out his wallet and pulled a card, handing it over.

John P. Brophy (Ph.D.) (NSPE)

"Jack"

Mining Engineer (Ret.)

Boise, Idaho

"Spent my life digging holes all over the globe," he said. "It's pretty boring in a tent in Ecuador, so I started reading when I wasn't digging or sleeping or drinking or whoring. I'm still reading. About three years ago, I noticed I had five or six million bucks ticking away and declared myself retired. I got hooked on JFK and have been digging into that. It seems to have taken over my life. I read your website for news every week. Anyhow, I finally worked out some stuff of my own and thought I'd come to town to check it out, see if it stands up to reality."

"So you're a Dal-Tex guy. I could put you in touch with a couple of other big Dal-Texers."

"Well . . ." said Bob. "Yes, but I am cautious—"

"I get it. You've got a theory, it's your intellectual property, you don't want it getting out. All of us are like that, halfway between hungering to share and fearing being ripped off. I'll go easy, no problem."

"You know everybody and everything?"

"I *am* the Kennedy assassination," Richard said, laughing. "I live and breathe this stuff, Jack. And I have the unfortunate problem of a photographic memory. If I read something, it's there forever. Or at least so far. Maybe it'll reach a point where one more fact makes my head explode."

Swagger laughed. Richard Monk was engaging, if weird, and didn't have that suspicious, feral quality that so many in the "assassination community" seemed to have.

"Offhand, what's the state of the art on Dal-Tex?"

"Well, for a time the people who owned it were generous in letting researchers tour it if they made an appointment. Their policy has changed lately, I suspect because of the fiftieth, and the attention is ginning up, and they're trying to rent out a lot of office space. I know the building manager; I might be able to get you in."

"That would be great," said Bob.

"To be honest, you shouldn't expect much. The whole thing has been gutted and rehabbed twice over since '63. Now it's modern, you know, kind of 'lofty,' very chic urban Greenwich Village vibe happening. They even built an atrium into the lobby that goes up all the way through the center of the building so it looks like the Bradbury Building in L.A. Very old-movie cool, but completely disconnected from 1963."

"The windows are still where they were?"

"Absolutely," Richard said, "and of course you'll confirm that certain windows line up almost perfectly with the angle and the trajectory of the head shot allegedly taken by LHO that day."

"Good. See, I get into it through the guns. I'm a shooter. I actually did a lot more hunting than whoring and drinking and feeling sorry for myself, and I've seen a lot of animals and even some men die when hit by a high-powered bullet, or even, believe it or not, a low-powered six-point-five. My work has been on guns and ballistics, and now the problem is to make it fit the possibilities of the day."

"Got it. See, I think it's good that you don't come into it with the preset conviction that 'The CIA Did It' or 'Dallas Right-Wing Oil Bastards Did It,' because that skews your thinking."

"Exactly."

"You know what, Jack? I'm way behind in my shipping. I more or less survive by mail order. Man, without the Internet, I'd be trying to get by on a major's pension from Big Green."

"Army?"

"Intel. Twenty years, mostly Germany. Anyhow, I'm thinking maybe we ought to meet for dinner and talk there. Is that something you'd be up for?"

"Only if it's on me."

"Great. Better than I hoped for. Where you staying? I can at least come to you."

"The Adolphus."

"Oh, then the French Room," Richard said airily, and Swagger knew it was a joke, for the French Room was the swanky hotel's glamorously decadent restaurant.

"Seriously, go down one block to Main, go up Main, there's a great Mex place called Sol Irlandés."

"Got it," said Swagger.

"See you at eight. It's an easy walk."

"Okay," said Richard, after a long grateful swallow of Tecate, "I didn't bring the file, because I *am* the file. But when you come back, I can pull all the pictures and references for you, or I can attach it to an e-mail and ship it to you, whichever."

"Great," said Swagger.

"Meanwhile, I'll call Dave Arons, who manages the building for its owners, Galaxy Capital Limited. Dave's okay, he gets it; I'll tell him you're an old friend, very trustworthy. He just doesn't want loonies parading through there in tinfoil hats."

"I left mine in Boise."

Around them, the dark restaurant hummed with commerce. It seemed to be a popular place, maybe because the salsa was so good. Swagger sipped his Diet Coke.

"By the way, they're playing down the connect to the assassination, even if they've got an assassination museum souvenir shop right there on their corner, at Houston and Elm."

"I noticed it," said Bob. "I didn't go in."

"They now call it 501 Elm, not Dal-Tex."

"Makes sense."

"Good marketing move, I think. Okay, right now Dal-Tex is featured in at least thirty-eight of the two hundred sixty-five formally recognized conspiracy theories. It's got the angles, and as you'll find, access and egress on that day was more or less easy. It wasn't closed down till twelve-thirty-nine or so, so a team could have gotten out pretty easy. But you probably know neither Bugliosi nor Posner, the two great Warren Commission acolytes who've studied all the theories, give it much time of day. They don't even bother to rebut it. When you think about it, maybe that's sensible. I mean, man, it would have taken some balls. Go into a public building, crack an office, pop the president, and walk out whistling 'Dixie' ten seconds before the cops arrive. Balls and luck. Over two hundred people worked in that building."

"Weren't most of them at Dealey, like Mr. Zapruder?"

"There's always some guy hanging around."

"Maybe they were disguised."

"Possible, I suppose. But disguised as what? A giant charm bracelet? No way strangers can disguise themselves as friends."

"'Giant charm bracelet'?"

"Sorry, Woody Allen line. Not funny if you don't love Woody."

"I must have missed it," Swagger said. "Anyhow, on the disguise thing, maybe it was long-term. The group rented an office before, and after the shooting stayed there for six months, when the lease was up. No, wait, dammit, the route wasn't known till the twentieth."

"That would free you up to the big deep-conspiracy thing, where some sinister force buried in government uses its tentacles to manipulate things into place far in advance."

"I'm an engineer. I have a distrust of big plans, because I've made my money troubleshooting when big plans go wrong, and believe me, they go wrong all the time. It's better to have a plan than not have a plan, but at the same time, no plan survives contact with reality."

"You sound military, Jack. I was in for twenty, I saw it happen all the time."

"I was in the marines for a—"

"The limp, Vietnam?" interrupted Richard.

"Nah. Ecuador. A piece of drill bit going a thousand feet a second. That was my real education. The engineering teaches you that a plan is a set of assumptions or diagrams that are wrong or impossible. Everything affects everything, everything changes, and you end up in a place you never thought you'd be."

"I agree."

"Still, dammit, the angle of any of six windows to that X on Elm Street gives us exactly the brain shot that killed the president. It's attractive to a conspiracy theorist."

"It is. You say your thing is ballistics?"

"Yeah. I think I've figured out some things as to how there could have been another gun, but no forensic evidence of it."

"Fascinating. But don't tell me, because you'll be angry at yourself in the morning."

"I wasn't going to. 'Intellectual property,' as you say. For a mining engineer, the whole world is secured by mineral rights. That's what I bring to the table, and it makes me kind of paranoid."

"That's fine. Also, as it turns out, I'm not much of a gun guy, and I'd have no way to evaluate it."

"That's a common failing in this assassination research world," said Bob, taking another sip of Diet. "Too many gun opinions by people who don't know a damned thing about guns. A lot of time has been wasted."

"I'll tell you why. Because it's so big. In order to make sense of it and make fair assumptions, you've got to have expertise in too many areas. The medical people know nothing about guns and the gun people know nothing about the Mafia and the Mafia people know nothing about the CIA and the CIA people know nothing about the Cubans and so sooner or later you're making judgments on something you know nothing about, and the result is always nonsense."

"Let me ask you, Richard," said Bob, "do you have a theory?"

"My problem is that I know too much about it. I can't judge anymore. I see the flaws in everything, the contradictions, the micro findings. I could do twenty minutes on the metallurgical analysis of the bullet fragments found on the floor of the limousine and whether it disproves a second-gun theory or buttresses it, and it's arguable either way. But I have no real opinion as to which side of the issue is correct. How can I judge? I wish I could forget some of the stuff I know, but I can't make it go away. It's my curse. On the other hand, it made me a good intel analyst, and it helps me in my chosen line of work."

"Got it."

"But since you're paying—do you mind if I order another beer?"

"Go ahead."

"I will share with you the one theory I've heard that explains everything. I may have made it up, I may have heard it somewhere, I don't know, it was just in my mind one day. Perhaps God put it there. It accounts for every nuance and inconsistency and witness confusion and everything. The only problem is, after I tell you, I'll have to kill you."

Where is this guy going? Swagger thought.

"I'm not going to live much longer anyhow, so you may as well fire away."

"Let me ask you one favor. Don't interrupt when I say something that doesn't accord with the thing we laughingly call 'history.' It'll all become clear in the end."

"I'm listening," said Bob.

"On November 22, 1963," Richard began, "a screwball Marxist loser named Lee Harvey Oswald, for reasons too banal to be believed, fired three shots at the president of the United States, who by utter coincidence showed up outside his workplace window one day. The first shot missed, because Oswald was an idiot. The second shot hit Kennedy under the neck, in the high back. It drove through his body, deflecting because of the president's heavy neck musculature, hit Governor Connally in the back, passed through him, and hit him in the wrist and finally the thigh. Oswald's third shot missed, because he was an idiot.

"Oswald is not important, but let's stay with him for a second. He panicked, raced downstairs, and there met a police officer named Marion Baker, who commanded him to halt. Oswald instead bolted by the officer and headed out the door of the Texas Book Depository, and Officer Baker drew and fired. End of Oswald.

"What happened to Kennedy is the gist of our story. His Secret Service driver raced to Parkland Hospital, less than five minutes away, and a very good team of emergency physicians got to work. It was touch and go, nip and tuck, all through the day and night. In the morning Kennedy finally stabilized. Though feeble from the devastating wound, he hung on, sustained by his incredible will to live and the good wishes and hopes of millions around the world.

"The recovery was slow and painful. Lyndon Johnson became acting president in his absence and ruled judiciously, as guided by Kennedy's advisers, and made no tragic, boneheaded decisions. No Vietnam, obviously. Meanwhile, Kennedy grew stronger and stronger each day. It was feared that his spine was damaged and that he would be paralyzed, but by the narrowest of margins, that proved not to be the case. During this time, his wife, Jackie, hovered like an angel at his bedside, and perhaps the power of her love was another force for the good in helping the man regain his capacities as he healed slowly over the months. He sat up in March '64, he took his first tentative steps in May, and by August he returned to the White House (LBJ, of course, had never moved in) and began to take up light duties. By the convention, in mid-August, he was able to give a rousing speech and was renominated by unanimous acclaim. He barely had to campaign and barely did campaign, and his opponent, Barry Goldwater, was wiped out at the polls in November. Less than a year after the tragedy in Dallas, he was re-inaugurated as president and began his second term.

"But he had changed. At first only his closest associates noticed it, but as his policy tendencies, uncontested because of the sheer charisma of his near martyrdom, became evident, the press and then the public noticed. It seems that he had 'seen the light,' as it were. The near-death experience altered him profoundly; the long months of solitude with nothing except his medical team and the enduring love of his wife had cemented that alteration.

"Gone was the anti-Communist cold warrior. Gone was the savvy political pro, not above a dirty trick or two. Gone too were the philandering, the drug excesses, the games of carrot-and-stick with the press for maximum advantage, the partying, the glamour, the whole sense of the glory of Camelot. Instead, he became an ascetic."

"A what?" said Swagger.

"Guy with great self-discipline, clear moral beliefs. True believer."

"Got it."

"Having come so close to death, he hated it and would have made it illegal if possible. In policy, that feeling of the fragility of life, the rapidness with which it may be taken away and the permanence that even a tiny act of violence leaves in its wake, turned him into a pacifist. He saw that war was wrong in the abstract and in the particular, that strength was a pitiful disguise for fear, that more was gained by reaching out with love than shunning while locking and loading. He immediately recalled the ten thousand American troops in the Republic of Vietnam, he canceled a hundred million in defense spending, he began to open avenues to rapprochement with Castro in Cuba and ordered the CIA to stop all its anti-Castro activities. He also forbade the agency from playing in the internal politics of numerous Latin American and African countries, all of which promptly went Communist, as did the Republic of South Vietnam, absorbed without struggle by the North

Vietnamese. It didn't matter to him that we 'lost' those countries; we 'won' by avoiding battle and the loss of our precious young men.

"His grandest ambition was to end our nuclear arms race with the Russians. The idea of millions cowering in fear across the globe because some mad general could push a button and end the world in nuclear holocaust, essentially on a whim, horrified and sickened him. That would be his crowning glory.

"In the years 1967 and 1968, his most ardent initiatives addressed the arms race, the escalating accumulation of atomic devices and delivery systems (their presence made the possibility of accidental annihilation all the more feasible). He offered the Russians everything he could think of, on bended knee, so to speak, anything to move away from the madness of mutually assured destruction that held the world in its iron grip, as the Atlases and the Poseidons and the SS-12s and 14s seethed and steamed in their silos all across the American West and the Siberian Plain, and the B-52s and the Tupolev Badgers held in their fail-safe orbits just outside of each other's airspace, twenty-four/seven, their high, feathery contrails against the blue blurry reminders of how close we were to the brink and how fragile were the mechanisms that seemed to guard our safety.

"As for the Russians, they wouldn't budge. Sure, some liberals in the politburo appreciated the opening for a softening of attitudes and lobbied to play along, but the hard-liners, astounded by how readily the president was acquiescing and how much he was giving up without recompense, counseled sternness, to see how much more could be gotten out of a fellow they thought was clinically insane, even if neither they nor anyone in the United States could say as much.

"Finally, as his second term was running out and egged on by liberal Eastern newspapers and new media that celebrated his willingness to defuse the bombs threatening the world and replace bellicosity with understanding, the president ordered the unthinkable. He ordered unilateral nuclear stand-down. To prove his sincerity, he would prostrate himself and his country to the Russians.

"He ordered the B-52s of SAC grounded. He ordered the computers at NORAD unplugged, as well as the over-horizon radars of the DEW line. He ordered the Minutemen in their silos defueled and began a program of warhead neutralization, removal, and destruction. He ordered the MX experimental program halted. At a certain date, he had done what he set out to do: He had removed the United States from its position as a nuclear power. He had achieved peace.

"At twelve minutes after midnight on Tuesday, November 5, 1968, the Russians launched."

"Wow," said Swagger. "Richard, this is getting a little weird, isn't it?"

"Jack, you promised not to interrupt."

"It's a good thing I'm not a drinking man anymore, or you'd have me all bourboned up by now. I'd be fighting sailors, talking to young women, and calling my kids."

"My whistle is dry. I need another beer."

"After destroying the world, I'll bet. Waiter!" He hailed the kid. "Get my father here another Tecate and refill my Diet, will you?"

"Sure. You guys want to see the dessert menu?"

"Hey, ice cream and nuclear firestorms turning me to ash, that's a great idea," Bob said.

Richard laughed. "Oh, it gets better."

The beer came, and Richard rewarded himself for destroying the Western Hemisphere with a swallow, while Swagger drained his own half a Diet Coke in tribute to the burning cities and civilians slaughtered in their beds by the millions.

"Okay, Richard," he said. "I guess I'm manned up enough to get on through this."

"You only think you can't handle the truth," said Richard. He took a breath and began again.

"Who can blame them? It probably wasn't even a decision made in the Kremlin. I'm sure it was some junior lieutenant general in some command bunker outside of Vladivostok. By the iron logic of his national philosophy and the Doctrine of Mutually Assured Destruction, he did the right thing. Once the 'mutually' is taken out of the equation, the sane thing to do is fire.

"In thirty minutes of sustained SS-9 warfighting, over a hundred million Americans perished. All command and control bunkers were hit, SAC-NORAD was turned to radioactive glass, but there was no point in wasting megatonnage on the silos because they'd been disconnected from the computer grid and the local commanders, the first lieutenants in the holes with the two keys, didn't have the flexibility to launch without command authority. Fail-safe, you know. Those weapons were redirected at smaller cities, so even the Dubuques and the Cedar Rapids and the Lawtons were fried on the thermonuclear griddle. So the Russians won World War III quite handily.

"Unfortunately, they didn't do so well in World War IV, which started the next day. Assuming the Brits would sit it out, they assumed wrong, and the RAF went in low and hard and turned Eastern Europe into a funeral pyre. For its efforts, the RAF's airfields were awarded secondary strikes from intermediate-range SS-7s, and since the airfields were attached to the island of Great Britain, another twenty or so million went up in flames.

"The Russians also thought they had the American carriers zeroed, but it turned out their subs were the ones on the zero. The American destroyers hunted and killed them like fish in barrels, and the carrier planes took out the Russian surface fleet with first-generation air-to-ship missiles, allowing the carrier medium bombers and attack planes to get close enough to roar up the soft underbelly of Redland at low level and deliver tactical nukes on all Red Army groups, tank concentrations, and any unfortunate cities in the neighborhood. Finally, one Boomer-class nuke missile sub that had been at sea and missed the fire that time got itself back into the game and launched without command. Sixteen Poseidons. A hundred and sixty megatons, COD. Returns not accepted. By the end of the first day of World War IV, the Russians had lost close to two hundred million people and their military structure had been utterly cremated.

"Then it looked like the Chinese, the Africans, and the South Americans would inherit the earth. Ha ha, joke's on them. A little thing called nuclear winter set in. One of those unintended consequences people are always talking about. I hate it when that happens. A blanket of radioactive debris filled the sky—I mean *everywhere*—and, robbed of sun, agriculture wilted and died where it grew. The temperature dropped forty degrees mean. The seas became oceans of poison. Marine life went the way of the dodo. Mutations, new plagues, new parasites, actual vampire attacks, all these microscopic nasties that had heretofore yielded to the killing power of soap and water flourished and multiplied and grew, killing yet more millions. The flu, black plague, cholera, you name it, ancient diseases not seen in eons came trotting out for their pound of flesh. Ovaries shriveled, and among the few million survivors, the birth rate fell precipitously. We were going down. We were dying faster than we were replacing, and nothing could change that demographic trend. By 2014, there was almost nothing left.

"There was only one solution. The remaining high-IQs agreed on it. With fewer than a hundred thousand people left on the planet, there was only one choice. In one of the most moving spectacles in human history, the world's remaining top scientists, engineers, physicians, soldiers, and thinkers gathered; it was like the Manhattan Project, a colossal undertaking underwritten by all surviving power structures, backed by all humanity, a concentrated species effort the likes of which hadn't been seen since Australopithecus crushed his first gazelle with a femur on the African savannah, with one goal; to find a way to use the power of science to save humanity.

"They had to send a man back in time."

"I think I saw that movie," said Bob. "I think it was called *Terminator*."

"Hmm, never heard of it," said Richard, taking a finishing draft on his Tecate, then raising his hand for another one. "Now that you mention it, I *might* have seen it a time or fifteen."

"I think I was with you until the time-travel jazz came up. I dig holes in the ground, long, straight holes. In other words, I live in and fight dirt. Dirt is about as elemental as you can get, Richard, especially when six miles of it are between you and what you're trying to dig up. So for me, time travel is a nonstarter. I just can't wrap my mind around it. I have to get off the boat right here."

"Jack, trust me on this—time travel, by the laws of physics, is theoretically justifiable. I'll spare you the math, but the secret is the position of the body in space. You see, if you sent a man back a hundred years from here, from this nice restaurant and among all these attractive young people, and he stepped into the here of a century ago, he would instantly die, because he'd be in outer space. Hello, no air, 5,000 degrees below zero, and pieces of shit flying along at light speed because there's nothing to slow them down. That's because the earth, the solar system, the whole shebang, nothing is where it was. It's all moving and moving fast. You have to first devise the mother of all computers to calculate exactly where *here* was a hundred years ago, and by particle beam transmission, that's where you send him. So when he gets there, there is a there to be gotten to."

"I'm getting a headache," said Bob.

"We're almost done," promised Richard. He took another long draft and resumed. "He wasn't a special man. But he had to be a hundred percent certain. After rigorous psychological testing, he was found, winnowed from the thousands who'd sworn they could do the deed. But in 2015 everyone knew the temptation to stay in the past would have been overwhelming. The past was so much better than the ever-diminishing present. They had to have a man with the integrity to destroy himself on faith for a world he'd never see, for children he'd never know, who'd not only die but, more tragically, perish from memory, a man who not only wouldn't exist but never would have existed.

"They found him. Maybe he was someone like you, Jack, tough and smart, salty, been around, walked with a limp, always with the watchful eyes, always slightly tense, as if he's ready to dodge a flying drill bit. That would be the guy. A hero, like Jack, with a limp from a wound he never talks about.

"They sent him back. He entered the past at twelve-twenty-nine p.m. CST on November 22, 1963. They sent him to the southwest corner of the Texas Book Depository, just beyond the Hertz sign. He had a minute or so to set up, and he'd been trained well. He didn't flinch. He didn't hesitate, doubt, fear, regret. Very capable, a Jack Brophy if ever there was one. Good with tools, even or especially guns. He had a rifle, nothing special, nothing complicated, and a nice midrange scope, and several rounds of ammunition. All of these were chance survivors of the nuclear wars, located at great cost and effort by our descendants in the year 2015.

"The hero on the roof put his well-zeroed scope on the head of the vital, attractive young man known as John F. Kennedy and saw the president take Lee Harvey Oswald's second round and flinch but not fall, watched his hands involuntarily rise to his throat in the nerve behavior known as the Thorburn position, counted to five, and squeezed the trigger. He drove a bullet into JFK's skull.

"In that moment, he disappeared. The rifle disappeared. All traces of the bullet disappeared. As it performed its killing duty, it ceased to exist. All evidence of the second rifle ceased to exist. And that's why nobody will ever 'solve' the case. A confused but still idiotic Lee Harvey Oswald was left to go *Huh?*, panic, and begin his crazed last run. Who cares what happened to him. What's important is that in the moment of JFK's death, the next hundred years ceased to exist, or ceased to have existed. JFK was dead; he wasn't wounded, he didn't recover, his brain had been turned to vapor, he didn't pull the troops out of Vietnam, he didn't beg the Russians for mutual concessions, he didn't unilaterally stand down from the brink, thus pushing us over the brink. There was no nuclear holocaust, no deaths in the billions, no nuclear winter, no collapsing ecosystem, no vanished agriculture, no poison seas, no demographic suicide, no second Manhattan Project; we got, as a planet and a species, something unknown—a second chance.

"That's where we are now, Jack, fifty years into the second post–November 22, 1963, reality. Vietnam. Watergate. Jimmy Carter, Ronald Reagan, Bush One, Clinton, 9/11, Bush Two, the war on terror, Iraq, Afghanistan, it's been one mess after another, Jack, but we haven't blown ourselves up, and billions of us still drink the water and breath the air. So maybe that lone gunman did us some good after all."

"Well," said Bob, "you promised me a theory, and that's a hell of a theory."

"See, most theories assume that had JFK survived, the consequences would have been positive. There's no way to make that argument. Just as likely, by that goddamned law of unexpected consequences, they could have been negative, tragic, even catastrophic. We can never know."

"Richard, you are either brilliant or insane, I don't know which."

"I'll bet you're not surprised to learn I've heard that line a few times before. Now chew on that one overnight, and tomorrow at eleven, show up at the lobby of Dal-Tex, and Dave Arons will take you through the building."

Swagger got back to the hotel with a headache, as if he'd been drinking. In a sense, he had been: Richard's science fiction story, with time travel and all that goofy bullshit. What the hell was that about? It had a meaning, somehow, but he couldn't see it.

He almost wished he had a drink, and as usual, the temptation to go to the bar, to have the one that would become two and then three and so on was still there, like a pilot light, something that never went out.

He had to think of something else. He had to put something between himself and his appetites and the craziness that swirled in his head. He pulled on clothes and boots, took the elevator down, and walked the twelve blocks in darkness and coolness and emptiness to

Dealey in a haste that belied the pain in his hip and the gracelessness of his walk.

He wanted to look at it again, see it in the dark, as form without detail, as shape. That nightmare site of so many crazies: the grassy knoll.

Without features, the small hill to the west of the plaza seemed utterly nondescript. He walked to it, climbed it, and watched the cars peel down Elm. He imagined himself as that legendary French gangster, the favorite candidate from one of the first theories, who somehow had lingered. A Corsican, the story went, like someone out of an old Hollywood movie, so degraded that he could kill the world's most beautiful and dazzling man. There he was with his M1 carbine, leaning forward at 12:30 p.m. that day, putting the front sight blade on the president's head and squeezing the trigger.

But—

No, it was wrong. The French killer couldn't have aimed at the president. The president was moving at an uncertain speed. His killer would have to aim ahead of him. He'd have to hold, what, six inches to the front to make that brain shot. It was called shooting on the deflection, and it took talent and practice. Some people never got it.

Most people assume that the Frenchman on the knoll had the easier shot because he was closer. In their minds, close equals easy, far equals difficult. Oswald was 263 feet away, the Frenchman 75. Clearly, these people hadn't done any wing shooting, or taken any shots at running game or men.

Swagger estimated that the theoretical Frenchman would have been on a ninety-degree angle to the vehicle, which itself was beginning to accelerate at an uneven speed. In order to place one shot— and he would be limited to one shot in order to preserve the false-flag operation—he would have had to shoot on the deflection. In skeet and trap and sporting clays, this is the hardest shot, called a "crosser," because it demands the biggest lead. It is mastered by shooting it over and over again to develop a feel for the necessary lead given the speed of the target. The Frenchman would have had to find the target, keep the rifle moving, pull ahead of the target a certain (unknown) distance, and then pull the trigger without disturbing the sight picture as he kept the rifle moving. Swagger knew that was hard enough with a shotgun, which blasts a pattern of shot covering a fairly wide area, but almost impossible except for the top professionals with a rifle, an instrument that puts a single bullet into a single spot. The odds on making that shot the first time out are extremely remote. No, they are not impossible, but it seemed unwise for a professional team to base its plan on one man hitting a near-impossible shot first time, cold bore, unless it had at its disposal some sort of shooting genius, and such men are rare and difficult to find.

As for Oswald, or whoever was back there in the building, whichever one it was, his situation was completely different. His shot, in wing-shooting terminology, was an outgoer. It's pretty easy. The target presents very little angle. The limo wasn't exactly at zero degrees angle to him, but as it moved down Elm Street and as he oriented himself in the window to track it, it was under five degrees. From his point of view, even through that poor-quality scope, it was trending right to left slowly, possibly even undetectably to him. Its main quality was that it was diminishing in size as it traveled farther in distance. Neither of these conditions required that he shoot on the deflection, demanding that skillful computation of lead. He could hold point-blank on the target, concentrate on his squeeze, and get his shot off. If the rifle was accurate and the sight aimed dead zero, then the shot was technically no harder than a benchrest shot at a rifle range. The difference in distances—75 feet versus 263 feet—was hardly meaningful. To Bob's sniper's brain, the shot from behind and above was far easier than a shot from 90 degrees at a vehicle accelerating at an unknown rate.

Swagger thought: Hmm, that's kind of interesting. The shot *had* to come from behind.

CHAPTER 5

S hower, dress, coffee, paper. The same khaki suit, still baggy. The same red tie. He noticed neither tie nor suit and headed out. Dal-Tex was eight blocks or so away, the same walk as last night's jaunt to Dealey, and he thought it would do his hip some good to walk it.

He made them easily enough. Two of them. One on foot, one trailing in a car, which looked to be an '09 Chevy. The car hopscotched, and the man on foot would change duties with the driver. One guy was black, in a black suit with no necktie, a porkpie hat, and shades. The other was dour and plump, in plaid sport coat and slacks, no tie, no hat, no glasses, sun or otherwise. They were not amateurs.

Bob walked down Main, swallowed by the glass-and-steel canyons that had not been there fifty years ago. As last night, he followed Kennedy's route, pungently aware that the style of modern air-conditioning climate control largely banished the open window from large building construction. No open windows in the sheets of tinted glass that rose forty stories.

It was all different for Kennedy. The buildings then were squatter, stouter things, constructed mostly in the twenties and thirties, lots of ornamentation and showy work, arches and cupolas and the other flourishes that cheap skilled labor could routinely produce in brick or stone. And windows. The close-in canyons of Main must have pushed JFK past fifty thousand open windows, and a shooter could have lurked in any of them. It was outside the limits then. Kennedy himself joked about it and drew smiles because it was such a fantastic possibility. He was just about out of windows too; beyond the depository, it was wide-open space all the way to the Trade Mart and the speech he never gave. The fifty-thousand-and-first window had a gunman behind it. End of story.

As had Kennedy, Swagger reached Main's jog at Dealey, and instead of turning left to follow Main, he turned right down Houston. A block brought him to the corner where he'd met Nick, where Houston crossed Elm and the two brick piles stood side by side, the Book Depository and Dal-Tex, almost twins: square girder and mortar palaces.

He looked hard at Dal-Tex. A biggish office building, seven stories tall, redbrick, flat roof, fairly elaborate with arches built into the brick, recessing the windows, thick stone slabs edging the roof, big windows that opened from the bottom up. He could see where new oranger brick had replaced a couple of chunks at the joinery of the Elm-Main corner, to sustain a new brand for the unit. That corner also sported the building's sole retail unit, the Sixth-Floor Museum souvenir shop and coffee gallery, though it was unclear if it was officially connected with the museum in TBD across the street, or if they had claimed the name as a marketing ploy. He noted that a fire escape, which in 1963 ran the height of the building on Houston Street, was gone.

Swagger's vision drifted leftward, across the gulf of Houston Street, and settled again on LHO's sniper's nest, at the sixth-floor corner window. From where Swagger stood at the corner of the two streets, the window seemed immense. It couldn't have been seventy-five feet away, and the downward angle wouldn't affect the trajectory because the range was so close. You point at the white shirt through that junky scope and pull the trigger and cannot miss; no bad trigger pull could jerk the gun far enough to make a difference, no wind deflection could push the bullet from its destiny, nothing could interfere with its flight into flesh.

He stood on the corner, again imagining the slow pivot of the big car as the driver wheeled it through the 120 degrees of the turn. It would have been all but stationary except for the slow pivot. And up there, behind Window 50,001, was the gunman.

Again: why didn't he shoot then? Wide-open target, straight angle into the high chest, Connally too far forward to interfere, Jackie to the right and out of the way, the shot *so easy.* A Boy Scout could have made it.

What was going on with LHO up there in his nest?

Another mystery, unknowable, unsolvable, that had died with Jack Ruby's .38 Special into Lee Harvey.

Swagger waited for the light to change, crossed the street, turned right and then left up the four steps, and entered Dal-Tex.

The first thing he felt was the openness. Looking up, he saw space, as an atrium scooped from the guts of the building exposed several floors of balconies and the wood trusses of the roof. Moving ahead to the security kiosk, he was greeted by a man in his forties, well dressed and pleasant.

"Mr. Arons? My name is Jack Brophy. I think my friend Richard Monk called you on my behalf."

They shook hands and Arons said, "Yes, he did, Dr. Brophy—"

"Jack, please."

"Jack, then. He did, and I like Richard, so I'll be happy to take you through and try to answer any of your questions."

Swagger peppered the man with inquiries. The first concerned the atrium, which, no, wasn't there in '63. It was the creation of a nineties refurb. The whole building, Swagger saw, had the kind of urban-hip tone of so many gentrified older units, and the new designer had stressed raw brick where possible, lots of plain white structural wood, simplicity and unforced elegance everywhere. The ceilings had been cleverly peeled of stucco, exposing the stout girders that were the frame of the building nested in the still-sound wood beams that also sustained the building's pressures.

"I'm guessing these three elevators were here before?" he asked as they rode up.

"Since the beginning," said Arons. "They've been rehabbed, of course"—the elevator was sleek stainless and teak, with mirrors for the vain—"but the shaft was always here, central rear."

"Got it. Were there ever any elevator operators? Particularly in 1963?"

"Not then, not ever."

"What about security?"

"Never. Not until recently, that is."

Swagger felt that the building was smaller on the inside than on the outside, even with the opened atriums and ceilings. Also, it was squarer; somehow you sensed the perfection of its symmetries inside, whereas from outside, it seemed longer one way, more rectangular.

They started on the seventh floor, and Arons took him to an unrented office suite that fronted on Houston Street, looking south to the Book Depository. Its roof could be seen twenty-five feet away, but more evident was the angle down Elm, exposing totally the street up to and beyond the X that marked the brain shot.

It didn't take a genius to see how easy that shot, or the back shot that preceded it, would have been from here. Moreover, the wide sill made for superb, almost bench-quality stability, and since the window was recessed in an encompassing arch, the muzzle wouldn't have been visible from the street nor, given the height, from the TBD across Houston, the only building on the horizon. The angle into the car and bodies would have been almost identical to Oswald's, depending on the subtleties of twist and turn of the president and the governor.

"And the windows? They've always been the kind that slid up and down, like these, not the kind that hinged outward?"

"Always up and down."

"And the floors? All wood, like now? Ever covered with carpet?"

"Just as you see it, except in those days, plasterboard covered the brick. Then as now, it was used for office space and storage. It was a much busier building, with a lot of garment wholesalers. They used it as a distribution center, so it was in one sense more a warehouse, particularly on the lower floors. The office suites were on the upper four floors."

Swagger wanted to see the angle from the front, that is, from the Elm Street windows. That was easily arranged, and he soon found himself facing down Elm from a more severe angle, yet if he stood to the left of the window and oriented himself to the street, he had an equally easy shot. Moreover, the shooter would have to be, by the mandate of the angles, concealed, as he'd be standing or sitting to the left and shooting out the window at roughly a forty-five-degree angle.

He also noted one of his watchers sitting on the park bench at Elm and Houston, right at the top of Dealey, where Bob had sat with Nick earlier. It was the black one, and he sat pretending to read a paper but in reality keeping his eyes nailed on the Dal-Tex entrance between the lid of his hat and the top of the newspaper. Bad craft. A smarter move would have been to amble down the street and set up against the Dallas Records Building across Elm, where he wouldn't have been so visible.

The roof was next. It was accessed through a narrow stairway at the top of the stairwell, then a horizontal door. Stepping onto it, you were invisible to any building extant then, for none had been higher than it in the vicinity. The roof supported but one structure, the elevator room, which was a freestanding brick pillbox centered in the rear of the building. It had clearly been rebuilt in one of the refurbs, and unlocked, it yielded a surprisingly minimalist interior, with three big units for hoisting, each attached to an electronic board, all of it evidently computer-controlled and run by robot program.

It would have been much smaller in '63, and Jean Marquez's evocation of a room jammed with gears and pulleys, with the naked winding and unwinding of the cables and the stench of lubrication, all of it dark and dangerous and crowded, rang true, even if the twenty-first-century iteration had become something a lot more high-tech.

And that really was that. No puzzles solved, but no possibilities rendered inoperative by reality. He thanked Dave Arons, shook hands in the lobby, and went on his way, awaiting the phone call on Nick's cell. It came when he was halfway back to the hotel.

"Have you picked them up?"

"Yeah. Black guy, porkpie, suit, no tie. White guy, chubby, no hat, plaid coat. Working out of a '09 red Chevy. Should I be worried?"

"No. They're local bozos. Ex–Dallas dicks. They work for Jackson-Barnes, the big detective agency. Their usual deal is following husbands to the love nest and getting some nice dirty ones. The dirtier the shot, the bigger the settlement. A blow job can cost Mr. Big a cool two million. Unbelievable. These guys are pretty good at following software millionaires and new-oil people around. They're overmatched by you."

"Who hired 'em? Richard?"

"Yeah. One of our agents has a source in their office."

"I wouldn't have thought Richard had the dough."

"See, that's interesting. He lives poor, he dresses poor, he's the complete assassination monomaniac, but he's worth over five mil and takes two vacations a year to, wouldn't you know it, Bangkok."

"Is he legit otherwise?"

"Everything checks out. Fifty-two years old. Brown University grad, went army intel for twenty, very good rep, some good undercover ops, mostly in Germany. The photographic-memory deal is apparently real, and he was valued for that. Faster than a computer. Married to a German gal, divorced. Retired a major in '04, showed up here in '05, set up the institute, got to know all the players, got them to trust and like him and view him as a harmless fuzzy-wuzzy nutcase but adorable. His vice appears to be porn. Not kiddie stuff, he's too tame for that. He buys a lot of DVDs from Japan and is a member of several 'Japorn' chat rooms, where he holds forth with great authority."

"Everybody has his little kink. Who pays for the 'institute'?"

"It's run on a yearly grant from the Thompson Foundation, a lefty outfit out of D.C. that also gives to big gun control, big green, big lib, and other similar entities. We can't trace it beyond that, so I don't know if the dough originates with them or not."

"Should I start packing?"

"No. These two Dallas flatfeet, as I say, are non-vi types. Both were in Vice, never did SWAT action. They wouldn't be involved in a hit. Too scary for them. They're strictly nine-to-fivers and want to go home at the end of the day and play with their kids."

"Okay, I won't even ditch 'em yet."

"Jackson-Barnes is almost certainly doing some deep data mining on 'Jack Brophy,' but the Justice Department work should withstand that easily. You'll check out. Richard will believe you're who you are. Then what?"

"Tonight, when Dumb and Dumber are home, I'll check out and disappear. I'll let Richard wonder if I've left or what. In a couple of days I'll catch him off-balance and start throwing some hardball at him. His next job, if he's something other than a paranoid, will be to get a pic or a print on me. I'll make sure he doesn't. Then we'll see what happens."

"I don't like that, Swagger. You're trying to goad the violence, and we may not be able to stop them in time."

"No, I'll stay in touch, and we'll set up a nice sting op when the time is right and see what we net."

"No guns."

"Not unless I know I'm being hunted. Then I'll hunt back."

Swagger spent another normal day, dropped by Richard's bookstore and bought three used books at the friends' rate, 25 percent discount—Bugliosi, Posner, and the abridged copy of the Warren Commission report; he owned them all but hadn't brought them—then went back to Dealey, sat, hung out, read yardage with a small Leica Rangefinder, walked this way and that. Then he went back to the

Adolphus, had an early meal, and went to bed. He was tailed the whole way.

At 4 a.m. he woke, showered, shaved, packed, and checked out of the hotel. He checked his suitcase at the hotel desk and carried an overnighter with the books and some fresh clothes, toiletries, and his .38 Super, mags, and speed scabbard, then slipped out a side door. He walked about nine blocks through a dark devoid of human activity, dodging the occasional police car whose attention he might merit, and got to Dallas's West End, a nightclub and entertainment zone a few blocks northwest of Dealey, where cabs were plentiful.

He arrived in twenty minutes at his destination, a randomly selected Econo Lodge on a road that led to the airport, and checked in, paying cash for a week so no one could trace him via credit card. He didn't think Richard had that capacity, but the big detective agency might. He called Nick's number and left his new address, then went back to bed.

Nick called at three the next afternoon. "My news is that the boys are going crazy trying to find you."

"Let 'em sweat."

"What's your plan now?"

"I'm going to chill here for a few days and hunker up and reread all this crap. As he said, it's so goddamn big, and no matter how you enter it, you get lost in the maze. I'm going to try out a more concentrated, less scattershot approach."

"I thought you had it nailed good by sticking with the rifle stuff."

"The rifle stuff is great as far as it goes, but I can't get beyond the timing issue. How'd they do it so fast? If it couldn't be done that fast, then the whole thing goes away, Lee Harvey's the bad boy, Robert Aptapton got smacked by a punk on meth, and Bob Lee goes back to his rocker, wiser but poorer. You could go nuts with all this stuff."

"Many a poor man has, I know, I'm one," said Nick.

"In a couple of days I'll pop in unexpectedly on Richard, and we get to the new game of now-he-sees-me-now-he-don't."

"Okay. Let me know what I can do."

That was that. Bob spent the three days poring over the three books, cross-checking, trying to find a pattern, looking for something that might tie everything together in a nice little package. A million others had done so before him, and like them, he failed. Nothing. No holes. Oswald did it, that was all, had to be, nothing else worked. Shot from Dal-Tex? On the wildest frontier of the physically possible but unsupported by any evidence whatsoever, except the generalized conceit that the third bullet came from behind and above, and certain windows at Dal-Tex were within the cone of trajectory that the computer age had imposed upon the reality of the event. No known photo existed that showed the upper floors of the building at around 12:30 that day, which would document whether or not a window had been open.

The one new fact was that someone had killed James Aptapton. If so, then maybe it was over something mundane, not the assassination of John F. Kennedy. Maybe Aptapton had divulged his theory, and that guy had recognized it as something new and special, wished it were his, and decided it was his. So he killed him in Baltimore for it. Murders have happened for lesser reasons by far, for pennies, for toys and gym shoes, for pride and prejudice, for honor and glory, for blow jobs and rim shots. Maybe it was Richard himself, though it was hard to feature someone so rumpled and disheveled as a badass killer. But maybe if "Jack Brophy" came clean with Richard, Richard might have some suggestions about who in the assassination community was capable of such a thing.

It was hard to know what to do next.

On the third day, Swagger could tolerate the inactivity no more and took a cab to an address in the suburbs that he'd found on the Internet. It was a huge sporting goods place called Outdoor Warehouse, and it lived up to its claim of holding nearly everything indoors that could be used outdoors. That included the hunting department, where, among the beautifully crafted new rifles and the black plastic assaulters and the endless variations of 9 mm, .38./.357s, and .45s in the gleaming showcases, he found a wide-ranging aisle of ammunition offerings and, between the 6.5 Creedmore and the 6.5 Swede, some boxes of 6.5 Mannlicher-Carcano. It was Czech or something, from an outfit called Prvi Partizan, but in the requisite 162-grain load. It was surprisingly cheap, at around fifteen dollars, and the thirteen-year-old behind the cash register up front displayed no sense of irony at the sight of a man buying a box of six-five Carc in Dallas, Texas.

Back in the room in the Econo Lodge, Bob opened the box, took out the twenty cartridges, and brought one close to his eye. It looked like a small blunt-nosed missile, all gleaming and reflective in the fluorescent light. The bullet was abnormally long, given the length of the case, and spoke of the nineteenth century with its blunt tip, which was the latest thing in the 1890s.

He looked at it from a dozen angles, trying to uncover its secrets. It was a lynchpin of sorts, close enough to the original to stand in for the bullet that LHO had nominally used.

Though it was the magic bullet, today it didn't look magic, just comically old-fashioned, with that rounded "meplat," the technical term for bullet point. He recalled the number of wounds it had inflicted, hitting the president high in the back, passing through him, hitting Governor Connally, passing through him, passing through his wrist and smacking his leg, all without doing much damage to itself. From a certain angle that bullet—Warren Commission Exhibit No. 399—did look as "pristine" as the one three inches from Swagger's eyes. But Bob recalled that from other angles, it became clear that the base of the bullet was severely mangled, crushed out of round by some impact, with core lead extruded from the interior by the impact. It was far from pristine but at the same time suspiciously intact.

Swagger had a melancholy fund of knowledge on what bullets did to bodies, his own and others'. To him, it was not nearly so mysterious when he considered that the bullet did not strike bone until it left the governor's body, when it struck his wrist, fracturing it, by which time it had slowed considerably from its initial muzzle velocity of two thousand feet per second and lost most of its power to crumple or break when colliding with hard structures.

Swagger couldn't get away from the *old-fashionedness* of it. It was old-fashioned by the standards of 1963. It was eighty-two years old in theory and design when it struck the president. Lots of folks missed that; it was just another bullet to them.

Another way to look at the bullet was to consider its origin and purpose. Too many fools had written about the event without reference to those two issues. Too many fools thought a bullet was just a heavy piece of lead screwed into a cartridge and sent arbitrarily on its way. In fact, even in 1891 bullets and their design and performance were among the most overengineered items in the human inventory, thought about hard and mathematically; long before men had indoor plumbing or hot running water, they had substantive mathematical treatises on ballistic performance, principles, and laws. Ballistics were always the first thing the state's mind turned to, not the last.

That bullet, like the one in its brass casing in his hand now, weighed 162 grains and consisted of copper gilding of unusual thickness over a lead core, 1.25 inches in length with a round nose. It was designed after great research and experimentation to perform a certain military job, which the Italian general staff believed would be of importance in the late nineteenth and early twentieth centuries. There was nothing arbitrary about it. It wasn't designed just "to kill" but to kill a particular enemy in a particular environment.

It occurred to Swagger that to understand WC399, he had to understand the military realities of the Italian army in 1891, when the round was adopted as the standard infantry cartridge, during the general European upgrade of that era from single-shot muskets to magazine-fed bolt actions, such as the Mauser K98, the French Lebel, the British Enfield, and eventually, the American Springfield.

Who was the Italian general staff planning to fight, and in what environment? The Italians have never been expansionist, and Mussolini was thirty years down the pike. They were not great colonizers with an overseas empire to safeguard, like the British or the Germans. Despite two pathetic forays into Africa, they did not see their troops fighting indigenous forces in Asia, India, or the Pacific. What they imagined was protecting the good life that was lived in their beautiful country, with its abundance of resources, its grapes, its pasta, all roasted by a warm sun.

The Italians of 1891 understood that the important battles to come would be defensive in nature. They would not invade. They would be invaded. Their task was to stop invasion in its tracks. Where would such a battle take place? The amphibious landing had not yet been attempted, much less perfected, so it seemed likely a foe—German or Austrian, most likely—would come overland. If you look at the map, that tells you much: the invasion would have to come through the Alps. It would be a mountain war.

In such a battle, who would an Italian soldier be trying to kill and at what range? Well, Swagger reasoned, the nature of mountain war is that the ranges would tend to be long. Just look at Afghanistan and its five-hundred-yard firefights. Mountain war would involve shooting uphill, downhill, across valleys. Except in rare instances, there'd be little hand-to-hand combat; targets could be expected in the two-to-four-hundred-meter range. That would dictate a bullet noted for its accuracy, which in turn would result in a long, thin bullet, so that the rifling could be counted upon to give efficient spin, with an unusual density so as to resist the unpredictable spurts of wind found up high. It occurred to him that was an excellent description of the M-C 6.5 in the ideal, although Italian manufacturing practices may have meant that the ideal was seldom achieved.

Who would the Italian soldier in the mountains be shooting at? The enemy would be a German or an Austrian mountain soldier, skilled in climbing, hearty, with a higher pain threshold, a more athletic demeanor, superb physical conditioning, an elite soldier. One more thing, the key thing: he would be heavily dressed. He would be wearing underwear, long underwear, heavy woolen pants, a heavy woolen shirt or battle tunic, probably a sweater or some kind of tight leather-and-fleece vest, a parka heavily matted (no Gore-Tex in those days), all bundled tight by belts and pack straps.

To kill him, what do you have to do? You have to penetrate him. You have to drive a bullet into him with such force that it will not deviate if it strikes a button or a strap or a canteen, that will not dis-integrate if it strikes a bone, but continues on its quest for heart or lungs or guts that lay deep inside the insulation. That is what the Mannlicher-Carcano was designed to do, and that is exactly what WC399 did on November 22, 1963. It was not an anomaly. It per-formed totally within its design characteristics.

Swagger saw immediately where his thought process had taken him. It was enough to drive a man to drink. If the second bullet per-formed to design specification, that meant that the third bullet did not. It disintegrated when it should not have. And that was the key question of the whole goddamned thing.

The true magic bullet of the JFK assassination was bullet num-ber three. It was a heavily encapsulated round designed to penetrate, not fly apart. It killed by penetrating, not by detonating. Moreover, at a range of 265 feet, it had lost a great deal of its momentum—from a high of 2,100 feet per second, it had probably dropped off to 1,800 feet per second. It hit the skull fully flush. Swagger had no difficulty understanding why the president's head yielded a massive, explo-sive wound upon impact, as the bullet would have pushed an energy wave through any material it encountered, and if that material were enclosed, the results inevitably would be explosive, but he couldn't see why the bullet itself would have detonated. There was no ballistic principle for such a thing happening.

Why did the third bullet explode?

CHAPTER 6

Richard Monk allowed himself a steak once a week, and on Friday, he went to the Palm in the West End. He had a nice martini (straight up, slightly dirty, olives), ordered the small filet medium rare with mashed potatoes, nursed his 'tini while the steak was seared, and then looked up in astonishment when Jack Brophy slid in across from him.

"Richard, I do declare, mind if I join you?"

"Jack, God, I thought you'd left. I tried to call you, and they said you'd left."

"I changed locations, that's all."

"Where are you now?"

"See, that's it, Richard. I'll be honest with you. I think I'm being followed."

"Followed?" said Richard with a little too much dramatic emotion driving the word from his lips.

"Two guys, I'm sure. Black guy, white guy, a team working out of one car. You wouldn't know anything about that, would you? You were in intel, you know how these things can be arranged."

"If I was in intel, I'd be a trained liar, right? So if I tell you no, you won't believe it. I don't know what to say except that if you look at it, why on earth would I have you followed, which, after all, would cost some money, and I don't have enough of the stuff to throw around like that. The piece of meat I ordered is my one weekly luxury."

"Okay, okay," Bob said. "Sorry, didn't mean it as an accusation. But let me ask you this: do you know anybody in the wide body of buffs, fanatics, researchers, whatever, who might follow me? I'm thinking I may have a valuable piece of intellectual property. Maybe you mentioned it to someone who mentioned it to someone who thought it sounded interesting and decided to look into me."

"Jack, I don't even know what it is. Something about guns, that's all."

"That's right," said Bob.

"Maybe it has to do with something else altogether, something back in Boise. Child support?"

"If my children can't support themselves by now, there's nothing I can do for 'em. I think the money manager sends my ex-wives their checks, so I believe I'm okay on that. No, my life's too dull for intrigue."

"Jack, no one's approached me, asked me any questions about you, anything like that."

"Richard, I'm just going to disappear for a bit. You okay with that?"

"Sure, Jack."

"I'll see you in three days at that Mex place on Main, twelve-thirty."

"You've got it, friend."

Of course, Swagger didn't show at the Mexican place, but two FBI agents did, and they confirmed that the operatives from the Jackson-Barnes detective agency were in place down the street with a Nikon and a heavy telephoto lens.

Swagger called Richard while he sat there, apologized for being unavoidably detained, and promised to make it up to him and that they'd meet soon, but he couldn't set a time because his schedule was so "fluid." He let three days pass and ambushed Richard in the parking lot outside the Y.O. restaurant, another famous joint just across from the Palm in the West End.

Richard was a little buzzed from the martini, and his belly was loaded with protein and carbohydrates. "Man, you show up at the oddest times," he said, perturbed, Bob guessed, because his photo team wasn't with him and there was no way he could call it in to them in time.

"I'm secret-agent man, all over the place. I think I dumped my followers. Let's get a cab and drive around for a while."

"Jack, maybe you're overdoing it a bit. I should tell you again, in the past three days, nobody asked me anything about you, and nobody's keeping an eye on me or anything. I do have something for you."

"Yeah?"

"I have a friend who has a gun as close as you can get to the Oswald rifle. It's a Mannlicher-Carcano Model 38 carbine, serial number CV2755, just eleven shy of Oswald's, from Terni. It's got the Japanese scope and mount, and it was ordered from Klein's just a week or so before Oswald ordered his, in March 1963. I'm guessing the same technician attached the scope to the rifle. You couldn't come closer. A wealthy collector I know paid over three grand for it. I think you'd find it interesting to shoot. We've even got some white-box 6.5 from Western. You know how hard that stuff is to come by."

"Nah," said Swagger. "See, it doesn't matter how 2755 shoots. It only matters how 2766 shoots. For a dozen reasons, a hundred reasons, they could shoot different by far. And you know what, Richard? In my theory, it doesn't matter a lick how even Oswald's rifle shot that day."

"Okay, I get it. Second gunman, second rifle. Another Mannlicher."

"Close, but no. Let me tell you this: I don't know why, I don't know who, but goddammit, I know how. Come on, let's get that cab and go for a ride. On me."

He herded Richard toward the street in a friendly-bear manner, and the younger man couldn't resist. If working for somebody, he had to maintain the contact; if the assassination nut he claimed to be, he had to find out whether the new info was cool.

They got in, and Swagger instructed the driver to drive around for a while on the meter, that he'd pay whatever. It was a great gig for the fellow, who rarely got a big ride this late at night. Off they went.

"Richard," Swagger said, "I want your judgment. Maybe I'm nuts and all I've got is bullshit. Or maybe it's part of the answer. Anyhow, I had a what-you-call-it, epiphany today, which makes me even more sure I'm on to something. It came out of something you said. Let me run this by you—"

"Jack, I don't know anything about guns. I can't make a judgment."

"You'll get this, Richard. Then tell me if it's worth hiding, worth looking for an author to partner up with, if it has any value book- or movie-wise. I don't know about that stuff; you do."

"Okay, Jack. I'll give it my best shot."

"Here's the key question. Why did the third bullet explode? In my opinion, nobody has answered that correctly. The best answer you get is, it exploded because it exploded. Bullets occasionally explode. You can't predict it, but you can't deny it. Get something moving that fast, anything can happen."

"What's your answer? Why *did* the third bullet explode?"

"You said, 'As it performed its killing duty, it ceased to exist,' isn't that right? The bullet from the future, which, in doing its duty, obliterated itself, its rifle, its shooter, and a hundred years of tragedy."

"I said that, yes. That's the crux of the conceit. It's kind of cool, I think."

"Richard, do you know what 'lingering' means?"

"Of course I do."

"I mean something that hangs around, won't leave your mind, seems always there, that kind of lingering."

"Yes, I know what that kind of lingering is."

"What you said, 'it ceased to exist,' that lingered for me. It lingered and lingered, and finally, I realized something. The third bullet. The one that hit Kennedy. It ceased to exist."

"So it did. To the eternal annoyance of the Warren Commission and the delight of conspiracy animals the world over."

"No, no. It wasn't an accident. Here's the point. *It had to do that*. It was engineered to do that. And because the engineering was sound, that's what made the conspiracy possible."

"Explosive bullet, huh? Just like *The Day of the Jackal,* with the mercury inside. Or I suppose—"

"No, no. No explosive, no mercury, no glycerin, nothing like that. All those leave chemical traces, easily detectable by the forensics of 1963."

"I believe the Warren Commission asked the FBI forensics guy about such a possibility, now that you mention it."

"Yeah, Frazier his name was, and as usual, he was both wrong and stupid. I'm talking about something else. What I mean is that the bullet itself, without changing its composition, its metallurgy, its anything, was engineered in such a way that it had to explode—it had to, that was the brilliance of it all—so that it left no record of its existence. It was the real magic bullet, only everybody was too stupid to figure that out."

"So what are you talking about? How do you make a bullet explode?"

Swagger said, "I'm talking about velocity."

He continued to explain to Richard, who sat rapt, as if he did know something about guns after all.

"Where are you?" Nick's voice came over the cell. It was a few days later. In the meantime, he'd stood up Richard at a planned meet, sent him a few e-mails asking whether he'd come across anything similar to his velocity theory, which Richard was presumably checking, and generally making an annoyance of himself without showing up anywhere to be photographed.

"I've switched motels," Swagger said, giving him the new address. "I'm closer in now, and I can get cabs easier. Man, am I wearing out the ATM, all the cash I've been using."

"Okay, listen to me," Nick said. New tone to his voice: official

G-man, dead-zero serious. "I want you to stay there. Under no circumstances are you to leave and expose yourself. Don't make me
send a car to bring you in and put you under protective; just comply,
okay? It's for your own good."

"What's happened?"

"This may mean nothing. I have no evidence it's anything other
than what it seems to be, but still, it's provocative. A black Dodge
Charger, brand-new, the big muscle-car variant with that super-
charged 370 Hemi under the hood, was stolen out of a garage in Fort
Worth yesterday. It's exactly the kind of muscle car that was used in
Baltimore."

Swagger said, "He's here. He's hunting me. Either Richard told
him, or someone is on Richard and knows what Richard knows. And
whoever it is, he doesn't like the velocity theory. See, Nick, this *proves*
it has to do with JFK."

"It doesn't prove anything like it. It proves a muscle car was stolen. Maybe it's in parts in some chop shop, or on the way to a soldier
of the Zeta cartel's garage in Nogales, or being driven around by a
couple of meth heads with chicken feed for brains. Those are all possibilities, and they may be more probable than this slightly improbable car killer, whoever he is, if he even exists."

"Ask James Aptapton if he exists."

"So. Here's what I require. You stay put. I mean put. Room-service pizza and Chinese food, lots of daytime cable, get to know your
housekeeping staff, that sort of thing. Meanwhile, I am going to put
together a task force. I want to bring Dallas Metro in, and since it
involves cars, maybe the Texas Highway Patrol. We'll figure out some
kind of sting, find a way to expose you under controlled circumstances, and when he thinks he's taking you—assuming he exists—
we'll take him. Bet he has some interesting beans to spill."

"Everything says he's a pro. He spills no beans. He shuts up, takes
whatever ride he gets without ratting, because he believes his outfit
will bust him somewhere along the line, maybe not this year but the

next. Those guys have made friends with that kind of math. It's the price they pay for the chicks and the coke and the respect, for being a hard guy. Nick, he won't tell you shit. By being here, he's already told you everything he's going to tell you."

"Ten years in Huntsville, followed by life in Hagerstown, that might budge him."

Bob sighed. "You're thinking like a lawman. Everything's leverage. Sometimes you have to send a message; that's the best leverage."

"Bob, I'm going to have you picked up if you pull any shit. You will go down. You have to play by our rules on this one. It could be a big bust. It all goes away if you go cowboy."

Bob saw that Nick was bluffing. It wasn't so. Dead, the pro would be just as much a trophy as alive, particularly if an FBI undercover put him under through Nick's supervision. And whoever he was, his identity would be his true testimony and point to a next step.

"Do I have your word?"

"Please tell me you'll set this up fast."

"It takes time, coordination between agencies. If he's after you, he's not going to go away. We haven't even spotted him yet. We'll put a net around Richard and see if he shows. If we nail him, we'll move on to the next step. I need time from you. And sniper patience."

"He'll pick up on that in two seconds."

"For God's sake, you—"

"It'll happen late, no traffic, no pedestrians. Tomorrow night, near Dealey, in some alley. He likes alleys. Have a rolling team set up, get there fast, and it's your crime scene. It'll be your kill."

"Or your death."

"This guy ran down a decent man who never did a thing except pay his taxes and educate his kids. Broke his spine in an alley. Now let's see him try that trick against some real competition. I won't lie to you, Nick. I'm not going to sit here in this goddamn room eating Chinese and rereading books for the tenth time. It's not my nature. My nature is the hunt."

Nick said, "I can't authorize this."

"I'm your undercover. You get all the credit."

"I'm hanging up. I cannot authorize this."

"But you will not pick me up, right?"

"Agh," said Nick in frustration. He hung up.

Swagger went to the closet and removed his small overnight bag from behind the spare blanket, feeling the heaviness inside. He opened it, picking up the stainless-steel Kimber .38 Super, taking reassurance from the familiar lines of the 1911 platform as designed by John M. Browning over a century ago, with its twenty-three-degree grip angle, its flatness, its ergonomic genius of safety and slide-release placement created in a world where the word "ergonomics" hadn't been invented. It was already cocked and locked, for what was the point of having a pistol if you couldn't shoot it fast? He knew that nine hardball +P Winchester 130-grainers were in the mag and a tenth in the chamber, bullets that had their own velocity attributes, moving out at 1300 with enough juice to puncture glass or metal and keep on the straightaway for a killing shot. The gun had a familiarity; its ancient frame was of the perfect width and boasted the perfect relation of grip to bore so that when it came to hand, it went on point naturally. Bob slipped a speed scabbard, a minimalist concealment holster that yielded pistol to draw in a flash, on his belt, along with a mag pouch that already concealed two mags. He cinched his belt, then slid the pistol into the holster so that it rested three inches behind the point of his hip but flat against his body.

He put on his khaki coat to conceal it. Then he put his lucky dollar in his pocket. His lucky dollar was four quarters Scotch-taped together. In the pocket, the four coins supplied steadying weight, but if he had to draw, he'd give it a swat, and the heaviness of the coins would pull the coat back and clear and straight, presenting the pistol to the same hand that came back to snatch and deploy it.

Then he called Richard and told him he had to see him tonight at eleven, at the bench outside the Book Depository.

CHAPTER 7

The Russian saw them. Two men sitting on the bench by the reflecting pool. The Book Depository was well lit at night from the front, so the two were bold and clear in the refracted glow. On top of that, the Russian's eyesight was absurdly superior, so the details leaped at him. No problem telling target from bait. Target was tall, angular. He looked like he'd been around some, been hammered here and there, even if his posture was relaxed. The Russian suspected he'd do better than the last one, that dish of pudding in the alley.

The Russian was parked out of the lights on Houston, across from the Book Depository near the tracks on Pacific. He had a good angle, and he was invisible to them. He hunted for signs of wariness but picked up nothing. The older man never looked around, his body language was not tense, he never swallowed or licked his lips, all tells of high anxiety. He wore a khaki coat, a red baseball hat, jeans, and a pair of boots. He was talking earnestly and listening earnestly.

Soon the chat would be over. Target would get up, and in whatever direction he went, the Russian would follow at a decent interval. The trick of the hit was the timing. No traffic downtown this late, and the police scanning radio indicated no presence of official vehicles in the vicinity. The plan was: wait for him to cross a street and head down a block. Then circle that block at speed with good angle control at the corners to beat him to the next intersection, get there before him, park with lights out. When he approached the intersection, he'd look both ways, probably wait until he had the green even though it was an empty weeknight, then start across the street. Find the angle of interception, accelerate through him (the Dodge did zero to sixty in 3.7 seconds) and smash him hard. Speed should be up to sixty-five by then. At the last second, as he turned to the noise, hit him with the lights, which would visually disorient him and freeze him in place. The kill was certain. There would be no time to react.

He waited, he waited, he waited. Occasionally, a cab pulled by, headed to the passenger-rich zone of the West End, not far away. Music and light issued from that neighborhood, but it meant nothing to the Russian. He sat in the dark corridor on the dark pavement in the dark car. On either side of him, two square brick buildings, dark as well, loomed. He had no idea what they were.

"Donahue seems to come the closest," Richard said. They sat as if stage-lit on the bench, near the reflecting pool filled with Scope, under the shagginess of the overhanging oaks. A cool breeze stirred the leaves above to low whispers in the night, perfect for talking conspiracy.

"He goes nutty at the end," Richard continued, "but it's a logical nuttiness. He's tried to answer your question: why did the third bullet explode? His answer is that a Secret Service man in the follow car with something called an AR-15, brand-new in '63, I don't know what it is, rose and accidentally fired after the second shot. That was the bullet that hit Kennedy."

"And being a thin-jacketed, high-velocity 5.56-millimeter round impacting at close range, it behaved differently than the much heavier Carcano 6.5 from six times farther out, and that it was indeed engineered to explode? Is that it?"

"Yes."

Swagger grunted.

"You don't like?"

"It's hard to believe that A) the agent could fire a bullet from an unusual-looking space-age rifle in front of, what, two thousand people, and that nobody would see it or hear it. Or B) on top of that, by the randomness of the universe, his muzzle would line up pointed directly at Kennedy's head."

"It's a theory with many difficulties, yes. As I say, discredited."

"You're telling me. I guess the point is, he has good analysis of the Carcano, and he was stuck as to a way to explain the behavior of the third bullet. That AR-15, what would later be called an M-16, seemed to answer all the questions, and it sure as hell was there, but he didn't realize it raised more than it answered."

"There is testimony that some people smelled burnt powder in Dealey. And it would explain the government 'cover-up' and why they would never admit that friendly fire killed JFK."

"I can't buy it. I acknowledge that gun accidents frequently turn on great anomalies, like a .45 that's never before doubled suddenly doubling, or a ricochet pattern that you couldn't duplicate in a million years. That does happen. But here you've got two, one at either end of the shot, appearing in front of two thousand witnesses, and no one saw it?"

"As I say, many problems. Still, you should read the book and see what you make of the first hundred pages. I think it accords with your idea, to the degree that I understand it and am capable of making such a judgment."

"Great, Richard. Richard comes through again."

"You wanted to see me. What was it? You didn't just want my report. I had the idea it was an emergency."

"I get these ideas and get excited. Here's my new one. It has to do with the angles."

"What about the angles?"

"It's very odd. Everybody who knows nothing thinks it's all about distance. Close shot easy, far shot hard. Well, that ain't true, and it especially ain't true when you're shooting on the deflection."

"Deflection? No comprendo."

"Deflection. Shooting at a moving target. You've got to solve the angle, that is, find a way to produce not a hit but an interception. You have to put the bullet where the thing is going to be. It's like nobody who wrote about the Kennedy assassination ever shot a duck on the wing. So it's all made up, assumptions, guesses, hunches."

"Hmmm," said Richard. "Interesting. All right, I'll bite. Tell me what you're getting at."

Bob explained it to Richard. "So, does it hold water? Does it make sense to you? I think this is the best one yet. How would I check it? Does it connect with anything else? Has anyone else thought of this approach?"

"Jack, I love the way you get all into this, and how it becomes so important to you that you have to discuss it at"—he looked at his watch—"ten after midnight. Offhand, it seems new to me."

"I thought you had a photographic memory."

"I thought I did too. You are testing the limits of it, however, so let me think about it overnight. Maybe do some checking. I do have a business to run, you know. Anyhow, it's late, and I'm no longer a monomaniac like you; I'm just a human, so I need sleep. I'll check, you call in the next few days, and we'll get together soon. Right?"

"Sorry, Richard. Okay, swell."

"Drop you somewhere?"

"No, I'll get a cab. I appreciate the way you humor me without really seeming to humor me. Your mother raised an honorable man."

"Thank you, Jack. Okay, I know well enough to know that I can't persuade you to accept a ride. I'll await your call."

They rose, shook hands, and separated, each heading off in his own darkness.

The Russian watched. The tall one crossed Houston and headed up Elm into the high buildings of downtown. It seemed he had a limp, as if someone had taken a hard shot at his hip. There had to be a story behind that! It slowed the old man considerably, and the

Russian winced at the clear discomfort the man felt while on the go. The Russian waited for him to drag his wretched, bent old body along until it disappeared behind the corner of the building to his left, waited twenty seconds, then turned on his lights, drove slowly and under control to Elm, and turned left. He could see the tall man half a block ahead, sending out vibrations of painful imprecision but at the same time holding not a care for security in his mind, lost in whatever internal drama consumed him, limping along.

The Russian timed it perfectly, made certain not to look at the man, since some people have a weird gift for feeling the presence of another's eyes upon them, reached him just as he was at the corner, and turned left. He drove at under thirty to the next block, turned right at the corner, and hammered it, aware only marginally that he was on the railroad tracks of Pacific Avenue, shooting up to sixty-five in three seconds to reach the next corner, found the ideal angle, and hardly lost a mile an hour on his controlled right-hand burn around the corner, then pulled up in the block with the intersection a hundred feet or so ahead of him, and halted, downshifting to neutral, putting his lights out. All was fine. It was no problem at all.

He waited, he waited, he waited. Time sometimes goes slow on the hunt. But at last his quarry arrived, ambling into view at the same distracted old man's pace, disfigured by the limp so that he had an odd comic bearing. The Russian cracked a rare smile at the old man's funny walk.

The Russian also had a gift for instantly computing interception angles. He knew not to go to the pedal at the man's first step into the street or even the second. He had time to check for beams from oncoming traffic out of sight, and he noted there wasn't any traffic. At the target's third step, he got the go-code from his deep brain and rammed the car into first, controlling the clutch with a virtuoso's touch, and a split second later, a really fast throw into second as the car's 370 horses roared into high gallop and got there as fast as anything on earth except a straight custom drag. The sound of the engine eating gas with a basso profundo growl and alchemizing it instantly into speed filled the air. The car lurched ahead so powerfully, it turned the hard edges of reality into a blur.

Swagger had the gun in his hand along his right leg, hidden behind his comically exaggerated limp, and at the roar, losing no time on surprise, none on regret, nada on indecision, and in his pure-killer move, beautiful and stoic and all-American gunman, he pivoted and, because smooth is fast, slid the gun up so smooth it moved at a rate that has no place in time, and his subconscious acquired the front sight exactly as it came to center, driver's-side windshield, and the pistol's double tap lasted but a tenth of a second, recoil not fast enough to catch up to fully firing fast-twitch muscles of the trigger pull, even as one muzzle flash became another and two pieces of hot brass spewed from the ramjet breech eight inches apart. The windshield yielded instantly into a haze of micro-fracture, the car careened right, ate up the curb, hit a building with the sound of metal crunching, flipped, and roared on its beautiful, glossy black flank along the sidewalk, chewing up pavement, spraying sparks and stone debris, ripping sheets of window out of storefronts, its hood bending and twisting like a burning piece of paper, at last halting in a heap of twisted steel, with the stench of gasoline, tendrils of steam and smoke arising from several wounds in the body and engine well.

In the quiet that followed, Swagger slipped the gun into his holster and grabbed his cell.

"Memphis," came the quick answer.

"I'm at Elm and North Market. He's piled up to the right, on the sidewalk, no citizen collateral, all of it clean. Get your team here fast, and get me the fuck out of town."

"What happened to him?" Nick said.

"Bring a body bag," said Swagger. "And a mop."

PART II

Mockba

"What it is ain't exactly clear"

CHAPTER 8

Moscow

It was a perfect twilight in utopia as couples strolled, children frolicked, lovers squeezed, dogs yipped, and intellectuals theorized in the park off Ukrainski Boulevard. They glided with the radiant happiness of those who were happy to be who they were where they were when they were. "Life, it's good" seemed to be the prevailing ethos. Lights winked in the soft darkness, more show than anything else, for in this urban playing field, there was no crime, or very little, nearly full employment, and low taxes. The dark for once concealed the construction frenzy of backhoes, bulldozers, and cranes as daytime Moscow reconstructed itself for about the thirtieth time in its long and convoluted history, this time giving capitalism a good shot even as the citizens ebbed and flowed through and around all the projects, dashing nimbly to avoid being crushed, either by the errant construction machine or that jet-black gleaming Ferrari whistling down the cobblestones at ninety per. Meanwhile, observing without comment, stone or steel men in greatcoats with those clamshell World War II helmets and the old red tommy guns, with their signature ventilated barrels and gangster-style seventy-one-round drums, stood fifteen feet tall every block or two, as if unsure whether this was what all their fighting and dying had protected and made possible.

Flanked by the nine-story banks of the Kutuzovsky 7 apartment complex and nestled under trees, the restaurant Khachapuri was operating at full meat ahead. It was a place that specialized in animal parts on sticks. They arrived glistening yet crisp, with the fat broiled out of them by raw flame, chunks of pure protein whose odor filled the air and made one think of Cossack camps along the Don after a good day massacring Tsarist infantry in about 1652. The restaurant itself had a Cossack quality, as it was an open-air tent affiliated with the kitchen of a bar in the building across the sidewalk, and a gathering place for those of the new generation seeking sustenance, vodka, and comradeship, at which it excelled in providing.

Swagger, of course, couldn't try the vodka, knowing he'd end up in Siberia with a new Uzbek wife and nine children, plus some really cool tattoos; he wasn't hungry, though the meat smells touched some primal thing in him; and the comradeship he sought was of a particular kind.

He leaned alone at the bar, drinking *koka*, as Coca-Cola was called here in the capital city, and watching the proceedings with a wary eye, not quite willing to buy in to it. Something held him back, history perhaps, his own as well as his country's and his culture's. It was hard to believe he'd been nurtured to hate all these people and they'd turned out to be so beautiful, energetic, and happy. Gee, folks, he thought, glad we didn't blow you to nuclear shreds in about 1977; that would have been a big mistake.

It was his second day in Moscow. The first he'd spent wandering from his room at the Metropol onto Red Square and around the area and being stunned for the first time by the sheer joy of the city, a dusty, ramshackle, still-makeshift-after-865-years place. The ranks of Stalinist apartment buildings, with their dour exteriors and their ancient memories of tears and slaughter, all had been invaded by retail at the ground level and boasted gaudy signals of various frivolous goods, every luxury car and perfume and fashion designer known to man. In at least seven points on the horizon, brand-new Dallases of steel and chrome pierced the sky, lording over the five-story flatness of the now-dead Communist reality at their feet. It was a true gold-rush city, even if over a millennium old and the site of a massacre hall of fame. He couldn't get over how the place throbbed.

He saw her then. She had the smart, tough look of a journalist, nothing to her of show or pretense, just a kind of irony playing through her eyes under her American hairstyle. She wore pants and a black T-shirt, as fitted the warm weather, and looked comfortable among the natives.

"Ms. Reilly? I'm Swagger."

"Oh," she said, "the great Swagger. Nice to meet a hero." Handshakes, tight smiles, a little awkwardness.

"I'm just a beat-up goat trying to stay on the wagon around all this potato juice," he said.

"The Russians do squish a nice potato. Here, I'll get us seated."

He followed her to the maître d's station, and the maître d' in turn led them through the tent, past family and office parties of swilling laughers and carnivores, to a smallish table at the margins of the place, which looked out on the recreations of the vast parkland, crosscut with walkers on both two and four legs and other sorts of relaxed civilians.

"You weren't followed?" he asked.

"This is exciting," she said. "No one's ever asked me that before. No, I don't think so. The Russians don't follow American reporters anymore. They're much more interested in making money."

"So I've heard. Anything's for sale in Moscow."

"Anything," she said.

"What about rent?" he said. "See, I want to rent the Lubyanka for a night."

She laughed. "Good luck with that. You must know oligarchs."

"Since I don't know what an oligarch is, I don't know if I know any. What are they, by the way? I saw that word in the English-language paper."

"Rich guys. Tycoons, billionaires, conspicuous consumers. Mostly ex-KGB goons. They were buddies with Yeltsin in '93, and when he dismantled the state economic apparatus, they butted their way to the head of the line and got all the pie. In short order, they became mega-rich. Pie, pie, pie, all day long. Now they drive around in gold-plated limos, marry flight attendants, buy American sports teams, try to get on Page 6, and generally run the place. Abramovich, Krulov, Alekperov, Vekselberg, Ixovich. One of 'em is married to Yeltsin's daughter, as a matter of fact. Will and I did a story on them. Petonin, Tarkio, a couple more I can't think of."

"The names would be lost on me anyhow. But it sounds typical. That's how headquarters towns always work. Anyhow, nice of you to meet me."

"How couldn't I? I did some checking, and if half the rumors are true, it's like meeting John Wayne and Ted Williams and Audie Murphy in one man. Plus, your daughter says you're a teddy bear."

It was through his daughter, Nikki, a TV news reporter in Washington, that Swagger had effected a meet-up with Kathy Reilly, the *Washington Post*'s correspondent in Moscow.

The waitress came, and the reporter consulted the menu, which essentially consisted of meat with more meat, some other kinds of meat, some usual meat, some unusual meat, and, of course, meat. Kathy Reilly ordered some meat.

"So you're working for the FBI, is that right?" she said.

"More or less. That's what Nikki believes, that's what the Russians believe. But they also believe my name is Jerry Homan and that I'm a special agent. I have all the credentials and diplomatic okays to back it up. I did meet with the State Department–FBI liaison guy at our embassy, and he thinks I'm who I say I am."

"Wow. Undercover stuff. This is turning into something glamorous. What's it all about?"

"Short version, I was asked to look into the death of a man in Baltimore by hit-and-run. He'd just returned from Dallas, where he'd been asking pointed questions. I went to Dallas and asked the same pointed questions. Sure enough, someone tried to kill me, hit-and-run."

"It didn't work out for him, I take it."

"Not exactly. Fortunately, I'd contacted an FBI agent in Dallas, a fine man with whom I've worked before, and he agreed to run me as a contract undercover even though I was the one who brought it to him. It was a thin fiction, but it held up. Then it turned out that the fellow who tried to kill me was what you might call a trophy. Russian mafioso, associated with something called the Iz-may-lov-skay-a gang here."

"Okay, now I'm impressed."

"That bad, huh?"

"Very bad."

"This character was wanted by Interpol all over Europe, he was wanted by the Moscow police, and he had relocated to a Coney Island outpost of the Iz-may-what's-it empire and was doing jobs for them and freelancing. Technically, I'm here to try to find out from this end who he was working for. Not which family, but who contracted with that family either here or in New York to hire him and for what reason. I've got an appointment with a top Russian gang cop in a few days to try to get some dope. We may talk to some snitches and so forth."

"You don't want to get too close to the Izmaylovskaya boys, take it from me," she said.

"I'm just going to ask some polite questions and go on my way. No need to mix it up with the locals."

"Sound policy. I will tell you, and you didn't hear it from me, that the oligarch Krulov is said to be most intimately associated with the Izmaylovskayas. His enemies had a way of disappearing or getting hit by vagrant untraceable cars."

"Krulov," said Swagger, marking it down internally.

The dinner arrived. It appeared to be meat. There were also suspicious vegetables, which Swagger avoided, and some soups, equally menacing. He did enjoy the animal he ate, whatever species it might have been, however it died. "It's very good," he said.

"She said you needed a favor. It happens that this is a perfect time. My husband is in Siberia—no, I didn't send him, he's covering an oil conference—and I'm sort of at loose ends, with only thumbsuckers due. So I can take you around, introduce you to people, if you want."

"I'm not sure you should be seen with me. These people are serious. That's why I asked to meet after dark, close to home, at a loud public place."

"Do you think—"

"I just don't know. I do know if you look into Russian mafia, you can get dead all of a sudden. I might have some skills that would help me get out of a tight, dangerous situation, but unless you've had a lot of SEAL training, I doubt that you do."

"Not unless it's slipped my mind."

"Nikki says you speak Russian well but that you read it *very* well."

"I can get by on the streets. I read it like a native."

"I'm trying to get hold of some records. Copies won't work; I have to see the actual files and try to determine to what, if any, degree they've been tampered with. I'm hoping you'll read them for me. Or at least scan them. I hope to arrange it discreetly, so you'll be in no danger of exposure. Is that a possibility?"

"I suppose it is. What are you looking for?"

"The Russian James Bond," he said. "Circa 1963. I can feel him. I can recognize his talent, his imagination, his will, his decisiveness, his creativity. He was their top agent, and in 1963, it's possible he pulled off the operation of the century. I've come to Moscow for him."

It was another box of a building, this one much bigger. No bricks, some sort of yellow stucco, maybe ten stories tall, with all the early twentieth- or late nineteenth-century gewgaws, like pillars and arches and stone window frames, its flat roof festooned with radio communications antennas. And it was gigantic, about a block wide, a huge chunk of real estate eating up land on an empty Moscow circle a mile from Red Square.

"That's it, huh?" Swagger asked.

"In the flesh. Or in yellow stucco. Source of evil, source of cunning, source of murder, violence, conspiracy, treachery, torture. It's a very bad place. You did not want to make people in that building angry with you."

"I get it."

"Nothing military in there," said Mikhail Stronski. "It's all secret-agent spy shit, games in games in games, always fucking people up."

It was the Lubyanka: former home of the Cheka, GPU, OGPU, MGB, NKVD, and KGB, and now FSB. During the purges, many were hauled here from Swagger's polished luxury hotel, the Metropole, which in the thirties housed the wreckers and oppositionists of Comintern, and in Lubyanka's cellars, they were shot behind the ear. No one knew what became of the bodies. Maybe they were still there.

"It's hard to hate a building," said Swagger.

"This one, no problem."

Stronksi was a heavyset man with a glowering face that seemed like a map of Eastern-bloc misfortune. He had wintry gray eyes under wintry gray hair and heavy bones, and looked as if he could crush a diamond between his fingers, or at least fracture it a little bit. He had a bear's body, yet at fifty-seven he moved with surprising grace. He had been in the same business as Swagger, but his outfit was called Spetsnaz, and he practiced the trade in Afghanistan—fifty-six kills.

An American gun writer who'd come to Russia to do a feature on the new Russian sniper rifle, the 12.7 mm KSVK, had found him and interviewed him; Swagger saw the story, contacted the gun writer, got the e-mail address and a recommendation, and reached out across the ocean to another high-grass crawler, another brother of the one-shot kill, another infiltrator and exfiltrator who knew too much about certain things but would never speak of them. Stronski had heard of Swagger—it was a small world, after all—so the two men were a natural fit, having killed for a king whom they later doubted, having lost too many good friends for a cause that now seemed to mean nothing in the world, yet sought for certain recondite skills that never go out of fashion.

"This woman, she's okay?" Stronski asked.

"She's not of our world, which I like. No games to her. I haven't told her everything; that's tonight. But she reads your language as well as a native—"

"I love her already."

"—and she's super-smart and tough. It'll be fine if I can get her to feel secure. Like all Americans, she'll fear the building."

The two sat in an elegant restaurant, called Spy for the irony (irony was as new to Moscow as capitalism), that fronted Dzerzhinsky Square and lurked three hundred yards across the circle from the Lubyanka. They were on the balcony of the third floor, eating blintzes and caviar and cold slices of salmon, Stronski throwing down vodka, Swagger trying to keep up with old-fashioned water.

"We fear that building too. A good young fellow named Tibolotsky, good operator, brave as hell, spotted for me in the mountains, he voiced doubts about the war. He was fighting it; his right, no? Someone informs KGB, and young fellow is disappeared. Wrong for him to fight so hard and end up in cell or worse. That is why I hate bastards so goddamn much."

"The politicals were always assholes," Bob said. "I lost a spotter, and politicals were involved. Any apparatus in the world, the politicals are assholes."

"It's true," said Stronski.

"You've made the arrangements?"

"I have. You have the cash?"

"Smuggled in, in my shoe. You trust this fellow?"

"I do. Not because he's brave but because in Moscow, corruption is like any commodity. He has to deliver or it gets out, and new business goes to the competition. So the market guarantees this lieutenant-colonel will shoot straight and deliver, not his own honesty, of which, of course, he has none."

"If Stronski says yes, I say yes. I trust Stronski."

"I am as crooked as all of them. I extend certain courtesies to Brother Sniper, that's all."

"Fair enough."

"Now put your hand under table and receive."

"Receive what?"

"You will see."

Swagger received. It felt like a Glock 19, loaded, from the weight, three- or four-inch barrel, no 1911 but nevertheless substantial in feel and lethal in purpose. The slide was steel, though ceramically finished for dullness and durability, the frame some sort of super-polymer. He held it out of sight under the table and looked down and saw that it was a near-Glock, dark and blunt, no safety, nothing to catch or pull on fast removal. It was a generation more streamlined than Glock's stolid Teutonic brick, and its ergonomics were better; it slid into, rather than fought, his hand. He turned it and saw the marking in Cyrillic, and under that in English on the slide, IxGroup, 9 MM. He slid it into his belt, behind the point of his hip, under the coat.

"I have enemies. Maybe they get on to you from me. Moscow is full of bad people. You can never tell. That gun, freshly stolen from factory, no serial number. If you get in trouble, use and ditch. It can't be traced."

"It's not a Glock?"

"GSh-18, better than Glock. Eighteen in magazine, double action, from the Instrument Design Bureau KPB, in Tula. Manufactured by IxGroup, meaning rich guy named Ixovich, one of our new big oligarchs."

"Just learned the word."

They made their plans.

You couldn't help but love the Metropole, the famous old hotel where Swagger had booked himself. Rich in history, it was also—at least in the new Moscow—rich in appointments, possibly restored to something like prerevolutionary glory. Everywhere glitter, glass, shiny brass, marble, full of beautiful people. Even the whores sitting in the bar were high-class.

Yet Swagger tried to see it as it had been in 1959, when it housed, for a few troubling weeks, the melancholy Lee Harvey Oswald, as the Russians tried to figure out what to do with him. In those days, before the fall of the reds and the infusion of Finnish capital, the hotel must have been a dump, smelling of cabbage, vodka, and sewage, dour and dank and grim. It fit the self-exiled American perfectly, a man with a dismal past and not much future, who'd as yet impressed nobody in his short life.

When he got to his room, Swagger found that Oswald wouldn't go away. The little hangdog mutt, radiating anger and self-pity, tracked him at every stop in the classy room that, in dumpier days, could have housed the would-be defector.

The whole thing turned on him, didn't it? You couldn't ask why. There was no point in asking why. The only question had to be how.

Don't think of him as a man, Swagger instructed himself. Think of him as an agent, a servo-mechanism, some anonymous hinge in history that did what he did, and you have to figure out how he did it. It wasn't as simple as waking up one day and deciding to kill the president. There were too many factors involved and too many questions to answer.

Swagger wished he had vodka. He wished he had a cigarette. Many a man had gotten through a bad night in the Metropole on vodka and cigarettes. Maybe Oswald himself, as the bosses figured out his immediate fate.

Little fucker. Who would have guessed?

Don't think about that, Swagger ordered himself again. Think only of the how.

Don't waste your time on his feckless, difficult personality, his pitiful upbringing, his learning problems, his attitude problems, his bullying problems, his endless string of small-time failures, his temperament, his vanity and narcissism, as all are on record. Anyone can look up Lee Harvey Oswald and conclude that he was exactly the type of lazy loser who might abandon the ongoing parade of nothingness that would be his life in exchange for eternal notoriety.

Instead, let's stick to the how of the act. Not did he do it, but could he do it?

Swagger tried to make contact with him through the only vessel that connected them, the one he loved and Oswald hated: the United States Marine Corps. After all, Oswald was a trained rifleman, as his scores attested, particularly in the sitting position, similar to the position he fired from in the Book Depository. Similar but not exact: different stresses, different angles, different muscles involved, and while some skills are transferable, position to position, some are not. His training—which, after all, had been five full years previous—was entirely restricted to the iron-sighted M-1 Garand rifle. Swagger remembered his own M-1, even to the serial number, 5673326, built by Harrington & Richardson. Oswald's had to be about the same: a nine-and-a-half-pound semi-auto with well-calibrated aperture sights, heavy recoil, and no necessary manipulation between shots. Both men had to master the fundamentals, as universally, the Marine Corps does a good job of building them in.

Swagger presumed Oswald had mastered the most basic of basics: solid position, bone-on-bone support, sling management, focus on sights, trigger s-q-u-e-e-z-e, breath control. Would that be enough? For one shot, possibly. But he missed his first, not his last, shot. Baffling. You would think it the opposite. Because after the first shot, it's all new again.

He's got to manipulate the bolt, which takes him out of position, he's got to refind the position on the fly, he's got to reassert his concentration, his breath control, his trigger squeeze. Rather than fighting him, the Carcano with its cheap-jack Japanese sights is overresponsive to his commands, because it is so much lighter than the Garand, at under six pounds. Then he has to reacquire the target through the lens of the scope. And since Garands aren't scoped, he's used to seeing the target in his peripheral vision as he brings the recoiling rifle back toward it on the shooting range. With the Carcano, after the first shot, he is looking at blur, so he has to do two things quickly. First of all, he has to refind the proper eye position so he's able to see through it clearly, and then he has to reacquire the target, which, being transported by vehicle at unknown speed, is in a different place. Still, Swagger had to admit, much of this is instinctive, and a relatively competent Marine-trained shooter such as Oswald, especially with a little practice time, ought to be able to bring it off. It was not likely he made the shot, but it was at least possible. You couldn't deny that reality.

Still, the scope presented a whole host of problems. For example, the FBI gun expert Robert Frazier testified that when the rifle and scope arrived in FBI HQ on Tuesday, November 27, 1963, the plate holding the scope to the rifle was extremely loose. Moreover, it was secured to the receiver by only two screws, although the metal of both the scope and the rifle receiver had been machined to accept four.

Why was the scope loose? Was that the condition under which Oswald fired the rifle? Frazier testified that he assumed it had been loosened in Dallas for fingerprinting; that is, disassembled, fingerprinted, then reassembled somewhat haphazardly. Yet no inquiry to Lieutenant Carl Day, the Dallas fingerprint expert, was ever made, so it is unknown in what condition Day received the rifle. It seemed odd that Day would have disassembled the rifle, because he was a salty old pro and would have known it was highly unlikely to find prints on the few centimeters of metal that the scope rings covered, and that the integrity of the piece as a whole was more important. It was also unlikely that, had he disassembled the rifle, he would have reassembled it haphazardly. It wasn't his nature.

Swagger knew that the screw-tightness issue was important because the looser the scope, the more it deviates from the point of impact. At each shot, it resets itself. Even a slightly loose scope equates to misses in the field, so a remarkably loose scope would make accurate shooting almost impossible.

However, at a certain point, the FBI was required to make accuracy tests with the rifle. According to everything Swagger had read, the rifle could not be zeroed—that is, its point of aim indexed to its point of impact—under any circumstances, as it was presented to the FBI shooters. A machinist had to grind out two spacers—called "shims"—that were inserted at some point, between the mount and the receiver or between the ring and the scope, to provide extra metal that would align the scope at an angle otherwise unattainable. Then the whole thing was tightened up for shooting. If that was so, it was highly improbable that Oswald, lacking those adjustments, could have hit the head shot.

Bugliosi suggested that it was a moot point, since Oswald would have diverted to the iron sights he was used to from his Garand experience. Highly unlikely. The nonadjustable battle sights on the Model 38 were set to the anticipated distance of engagement, which was three hundred meters. To hit the small and diminishing target in the back of the limo with iron sights, Oswald would have had to know the distance, would have needed much experience discovering the relationship of the point of impact to the point of aim, would have had to display unusually sound, to say nothing of quick, math skills in estimating how much below the target he would have to hold to hit at 263 feet with sights regulated to 875 feet, known where that spot was on the blank of the limo trunk behind the president—it would have been a low hold, a very low hold—and squeezed off the shot precisely. Very few people could make that shot on the first try.

Sitting there in his room, vodkaless and cigaretteless, Swagger came to a conclusion: it was not impossible but was highly unlikely that the shot could have been made by Oswald. And that led him to another key question: why did Oswald's shooting, over the course of the engagement, as his own desperation increased and the distances expanded, improve radically?

Same meat, different restaurant. This one was a sort of porch to a classic old-Moscow property on a busy downtown street, open-air, and the patrons sat on cushions instead of chairs, lounging like pashas as the skewers loaded with animal were brought, along with spices and other vivid treats. Hookahs were available, and the Russians, not having received the cancer memo yet, greedily sucked on them or on cigarettes. Meanwhile, just outside, a backhoe struggled with the hard earth; to get into the restaurant, you had to walk on a wooden board over the shattered concrete. If the backhoe happened to squash you, it wasn't your day. It was like a Panzer out there, hard to ignore.

"Sorry I'm late," said Swagger, showing up at five after the hour.

"It's not a problem," said Kathy Reilly, putting away her Black-Berry.

"Were you followed?"

She laughed. "I wish. My days are so routine, a little excitement like that couldn't hurt."

"It could," he said, "and I hope to spare you that. You were fol-lowed—by me. That's why I'm late. I tailed you back to your build-ing a few nights ago, then picked you up tonight as you left and was with you on the subway and everything."

"I— I never saw you," she said, a little nonplused.

"I followed you to see if anyone else was following you. The answer, both the first time and tonight, was no. So we're clean, I think. We can continue, if you'll still play."

"Oh, sure," she said. "It's so Cold War. I love it. Have you arranged for the files?"

"Absolutely. I know they'll be there."

"Great. And where is there?"

"The ninth floor. They centralized their archives a few years ago, with the idea of moving them all to digitalization. But the budget never caught up, so it's still old paper, some of it a century or two old. Very delicate. Fortunately, we don't have to do a lot of digging. We're just going to look at one month, one year."

"You said 1963."

"September. Maybe October, maybe November."

"Of 1963."

"That's right."

"And where is this archive? Ninth floor of?"

"Lubyanka."

He waited. Her eyes stayed calm, maybe fell out of focus for a fraction of a second, then returned to the full-on gaze.

"I take it you're not joking?"

"No. Please, it takes some getting used to."

"You'll have to explain."

"We're not parachuting onto the roof or shooting our way in. We're not blowing a vault or tunneling up from underground. We're traveling by that glamorous transportation means called the elevator."

"I don't—"

"Money. I've bribed, through my friend Stronski, an SVR lieutenant colonel. To show you how serious I am about this, I'm giving him forty thousand, American cash. Mine. Not the FBI's; mine, hard-earned."

"Swagger, you spent forty thousand dollars of your own money on this?"

"I did. I'd do it again. I gave a woman my word I'd look into the death of her husband. I ain't near where I have to be on that one. There's other issues too. Anyhow, to me, the money don't mean a thing. I'll spend it all if I have to. I gave my word, I got myself engaged, and maybe there's some other memories yelling at me. I'll do what I have to do."

"'Crazy with honor' is the phrase that comes to mind. Did you step out of a thirties movie?"

"Ms. Reilly, I don't know enough to know what a thirties movie would be. I only know what I've got to do."

"You are so insane, it's kind of impressive."

"Maybe so. Anyhow, enough on me. Let's get back to tomorrow. Let me tell you, if Stronski says it's guaranteed, it's guaranteed. It's safe."

He explained the details. "The lieutenant colonel himself will give us ID badges and escort us to the ninth floor. He will show us where we need to be. We have six hours. No photos, no notes. All by memory. What we're looking for isn't that big a deal. As I say, the Russian James Bond. We have to find out if he visited or worked in the Mexico City embassy in September through November of 1963."

"See," she said, "that's the other thing."

"I know it is. You see what this is about."

"I know Lee Harvey Oswald went to the Mexico City Russian embassy sometime in 1963, trying to get a visa or something. He failed, I guess. I think it's all been looked at."

"It has. Over and over again. A man named Norman Mailer even managed to interview all the KGB people and examine the records. There's nothing there. Case closed. History reclaimed. End of story. That's what I believed too, until a few weeks ago."

"And now you believe a Russian James Bond killed JFK?"

"No. I don't know enough to believe anything. I will tell you, however, why I think that if—I do say *if*—there was some kind of game being played, it had to be played through the Russians. Maybe in a big way, maybe in a small way."

The waiter cleared the plates.

She ordered a vodka tonic. "I think I'll need this."

He stuck with *koka*. "A few weeks ago a piece of information came to me. It was too mundane for anyone to have made up. There was no profit in it, and it was transferred over the years through completely normal, workaday people, none of them troublesome in any way, all of them sane, productive, middle-class. It was about a tread-print on the back of a coat. Stupid, huh? Briefly, it suggested that a rifle may have been present in something called the Dal-Tex Building in November 1963. Dal-Tex is right across the street from the Book Depository, and its windows give virtually the same angle on the limo on Elm Street as the sixth-floor 'sniper's nest' of the Book Depository. The treadprint suggested the presence of someone I know about who was a superb rifleman."

"He would be the second gunman?"

"Possibly. Just barely possibly. But the coat could have also been owned by an old-boy Texas pheasant hunter, and it was his daughter's bicycle that put the treadprint there. Still, worth investigating."

"So that was what the man went to Dallas to investigate. Then he got killed. Then you went to Dallas. And a Russian tried to kill you. Is that how the Russians come into this?"

"Possibly. It's another indicator that somehow in this thing, all lines of possibility run through Russia. But the fact that the guy who tried to kill me was Russian wasn't the thing I zeroed on.

"What I've done is, I've tried to isolate hard data points from the Warren Commission report, that is, the things that we know happened, times, dates, places, all multiply verified. And I've tried to triangulate from that a possible scenario by which someone besides Oswald could have been involved. I have worked hard trying to find the intersection of certain streams of information that were necessary for anyone trying to kill Kennedy. If I can find a place and a time where all the lines come together, that would be the place to start. My only technique is trial and error, try this, try that, try something else. Believe me, I ain't no genius. But I've come to something. And that something has to be at the Soviet embassy in Mexico City in the late fall of 1963."

"Tell me. Wait, the vodka hasn't arrived. If I'm going to spend ten years sunbathing in the Gulag archipelago, I'll want to know why."

He waited, composing his thoughts. The vodka and the new *koka* came. She took a swig. "Very good. The world is nicely blurred. Please proceed."

"If anything of a conspiratorial nature happened," Bob said, "it had to have sprung from the intersection, by chance, of five elements. I say 'elements.' They tell me it's a lousy word because it means 'stuff.' That's because the five things are different in nature, and no word other than 'stuff' collects them all."

"I'm listening."

"The first four are pieces of information. Three are related but separated in time. One is completely unrelated, from left field, and it arrives real late. The fifth isn't information at all; it's a personality."

"Okay. I can follow that, and I get lost in Agatha Christie, much less le Carré."

"First bit of information: someone had to know that a man named Lee Harvey Oswald existed. And that he was kind of a pathetic screwball with dreams of glory that his sad little life couldn't possibly support. Who would know that?"

"His mom? His poor wife?"

"The second thing they had to know was that he had homicidal tendencies. He was violent. It went with his loser personality. They must have known that he had a rifle with a telescopic sight and that on April 10, 1963, he had taken a shot at and missed Major General Edwin A. Walker."

"I think I remember that."

"Walker was a right-wing general who had just resigned in scandal when it was learned he was indoctrinating his troops—the Twenty-fourth Infantry Division, in Germany—with John Birch propaganda. He was briefly notorious. As a civilian, he was even more annoying to many people: he gave speeches, he made accusations, he showed up at various civil rights demonstrations and was violently segregationist, he called Kennedy pink, the whole nine yards."

"Okay. Oswald took a shot. Someone mysterious and conspiratorial knows that."

"The third thing they had to know was that he worked in a building on Elm Street in Dallas, Texas, called the Texas Book Depository. But since he didn't start working until October 14, they couldn't have known until then."

"Who is *they*?"

"That's where we're going. Who would care enough about this little schnook to record those pieces of information? The FBI questioned him, the CIA debriefed him, but both dismissed him as a twerp, unlikely to be of any consequence. They had no idea about the Walker shooting."

"I have you."

"The late piece of information was that on the afternoon of Tuesday, November 19, 1963, the *Dallas Times Herald* announced that JFK was going to be parading down Elm Street in front of the Texas Book Depository at twelve thirty in the afternoon on Friday, two and a half days later. Remember this—they couldn't possibly find Oswald in that short amount of time. And they couldn't possibly have predicted that Kennedy would pass within seventy-five feet of this screwball. So, you ask, who knew all that about Oswald? Not the FBI. Not the CIA."

"I know the answer. I know what you want me to say."

"Of course. The Russians. He'd been to them. He'd begged them to take him back. He said he'd do anything for them. I'm sure he bragged about the shot he'd taken at Walker as the proof of his willingness to serve. They knew. They had to know. But all that was in September. He didn't start at the depository, as I say, until October 14. How'd they know he was working there over a month later?"

"I don't know."

"This is where the Russian James Bond factors in. The fifth element."

"Hmm," she said.

"Someone who would see the potential in Oswald after the Walker shot and establish a clandestine communication. So he would be up-to-date. He would know Oswald was working at the Depository. See?"

"I see theoretically."

"We need a certain personality. Actually, I say James Bond, but I'm being inaccurate. James Bond is an operator. We don't need an operator. What we need is a case officer. Do you know what a case officer is?"

"I've heard the term, but that's about it."

"He would be the guy like the movie producer. He has the vision. He sees the possibilities. He sets the goal. His talent is putting a team together to get the job done. He keeps everybody focused. He adjudicates. He administers. He finances. He hires, he fires. He's the tough guy, not the creative guy. He does logistics. He gets everybody there when they have to be there. He figures out cover stories, escape routes, all the petty details that the specialists are too good for. He's the guy who makes it happen. He's the guy we're looking for."

She said nothing.

"Here's what I'm seeing. Maybe this isn't exactly how it happened, but I'm guessing it's close. Oswald does his crybaby number for the KGB and, of course, is laughingly turned down. Ha ha, what a schmuck. But there's this guy—maybe he's GRU or some other branch of the apparatus—and he hears about Oswald, particularly the part about trying to hit General Walker. And unlike the stooges, he thinks, You know, this guy has possibilities. So he tracks him down in Mexico City, which would be easy, as there's a whole Sunday, September 29, when we don't know what Oswald did.

"He says, speaking in Russian lingo that would astound Lee, 'Say, Comrade, let me buy you a beer.' He says, 'You know, they all think you're a loser, but I'd like to give you a chance. If you want that chance, you have to clean up your act. None of this letters-to-the-editor bullshit, none of this Fair Play for Cuba bullshit, none of this reading the Party newspaper in the cafeteria. You get a job, you live straight, you work hard, you put your 'radical past' behind you. Your goal is to get a job in the next ten years in aeronautics, defense, high-tech engineering, medicine, something where you can do us some good. Can you do that?'

"Oswald is flattered. Nobody's ever trusted him before, thought he was worth a damn. 'Yeah, sure,' he says. The guy says, 'Look, I'm giving you an address. You can send me a letter there. Any place I am in the world, I will get that letter quickly. Now go home, get to work, and keep me up-to-date.'

"Oswald goes home. He gets the Book Depository job. 'Dear Comrade, I am now gainfully employed at the Book Depository at blah-blah Elm Street. My plan is to remain here five years, complete high school, be a success, put all crazy radical childishness behind me, and then maybe begin some college as a way of getting into the sectors you need me to be in. Yours truly, Comrade Lee Harvey Oswald.'

"Our guy's got one of those case-officer minds that doesn't forget anything. It happens. The really talented guys have them. When he finds out Kennedy's going to Dallas, he thinks of Lee Harvey, and when he sees the route—two and a half days before—he sees he's got the chance of a lifetime. He'll never have another chance like this. He flies to Dallas, he meets Lee on that Thursday, he says, 'You've got to do this, Comrade.'"

"But would KGB—"

"See, maybe it's rogue. Maybe he knows the general committee would never say yes. Too risky. But he doesn't see it as risky at all. And he can take out a guy who's making noise in Vietnam and putting pressure on Cuba and looking for a place to draw a line in the sand and replace him with a Texas guy who knows nothing about foreign policy and just wants to be the next FDR. It's easy as pie. He can do it."

She said, "It sounds original. But I don't know enough to point out your errors."

"Oh, they're there. For one thing, this whole thing started with someone looking at the Dal-Tex as the site for another rifle. So if there's another rifle, there's a complex ballistic-deceit issue involved. I'll spare you the details, but no one could have figured out the complexities of it, recruited another shooter, found him the place to shoot, and gotten him in and out without a hitch in two days. Not even the greatest case officer in the world. It can't be done. That's the crucial issue of the assassination. How did they set it up so fast? The route wasn't known until the nineteenth. I just can't get by that."

"Maybe . . ." she started. Then, "No, I don't know."

"Anyhow, that's why I'm here; that's why I'm hoping you'll help me. There's not much else I can say, Ms. Reilly."

"I told you, it's so cold-war, how could I turn it down? Maybe, maybe, maybe somewhere down the line, there's a story in it for me."

"If there's a story, you'll get it."

Was she sold? Enough to do the job, which, after all, was only scanning old files, looking for records of visits by Soviet intelligence personnel to one embassy over a relatively short period of time.

Nothing to it.

CHAPTER 9

The Russian spoke, Stronski translated.

"You will not be challenged. You may run into others in there, for the library is never empty. They are simply other spies who've paid the same price for their few hours of gnawing at the scraps of history. They will not see you, nor should you see them."

The officer led them to a dedicated passageway—no other entries were placed along its way except at the end—and to that last door. Again, it had that old Commie look, the steel, the harsh lights behind cages, girders with rivets everywhere, the smell of paint and iron, the sense of muscular, even brutal industrialism as aggression.

The officer did discover a bright plastic keypad, self-lit, a concession to the modern era. His fingers flew across the pad, and the door clanked ajar.

He led them into a final chamber. This one had a sense of hospital to it. The officer pointed to a box of fresh-pressed surgical green utilities, and they pulled them on over their clothes. A mask slipped over nostrils and mouth, a rubberized surgical cap to contain the hair. Gloves came next, rubberized as well, tight and thin, to handle the delicate papers. When they were sealed off in their operating-theater garments, the officer took them through a last door, and they felt the temperature drop twenty degrees.

Swagger blinked to adjust his vision to the greenish hues. It seemed they were on a metal balcony of some sort, restrained by a railing from a twenty-foot drop to the floor of the place itself, a vast, hushed space with metal racks on two levels, cut by steel stairways running this way and that, the whole thing seeming to extend to infinity or whatever was beyond the realm of the greenish lights on the far side of the opening. Clearly, the cavern occupied the entire eighth and ninth floors.

Swagger beheld the belly of the red beast: a vast room with crude steel shelving sustaining boxes, each box labeled and containing a forced mass of good old paper-and-ink documents. How many coups, how many deceits, how many black ops, how many wet ops, how many pix of fat diplomats with whores sucking their cocks, how many assassinations? All chronicled here, so it wasn't a belly, it was a memory, a part of the brain loaded with forgotten info, hard to access, buried deeply away, barely acknowledged.

"Sixty-three, Mexico?" the Russian officer said.

Swagger nodded.

"Okay, you come."

He led them downstairs and into the maze of two-leveled shelving, turning so many times that Hansel and Gretel would have become lost. Now and then another pilgrim would pass in the green night without acknowledgment. The officer turned at last down an aisle no different from any others. He spoke in Russian to Stronski, who translated.

"He says during duty hours, clerks process requests from SVR or army intelligence officers of rank, take the box, find the file, check it out, and present to officer, who can only read in reading room, also on ninth floor. You do not have it so easy. You will have to find your own files, pull your own documents. Sorry for dust, sorry light is not good, sorry no place to sit, no bathroom, no Coke machine."

The two Americans nodded.

The Russian spoke again through Stronski.

"Rules once again. No pictures, no notes, no Xerox machine, all must be memory. Replace everything. Delicacy, please: no tugging, no folding, no forcing. You must respect the material and make allowances for its age and brittleness. You are interviewing an old man, and his attention may wander, do you see? You yourself, do not wander. Do not leave this area. Do only business you have paid for. Be honest, diligent, and bring glory on your cause, whatever it is. I will come get you in four hours."

"Ask him," said Bob, "if this is all agencies, including, I'm guessing, not only KGB but GRU as well as specialized military teams, or just KGB."

The Russian listened and, in time, responded.

"I don't know. The idea initially was to consolidate, all by hemisphere and target country, all of it in one place so that access would be better and those who had to know could find all from one area. But budget ran out before it could be completed, and I am not certain if consolidation project got to '63 or not. Also: this is only 'offensive' materials, that is, initiatives generated by heroes of the past. 'Defensive'—that is, 'counterespionage,' in response to something done by main target and others—would be on different floor. That is not so interesting, just notes of suspects being followed, wiretaps being uncovered, traitors found and executed."

"Would I be able to get in there at some later date?" asked Swagger.

"I will take it up with committee," the officer answered, then laughed at his own joke. "All things are possible for a man with cash in his pockets."

"Excellent," said Swagger.

"I will see you in four hours," said the officer. "Not a second longer."

They worked on their knees, as if in genuflection to the material before them.

"Station 14Alpha (1963)," read the marking on the box. That would be it, the Mexico City KGB reports, that year, that place. Stronski removed the box and set it on the floor for inspection, and they crowded in close. This, as much as anything, was what Bob had come for: to see the thing, to check it for evidence of tampering.

He bent and looked at the cardboard box full of papers, all held in coherence by a red ribbon illuminated in the beam from Stronski's flashlight. Bob went lower, looked carefully at the knot. "Has it been untied and retied a lot?" he asked.

His two colleagues closed in as well.

"I can see the worn-flat signature on two of the intersecting ribbons that suggest it was untied once," said Reilly, "but it doesn't look as if it's been subject to chronic tying and retying. I'm guessing that when Norman Mailer was here in 1993 or '94, that's the last time the box was opened. They untied it, found and removed the Oswald reports from the KGB goons, and took those to him in the reading room."

"Does anybody see signs of disturbance since then?"

All looked as Stronski rotated the beam across the messy surface of the raggedly stuffed-in paperwork. Tatters and flags stuck out unevenly; a corner or two peeped out at the edges. Stronski gently ruffled the uneven edges, as though pushing his hand through sheaves of wheat, and fluffy clouds of fine dust puffed outward, roiling in the flashlight beam.

"It does not appear to have been disturbed recently," said Swagger. "Everybody agree?"

"Let me compare with others," said Stronski, and leaped up with his flashlight and walked a few feet, making random examinations. He returned. "It is same. Dust, chaos, paper disintegrating at the edges."

"Okay," said Swagger. "Now what do we see?"

"I can see divisions, I'm guessing by month," said Reilly. "Do we start with September, when Oswald showed up?"

"That makes the most sense," said Swagger.

Reilly pointed to the appropriate cardboard separator that demarcated the adventures of September, and he pulled it out as gently as possible, amid more clouds of dust and flecks of disintegration as the paper—at least at its edges—eased toward oblivion. Three sheaves extended a bit from the more neatly collected mass of April reports. They were an obvious starting point. He pulled them out and held them open.

She examined the first. "This is just the September 27 report by Kostikov on his immediate discussion with Oswald. It's been published by Mailer, I have the book. Standard stuff."

"Would you do me the favor of examining this one for any info that Mailer might not have published or missed?"

"Sure." She read it carefully. "I don't see anything."

"Anything on claims or boasts by Oswald?"

"No. His intensity comes through, his seething anger, his disappointment that they don't greet him like a brother, but there's no specific dialogue or claims."

"You're sure."

"Absolutely."

Swagger considered this carefully. "But is there a transcript?"

"No," she said. "It's based on notes, not recordings."

"Okay, fine. I get it. Let's go to the next one." He slid the next file over, and her eyes attacked it.

"This is a report by Nechiporenko, another KGB, the next day, on the disposition of the case, the rejection, Oswald's anger and unpleasantness."

"Please read for any indications of boasts or claims."

"No, nothing. But there is a second page." She read it, her eyes scanning hard behind her glasses as Stronski tried to keep the light steady. "Okay, this is a summary by a third KGB, I'm guessing the boss, his name is Yatskov, he's a jock. Oswald comes back a second time, Saturday the twenty-eighth, shows up at the KGB-GRU volleyball game, and Yatskov is there and takes him into his office. Oswald is beside himself by this time. God, he even pulls a gun! Yatskov takes it from him, and the idiot collapses crying on the desk. The only thing that Yatskov can do is tell him to submit for a visa through regular channels, and no, he can't get in contact with the Cubans for him. Meanwhile, Nechiporenko shows up and pitches in. Then Yatskov gives him the gun back! And leads him out. Pathetic."

"No boasts, no claims?"

"Why is that important?"

"I have to know what he told them about himself that might be interesting to the James Bond guy I'm looking for."

"The gun, doesn't that signify something?"

"Possibly. But no transcripts, no specific language, nothing like that?"

"No."

"Okay, then, that's that. Next move: we scan, start to finish, looking for visitors to the embassy; by that I mean intelligence professionals not assigned to it but arriving and departing around the same time, the last week in September. KGB, but also GRU or military as well. SMERSH, even, why not? Maybe there were units of intelligence I don't know about, connected with the air force or strategic warfare or signals intelligence. Intelligence outfits are like mushrooms."

"They grow in the dark and thrive in shit?" said Reilly.

"I thought I made that line up, but I guess I didn't. Are you ready?"

Both nodded.

"Mikhail, you hold the light. I will pull the documents one at a time and turn the pages. Kathy, you tell me when you have the gist of the page, and we can go on."

That was what they did for three hours, with breaks for sore knees, eye fatigue, backaches, and on and on. It was not fun. It seemed to last six or nine rather than three hours.

Finally, she reached her verdict. "Agriculture reps, diplomats, doctors, lawyers, but nobody is in the official record as a case officer, an agent, a recruiter, nobody who seemed remotely like an operator. Maybe the Russians used codes within their own top-secret documents, and when I see 'Dr. Menshav the agronomics professor,' that means 'Boris Badanov, special assassin,' but I doubt it."

"I doubt it too."

They had done all of September, then the October and November files, through the assassination. That event produced its own tonnage of paper and demanded its own box, but Swagger saw no point in looking at it, since everything after the fact was meaningless.

"No sign of James Bond," said Reilly. "No sign of any cogitation, activity, meetings, anything that would suggest the embassy was anticipating or knew that someone in its own sphere was involved in what would happen on November 22. No sign of any contact with outside agents from outlier espionage groups, no suggestion of special 'visitors' from Moscow."

"Did you see the name Karly Vary?" asked Stronski. "It's the Spetsnaz and KGB training site on the Black Sea; all 'wet' operators go through there for technical expertise and are held there on downtime."

"No Karly Vary," said Reilly. "Not a whisper."

"Red bastards probably killed your president anyway," said Mikhail. "They like that shit, they pull it all over the world."

"If so, it was entirely out of the embassy sphere, and none of the bureaucrats noticed anything out of place or out of norm," said Swagger.

"Mikhail," said Reilly, "the reports are consecutively numbered. I kept careful track." She had noticed something Swagger hadn't. "That means nothing could be inserted or removed without retyping the entire file that came after. I don't see any difference in the tone or state of the paper to suggest that new paper was added sometime. Also, the typing is clearly from the same typewriter, and I got so that I recognized the font, particularly since the H was clouded under the bridge. That typewriter—some poor Russian girl had the job of typing more than forty pages a day—was used all the way through. I can recognize her style. She was a little weak on the last two fingers of her left hand, and those letters were always a little lighter. But she had Mondays off, and a much less gifted typist took over, more typos by far, more uncertain on the right side of the keyboard, so I'm guessing the substitute was a lefty."

"Wow," said Swagger. "Kathy, you're in the wrong business. You should have been an intelligence analyst."

"I've looked at a lot of Russian documents, a lot of reports. I get used to the style, the diction, the nomenclature, even the bureaucratic culture. It hasn't changed all that much since '63, even if everything else has. This has the feel of the authentic, so I don't think there's any suggestion that someone came back to it and tampered with the evidence to hide James Bond's visit."

"That damn James Bond," said Swagger. "He's never around when you need him."

The next day, Swagger as "Agent Homan" had his sitdown with the ranking gang specialist of the Moscow police, who, well known on the international circuit and a Moscow rep to Interpol, spoke fluent English. They sat in the inspector's office, glass-enclosed, off the usual bright, impersonal ward of the organized-crime squad on the third floor of Moscow's central police station.

"This fellow Bodonski, he was a nephew of the Izmaylovskaya boss, or in their language, *avtoritet*, also a Bodonski," said the inspector as they looked over the thick Bodonski file and Swagger saw a photo of the man he'd killed. Bodonski had been handsome, dashing, even, with thick sweeps of dark hair and piercing eyes. He must have had the gangster way with women. The last time Swagger had seen him—which was also the first and only—his face had been pancaked into the steering wheel of his car, and what flesh was visible in the nest of crushed plastic and bent steel looked like the rotting fruit of a watermelon smashed against a brick wall. Too bad for him.

"He was a tough guy, very capable," the inspector continued. "If someone topped him, whoever did it must have been a tough guy in his own right."

"Inspector," said Swagger, "he just shot him. It wasn't a fight. A gun is always tougher than a man. Even a man in a car."

"The car was coming right at the man, as I hear it."

"Yes, that's true."

"So that man, if he panics and runs, as most will do, Bodonski breaks his spine in two. He did it enough here. We have him for at least fifteen hits, which was why his uncle suggested he get out of town. Anyway, your man on the gun, he didn't panic, he stood and fired well. Bravo. My compliments."

"I'll tell him you said so."

"This Izmaylovskaya is the toughest of the gangs in town. Most of these outfits, they call themselves a *bratva,* meaning 'brotherhood.' It gives them some gentility, like a guild or something, a group of business associates looking out for each other. Not the Izzies; they just go by 'gang.' Their specialty is applied force. Murder for hire, extortion, human trafficking. The dirty end of the stick. Much more disciplined, much more violent, much scarier. They're smaller—three, four hundred, maybe—than the brotherhoods, which may have as many as five thousand men. They're not Jewish, they make no show of religious belief or ethnic identity. Hard guys, killers, danger boys. They take their money up front, lots of it. You want to swindle a financier, you go somewhere else; you want to murder your boss, the Izzies are for you."

"Any connections? Gangs usually flourish where they have some kind of semi-official connection with power."

"Only rumors. Nobody talks. You only get out of that gang the way Bodonski did, on a slab in the morgue. Nobody gets inside, as each rank is tattooed with a code of stars and dragons, and all the codes have to be perfect or you go swimming in the River Moscow with a zinc sink chained to your ankle. I'll be honest: it's a thing I can't look into closely or I'll be the one with my spine broken in two on the street, but the rumors say they have an affiliation with oligarchs. The one most usually named is Viktor Krulov."

"I heard the name before. I think we have oligarchs too."

"Yeah, everywhere, the same smart guys figure out how to get to the front of the line and get all the potatoes. They get so big, you can't stop 'em. If I go against an oligarch, I don't mind telling you, my wife is looking for a new husband."

"Let me ask you this: since there was no personal reason for this Bodonski to hit our undercover, clearly, he was a professional doing a job. How would you go about hiring him? Would you do it from Moscow, or could you do it from New York?"

"Good question, which I will have to look into. See, with other groups, much bigger groups, there is more sophistication. They have lawyers, brokers, advertising directors, journalists all on the payroll. Many ways to approach them, to slip through that portal between legal service and illegal service, like a murder. With the Izzies, it's different: they're so small, they're so specialized. You would have to know exactly who to go to. There would be one guy, that's all."

"Do you have a source who could tell you the name of that guy in New York?"

"Again, I'll put it out. How long are you going to be here? You want to go on raids, we do a ceremonial raid once a week so it looks like we have a chance of enforcing the law against the *bratvas*. It's a big joke; everybody laughs and goes out drinking together afterward. Certain sums are passed. Do I shock you?"

"No, I appreciate the honesty, Inspector."

"Agent Homan, I don't want to represent myself as a hero above it all. I take my envelope too, I know the rules, I know what can and can't be asked and what will and won't be answered."

"Am I getting you? You will 'ask' about that name I requested, but you won't really *ask* about that name. Is this the message I'm getting?"

"I'm trying to be honest and don't want to get your hopes too high."

"It's not a problem. You have to do what you have to do. You live here, I don't."

"This I can tell you. You say two killings, one in Baltimore, one in Dallas. For a known man with a high rep, Bodonski would expect big dollars, plus expenses. I'm thinking fifty thousand dollars for one, maybe a discount, only twenty-five thousand dollars for the other if business has been done before. Not small change. Whoever paid, he had big money to spend, and he had highly sophisticated connections. He is not a small fry. This is not something that would be arranged to punish an adulterer, squelch a debtor, get a store owner to pony up his monthly. This is quality work, big-time stuff, usually for other bosses, big debtors, well-guarded politicians."

"You've been a great help, Inspector."

"Wish I could help more, Agent Homan. Do give my congratulations to the shooter. He was a man in a million."

"So I will," said Bob.

CHAPTER 10

The man wore the baggy, nondescript workingman's grunge so common in Eastern Europe and Russia, corduroys, an untucked plaid shirt, an indifferent burgundy jacket of some Chinese miracle fabric whose zipper didn't quite work, a watch cap pulled low over his eyes. He carried no luggage, though anyone with a close eye for observation might have noted a bulge on his hip, even possibly suspected that it represented the sleek lines of an IxGroup GSh-18. But nobody had that close an eye. He was too ordinary.

He was one of Moscow's unseen millions. The cheekbones suggested Magyar or Tartar; the gray hair, full and brushy, suggested good genes; and he kept his mouth closed because his teeth were too bright and he knew few Russian factory men used Crest White Strips. He had picked up a pair of red and white Nike rip-offs made in Malaysia, and he walked like any of the proletariat of the earth, head down, hands stuffed disconsolately into his jacket pockets, not quite homeless but seemingly without destination, past or future. Flashing Russian Federation ID, he checked in to a workingman's hotel in a zone far out of the flashier precincts of the new Moscow, disco king, BMW and Porsche capital, Armani outpost of the world. There he sat in his room and waited for four days, eating mainly from food-dispensing machines in the Underground station nearby, where his lack of Russian wouldn't cause problems or be noted, nursing his scraggy beard and unkempt hair. He let his teeth turn yellow with disinterest and the hair in his nostrils grow repulsively.

He had one companion on this journey into shadow: Lee Harvey Oswald. The killer would not leave him alone and haunted his dreams.

Swagger could not stop thinking about him; it seemed just when sleep was deepest, Lee Harvey would poke him in the ribs and start muttering in his ear. Actually, it was his subconscious muttering in his ear, and the damned thing was no respecter of regular work hours.

So Swagger blinked awake in his Russian shithole, more like a fifties-man-on-the-run hideout than anything, and a voice was muttering to him about the timing.

The timing, it kept saying, the *timing*.

The timing was 4:17 a.m., that was the timing.

But no sleep returned, and the voice grew louder, and he saw that the muttering came from his own throat.

Timing. Timing! Timing: this is where most conspiracy theories wander out into the ozone. Because the time schedule was so fucking fast from the evening of November 19, when the route became known, to the early afternoon of November 22, when the kill shot was delivered—sixty-six hours—a great number of things had to happen very quickly. Those who wanted to believe in conspiracy could only ascribe that kind of speed and efficiency to the result of deep government intrigue. Someone in "deep government," in a shadow department of great but unseen influence, was able to arrange something far in advance so that immaculate long-range planning could be initiated: Oswald had to be found and brought under discipline, a job for him had to be arranged, and that job had to be on the motorcade route that itself had to be forced on the Kennedy people. Since only CIA was paid to do such things professionally, quite naturally, CIA was almost always invoked. Since both CIA and FBI had previous knowledge of, ran files on, and had dealings with Oswald, their presence could be quite naturally inferred. But that was all shit.

The hard data points of the assassination totally dismissed any deep-government intrigue; rather, things happened as they do normally: by chance opportunity, by whimsy, turning on someone's eavesdropping.

Swagger felt he was on to something. He ordered himself to begin at a beginning: how did Lee Harvey Oswald end up in the Texas Book Depository on November 22, 1963? Swagger recalled Posner and Bugliosi. The first hard fact that would never go away was that he got the job before there'd been any announcement that JFK would come to Dallas at a specific time and date (there was a general acknowledgment that the president, for political reasons, would have to make a Texas trip "in the fall"). So any idea of "placing" Oswald in TBD was absurd on its face. What would be the point of placing him in *any* building in Dallas against the faint possibility that the president might someday drive by? Don't make me laugh. And that becomes even more ridiculous in view of what actually happened.

He got that job the way most people get most jobs. Someone who knew that he was looking for work heard a certain place was hiring, made some phone calls, notified Lee, and Lee showed up in a place he'd never heard of, was hired in the lowliest of positions—essentially a stock boy—and started work the next morning, Wednesday, October 16, at $1.25 an hour. Were these CIA or military-industrial-complex shadow agents or even Men from U.N.C.L.E. or SPECTRE manipulating bureaucracies to bring killer and victim within range? Hardly. They were the redoubtable Ruth Paine, a sublimely decent Quaker gal who had met and taken a liking to Marina Oswald and was trying to help her by helping her husband, whom she didn't like much—she had a nose for character, that one—and Roy Truly, supervisor of the Book Depository, who was always filling his staff of clerks with transients, knowing that the jobs were perishable and demanded little except a strong back and a willingness to do boring, menial work. In fact, Truly was responsible for another facility and assigned Oswald to the Dallas building only on a whim; he could have as easily sent him to the suburbs. By what secret method did the U.N.C.L.E. agent Ruth Paine learn that Truly was hiring? She heard a neighbor's son had just been hired there!

Swagger was now up, walking about, the muttering getting louder.

Later that week, the White House announced that there would be a fall trip. But planning didn't begin on the trip for some time. Agendas had to be worked out and translated into schedules, which had to be coordinated with Texas officials as well as the vice president's office. All this took time and negotiation, and it wasn't until November 16 that the Dallas Trade Mart was selected as the site for the president's 1 p.m. luncheon speech. The Secret Service advance party didn't arrive in Dallas until the seventeenth, to begin the more intensive preparation for the trip; and it wasn't until the nineteenth, when two Secret Service officers and two ranking Dallas officers drove the routes from Love Field, where the president would arrive on the twenty-second, to the Trade Mart, that a certain route—the one that took the president down Main, to a right-hand jog on Houston, to a sharp left-hand turn down Elm to access the Stemmons Freeway entrance—was selected.

At best, a "mole" representing the deep-government conspiracy could have alerted the kill team the night of the nineteenth; but in all likelihood, the killer (or killers) didn't find out about it until the next morning, when the route ran on the front page of the *Dallas Morning News.* Since Oswald was in the habit of reading day-old newspapers, he probably didn't learn about it until November 21, the day before.

Swagger tried to advocate against himself for a bit. If indeed there was a conspiracy planning to kill JFK in Dallas long before Oswald entered the picture, he thought, it would have had a maximum of the night of the nineteenth, the days of the twentieth and twenty-first and half a day of the twenty-second, sixty-six hours, to do the following:

Find and recruit Oswald and get him committed to the sixth-floor Book Depository shot.

Learn what kind of rifle he would be using.

Develop a method of ballistically "counterfeiting" the rifle that was so successful, it would withstand nearly fifty years of the highest-tech scrutiny, with the tech getting higher every decade.

Find an alternative shooter who could make the head shot on the president that everyone who knew Oswald would consider well beyond his modest range of talent.

Find an alternative shooting site whose angle to the target was close enough so the trajectory of the counterfeited bullet wouldn't give the game away.

Plan and execute an entrance and exit with such precision that it would go unnoticed in the hubbub.

One more thing occurred to him, and he wondered why his gun-soaked brain hadn't come up with it earlier: the rifle would have to be silenced so its noise wouldn't give away the existence and locale of the second shooter. Silencers, more accurately "suppressors," are not easy to come by. In the first place, they are Class III items, controlled by federal regulation, like machine guns. It's probably safe to assume that, as with machine guns, professional government espionage agencies and underworld organizations have access to them, but procuring them quickly and testing them for effectiveness and their influence on the point of impact demands time that these theoretical conspirators didn't have. Also, a sudden search for such a device is certain to have attracted notice, and even in (or particularly in) the underworld, people talk. If circa November 20, 1963, a search of underworld inventories for a rifle suppressor had been suddenly run, snitches sure as hell would have squawked to the police as a way of sliding a few months off a breaking-and-entering sentence. So the suppressor remains completely mysterious, another item that could not have been obtained in the time frame without having left a record.

BANG! BANG! BANG!

He looked around, startled. It was someone in the next room pounding on the wall. Something was yelled in Russian, presumably "Shut up, asshole."

Swagger took the hint.

He turned off the light and crept back into bed, and this time sleep was awarded him. But he had a new conclusion to add to his mental inventory: they'd have to be the best team ever assembled in order to bring it off.

On the fifth day, late in the afternoon, he took a roundabout walk to the Underground and headed into another precinct of Moscow.

He arrived at the flea market late. Most of the tourists had left, there was little activity, and already the merchants were rearranging their wares and closing their booth fronts. It was another maze, as avenue bisected avenue on a square mile, all of it with the appearance of something temporary that had become something permanent. Most of the structures were low wooden booths, possibly walled or awned in canvas. The plaza of low-end retail was dominated by a central building in the old style, with the typical onion-shaped dome of gold gilding, which rose on a tower from a complex structure that could have been a monastery or a refurbed software outlet. The flea market was the place to go for nesting dolls, which had come to represent the universal symbol of Russia, and shop after shop offered them in dazzling variety, including those boasting the symbols of great NFL teams, as each doll inside revealed a new and smaller icon of gridiron greatness. Ceramics were another popular sales item, as were watches, particularly the Russian diver's model with the screw-on cap chained to the case protecting the winder, jewelry, knickknacks of all sorts, imitation icons, photo books, and store after store of medals and badges where you could pick up a Panzer-killer award with three bars, signifying that you had knocked out three Tiger IIs in the ruins of Stalingrad.

Swagger dawdled here and there, setting up switchbacks and ambushes to check if he was being followed. Finally, satisfied that he was at least for now unobserved, he found a corner, navigated a street and then another, and found his destination, a surplus-military hardware shop that sold ponchos, helmets, bayonets, T-shirts, boots, tunics, everything that spoke of war, including some old Marine Corps helmets with the jungle-green camouflage cover. He slid up, pointed to the pile of helmets, and said to the proprietor, "I'll take six of them, please."

The man looked up from his newspaper, took a second to comprehend, then said, in English, "Jesus Christ, Swagger."

That he spoke English was no surprise, since the flea market's economy sustained itself on tourism, so if a fellow wanted to make a living, he had to know the language of the people with the dough.

"I have to see Stronski."

There was nobody else around, though down the way, an old woman was closing down a nesting-doll joint, delicately stacking the ornate doll faces back on the counter so they would be enclosed when she lowered the shutter.

"Man, do you know you are the most hunted guy in this town? Here, look at this."

He shoved over a piece of paper from the mess on his counter, and Swagger beheld himself, sans the beard and low cap, in a kind of Disney caricature.

"My eyes aren't that close together," he said, and in a second tumbled to the rest: how had they—never mind yet who *they* were—gotten this out so fast, so completely, so nearly lethally? How did they know? The intelligence operation was superlative. Whoever put it together—the red James Bond again?—knew what he was doing.

He felt his anxiety level raise six degrees. "Is it shoot on sight or anything like that?"

"No," said Stronski's man. "Person of interest. The instructions are 'detain for questioning.' They had these all over the place four days ago."

"Figures. Three days ago I went and saw a cop, and his eyes lit up when he looked at me. I didn't know why, but I had a feeling he'd seen me before and was interested in continuing the relationship. I thought it was time to blow town fast. I've spent the last four days in a crummy room in the crummy suburbs, sneaking out at night to buy clothes from used-and-maybe-washed places."

"And here you are now. The underground man. You could be some Raskolnikov lurking in an alley with an ax. Who'd notice you except for the height?"

"Where is Stronski?"

"You never know where Stronski is. He hides well. He was a sniper."

"So I've heard," said Swagger.

"We'll disappear you."

It became a progression of squalors. He was shunted from place to place in darkness, by friends of Stronski's, who had no names and issued no instructions. Some spoke English, most did not. He stayed in a room in a brothel and heard people fucking all night. He stayed behind a Laundromat in a room of near-unbearable heat with lint floating in the air. He stayed in the cellar of a Star Dog place that sold imitation American hot dogs. He had one. It was good.

Always, it was the same: at a certain time in the evening, a new man showed, picked him up, and drove him through dismal streets to another dismal hovel. Without a word, he was dropped, entered, shown by his new host his deluxe suite for the night, and there he spent the next twenty-two hours. A farmhouse, a suburban garage, another brothel, the rear of a pawnshop, on and on, for what seemed weeks but was shy of one. Time doesn't fly when you're not having fun. He lived in a cold fusion of nerves and shallow sleep, knowing in his heart of hearts that he was exactly where no man should be, hunted in a country whose language he didn't speak, whose streets he didn't know, and whose culture baffled him. He knew also: I am too old for this. But it was a thing he had to do. He had given his word. Crazy with honor? Nah. Stubborn was all, an old crank's privilege.

Food was brought or bought, but nowhere within the whole elaborate structure of escape and evasion was there a cash economy, and no one wanted or would accept payment.

On the seventh day, he was dropped at a bar and told "fourth booth." He entered a dark place full of bitter, isolated drinkers, found his way through the low lighting and the cigarette smoke, slid into booth no. 4, and indeed, there was Stronski.

"My friend," said Stronski. "Still alive by the narrowest of margins. They're hunting you everywhere."

"Do we know who 'they' are?"

"Powerful enemy, whoever. The Izmaylovskaya have called in a lot of favors and essentially control a large part of the police apparat. You never know which cop is your friend, decent, honest guy, and which is Izzy, who will make a call and send the killers on your tail in a second. The main thing is, we have to get you out of here. That is why I have you moved around, wait until the novelty of manhunt has worn off and watchers aren't so watchful."

Swagger nodded. "Good strategy."

"I think," Stronski said, "now it's good to go. You rest tonight, tomorrow you will be taken to truck yard and hidden in long-distance trailer north, out of Moscow. Long ride, my friend, over seven hundred miles. You'll make it out soft route on the Finnish border. I have friends there too. Finland, Sweden, you home safe with warm memories of Mother Russia."

"No," said Swagger.

"No? What the fuck, brother? Is it money? No money. It'll cost you nothing! This isn't about money, at least your money. This is business. I back you, I give you my loyalty, no matter what it costs short-term, people have to know Stronski can be trusted. That's my long-term. I got you into Lubyanka, I'll get you out of Russia, everyone says you go to Stronski, you get what you bargained for. He is man of trust. In my business, that's money in the bank."

"That's not it. I still have business here. There's a last detail that has to be nailed down, and I'm not leaving until I've nailed it."

"Swagger, are you nuts? These Izzy birds are gunning to kill you. They are not going away soon. They will in time track you down, it has to happen. Somebody will see, somebody will call, gunmen will show. Don't matter if you're in nice restaurant, in park, in orphanage, it don't matter. In they come, blazing, killing any and all in the way, and that's you on the floor, leaking. Nobody wants to leak."

"I don't want to leak. But I can't move on unless I cover one more thing."

"Goddamn, Swagger, you are a stubborn bastard."

"I need to get back into the Lubyanka."

"Jesus Christ! That's the one place they look hardest for you. You'd be the one hundred thousandth killed there, but the first sniper. You want that record?"

"Of course not. But I don't mean I'd go myself. I mean my representative. I have to get a man in there. Get him in there to check a certain thing. Then I am out of here."

Stronski's blunt face showed frustration. "Swagger, go home. Tell me what it is. I will find out. I will let you know. No need to die for something so small."

"No, I have to debrief the guy who goes in. I have to see him, talk to him, ask him stuff so I trust him. So there are no doubts. That is why there is only one man for the job. That is you, Stronski."

"Jesus Christ, you'll get me killed too in your madness over something that happened fifty years ago. Crazy, man, crazy."

"I have to trust the guy. I trust Stronski. Then we have to have a sit-down afterward in some safe place in Moscow for a debrief."

He did trust Stronski. Also, knowing Stronski, he felt he could read the man's face more than he could read a stranger's.

"Money. You know the price that shit charges? And that was after haggling."

"I don't care."

"Man, you don't. I never thought I'd meet a guy who didn't care about money, but that's you, brother."

"Maybe it won't be as much. It's just you, for under an hour, not the three of us in all night, prowling, two of us American. And you're not in the big room, you're in that other room, the counterespionage annex on the other floor."

"If I do this, you'll go home?"

"I'll walk into the American embassy and turn myself over to the

Marines. They'll get me home easily enough. No Finland border stuff, no crawling through the snow. I'm way too old for that."

Stronski shook his head in doubt.

"We'll set it up," Swagger said, "so that I meet you somewhere public close by the embassy. We have our debrief chat, that's that, shake hands, and I walk into the embassy. They'll cooler me for a day or so, but they'll verify me through U.S. sources, the FBI will okay it, and I'm out of here. Does that work for you?"

"What makes you think I can do it? I am sniper, not professor. That Kathy, she was good, she would get it, but me? Suppose I can't find it?"

"I'm sure you can."

"What would it be?"

"There has to be a security sweep every few years. All services do that. I have to know to what degree the embassy in Mexico City, particularly the KGB suites, were penetrated in 1963. That was the game back then. Microphones all over the place, in the most amazing locations. Stalin's eye, Lenin's beard, the men's room urinal. That place, the American place, all the places all over the world, they were radio stations broadcasting twenty-four hours a day, and not far away we had a little roomful of listeners writing it all down or monitoring the tape recorders. There were no secrets, at least not until cyber-cryptography came in, and that probably didn't last too long either. I need confirmation that anything Oswald told the KGB goons wasn't private. That is, it reached other parties."

"I think I know who you're talking about," said Stronski.

"Yes. The red James Bond didn't have to be red at all. He could have been a listener. And who was he listening for? He could have worked for the CIA."

CHAPTER 11

I t cost ten thousand dollars, and that was after much haggling. Give it to Stronski, he drove a hard bargain and finally got his price. Swagger was driven in the back of a delivery truck to a Bank of America ATM in downtown Moscow—he was too tense to ponder the ironies—and took out the money after having arranged it via satellite phone call with his banker in Boise. The miracle of modern satellite communications: he, in the back of a bicycle shop in Moscow, calls a man in Boise who calls Atlanta so that a computer transaction is verified back in Moscow, and the next day, with the PIN, Swagger walks away with the cash, gets in the delivery van, and heads back to the bicycle shop.

Then it was wait, wait, wait, more days fled by, days of nothingness and boredom that did nothing to alleviate the crush of anxiety. Too bad he no longer smoked or drank—either crutch might have provided some mercy—but it was a thing of staring at the ceiling as the plaster crumbled away while time decayed slowly. He cultivated an interest in a soccer team, wondered when the NFL would get to Moscow, tried not to think of his daughters and his son and the fine lives they were building, missed his wife, mourned his dead (always), thought about certain flavors, colors, and smells, and more or less concentrated on existence. His only companion was the pistol, brilliantly engineered by the Instrument Design Bureau, flawlessly manufactured by oligarch Ixovich's IxGroup. He stripped it, examined it, dry-fired it, drew it, grew proficient and familiar with it, learned it in all the ways a man can learn a gun without firing it, which happen to be considerable.

His nighttime visitor, Lee Harvey Oswald, stubbornly stayed away. No ideas, no insights, nothing. Swagger tried to nudge the work along by sitting at the desk of one hole where he stayed and writing LEE HARVEY OSWALD three or four times in the margin of a Russian magazine about health food. The pen wouldn't work, the paper was too glossy, and nothing came of it.

Or maybe something did.

That night, as before, he swam from unconsciousness in the dark and felt the presence of the other man. Lee, you fucking little monkey, what are you up to now?

The chilly punk bastard was silent and smug, as always, and Swagger scoffed as if to play hard to get and sailed back into sleep, but then it started.

He saw the creep in his sniper's nest, hair a mess, limbs a-tingle, full of hunger for glory and immortality, on his sleazy, tiny rifle.

What the fuck are you up to, you little bastard?

The first question that came to mind was: why did he wait until the limousine had turned the corner off Houston onto Elm and was obscured in the few trees in the area to take (and miss) his first shot? What a moron!

This one had stuck in Swagger's craw since he'd stood in the sniper's nest. It spilled over him again. What the fuck? What's going on here? Any shooter looking at the situation would know that he was assured one clear, unhurried shot before any kind of reaction took place. He would not choose a shot through the cover of trees at a moving target. Rather, as Swagger had chewed on a million times or so, the best shot was when the limousine had slowed almost to a standstill as it was rotating around the left turn directly below Oswald. At that point, the president was at his closest to Lee Harvey, around seventy-five feet. His chest and head were plainly exposed. The angle was roughly seventy-five degrees, so the trajectory ran well over the windshield of the limousine and the windscreen that cut off the driver's compartment from the passenger compartment. It was the literal fish-in-a-barrel shot, and it was so close that difficulties with the scope alignment or even the three-hundred-meter battle zero of the iron sights wouldn't move the bullet placement outside of the lethal zone. That had to be the shot Oswald planned to take.

That was in fact the shot he tried to take. Consider that when he arrived on the sixth floor that morning, he had his choice of windows. There were six. Why did he chose the left-hand corner? Because it gave him direct access to the turning automobile immediately beneath him. It was the right choice. If planning a shot farther down Elm Street, he surely would have chosen the right-hand window: it was the building's width closer and, in terms of the curve in Elm Street, gave him less deflection to the target. It seemed that even Oswald, fired up on a wave of egomania and sense of destiny as he was, doubted his ability to make a deflection shot at close to three hundred feet, which was what his choice of the left-hand window ultimately committed him to doing. It was difficult to believe he could hit that shot if he didn't think it was within his powers and had planned to avoid it.

Knock knock.

Hello, who's there?

An insight.

Swagger realized the little creep in the nest had *tried* to take the closer, easier shot, and his failure to bring it off—consistent with his goof-up's personality and his tendency to fall apart at big moments— was what determined the outcome of the next eight to ten seconds. Oswald prepped for that shot, put his scope squarely on the president's chest, and at the moment of minimum movement and maximum proximity, pulled the trigger to discover that the rifle would not fire.

Had he put the safety on his loaded weapon and, in the heat of the moment, forgotten to remove it? The safety on a Mannlicher-Carcano is a devilishly small thing, poorly designed and not for battle usage. It's a button located under the bolt plunger at the rear of the receiver. To manipulate it, you've got to break your hold, look at the fucking thing, and carefully guide it out of one condition and into the other. The idiot whom the other boys called Ozzie Rabbit snapped dry, panicked, went through the process, then went back into the shooting position, aware that he was already behind the action curve. His first shot may have been premature, as he was hunting for a target through the trees and stacking the trigger for the final pull, and the M-C trigger, unlike most of the age, is surprisingly light.

The rifle fires. He knows it's a clear miss and now the clock is ticking on his effort and his old friend failure is nipping at his heels again. He rushes through cocking the weapon, reacquires the position, and is amazed to see the car emerge from the trees into plain view with almost no reaction from occupants, security, or crowd. He throws the crosshairs onto the president—this is his most likely shot to hit the brain, as the president is much less than two hundred feet away; the angle is beneficial to Oswald, producing little lateral movement and only slight diminishment, probably not even noticeable through the cheap glass of the inferior optical device; and he's on much firmer ground regarding the trigger pull, knowing exactly how much slack to take out to get the trigger to stack up at the point of firing and when to exert that last ounce of pressure to fire.

And he misses again.

Of course, that's the famous magic bullet, and not only does he not miss, he puts a bullet through two men. It's not God's point of view that matters, however, but Oswald's point of view. The president does not react spastically to the bullet strike; rather, he makes a little jerk, which, being lost in the blur of the recoiling scope, Oswald may not see. By the time he gets the rifle cocked and is back to the target, he sees—nothing. That is, the president doesn't collapse, tip, tilt, implode, pitch forward, splay his arms. Instead, he begins a slow, subtle forward lean, and his hands go toward his throat, but not with any wounded-animal instinct or speed. Oswald cannot see any indication of a hit and must think, You idiot! Another fuckup! And he must think, What the hell is wrong with this scope? I was right on, and I missed. Is it all fucked up? Where do I hold to make the shot?

Given that psychological reality, Swagger found it mind-blowing that Oswald recovered enough to reacquire the target after running the rough action a second time, and though the target was smaller, his psychological condition possibly more scattered, his doubts about his system more intense, his fear of failure even more concentrated, he managed the perfect brain shot.

What the fuck? How did this schmuck go from two strikes to a home run? How did he recover so fast and pull it off? You can look for years at his record for any hint of such a moment and be bewildered. There is nothing but utter failure; random mediocrity is his best accomplishment.

Swagger sat back, astounded that he was sweating and that he'd been transported to a faraway place and time. Now he was back in a sordid room smelling of piss and puke, sleeping on a dirty mattress, man on the run all the way.

Yet the dreamscape of Lee Harvey Oswald killing a president would not abandon his head. In another second, it took over his brain and Swagger was back among the boxes, smelling the burnt powder, standing next to the little prick who brought such shame on all of us who call ourselves shooters. The question, eternal and lingering: what the fuck?

Was it simple sniper's luck that he hit that last shot? It could have been. The wild shot can hit as accidentally as it misses. The bullet doesn't know where it's going, what's on the other end. It just goes where the physics tell it to go, and that can be into a brain or a curb, whatever.

Swagger understood that this idea sucked: nobody wants the key moment of the late twentieth century turning on nothing more than a nobody loser's one stroke of luck. But maybe that was what happened.

Luck or whatever, Oswald has just shot the president in the head. Freeze the moment, which is the most interesting moment in the entire event. He has just seen his bullet detonate the president's head into a geyser of brain matter and blood. Even if he lost specifics of the image in the recoil, when he comes back on target out of the recoil stroke, he sees chaos, panic, and hysteria in the back of the car. And what does he do?

He cocks the rifle again.

Excuse me, but what the fuck?

Why?

Does he mean to shoot again? Is it pure reflex? It wasn't learned in the Marine Corps, where his M-1 automatically reloaded itself. What is his motive? Most good hunters have trained themselves to cock again for a fast follow-up, but by no means is this ass-clown an experienced hunter, and there's no indication that he's hunted in five years. Or does he need a motive at the time? Maybe it can't be explained; it just is, it happened because it happened, and to look for motive is to see him as rational when he was an irrational man at an irrational moment.

Still, it seemed to Swagger, aware of the sniper's instincts after the kill, in that situation, his task done, Oswald now knows that his chances at escape can be measured in mere seconds. It seems far more likely that instead of cocking the rifle, he abandons it, exits the nest, and beelines toward the only stairway, which is over ninety feet away diagonally across the empty space of the sixth floor.

He doesn't do this.

Instead, *he carries the rifle with him, loaded and unlocked, across the floor those ninety-odd feet.* Suppose he meets a colleague? Suppose someone sees him from a building across the street, the Dal-Tex Building or the Dallas County Records building, both of which have floors and windows that look directly onto his area? At that point he is acting more like a marine on combat patrol, fearing ambush, than he is a fleeing assassin.

He reaches the stairway directly in the floor at the other corner of the building, and realizing he can't reenter the world with rifle in hand, he shoves it between two boxes there at the stairs, where it will be found, fully loaded, shell in chamber, an hour or so later.

Why does he cock the rifle after killing the president? Why does he carry it with him as he proceeds across the floor? These issues seemed to bother nobody. They bothered Swagger.

Finally, enough time passed so that Stronksi felt safe enough to set a night; he met Swagger again, this time in the back of a van, to arrange the debrief and pass over the money.

"You swear," said Stronski, "that after I have this thing for you, we will proceed directly to embassy, I will watch you enter, and can then finally relax, knowing I served you as you required and lived up to all promises."

"Absolutely."

"Now tell me where to meet."

"No."

"Swagger, you are such a bastard. Such a stubborn son of bitch. You don't trust me?"

"What choice have I got? But let's take elementary precautions. Though troublesome in the long run, they will cut down on the yips, and we can concentrate on our work."

"You talk like general. All the time soothing, reasonable, and probably right. Goddamn you, man, you are a hard friend to have."

"I'm just a country boy scared of city slickers, that's all."

"I don't know what 'slicker' is, but I get the meaning. So when we settle on place?"

"I will call you on a cell that morning after you are out of the Lubyanka. I will give you a street. You will drive down it. At a set time, I will call you with a turn to make. I will guide you by me in this way and make sure nobody follows. I may do that two or three times. When I am certain you are alone, I will give you the destination, my choice, and you will be dropped. We will chat, then head by another cab to the embassy. Is that acceptable?"

"You have a cunning Russian mind. No rush to do anything."

"It's how I earned a glorious retirement in the basement of a bicycle shop where I watch the plaster slowly fall from the ceiling."

"It is not very interesting, I am sure, but still, I am sure it is more interesting than death."

"It is."

Swagger gave him the envelope: ten thousand dollars in rubles.

"I hope what I get for you is worth that. There are no refunds," said Stronski.

"I understand. I take the risk cheerfully."

"I wonder: why do you do this, Swagger? The money it costs, the danger you run, after all you've been through. It's so insane. I can make no sense of such a thing. Vengeance. You took the death of this president fifty years ago so seriously, the pain is so deep?"

Swagger laughed. "Frankly," he said, "I don't give a shit about JFK."

Three days later, Stronski called at precisely 7 a.m.

"I have it," said Stronski. "It was fine. Walked in, found the Second Directorate volumes, found the right year, found the report, broke the rules by writing it down, he never asked or wondered, got out easily, now I am with driver."

"Anyone following?"

"Hard to tell. It's crowded. All Porsches look the same. But no, I think not."

"Take a few more turns around the town. I'll call back shortly and give you a boulevard."

Shortly, Swagger called. "Go to Bruskaya, then go north on Bruskaya."

"That's seven miles."

"I will call in half an hour."

Then it was "Bruskaya to Simonovich, left on Simonovich."

Swagger waited forty minutes. "Simonovich to Chekhov. Right on Chekhov."

He himself stood in an alley on Chekhov and watched as Stron-ski's black Cherokee roared by. He watched the busy Moscow traffic flow that followed, looking for cars with intent pairs of middle-aged men, their eyes hammered to the vehicle they were following. He saw nothing like that, mainly commuters as glum as those on any freeway in America, truckies cursing the schedule, buses driven by women, a few cars of youngsters too full of booze and vitality to notice how early it was.

He moved a block, rerouted Stronski around another street, brought him by, and again noted no professional followers; this time he looked for repeats from the first batch of vehicles he'd monitored. He found none.

"Okay," he said, "you've heard of the Park of Fallen Heroes, near the Tretyakov Gallery?"

"I know it well."

"I will meet you there in an hour. I will take the Underground to the Okty—er, Okty—"

"—abrskaya station. Yes, it's a few blocks."

"See you at"—looked at watch—"nine-thirty or so."

"Sit in front of Comrade Dzerzhinsky. He will appreciate the company," said Stronski.

Possibly Comrade Dzerzhinsky did enjoy the company. He had no one else there. He stood on his pillar twenty feet above the ground, wrapped in a swirling greatcoat, his strong face ascowl with con-tempt for the world he looked upon. The man had ruled from the same altitude in the center of the square named after him, where he had commanded the ceremonial space before the Lubyanka, whose apparatuses he had invented as founder of Cheka in the early days after the revolution. He was the first of the Communist intelligence geniuses, if Polish by birth, and had helped Lenin cement his hold and built the machine that helped Stalin sustain his. He ruled from that spot in stone certitude for years, radiating the red terror from each eye.

Now, covered in graffiti and bird shit, he commanded nothing. Look ye mighty and despair, was that the message? Something like that. After the fall, he had been removed to this far place, a glade behind the Tretyakov art gallery. He had become a perch for the avian citizens of the state, and he looked out on a small patch of grass and bush in which other dead gods had been dumped, including about twenty-five Stalins, some big, some small, all broad with the muscular mustache and the wide Georgian cheekbones but all turned somehow comic by their extreme proximity to the earth. It was as if the Russians were afraid to throw out the icon that was the Boss, but at the same time they couldn't honor him with a dictator's height from which to command fear and obedience. So, low to the ground, sometimes swaddled in weeds, sometimes noseless or otherwise defaced from street action at various colorful times, he looked, in his rows on rows, like a mysterious ancient statue, unknowable, mysterious, vaguely menacing but easy to ignore, and he was ignored, for of the many beautiful Moscow parks, this was the least beautiful and maybe the least visited. It was unkempt and overgrown, unlike the formal perfection that was within the Kremlin walls. It was strictly an afterthought.

Swagger sat in almost perfect aloneness with the stone men. Sparsely visited in normal time, the park was even more desolate this early. He felt secure from his hunters: he had not been followed on the Underground, he had not been followed on his walk over. He checked constantly and knew himself to be unmonitored. It was a matter of minutes before Stronski arrived, and then he could go home and get on with it. He yearned for a shower, American food, a good, deep sleep, and a fresh start. Maybe all this shit would begin to swing into focus after he got away from it for a while. He knew he had to persist in his nighttime journeys with the creep Oswald. Who? What? How? Why? Nah, fuck why. Why wouldn't make any sense. Only how mattered.

Oswald went away, and Swagger returned to man-on-the-run

guy. He looked up and down the sidewalk; from the direction of the Tretyakov, a museum whose modern fortresslike walls could be seen through the trees, he saw Stronski approaching. He had read Stronski's file, which Nick had obtained through CIA sources; he knew that Stronski had his finger in a hundred dirty pies, but everyone in Russia did. Some didn't have so many pies. He also knew Stronski was known as a reputable assassin. He always delivered, he never betrayed. His stock in trade was efficiency combined with trustworthiness; he worked with equanimity for whichever *bratva* needed a job done, never tarnishing himself with their affairs, never playing their games.

So Swagger trusted him as well as he trusted anyone in this game.

"This is Petrel Five at Tretyakov, do you read?"

Static crackled over the handheld radio set, but the young man on the roof of the Tretyakov waited patiently until it cleared.

"—have you loud and clear, Petrel Five, go ahead."

"Ah, I think I see Stronski."

"What's your distance?"

"About four hundred meters. I'm on the roof. He's got Stronski's hair, his build, muscular, he looks to be about the age."

"Where is he going?"

"He's in the park, just like you said. No rush. No worry. No indication he realizes he's under observation."

"Okay, drop out of sight, let the situation settle. Come back up in three minutes and tell us what you have."

"Got it."

The young observer did as he was told, sliding into repose below the edge of the wall at the roof's precipice. He was by profession a construction worker in one of the companies that the Izmaylovskaya mob owned, but he and many others had been pulled out for observation duties on sites known to be favored by Stronski. This was quite exciting for him, for like many young men, he dreamed of gangster glory, of running with the feared Izzies on their violent adventures in Moscow. The chicks, the blow, the bling! It was the same for gangsters everywhere.

He rose, looked through his heavy binoculars, had a moment of panic, and then made contact.

"Petrel Five."

"Go ahead."

"He is sitting on a park bench with someone. Yes, now I see, a taller man, at least his legs are longer. Thin, not so big as Stronski. Workingman, probably, not a Westerner. Doesn't look like an American."

"Can you see his face? His eyes?"

"Let me move a bit." The young man slid down the wall of the flat roof, coming to the corner. This would give him the best angle.

"I can now see they are sitting before the statue of Dzerzhinsky."

"The eyes."

He dialed the focus carefully, hoping to squeeze a bit more resolution out of it.

"The eyes," he said. "Very wary. Hunter's eyes."

"Good work, Petrel Five. Now stay undercover."

"First the good news," said Stronski. "The good news is that there is no bad news."

Swagger nodded. He waited for it.

"In those days, KGB started a program where a Second Directorate technical team was in constant rotation, station to station, the world over. That's all they did. They stayed a few days, a week, they did a complete sweep, using every electronic countermeasure and tracking device at their disposal, and they issued a report to center with copies to the KGB resident in place. A Comrade Bukhov seemed to be in charge. Very thorough man, very patient, very wise in the ways of concealed microphones, wires, long-distance amplified eavesdropping, the power of batteries."

Swagger nodded, listening hard.

"Soviet embassy, Mexico City, 1964 inspection, twenty-three listening devices found, eighteen of them removed, the point of leaving five, I suppose, to feed bad information to your eavesdroppers."

"So in 1963—"

"Your people had it all. Everything in that building, your people heard it."

Swagger nodded. "Of course," he finally said, "that was a lot of info, most of it routine, I'm sure almost all of it routine. I wonder how carefully the work product was examined, who made the initial discrimination; probably someone low on the totem pole, and then what they winnowed out got passed upward to senior officers."

"Very good questions, my friend, but answers will be found in Langley, not in Lubyanka."

"Was there a '62 report?"

"No, the program started in 1962, and Mexico City being not exactly a big priority, the team didn't get to it the first time until '64."

Again Swagger considered.

"I saved best for last," said Stronski, so pleased with his success. "Comrade Bukhov, very professional, very thorough, as I said, includes offices that he had found penetrated, and chief among them was that belonging to Yatskov, senior KGB and supervisor of Kostikov and Nechiporenko in Mexico City and first interrogators of Mr. Lee Harvey Oswald."

Swagger let out an involuntary sigh. "That means that CIA had access to whatever Oswald said the last day, when he was so distraught and pulled the gun. He was in Yatskov's office."

"I suppose that is conclusion you could draw. I only tell you what the records say about wire operation at the embassy at the time."

"What it proves," Swagger said, "is that someone in the Agency could have known about Oswald's hit on General Walker. It is not proved, but it cannot be ruled out."

"You're the genius. You're the—" He went still.

Swagger picked it up immediately.

"Two," said Stronski in the same even tone, "coming from around the bushes behind us, heavy coats, I cannot see hands. You have that pistol?"

"I do," said Swagger, his mind gone instantly tactical. Was this a setup? Had Stronski betrayed him? If so, Stronski could have pulled a pistol and finished the job in one second. He wouldn't have placed himself in the kill zone. In an odd way, a clarification had been issued. On the point of bad action, Swagger felt a wave of inappropriate enthusiasm. He could not help but smile.

"You laugh. Swagger, you are crazier than even I."

"This is the only shit I was ever any good at," said Bob, still smiling. He scanned for threat, immediately seeing two men, also in heavy coats with obscure hands, coming at them from the same direction that Stronski had come, from the Tretyakov, maybe moving with a little too much energy for so early on a sunny Moscow morning in such an out-of-the-way place.

"Two," he said, "my twelve o'clock."

"And two more make six, heading in from other entrance, just passing by Dzerzhinsky's statue on the right. Are you hot?"

"I'm hot, but no reload."

Neither body posture had altered, neither man had swiveled his head or signaled sudden anxiety through tensed body. In fact, Stronski laughed, and as he did, he reached over and shook Swagger's arm in mirth, and Swagger felt something heavy slide into his jacket pocket and knew it to be an eighteen-round magazine for his GSh pistol.

"No cover here," said Stronski, laughing, "and they've got baby Kalish, I'm sure. On three, draw and fire, then break around the bench, run straight back to cover."

Swagger knew what was back there sixty feet or so: Stalinland. Row on row of stone Joe, wisdom in his eyes, sagacity on his face, mustache flowing like the Don, hair thick as the wheat fields of Ukraine.

"I lay down fire, you move. Get into the Stalins. Good cover, you can move, will stop their rounds, you can get shots. We'll see if they have guts to come against our guns when we are on the sights and shooting calmly."

"Let's kill some bad-asses," said Swagger.

"On my one, three, two, one—"

It happened so fast after such a long wait. The Izmaylovskaya kill team had sat in a Mercedes limo behind the Tretyakov, a glossy black beast of a car with three ranks of leather seats, smelling of new car and also of perfume, as if someone had a woman there recently. But not now. Two men in the front, two in the middle, two in the rear. Very tough, very good men, had done wet work all their lives, first in Spetsnaz, then for the mobs, and now as dedicated Izzy hard guys. It was a great life, and they had everything that the kid code-named Petrel Five dreamed about, blow, chicks, and bling. They had bleak faces and small dark eyes and wide Slavic cheekbones and frosts of gray hair, and each weighed over two hundred pounds. Each could bench his weight and was expert at Systema Combat Sambo, an advanced Russian and deadly martial art. All had scars, mended limbs, jagged knuckles, memories of death in cold or faraway places or, more recently, in back streets or nightclubs. To see them was to fear them, and the exquisitely tailored dark suits they wore over dark shirts—some black, some chocolate, some dark blue—warned the world to step aside.

Each carried what is commonly but incorrectly called a Krinkov, or "Krink" in the vernacular, the preferred weapon of choice of the late Osama bin Laden and perhaps the instrument he was reaching for when SEAL Team 6 popped his balloon. (These men had done a lot of that sort of work themselves.) It was a short-barreled AK-74 variant with a large, almost bulbous flash hider, a folding stock now cranked tight along the left side of the receiver, and a wicked, curving plum-colored mag of thirty 5.45-mm high-velocity steel-cored cartridges. It was secured by shoulder sling under the heavy Armani overcoats they wore, and in each voluminous pocket were a few more mags.

The news came to the team leader when he answered his cell in perfunctory language, without drama or excitement; they were professionals at this, none of it was new.

"Oleg, we've got a confirm. They're on the bench at the Dzerzhinsky statue. You set to roll?"

"On our way, Papa Bear," said Oleg, tapping the driver hard.

Behind him, he heard the sound he loved best in the world, which was the *klack* of bolts being racked as they were slid back to turn the gun hot and ready. He himself made that wonderful adjustment, feeling the slight vibration as the bolt slid back, permitted a cartridge to pop into place, then rammed it home to the chamber, the firing pin held tense by the trigger. His fingers inspected while he called out the commands to his team, as he had done in the mountains so regularly: "Bolts back, safeties off, full auto engaged."

"All positive," came the ragged response.

The heavy car gunned to life but did not jump into the traffic. As in all action, smooth is fast, and the Izmaylovskaya driver was an equally experienced pro. He slid arrogantly into the traffic, accelerated, made the proper turns while obeying all laws, and in a few minutes pulled up to the margins of the park.

Oleg spoke into his phone. "Papa Bear, we're set. Still a go?"

He heard Papa Bear speak into another phone and then come back with "Yeah, he's still got them sitting there like birds perched on Felix's cold nose. Go rock their world."

"Showtime," he said to his boys.

The car slid to the side of the road, and two men slipped out. They'd hold a few seconds, the other two two-man subteams would get out at two other spots around the perimeter of the Park of Fallen Heroes, they'd coordinate the walk-in, and then they'd converge on the bench. All would go to guns, the shooting would be over in seconds, and in the stunned silence, they'd return to the patiently waiting limo, which they knew would go unseen by any of the hundreds of witnesses in the roadway, including Moscow police or militia.

The car deposited the second team, turned a corner, and drove fifty yards to deposit the third. The driver began the heavy labor of a U-turn meant to move him back and place him at the exit to the park closest to the bench, out of which, if all went well, the six shooters would soon emerge.

All did not go well.

Pistol up, two hands, front sight, front sight, front sight and press, the jerk of the recoil snapping the pistol up a bit, its slide in supertime hard back, a spent shell a blur as it spun away, and then Swagger found the front sight again and followed up with another to the midsection, cranked right a degree or so, and hammered two more nines into the partner, who was unlimbering his Krink, and watched that one blur spastically while his nervous system announced he'd taken hits and he staggered, the Krink dropping but not falling as the strap held it.

Swagger heard the reports behind him of Stronski, his own GSh-18 rapping as he fired a suppressive spray, having more targets and not being able to aim after the first.

Swagger's old legs drove him off the bench and behind it, and he was stunned to see that though he'd hit and slowed them, the two on his side had not pitched to the earth. He fired again even as one of them, in a lurching move, jerked on the Krink's trigger and chopped up a cloud of dust and debris at his own feet.

"Go, go, goddammit," yelled Stronski over his own new dialogue of shots; Swagger was too excited to feel his age and ran like hell, low, with first a zig and then a zag and then a zig and was in seconds, it seemed, absorbed by the formation of Joes in Stalinland. He fell behind the nearest, went prone, and shooting with the earth as his

sandbag, fired at the smears of men to the left moving and shooting, scattering as they looked for cover, their chopped-for-handling
assault weapons jerking arcs of unaimed fire into the air to cascade
wherever. Stronski ran, and Swagger held on the head of a man who'd
wisely dropped to kneeling to steady his front sight for an aimed shot,
but Swagger fired first, careful on the press, and saw a splat of gas-
inflated shirtfront to mark a hit high in the chest; the man staggered
to his knees, dropped his weapon, and seized it again. Swagger fired,
and the man went sluggishly, reluctantly to earth. He seemed so disappointed.

Swagger looked back. One of the first two he'd hit was down,
finished, but the other—though his black shirt, now wet and heavy,
clung tightly to his chest—staggered ahead, weaving the Krink with
one hand, bull-crazed by his job and meaning to finish before he bled
out. Holding carefully, Swagger managed to press one off that blew
a jet of mist from the man's broad forehead. He fell like a toppled
statue.

A strange ripping sound went stereophonic on Swagger as a spray
of stone or marble frags lacerated his cheeks and hands. He turned
and saw that two of the original four to the left had taken positions
behind the bench and were laying out fire into the fleet of Stalins,
ripping through nose and mustache and wavy Georgian hair, blowing out all-seeing eyes, ripping the comfy pudge of sanctimony that
in some variations bunched the Boss's cheeks. One Joe split radically
in two, its lesser half dropping to Earth; another, of porous material,
simply evaporated into a fog of dust as, hit centrally, it shattered.

"Go back, go back," screamed Stronski from an adjacent Joe head,
and Swagger, usually the yeller of orders in such situations, obeyed,
crab-walking back a rank to find another stout stone Joe behind
which to crouch even as he heard full-metal jackets hum through
the air and was aware that, around and behind him, the whole world
was dancing and crumbling to the jig of velocity. Situated and alive,
he rose, and though he could see only flashes and that thin scrim of

burned chemistry that accompanies multiple smokeless powder discharges screening the bench, fired the last five shots of his mag at the bench, hearing the protest of punctured wood as his bullets bore into the bench slats.

Stronski, under that distraction, scuttled backward, hooked behind a Joe, and slammed a new mag into his GSh. Swagger's, similarly hors de combat, received the same treatment, and dropping the slide on a fresh eighteen, he hoisted it before him to hunt for targets. He heard Stronski yell in Russian.

"I call them fucking gutless Izzy dogs, tell them to come visit me in the Joes and I will kill the rest of them and fuck their asses when they are dead, hah!" he translated in the next lull.

A new fusillade ruptured the blasphemy, and more stone fragments sang as they pranced from the various Joes that the high-velocity bullets pockmarked.

"He's coming around," yelled Swagger, seeing that the two on the bench were covering for a brave guy, cutting right and hoping to ease among the Stalins from that flanking point of entry. Swagger rose, guessing the gun smoke, floating debris, and floating slivers of grass and brush would give him a little concealment, and set to intercept. He dropped back a row of Joes, cut right, ran low, paused as he waited for the shadow of the gunman, then stepped out on the diagonal and fired twice into the approaching killer's heavy chest, then fired a finisher into center forehead. It was not pretty, but it was final. The gunner went down hard, headfirst, feet flying up with such force that a Gucci loafer popped off one. Swagger scurried, leaned forward, and retrieved the Krink, deftly unlinking the sling catch.

Swagger rose and, as steadily as possible, emptied the mag, about fifteen remaining rounds, into the bench where the last two bad boys hid, this time rendering it further useless under splinters and dust. One of them rose to run, and Stronski leaned into a sight picture to take him. He fired once and his pistol jammed, its slide stuck halfway back.

Swagger swung to take the runner down with the Krink, not remembering it was empty, and pulled on nothing. He dropped it, shifted the pistol to his right hand, and suddenly felt a horse kick in his hip as a pelting spray of frags and superheated dust flew upon him.

He rolled left into the fetal, locked his elbows between his knees, and found the man who stood over the defenseless Stronski and pressed just as that guy got another mag into his Krink and was about to massacre the sniper. Swagger hit him in the eye, blowing it out, and the man twisted like a dancer and corkscrewed earthward.

Swagger turned back on peripheral motion and settled in for a shot on the surviving gangster now fleeing, saw civilians across the street behind him, possible friendly-fire casualties, and opted not to shoot. The big guy, all athlete and amazingly fast, made it out an exit and dove into the open door of a sleek black limo, which burned rubber on the acceleration.

"Dump guns, get out of here," commanded Stronski.

"You've been hit."

It was true. The left side of Stronski's white silk shirt bloomed the dark spread of blotted blood.

"It's nothing, you go, get out of here. Do it now! I am fine. I cannot run much."

Swagger dropped the pistol, pulled his watch cap low, and started to walk forcefully away, crossing a street, finding an alley, cutting down it, finding a broad boulevard. Police cars roared along it, looking for a turn to the park, which, as it developed, was not accessible from that thoroughfare. Two passed within feet of Swagger, but in them, youngish men seemed alarmed and unaggressive, unwilling to get any closer until they were sure the shooting had stopped.

Finding a small restaurant, Swagger tried to look cool. He said, "*Koka*," and waited as the drink was brought, hoping no one noticed that he was hit too.

CHAPTER 12

Reilly e-mailed her boss at Foreign. "Seems to be a big shoot-out downtown here. They say five dead in an assassination attempt. Some mafia deal. Interested?"

She heard back in a bit.

"Sounds routine. Happens here all the time. Pass, thanks. Stay on that Siberian gas thing for the time being. Maybe if Putin comments on shoot-out, set up a Sunday thumbsucker on Russian mafia—getting more violent? Think about it."

So she went back to tap-tap-tapping. ". . . while concerns about the danger of cold drilling for natural gas under the Siberian tundra continue to rise after last month's blast, Petro-Diamond spokesmen argue that the explosion was a fluke. Moreover, they say the billion-dollar energy firm will stick with recently announced plans to expand drilling operations beyond the Nebeyaskaya range in the Arctic Circle."

Her cell rang. She saw the number was local but didn't recognize it. "Hello?"

"Hey," she heard Swagger say.

Normally able to handle cops as well as grieving widows, angry generals, and romantic drunks, she was momentarily nonplussed by the voice, arriving as it did from a man who'd vanished ten days before.

"Where are you calling from? Why are you here? I thought you'd left."

"I'm in the parking lot. I'm under your car, actually. Flat on my back."

"What?"

"I seem to be bleeding. I made it here on the Underground. I had to get flat or even this small wound could empty me."

"Jesus Christ, Swagger. You! You were in that gunfight. I should have known."

"I think I'm the missing bodyguard."

"And that was Stronski?"

"Stronski and Swagger, the two of us, both old guys, against the world. How is he?"

"They say the purported target is all right. Wounded, but expected to recover."

"Very good news."

"Okay, stay there. I'll come down and get you. I need to get you to a medical—"

"No, no. It just tore through some muscles and skidded off the steel ball I have for a hip. That's all. Bandages will do fine. In a few days, maybe you can dump me at the embassy, and I'll be all right. Some corpsman will sew me up. The FBI will verify me, and they can ship me back more or less in one piece. I don't want any police interviews, believe me."

"Swagger, you have *such* a talent for getting yourself into bad shit."

She got down to the dark lot to find him wriggling out from underneath one of the small Chevys that the *Post* provides its reporters in Moscow. Once he got himself upright, he was able to move without much more of a limp than he normally had, though looking closely, she saw the small bullet hole and a dark stain that suggested some blood loss.

"No arteries, no veins. Like a whack from a baseball bat. My whole side'll be purple for a month, but once the laceration heals, it'll be fine."

"You've been shot!" she said. "It can't be fine!"

"I've been shot before. Please, it's not a big thing. My main worry is Stronski now."

"He'll be all right."

The small elevator took them up seven flights. They turned through a metal door that could have guarded a bank vault and walked into a spacious double living room apartment laden with sofas, icons, books, textile hangings, art, all of it in splendid taste. Swagger had nothing to compare it to; he had never seen such a den of the mind as opposed to the body, but he imagined it as the kind of place some sort of fancy professor might keep.

"Nice," he said. "Lots of books. Bet you've read 'em all."

"Not hardly. The office is through the door down the way; it's another apartment, rigged for business with our computers, which are tied in to the *Post*'s in Washington. It's like I'm twenty-five feet away from my boss, not four thousand miles."

He flopped on the sofa, not that interested in miracles of modern journalism. "This is fine for me. Maybe in a few minutes I'll head into the bathroom and take a shower. The bleeding seems to have stopped. I can feel it stiffening."

"Do you want anything to eat or drink?"

"You know, I am hungry."

She fixed him a sandwich and a *koka,* which he greedily consumed. Then he told her all about the event.

"God," she said, her face alarmed, "how can you be so calm? All those men trying to kill you, and it's some kind of a joke."

"Sooner or later, somebody will manage it. Or I'll fall off the porch and starve to death like an old stag with a broken leg. It'll happen. I've seen it enough. It's a fact. I just want to get this one done, though. That would be enough."

"How did they find you?"

"They didn't follow either of us. Maybe they had a GPS planted on Stronski, but I doubt it. I picked the spot, he didn't, and he didn't know about it early enough to notify anyone, and neither could anyone else in his outfit. So my guess is they had a bunch of likely Stronski places under static observation, with a kill team near each one, and when we showed up, they got into action in a few minutes. What that tells me again is what someone else said: someone is spending a lot of money on this. Only governments have money like that to spend, or oligarchs, or Hollywood directors."

"I doubt Steven Spielberg has it in for you."

"You never can tell."

"You'd better get some sleep. Do you want to move into the bedroom?"

"I'll take the shower, sack out. I should be okay to move tomorrow. You won't tell anybody I'm here?"

"If I told my editors I had a guy on the couch shot up in a Russian mafia gunfight who was investigating the Kennedy assassination, they'd ship me to the Anne Arundel county mall in two minutes."

"I don't know what that is, but if you say it's a bad thing, I'll take your word for it."

He lay on the sofa. Escape. I made it. Tomorrow I'm safe, the Moscow thing is over, and nobody's hunting me. He tried to relax, and in a bit, fed and showered and only marginally uncomfortable from the hit on his steel hip, he fell into a restless sleep.

But escape was the theme of the evening, and as he tried to draw some pleasure from his own, his mind naturally went to his buddy Ozzie Rabbit. That guy had been on the run too, although he never made it. Swagger, reliving the sense of crushing dread that had accompanied him on the walk out of the Park of the Fallen Heroes, came awake in the Moscow apartment. He knew sleep would not visit again. But Ozzie Rabbit would.

He rose, went to the window, and looked down across the open park between the buildings in the complex, while on the horizon, those various new Dallases that were the future of Moscow rose and sparkled against the dark of the night. He could barely make out his own image in a trace of reflection on the window; he saw a specter, a shape, haunted by the nearness of death.

In time Lee Harvey moved in and sat next to him, face dull (as it always was, except when he got shot), hair a mess, skin pasty, broadcasting distress and melancholy and yet defiance and pure psycho anger. Man on the run, 11/22/63.

He makes it out of the Book Depository, though he is briefly stopped by a policeman, and heads up Elm Street. He has skipped out seconds before the police arrive in force to cordon off the building and search it. He continues on Elm Street, passing the Dal-Tex Building, disappearing into the crowd, and four blocks later jumps aboard a bus heading back down Elm Street. He is so determined to get aboard this vehicle that he stops it in the street and hammers on the closed door for admittance.

That was a mystery in the classical assassination canon, Swagger knew. Many wonder why he chose to go back in the direction he came from, back toward Dealey Plaza, the site of the assassination, where crowds and policemen were collecting in large numbers and traffic, as a consequence, was backing up.

Some say he had no plan at all, he was a moron in a panic, he took the first chance he saw to get out of the area.

On the other hand, it *is* the no. 2 bus, and its destination is not arbitrary. It will take him past the Depository, under the triple overpass, over the Trinity River, and into Oak Cliff, the area of Dallas where his roominghouse is located.

Swagger realized: Peculiar. It's clear he has no escape plan in place. This means either, first, he's an idiot, acting irrationally, beyond comprehension; or second, his original escape plan is ruined for some reason, and the only thing he can think to do is return home. He counted on something happening, and it has not; now he must deal with that reality.

The bus soon runs into traffic as it approaches the chaos of Dealey. Oswald hops off, cuts a few blocks across town to a Greyhound station, and catches the only cab ride of his life.

Swagger had a new thought: This known fact has been under-commented on. Oswald is at the Greyhound station, he has dough in his wallet, and hey, it's a *bus station,* right? So there are buses leaving regularly for other cities in Texas. Yet he does not buy a ticket and climb aboard. It's true, he may know that it's a matter of time before law officers arrive, check on last-minute ticket purchases, and send messages to the highway patrol to waylay buses. But if escape were his goal, given the way his world was about to be closed down, wouldn't that be his best chance, to scurry away before the manhunt net was thrown out?

No answer presented itself. Swagger continued narrating to the two figures in the dim window that overlooked the Russian nightscape.

It is known that Oswald takes the cab to his roominghouse in Oak Cliff. He's smart enough to have it drop him a few blocks away, so he can recon for law enforcement activity before blundering in. That suggests that the roominghouse is a rational destination, something he's thought about and decided makes the most sense given the problems he faces. He knows that it won't be long before a canvass of employees is taken at the Texas Book Depository and his name comes up and he's ID'd as missing. He knows that eventually—but not how quickly—the police will connect him to the recovered rifle. The cops could arrive at any second. Yet he takes the chance to go to his roominghouse, to beat the police response, in order to get one thing: his pistol.

Who did he think he was, Baby Face Nelson?

The next day, right at 5 p.m. when the office closed, she pulled up to the American embassy on Bolshoy Deviatinsky Pereulok, and he peeped up from the well of the front seat where he'd been crouching and opened the door. The marine guards were twenty feet away across the sidewalk, so he felt quite secure.

"You were great," he said. "I can't thank Kathy Reilly enough. If anything happens with this, I'll try to repay you."

"Swagger, get out alive. That's all the repayment I need."

"Good idea. Here, can you get rid of this?" He pushed the pistol across the seat toward her, wrapped in newspaper. "Just dump it in a trash can. It can't be traced. Sorry, but I had to carry it until now."

"It's loaded?"

"Extremely."

"I'll throw it in a river."

"Much better. It's a great little gun. Saved the geezer bacon. Your friend Mr. Yexovich knows what he's doing."

"Ixovich. The oligarchs are all-wise. Plus, they give great parties. Endless caviar."

He leaned and kissed her on the cheek. "Kathy Reilly. The best."

"I'm sorry it didn't work out."

"Oh, that," he said. "The trip."

"The trip. You paid, what, forty thousand dollars in bribes—"

"Fifty. There was another installment."

"You paid fifty grand in bribes, you got hunted like an animal for two weeks in the Moscow demimonde, you lost about twenty pounds, you got shot, and you didn't find your red James Bond."

He smiled. "That's true. But it reminds me, I swore to set something right with you. Please don't hate me, but I lied to you. Or rather, I played you a certain way."

"Why is this not a surprise?"

"I told you I wanted to find the red James Bond—actually the super case officer. That was to motivate you to make that your goal, to try to see him everywhere, in every file and every report. You tried your damnedest to make me happy. But you failed. Except you succeeded. I wanted your best effort, because then I knew if you couldn't find a red James Bond, there really wasn't a red James Bond. See, a red James Bond screws everything up. He muddies the waters, makes all the linkages problems, confuses the lines of command, brings in foreign guys, makes the thing international and not home sweet home. It's all spy-movie then, and I'm a lost puppy. So I was hoping to Christ he didn't exist. But before I could move on, I had to make sure he never existed. He had to be eliminated. A lot of it is about elimination. It all traced back to the Soviet embassy, but as it turned out, the reds were conduits of information, and basically, everything they told that guy Mailer was true. Their role is small: their Oswald info was intercepted by the real killers. Now I can go after them."

"If you can find out who they were, you mean?"

"Oh, no, Ms. Reilly. I know who they are. I've always known who they are, from the first second. That bicycle print; remember it? It's actually from a wheelchair. I know the guy."

"You know who they are?"

"I even know his name and what happened to him. I saw his body."

"He's dead?"

"Yeah, but he wasn't the brains guy, the case officer. He was just operations. I think the case officer is still around, because he keeps trying to kill me."

She looked at him, dumbfounded. "I don't— I don't know what to say."

"You don't have to say a thing," he said. "There's nothing to say anymore. It's time to hunt."

PART III

Back in the U.S.A.

"There's a man with a gun over there"

CHAPTER 13

I t's a peculiar way to run an investigation," said Nick.

Swagger couldn't think of an answer. His hip had been sewn up, a process that essentially involved tying two slabs of scar tissue together with hemp thread, the highest, strongest magnitude, with a needle that looked like a stainless-steel flagpole; he'd been loaded with antibiotics, and the State Department, with FBI intervention, had found space for him to return from Moscow, quite the worse for wear, aboard its weekly diplomatic flight. Complaints had been filed; FBI agents were not permitted to work undercover in Moscow, much less shoot up parks with well-known gangsters, leaving bodies all over the ground. If the new director hadn't been so busy giving speeches and interviews, he might have objected and brought heat and smoke on Nick, not his favorite to begin with, but he missed the boat on this one, so for the time being, it went officially unremarked upon.

Now Swagger sat in his living room in Idaho, hip sore and swaddled in bandages, in the silence of his disapproving wife and daughter, while Nick upbraided him.

"It's not the diplomatic embarrassment I care about. I'm too old to give a damn about that. But this technique you've come up with is pretty spectacular. You find a target. You run at it in full aggression, guns blazing, daring it to destroy you. It makes that attempt, and somehow, by luck, talent, whatever, you survive and proceed to learn what can be learned from the assassins whom you've just killed. Does it ever occur to you that you're too old for this kind of shit, that sooner or later your luck is going to run out, and when that happens, it will be tragic, as well as a mess for all involved?"

"It never occurs to him!" Jen hollered from the kitchen. "He is self-destructive and stupid."

Bob didn't answer her either; he couldn't. "I didn't plan on the gunfight," he explained to Nick. "That was their idea. It came, we dealt with it, and we prevailed. We were armed, we reacted faster than they expected. We won the fight to the action curve. Honey, can you get me some more coffee?"

"Get it yourself," came the call from the kitchen.

"I'd say your wife is a little perturbed."

"Can you get Nick more coffee?"

"He can get it himself too."

"There you have it," said Bob. "At any rate, I feel we made substantial progress. I feel I have cleared the brush away from any high-level Soviet involvement in this thing, and that any information that was in play in '63 may have originated in the Soviet embassy in Mexico City, but it was available to other parties."

"Meaning Agency."

"They were the ones who were listening."

"Now you want to focus on the Agency, 1963."

"Yeah, I know, there's not much left of that place at that time. It was so long ago. Everybody's dead. Still, if people in the Agency knew Oswald took a shot at Walker, which they could have learned from their intercepts, that made certain things possible. They used the same model in 1993 in their operation against Archbishop Roberto-Lopez. Manipulate a patsy into place with a known rifle, engineer some sophisticated ballistic deceit, have the backup shooter make the kill shot that the patsy couldn't be trusted to make, then betray the patsy. It was the same goddamn thing."

"It's a lot of could haves, might haves, possiblys, and maybes," said Nick.

"There was nothing *possibly* or *maybe* about the bullet Lon Scott was about to put into me, and there was nothing *possibly* or *maybe* about the bullet you put into him in 1993. You tagged him before he tagged me, maybe by a second."

True enough. Nick remembered the six-hundred-yard shot, the way the dust or debris vibrated into a puff when he put the bullet into the man and watched him slump back and disappear into his hide. Later, he remembered looking at him, crushed, so still, just wreckage. Great shot, somebody said. It wasn't till later that Nick learned that Lon was wheelchair-bound, and though confined to the steel trap, had fought his way admirably to a righteous life, that is, until the end.

"The ops were similar, yes. But there's something in Latin that means 'Just because it came first, doesn't mean it caused it.' In other words, they could have planned 1993 on the model of what they thought happened in 1963 or what could have happened in 1963. Nothing that happened in 1993 proves anything about 1963."

"It's too goddamn provocative to be left alone. Agree with me on that. That's the favor I'm asking. You've come this far. It's worth a hard look, and people seem to be trying to kill me because I'm taking that hard look. And you remember the 1993 people even better than I do. One in particular."

"I remember him," said Nick, thinking of the frosty figure of a man called Hugh Meachum, who supposedly represented the "Buddings Institute of Foreign Policy" but clearly spoke for a larger, more secretive entity when he tried to convince Nick to testify against Bob.

"So . . . are you going to help me?" asked Bob. "I know you've gone way out on a limb, but the fact that twice, high-priced, highly connected killers have tried for me, and that previously one of them killed James Aptapton, is evidence that we're close to something."

Nick shook his head.

"I know you've never really believed in this," said Bob. "I'm not sure I do either. But I don't know what to do except push ahead. Here's one idea. The people who tried to take Stronski and me out were from an outfit called the Izmaylovskaya gang, known to be the most violent of the Russian mobs. They seem to be, by reputation, connected to an oligarch named Viktor Krulov, very powerful international presence, that sort of thing. Could we run a deep cyber-search of Krulov? See what connections he has to American businesses. My assumption is that whoever hired the Izzys had to do so under the auspices of Krulov. So if we get a shake-out on Krulov's business affiliations in the U.S., we'll know who was capable of making such an arrangement. There's also one named Yeksovich. No, no, dammit, Ixovich. Weird name, huh? He owns some gun companies, and that might tie him to arms exports that might involve criminal activity and possibly the Izzies."

"Yes, I will look into Krulov and Ixovich."

"Okay, the next thing is Hugh Meachum."

"He died in 1993."

"Officially. That has to be looked at carefully."

"I have. Unlike John Thomas Albright, whose life as Lon Scott was clumsily hidden, everything about Meachum's death is perfect. All t's crossed, all i's dotted. I looked very carefully at the public documents, and they are complete," said Nick.

"But he was a spy, one of the best. He would be good at that."

"You can't say that lack of evidence is evidence. Then it all goes crazy. That's why all the conspiracy theories are bullshit. And I can show you his ashes."

"Can his ashes be read for DNA?"

"No."

"Aha!"

"Swagger, it proves nothing."

"It was a joke."

"He has three sons in the Washington area. They appear to be outstanding men, above reproach. I'm reluctant to engage them. Until we have something definite on Hugh Meachum, and we're far from that, I have no plans to visit or otherwise agitate them. This is America; they are not responsible for anything their father may or may not have done."

"Agreed," said Swagger. "That would leave only other vets of Clandestine Services from the early sixties."

"Most are dead. These are guys who lived hard. They fought the Cold War. And, it should be noted, won it. Paid a high price in alcoholism, divorce, breakdown, suicide, heart disease. Through the Retired CIA Officers Association, we have been able to locate only one, and he's been institutionalized for over five years."

"Agency records?"

"Hard to access unless you've got something to trade or hard data. You've done them favors, maybe you could get in contact."

"I don't know anyone there since Susan Okada died. And I hate to play that card."

"I don't blame you."

"I have an idea, though."

"You attack the CIA with an M-16. When you're captured, you escape and recapture your capturers, and we interrogate them."

"Exactly. That's it. What could go wrong? No, no, it's actually subtle."

"This I gotta hear."

Swagger flew to Washington a few days later. It was a wretched flight through lightning and cloud, not smooth, and as usual, his mind would not settle down. He tried to nap, couldn't, got up and went to the bathroom, earning displeasure from the flight attendant because the seat-belts sign was lit.

He returned, sat back, glad he had gotten an aisle seat, and tried once again to relax, tried again not to look at his watch or disturb the person next to him, Lee Harvey Oswald.

Of course not. Just a slumbering American male, teacher, salesman, lawyer, father, uncle, brother, what have you. Mr. Ordinary. Sleeping through it all.

But his hair was slightly disheveled, maybe that was it, like Oswald's, and the next thing Swagger knew, he was back on the run with Ozzie Rabbit, who, despite the fact that he is the object of a citywide manhunt and has only a limited amount of time to escape, has risked everything to return to the one place the police will expect him at any second to retrieve his revolver.

Why didn't he have it with him in the first place?

A gun makes a man comfortable. Swagger remembered his own recent adventures with the .38 Super in Dallas and Comrade Ixovich's GSh-18 in Moscow. Not using them, having them. The weight, the reminding pull on the waistline, the density, the pressure of the hard metal against the flesh. If you knew someone was going to try to kill you, that pressure was what let you operate. You were armed. You could fight. It was the enabler of all those who, for whatever reason, knew they would travel in violence's way.

Oswald knew that up front. He had to know that. Yet he didn't carry his pistol with him, even though it was designed for that reason.

It was, after all, a midframed revolver with a snub-nosed barrel, built explicitly for undercover use, for concealment. It's the gun you carry when you can't carry a gun. His ability to hide it really wasn't an issue. While the gun—a Smith & Wesson .38 Special of the model known as M&P, originally chambered in the less powerful British .38 S&W round, then rechambered for the more powerful Special, its barrel cut down for that "detective" look—is no derringer, it can be easily concealed. After all, that is its point. For example, he could (as he did later) have tucked it in his belt, under a shirt or sweater. Since nobody was looking for it, it would have been an easily sustained deceit. Or he could have taped it to the barrel or the forestock of the Mannlicher-Carcano and concealed it in the same paper sack that held the rifle. He could have taped it to his own ankle. He could have hidden it in a sock and secured the sock to the barrel. Lacking tape, he probably could have hidden it in the pocket of loose-fitting pants and kept his hand on it to keep its weight from distending the trousers, attracting attention. He could have carried it in a readily secured lunch pail or bag.

He knew he was going to shoot the president of the United States. He knew he was going to be the object of a big-time manhunt. He knew armed policemen would be hunting and ultimately confronting him. He probably dreamed of a glorious death in a blazing gun battle at the hands of law enforcement as the fitting climax to his heroic sacrifice. Yet he leaves his snub-nosed revolver at home.

This struck Bob as either the product of a mind too deranged and incoherent to have brought off the assassination in the first place or, at the least, a curiosity.

The fact that he didn't bring it was superseded only by the astonishment that he went back, an immense risk, to retrieve it.

So here was a question: *what happened that made the revolver so valuable after the assassination?* Clearly, something happened. Clearly, Oswald's circumstances changed, and his thinking and tactics changed.

Swagger listed the things that his subconscious had brought to his attention: three odd behaviors in a few minutes, from 12:20 to 1 p.m., November 22. First, from two abject failures, Oswald makes a great recovery and shoots on the president. Then he arms himself for a ninety-foot walk across an empty room. With the manhunt tightening around him, he passes up a bus out of town and takes an incredible risk to get home and arm himself again when he could have been armed all along.

"Excuse me," said his seatmate. "I have to go to the john."

"Sure," said Bob, and radio contact with station KLHO was lost.

The house looked like a book, a slim volume packed into a shelf of larger, more intimidating tomes. The others were mansions set back from the brick sidewalks of Georgetown, under the place's looming elms, but this humble dwelling was like a ragged paperback squished between the heavier works. It was a wood-frame, with white shingles and a mansard roof and a sidewalk around back, where perhaps someone once built a modest garden. The shutters were black, the door was red, the number sixteen stood out in brass next to it, and when he knocked, a man his own age answered.

He put out his hand. "Sergeant Swagger? Or do you prefer 'mister'?" he asked. The man appeared unlikely to have been shot at and looked comfortable in a professorial way; he wore corduroys, a blue button-down shirt, wire-rimmed glasses. His hair was a softly tousled white, as if on some bird's breast.

"Mr. Gardner, thank you. Bob is what I prefer."

"Please, then, come in. Call me Harry. I'm very pleased about this. I love to talk about Dad."

"That's what"—Bob mentioned a name—"told me."

The fellow named was an editor in the Washington bureau of *Newsweek,* to whom Bob had arranged an introduction via a mutual friend, because the editor's first book was called *The New Heroes: The CIA's First Generation of Cold Warriors,* a multi-biography of some Agency stars of the postwar years.

Gardner led Bob into a well-furnished if old-fashioned living room, revealing the house's surprising depth, then to a study lined with books. He taught at Georgetown University Law School some blocks away.

"Please, sit down. Coffee, something stronger?"

"No, thank you."

"I've been told you almost won the Vietnam War single-handedly."

"No sir. My one accomplishment was to come back more or less intact. All the truly brave men died over there."

"I'm sure you're too modest. I heard the word 'greatness' whispered."

"The whisper should have been 'lucky old crank.'"

Harry laughed. "Very good answer. Anyway, Dad. You wanted to know about Dad. He was a hero in his way as well."

"I understand. What put me on to your father were the several references to him in the *New Heroes* book. He was Boswell, the biographer. He put together fictitious lives that the Agency forgers documented—legends, I guess they're called in the trade—and as these fictitious men, our people went out and penetrated or at least operated in dangerous areas."

"Dad never lost a man. No agent who went underground as a Boswell construction was ever arrested or tortured or imprisoned. He brought 'em back alive. He was very, very proud of that."

"Yes sir. As well he might be."

"But I have to tell you, Bob, Dad was also discreet. Believe me, I should know, I tried to write his biography. I went through everything. All his papers, all his notes, all his diaries, all his unfinished novels. The man committed nothing to paper, and when I was growing up, in this house, mum was the word. He never brought work home with him, which is another way of saying he was almost never home because he stayed in Langley eighteen hours a day."

"I see."

"I don't know if I can be of help to you. I just don't know a lot. Maybe if you told me specifically what it is you're after."

"Yes sir," said Bob. "There is a slight possibility, and I can offer you no proof, that somewhere in the world a man is living under a 'biography' that your father assembled for him. It still hasn't been penetrated, as an example of your father's genius."

"Wouldn't it be in the Agency work-name registry?"

"If he exists, he would have managed to remove it. He was a sly dog, this guy."

"All right. Can you tell me his name?"

"You'll scoff. According to all documents, he died in 1993."

"Hugh Meachum! Yes, Hugh was capable of something like that. Hugh was the best. My father loved Hugh. Hugh was the ideal agent: bold, cunning, unbearably brave, but nothing like James Bond, whom Dad loathed. Hugh was smart and never showy. He didn't need recognition or glory. The work was reward enough. He was like a priest, a Jesuit, I think. Intense, not macho, dryly witty. Many a time Hugh has sat in the chair you're sitting in now, drinking my mother's wicked vodka martinis, his beautiful wife, Peggy, over there, Dad and my mother here on the sofa, the four of them laughing like hyenas."

"Hugh was quite a guy, no doubt."

"Anyhow, he would be, what, eighty-five or so if still alive."

"Eighty-two. Born in 1930."

"Old-school spy. Raised in France, spoke Russian, French, and German flawlessly, Yale lit major, turned out to have the gift for the game."

"That sounds like him."

"I can't tell you anything specific about Hugh. Neither Hugh nor Dad would talk about specifics. They were so disciplined, it couldn't have happened or been committed to paper. They distrusted journalists, even if at one time Dad was a journalist."

"It's more a mind-set. By that I mean your father had a technique for building a legend. It may have varied case by case, but it had tendencies. It had patterns. It had technique. Possibly you would know that, or you could have discerned it or inferred it. So if you could talk about that subject, you might give me some road signs I'd be on the alert for as I continue with my inquiry."

"I'm not going to ask you what for. If you're vouched for by the right people and you fought hard for your country, then I'll take you at face value."

"I would tell you if I could. Thanks for not making me cook up a lie."

"If it's about the war, then I can tell you Hugh was against it, that I know. I heard him arguing quite explicitly with Dad. He'd been over there early; I'm guessing he was involved in the plotting against Diem, so Hugh was definitely a good guy."

"See, I didn't know that. Very interesting," said Swagger, thinking, That's one for the bastard. He may have killed Kennedy, but he tried to keep me alive. "Anyhow, as a result of my investigations, I've come upon some indicators that Hugh might be alive but underground for one reason or other."

"Yes. A man like Hugh made a lot of enemies."

"He can clear up some things if I can get him to talk."

"If Hugh doesn't want you to catch up with him, you won't be catching up with him. He's that clever. Maybe in his old age, he'd spill his secrets. And they'd be many and interesting. He does know a lot about Vietnam—he tried to stop it, failed, and then waged it hard as any man. Any man except possibly you. He had three tours in heavy danger. He was a wanted man. And the two of you—boy, I'd like to be a fly on the wall during that conversation!"

"I'm just an Arkansas farm boy. I wouldn't say much."

"Sure. Anyhow, Dad. How would Dad proceed in building a legend? That's the issue, right?"

"Yes sir."

"It depended on whose influence he was feeling most keenly. He was remarkably sympathetic, picking things up from the air, it seemed. A movie would stimulate him, and he'd draw on images from it. Something would happen in the news that would set him off, he'd learn a new name, it would buzz around in his head until he found a way to use it. A painting could do it, and he was an inveterate museumgoer. He was a stimulus junkie, needed provocation to work. Do you have a time frame?"

"I'm guessing—middle seventies, early eighties. Vietnam's over and done, no one wants to think about it. China's coming up."

"Dad was not one they'd go to for something Chinese."

"It could be American."

"It could be. But again, not Dad's forte. He was classic himself, old espionage. Ohio State, but he could hold his own with the snooty Ivies."

"Russia, East-bloc countries, the Cold War. The old standbys."

"The eternal enemy. Okay," said Harry Gardner. "That would be Dad. Got it. One word: Nabokov."

Bob blanked, and knew his eyes registered emptiness.

"Nabokov, the writer, the genius."

"Well, sir," said Bob, "one of my embarrassments is how poorly educated I am. I have tried to catch up, but a day doesn't go by when I don't humiliate myself by exposing my ignorance. I never heard of any Nabokov. I even had to look up Boswell to figure out what it meant."

"Vladimir Nabokov. White Russian, born at the turn of the century. St. Petersburg. Lost it all in the Revolution, and the family fled to Paris, where all the White Russians went. Cambridge education. IQ 353 or something like that. Spoke English, French, and German as well as Russian, spoke 'em all brilliantly. Wrote intricate, troubling books, usually about intellectuals, with always an undercurrent of dark sexuality and violence. Probably regarded humans as another specimen to be mounted on a needle and studied. He was a butterfly collector too."

"Your father was an admirer?"

"A devotee. As was Hugh. They'd rather sit in this room and argue Nabokov and smoke and drink and laugh than almost anything. So whether it was conscious or unconscious, I'm betting that any work product Dad turned out was touched by Nabokov's influence. And what would that be?

"Nabokov loved all the candy corn of prose, puns, allusions, cross-linguistic wordplay, wit for wit's sake. I'll give you an example. You've heard of *Lolita*?"

"Old man, young girl. Dirty as hell, that's all I know."

"Believe me, it's the cleanest dirty book ever written. But the bad guy is a TV writer named Clare Quilty, Q-U-I-L-T-Y, who ultimately steals Lolita from Humbert and uses her for his own purposes. Nabokov loves to play games with the names and at one point has Humbert muse in French something like 'that he is there,' and in French it's *qu'il t'y,* that is, Q-U-apostrophe-I-L-space-T-apostrophe-Y. You see how it works? It's a pun but in two languages, the phrase in French, the name in English."

"So a Boswell work name would have a pun in two languages?"

"This is literature, not physics, so nothing is definite. It would be a hint, a shade, a ghost of a meaning subtly brushing against a word. If the name were a Russian name—this is a real simple example—Dad might have come up with Babochkin. That means 'butterfly man,' and Nabokov was known as a world-class butterfly collector. So anyone looking for a giveaway who happened to know that Dad, in his Nabokovian phase, was the author of the legend and spoke fluent Russian might look at a list of names, and immediately, Babochkin would stand out. It would be a dead giveaway. Of course, that's the principle as enacted at a primitive level. If he were doing it for real, it would be much subtler and go through a batch of meanings and languages before it gave up its final meaning. It would bounce-bounce-bounce all over the place. And no one would ever get that last meaning because you'd have to know such a broad range of disciplines, languages, cultures. That was the sort of thing he liked to do."

"I think I got it," said Swagger.

"Would you like to see Dad's office? I kept it the way he had it when he died. I think it's a kind of portrait of the way his mind worked. You might enjoy it."

"Great. That'd be very helpful."

"Okay, come this way." Harry took Swagger up a narrow, creaky back staircase, down a crooked hallway, and into a room off to one side, with a window staring at nothing except the vines on the house next door. Bob looked: this was the mind of Niles Gardner, creator of legends, who always brought 'em back alive.

"This is where Dad tried to write his novels," Harry said. "I'm afraid it never worked out. He was a brilliant beginner, but whatever it is that brings the writer back to the chair week after week and month after month, Dad lacked. He didn't have it in him to finish. By the time he was halfway through with anything, he'd changed so much intellectually that he no longer recognized the person who began the story and had no sympathy for him and the characters he'd created. A lot of geniuses never finish their novels, I guess."

"It's too bad," Bob said. "He must have had a lot to say."

The wall-to-wall, ceiling-to-floor shelves were crammed, spine out, with books, books, more books, arranged alphabetically. Many were foreign, and of the ones in English, Bob recognized no titles except some Hemingway and Faulkner. A couple of incongruities stood out. For example, there were four ceramic bluebirds on one of the shelves, papa, mama, and two babies. There was a surprisingly sentimental picture, or more of an illustration, of six green elms against a countryside. The oddest thing of all was on the desk, piled with pages of typescript. An old Underwood typewriter, battleship-gray and weirdly tall and complicated, stood in the center. On the desk were jars of paper clips, pens—and a pistol.

"I see what you're looking at. Yes, for some reason, Dad glommed on to this old thing and wouldn't let go of it."

Harry picked it up carelessly by the barrel, and Bob recognized it as a C-96 Mauser, commonly called a "Broomhandle," for it carried that shape in a grip that plunged almost at 90 degrees from the intricately machined receiver. The handle was freed up to be unique because it had no responsibilities for containing a magazine; the magazine was contained in a boxlike structure ahead of the trigger. The barrel was long, the whole thing oddly awkward and beautiful.

"I'm sure you know more about these things than I do," said Harry, handing it over.

Bob pulled back the bolt latch on the receiver—it was so early in the evolution of semi-automatic technology that it didn't have a slide—to expose the chamber, revealing the gun to be empty. "Mauser Broomhandle," he said.

"Yes, exactly. Winston Churchill carried one in the cavalry charge at Omdurman in 1898, when it was the latest newfangled thing. I think Dad kept it around because it reminded him of classical espionage. You know, Europe in the thirties, Comintern, the Storm Petrels, the recruitment of the Cambridge Four, the Gestapo, Gauloises, POUM, the novels of Eric Ambler and Alan Furst, that sort of thing. That was when espionage was romantic, and he loved that part of it, as opposed to the cruel war he was engaged in fighting, where the stakes involved nuclear exchange and maybe global annihilation."

Swagger looked at the old pistol, feeling its cavalryman's solidity. Loading was problematic, especially on horseback: ten rounds held in stripper clips had to be indexed into grooves in the magazine, then forced down into the gun by a finger's pressure. You wouldn't want to do that with dervishes whacking at you. Swagger turned it this way and that, somewhat charmed by its ugly beauty or its beautiful ugliness. He noted the number nine cut into the wooden grip to signify its calibration.

"You won't mention the gun to anybody, will you? Definitely illegal by current D.C. law."

"Your secret is safe with me," Swagger said.

"I have no objection if you want to stay here and go through the papers to your heart's content. I will tell you that when Dad died in '95, a team from the Agency came and went through everything. They took a few papers, that's all, but they assured me that everything that remained was of a nonclassified nature."

"That's very kind of you, sir," said Bob, "but for now I don't think it's necessary. Maybe when I have more information somewhere down the line and have something exact to look for, then I might come by again, if the invitation is still open."

"Anytime. Anytime. As I say, talking about Dad is always fun for me. Those were great days, that was a great war he fought. We won that one, didn't we?"

"So they say," said Bob.

In his Washington hotel room that night, Bob didn't need to sleep to get to the subject at hand. Old man Gardner had raised it himself. Pistols. His was an ancient thing, from the Jurassic of the semi-auto age two centuries earlier. Yet it meant something to the old guy, even if he wasn't an operational type who might have used it in hot or cold blood, hopelessly obsolete or not.

Swagger opened his laptop, went online, and quickly acquired the basic info about the C-96 pistol, confirming what he knew with more details. He also learned the source of the nine on the grip, seeing that during World War I, the inscription was the Prussian way of informing the troops that this variation was a 9 mm instead of a Mauser 7.65 mm, like the earlier 96s. The thorough Germans even painted the nine red, and the pistols became known as "Red Nines," even if old Gardner's red had worn off. Then Swagger had a thought: Red Nine. Four bluebirds, Blue Four. Green trees, Green Six.

Bob wrestled with that. Radio codes, somehow? Map coordinates? Agent work names? A way to remember the number 946? Or, er, 649. Or 469.

He came up with exactly nothing except a headache and a feeling of stupidity. This wasn't his game. He went back to his game.

When he tried to price the Red Nine on the GunsAmerica website, that vast repository of used firearms, he came across something else: a S&W M&P .38 of exactly the sort Lee Harvey had gone all the way home in the middle of a manhunt to carry. It rolled up the screen, and Bob fixed on it, recognizing the sweep and balance of the brilliant Smith design, which had lasted over a century, the odd orchestration of ovals and curves arranged in a stunningly aesthetic package that achieved, as had just a few other handguns, an accidental classicism.

How odd it was that Oswald had risked all to go back for a gun he could have brought with him. Try as he had, Bob hadn't cracked that particular nut. Maybe Oswald was going to head to General Walker's and take him out too, as his last beau geste to the world he was leaving behind. Maybe he thought, if trapped, he could administer his own coup de grâce?

The only coup de grâce he administered was to a poor man named J. D. Tippit, who, like Bob's father, had done his duty and caught a slug for his trouble.

J. D. Tippit was the forgotten victim of that bloody day. A Dallas policeman, he was armed with a description of the assassin—it nailed Lee Harvey to a T—and ordered into Oak Cliff, closer to downtown, to patrol and scan. He spotted a man who matched perfectly. The fellow walked, perhaps too hastily, up Tenth Street in Oak Cliff. Tippit trailed the walker from his squad car, then halted and hailed him over. Their conversation is forever lost. At one point it seems that Oswald satisfied the inquiry, left the squad car, and began to depart. But Tippit had a second thought, called, and got out of his car. It does no good to wonder why, in that age of less politically correct policing, he didn't brace the suspect more aggressively, at gunpoint, and put him in cuffs before sorting things out. He chose the courteous way and took three bullets as a consequence.

But what was odd wasn't Tippit's politeness, Swagger thought, with the silhouette of the stubby revolver before him on the screen, so much as the intensity of Oswald's homicidal response. It is known that the man had a temper and was prone to and not afraid of interpersonal violence, as frequent arguments and fistfights attest, but at the same time he was a yakker, a talker, a debater. He may have had or believed he had the skills to talk his way out of anything. He may have thought he'd done so. When he was hailed a second time and saw the officer emerging from the car, he never deployed those skills. His whole personality was based on them, his sense of self. Yet he abandoned them and drew and fired.

A case can be made: he snapped. He was a fugitive on the edge of rational control, his mind wasn't working properly, and he saw that he had to act or wake up on death row. In a panic, he did that. Swagger thought: I suppose that makes sense, at least as much sense as anything, even if it contradicts his basic character.

But what happened next is even more peculiar and out of character. Why did Oswald walk to the prone body and fire a last shot point-blank into the head? You might say execution-style, but that would be wrong. It wasn't style, it *was* execution.

It seems to have attracted little attention, but it puzzled Swagger deeply. He might concede that a fleeing man in a panic with no impulse control and abject fear for his life would draw and shoot. Almost certainly, he would turn and walk away rapidly. He is killing to live.

That is not what happened. Instead of turning, Oswald deliberately closed the ten feet of distance between them, bent over the fallen man, and delivered the brain shot at such close range that he could see the face as he drove the bullet into the head, see the spew of blood and the fall across the body of that utter stillness that marks the dead from the living. Why? It makes no sense in terms of his situation, and it really makes no sense in terms of his politics and previous behavior.

He never hated JFK. He wasn't a punisher, a psychopath, a coup de grâce giver, a scalper, a Bushido warrior who took the skull knot of his fallen adversary. His killing never had that personal edge of contempt. Yet in this instance, he goes the extra effort to lean over and deliver the final expression of contempt with the brain shot at close range.

Why?

The next day was the first stop on what Swagger thought of as the Hugh-Lon Grand Tour. From Georgetown, he traveled to Hartford and went through birth records, finding out that indeed a Hugh Aubrey Meachum was born in 1930, to Mr. David Randolph Meachum and his wife, the former Rose Jackson Dunn, both of whom listed their address as American Embassy, Paris, France. He found Lon as well, born five years earlier to Jeffery Gerald Scott and his wife, the former Susan Marie Dunn, address Green Hills Ranch, Midland, Texas. Evidently, the Dunn sisters preferred that their beloved Hartford OB-GYN deliver their children in the comforting confines of Hartford Episcopalian Hospital.

On then to New Haven, mostly decayed old city but part of it medieval university, with real ivy on the towers and buildings clotted with elm and oak, the whole thing a delusion of propriety and yet oddly comforting. He didn't bother with Yale itself. Who'd cooperate with a cranky geezer with a cowboy accent and boots, who looked like Clint Eastwood on a bad-hair day? It probably intimidated him a little too, maybe the only thing that ever had.

The public library was more accommodating; it had bound copies of the *Yale Daily News* that yielded information without attitude, and paging through the lost and forgotten record of elite success on the gloried fields of New Haven had a weird feel, as if he were on a different planet so far from the squalor of his own upbringing in the hills of Polk County, Arkansas. But Yale in the forties: what a glorious place it must have been, as half the faces later achieved, under the camouflage of more chin and less hair, national distinction of some form or other. Of the cousins, Lon Scott was by far the more outstanding, particularly as a fullback and linebacker for the Bulldogs. Many old photos showed that particular form of American male beauty, the square, symmetrical face, the strong nose and jaw, the ease of smile and warmth of eye. Confidence: it was born into this man as surely as his blond hair and the aquiline blade of his nose, broken once to great dramatic effect on some ball field somewhere. Swagger remembered Lon—then calling himself John Thomas Albright—stuffed in his hole on the ridge over Hard Bargain Valley in the desolate Ouachitas of 1993, head destroyed by the energy of Nick Memphis's six-hundred-yard shot. It came to that? Yes, it did. So sad. Three touchdowns against Harvard, led the league in points scored (few field goals in those days except by the rare drop kick), to say nothing of his spring glories, where, for four years running, he won the Ivy rifle championships in standing and prone. It was too bad the war couldn't have lasted a little longer, for Lon's skills at riflery and football would have done the American forces good wherever he served.

There was much less of Hugh five years later. He'd been no macho jock dominating the back pages of the *Daily,* only a sub on the Bulldog basketball five. Besides the cage mediocrity (best game: eight points against Brown his senior year), he appeared in only one other notice, his election to the board of the *Yale Review,* though Bob couldn't force himself to look that up and see Hugh's undergraduate poetry. Hugh was smarter: he graduated with cum laude honors; Lon did not.

Back in Washington, Swagger had the entire fifties-sixties run of the National Rifle Association's *American Rifleman* publication shipped to his hotel room off an Internet purchase. He spent nights going through the volumes, tracking Lon's early run of brilliant victories in competitive shooting at the national level, even finding a picture of Lon standing with a trophy exactly where Bob stood with the same trophy twenty-five years or so later. Bob had no father to stand behind him, but Lon's beamed proudly from behind his so-accomplished son, who, in just a few years, he would paralyze from the waist down.

By day, at the Library of Congress, Bob combed the gun magazines of the same fifties-sixties for Lon's work as a writer, as an inveterate reloader and experimenter, as a rifle intellectual, if such a thing existed, and saw that he was as revered as Jack O'Connor, Elmer Keith, and the others of that golden age. Bob could find no mention of the paralyzing accident, or the supposed "death" in 1965, but after a several-year interval, the byline John Thomas Albright began to appear and did so steadily for the next twenty-five years.

That left one more stop: a visit to Warren, Virginia, near Roanoke, where Lon "died." Swagger learned there only what he already knew: the death was a thin counterfeit, all the documents forged, all the newspaper accounts based on a funeral-parlor press release. The body, naturally, had been cremated, the ashes scattered.

Suddenly, there was no place left to go. No one was following him. Nobody was cyber-mining him. Nobody was trying to kill him. It seemed that when he had lost Hugh's scent, Hugh had lost his, even if it wasn't clear whether Hugh Meachum existed.

The Memoirs of a Case Officer

BY HUGH MEACHUM

"You can always count on a murderer for a fancy prose style," writes the great Russian novelist Nabokov. Well, we'll see about that.

I am undisputedly a murderer, but my prose style has been abraded of its sparkle, if there was ever sparkle to begin with, by four decades of filing largely unread administrative reports, a few research papers, too many after-action reports. My daily vodka intake hardly helps matters, nor does the arbitrariness of my memory. Speak, memory, I command; it responds with vulgarity. The issue is whether my old and creaky imagination will be stimulated by recollection and at least propel my words to the level of readability, or whether this record will disintegrate into drivel and incoherence. That would be a shame. I have much to tell.

For though I'm a dismal writer, I'm a great murderer. I've never pulled a trigger, but I've sent hundreds, maybe thousands, to their deaths in that bureaucratic intelligence-agency way: I've planned and authorized assassinations, raids, and commando assaults, the necessary by-product of which is murder. I supervised Phoenix for a year in Vietnam and made a jaunty figure with a boonie hat and a Swedish submachine gun slung under my arm, even if I never fired the damned thing, which was annoyingly heavy. Phoenix probably killed at least fifteen thousand, including some who were actually guilty. I put together and managed from close at hand all manner of paramilitary black operations, involving every sin known to man. Then I went home and slept in a warm bed in a very nice home in Georgetown or Tan Son Nhut. You're probably right to despise me. But you don't know the half of it.

I am also the man who murdered John F. Kennedy, thirty-fifth pres-

194 • STEPHEN HUNTER

ident of the country in whose services I labored so bloodily. I did not pull the trigger, but I saw the opportunity, conceptualized it, found the necessary arcane talents to staff it, recruited those talents, handled logistics, egress, and fallback via safe routes and counter-narrative alibis, also, as it turned out, unnecessary. Moreover, I was in the room when the trigger was pulled. Then my shooter put his rifle away, and we left to be quickly absorbed in the public frenzy of grief and mourning. Nobody stopped us, nobody questioned us, nobody was interested in us. By four o'clock, we were back at the bar at the Adolphus.

It was, as you must know, a perfect crime. No six—or was it eight or ten?—seconds in American history has been more studied than those between which Alek, poor little mutt, fired the first shot (and missed) and my cousin fired the last shot (and hit). Yet in all the years and against all investigation and attempts to comprehend, in all the theories, in the three-thousand-odd books by clowns of various mispersuasion, no one has ever come close to penetrating our small, tight, highly professional conspiracy. Until now.

I sit on my veranda. I am eighty-three healthy years old and hope to be around for at least another twenty. Before me the meadow, the valley, the purple forests, the river. The land is mine as far as the eye can see, and it is well patrolled by security. In the large house behind me are servants, a Japanese porn-star mistress, a chef, a masseuse (and occasional mistress), a gym, nine bedrooms, a banquet room, an indoor pool, the most elaborate entertainment center on Earth, and an array of real-time communications devices by which I can administer my empire; in short, the products and perks of a vastly remunerative and productive life. I'm worth more than several small countries.

At long last, five decades later, there is a tremor in my world. A threat. A possibility. A chance of discovery and destruction, even vengeance. It has impelled me to sit out here in the warm sunlight with a yellow tablet of legal paper and a cupful of Bic ballpoints (though I'm a traditionalist, I'm not so goofy as to insist on a fountain pen) and tell the story in my own hand. At any moment in the next few days, a phone will ring and tell me if the threat has gotten larger or has gone away forever. But as I'm a man who generally finishes what he starts, I expect that no matter the outcome of the drama being played—again, at my insistence and according to my instructions—I will finish this manuscript. Assuming I haven't been interrupted by a bullet, I will consign it to my safe. Maybe when I die, it will become known and shake the foundations of history. Maybe it will disappear, tossed into the furnace like Citizen Kane's sled. That's beyond my control and therefore beyond my care. I know only that now, for the first time, I will set it down. Speak, memory.

Though I am naturally reticent, resolutely shallow, and not one for self-analysis, I feel obligated to produce a few brisk paragraphs of pedigree record-straightening. I am Hugh Aubrey Meachum, of the Hartford Meachums. It's old Yankee machinist and tinkerer stock, with branches in the hardscrabble farming that Connecticut offers. My forebears were known for a shrewd eye on the dollar and opportunities to make it; quiet, severe faces (men and women); good hair; and taciturnity, with a black streak of alcoholism and melancholy evincing itself a couple of times in each generation. Given that as my stock, I was more fully formed by three mentors, about the first two of whom I will say just a bit.

The first would be a man named Samuel Colt. I was wise enough to pick as a great-great-grandfather an otherwise odious tyrant named Cyrus Meachum, who did one intelligent thing in a legendarily grim life as a Hartford hardware-store owner. He believed in young Samuel Colt and his twirling new gizmo called the revolver, and invested in the sprout's first Connecticut plant (the first of all, in New Jersey, had failed). It was an excellent career move, as all of us subsequent generations of Meachums have benefited from the colonel's invention, in a never-ending supply of just enough moolah to let us do what we wanted instead of what we needed. We had the best of schools, the best of holidays, the pleasures of big houses on hills under towering elms and of hearing the peasantry call our fathers "sir." We rode the genocide of the Indians, the elimination of the Moros, the whipping of the Hun, the destruction of the Nazis, and the Greater East Asian Co-Prosperity sphere to financial independence, happily. A few of us died in each of those campaigns, and my father, a career diplomat who served in the State Department before the war—in Paris, where I was raised, 1931–1937, where I picked up the language easily and totally—and in an outfit much heralded and, like all intelligence agencies, almost wholly worthless, called the Office of Strategic Services, which was actually more Red than Moscow was in the thirties! Then back to State for a genteel gentleman's career. Thank you, Colonel Colt, for underwriting it all.

Here I should insert a footnote about the language that I learned "easily and totally." It was not French, though I speak French. It was Russian. My nanny, Natasha, was an exiled White, a duchess, no less. An exquisite and cultured lady, she moved in high White circles, and Paris before the war was the White Russian Moscow, with the largest population of exiles anywhere on Earth. They were brilliant if deluded people: immensely cultured, extravagantly cosmopolitan, charming and witty and bold to a fault, of extremely high native IQ, generously seeded with genius, indefatigable in battle and literature. After all, they produced not only the great Nabokov but Tolstoy and Dostoyevsky as well. I may have even, as a small child, attended a soiree where N. himself was present, though I have no memory of it. So Russian was my first language, with a bit of aristocratic frost to it; meanwhile, my parents were busy doing the Paris scene, all but ignoring me, for which I thank them. Natasha's lessons were far more meaningful and lasting than anything they could have taught me. This will explain much of what is to come in the tale ahead.

My second mentor was a man named Cleanth Brooks, of Yale, where I majored in American literature with a view toward going to Paris and working with some Harvard boys on an enterprise they had started up that seemed damn keen to me, called the *Paris Review*. Dr. Brooks had his problems, about which I will remain discreet, but he was the founder and high priest of an early-fifties discipline called the New Criticism. It held, with Spartan rigor, that text was everything. It didn't matter what you read about a fellow in *Time* or *Life*, or what movie star he'd married or whether his dad had beaten him or his first wife had belittled the size of his dinger, none of that mattered. *He* didn't even matter. Only the text mattered, and it must be examined closely, under laboratory conditions, without regard to personality or psychology or voodoo-hoodoo or what have you. Only then would its message, its meaning, its place in the universe, if any, be teased out. I loved the discipline of it, the zeal of it, the sense of probity. I suppose I longed to apply it to life, and I suppose I did, in some fashion.

Enough of those old ghosts. My most powerful mentor was a famous man, a glamorous man, a brave man, a man who sent me on my way. I must address him at some length for you to have any grasp of what happened and why in 1963.

His name was Cord Meyer. He recruited me on my father's recommendation, spook-to-spook as it were, from the University of Pennsylvania, where I was a graduate student in lit and alone insisted on the seriousness of a pornographer named V. Nabokov, to the Plans Division of the Central Intelligence Agency, where I was to toil and happily murder by proxy for forty years, every second of every day spent in the idea—or possibly delusion?—that I was helping my country against its enemies, that I was living up to the standards of dead Meachums the world's battlefields over, that I was ensuring all those big words that made Hemingway cringe in the rain, such as "freedom" and "democracy."

Cord was a toot and a half, believe me. I still have dreams and nightmares about him; I'll never escape him. Perhaps you know the story: he was one of the most famous men the Agency ever produced, and, I would say, having known most of them, the best. He was thrice touched by fire when I went to work for him in 1961. He had first of all lost an eye as a marine officer in the Pacific. Cord never discussed it, but we are given to understand that he saw the hardest of hard combat, even the gory squalor of hand-to-hand with bayonet and entrenching tool against a desperate enemy. Cord was too diffident to wear an eye patch, knowing that it would make him too famous too young. He simply slipped a glass orb in the vacant socket, and only a man studying him would notice. It was the idea of the eye gone on Iwo or Entiwok or one of those god-awful, never-heard-of-again places that was far more powerful than a showy patch would have been.

His background after the war is probably pertinent. He emerged a pacifist, having seen too many bayonets crammed into the bellies of teenage boys who'd never gotten around to getting laid. He was attracted to the idea of one-world government, so that nations wouldn't send fleets of boys with bayonets after one another on flyspecks in far oceans. He was active in the United Nations movement and labored sweatily in service to that dream. Somehow, around 1948, after three years of hard work, it dawned on him that the whole outfit had been infiltrated and taken over by Commies and that it would henceforth work exactly the opposite of its intended mission—that is, it had come to exist to enforce the hegemony of the red over the blue. Disillusioned, he made contact with Mr. Dulles, who, duly impressed, offered him a position.

He had a talent, a nose for it. Within five years he became head of Clandestine Services, in the Directorate of Plans, and if you don't yet know, Clandestine was where it all happened, a hatchery for mayhem. Other outfits would call such a unit "Operations," and it would acquire flashy nicknames like "The Ranch" or "The OK Corral," and its operatives would be called "cowboys" or "gunslingers" or some such. It never looked as deadly as it was: a bayful of mild-looking Yalies (a few Princetonians and Brownies thrown in, the odd nonpedigreed genius with special skills) with narrow ties (never loosened), horn-rims or black-framed heavy plastics, Brooks Brothers dark gray or summer-tan suits, Barrie Ltd. pebbled brogues or loafers, as dull as the Episcopal ministry. On weekends, a lot of madras, rather lurid Bermudas (red was popular, I recall), old Jack Purcell tennis shoes, usually battered orange by clay courts, khakis, old blue button-downs, maybe an old tennis shirt. Little would one know that behind those bland eyes and smooth faces lurked minds that plotted the downfalls and upswings of tyrants, the murders of secret-police colonels, an invasion or two, and a coup or three.

Back to Cord, wizard of Clandestine. His second immersion in flame was not cool or enviable. It was awful. In 1958 he lost his second child, a nine-year-old son, who was fatally hit by a car in, of all places, the spiritual home of all us Yalies waging the Cold War, Georgetown. The loss of a child is something I cannot fathom. As emotion embarrasses me, I will not linger on it, nor try to conjure its effects on him. It cannot have inclined him to a merry view of the universe.

It was his third tragedy that made him famous, pitied, beloved, scorned, doubted, mistrusted, suspected, and yet somehow vivid. He was, in his way, a pre–George Smiley Smiley, in that his public cuckolding served allegorically for the earnestness with which he loved his country and the disdain with which it repaid him. The name of his disaster was Mary Pinchot Meyer.

I suppose she could be termed a transitional woman. She came too late to be called a beatnik and too early to be called a hippie. "Well-bred bohemian," though it has no public cachet, is probably the most accurate term. It goes without saying that she was beautiful, that she had the social ease being well bred confers upon its progeny (why do I insist on "progeny" instead of "children"? fancy again!), that she had beautiful flashing legs, that most everybody fell in love with her, that she was witty, effervescent, charismatic, that she had a great mane of hair, tawny and thick, and that lipstick looked redder on her than on any woman in Washington. She must have been sexually precocious, she must have loved danger, she must have had in her the seedlings of feminism and a need to be a person outside the illustrious reign of her husband as warrior-king of the Cold War and smartest of the very smart people who coagulated in then-seedy, dumpy, but somehow glamorous-amid-the-rot Georgetown.

She left him in 1961, citing the usual suspect of that age, the catchall "mental cruelty," whatever that meant, and I suppose it means anything its attorneys want it to mean. Did she begin her famous affair before or after the divorce? Was Cord officially cuckolded, or did the two lovebirds have the courtesy to keep it legal until the papers were served?

No one will ever know, and it's doubtful that Cord ever told anyone. He never told me.

The two were Georgetowners before 1960. It is known that she was friendly with and passed time with his gorgeous if slightly vague wife. Moreover, they must have seen each other in the streets, perhaps at the grocery, perhaps at the various drunken lawn parties to which their set, our set, "the" set seemed to gravitate, all the bold young shapers of the future, all the technocrats of the fashionable agencies (and our agency was very fashionable, while the poor boobs of the FBI were not), and all the young, ambitious journos who would write books about us and end up richer and more powerful than any of us.

It is not known when Mary Pinchot Meyer began to sleep with John Fitzgerald Kennedy, before the November 1960 election or after; nor if they waited till the divorce was final. But have at it they did, and she is credited with at least thirty visits to the White House during his three years, at many odd times of day or night. It was such a terribly kept secret in the Washington of the era that it could hardly be called a secret at all, although perhaps she was most in the dark, for she may never have quite caught on to the fact that if he was sleeping with her, he was in the meantime trying to bed every vagina between Baltimore and Richmond, with the odd movie-star bang thrown in for good measure. Other rumors swelled in the wake of the two. She had some mysterious connection to the least interesting man of the period, Timothy Leary (Harvard, of course! agh!). So it was said that she brought LSD and marijuana into the White House and introduced the president to them, in hopes of somehow lessening his childish aggression. Apologies, I have no inside dope on this and mention Mary only because she was part of Cord's glamour and because this was one more reason why Plans—not the Agency as a whole, as there is no Agency as a whole, only a loose confederation of tribes, some of whom get along and some of whom do not—was not a big Kennedy supporter.

Possibly I will address that later; let me just assure you that as far as I am concerned, sexual jealousy was not part of the equation—it would not be recognized under the New Criticism—and that I, little Hugh, latest of Cord's Yale wonder boys, was not secretly in love with Mary. I always loved Cord, I never loved Mary (and let me hasten to add, I had NOTHING to do with her murder in 1964 or whenever it was); I did what I did for the dreariest of reasons—a policy dispute. Again, you'll have to suffer my fancy for prose another few pages before I discuss that.

So I did not murder JFK to punish him for sleeping with Mary Pinchot Meyer, the former wife of my boss and mentor and a far better man, in all respects, than he was. Too bad; it would give a nice spin to what follows, would it not, if the assassin of Camelot turned out to be the noblest of them all, and the man he slew the rankest of dogs? It would turn popular history, where by default I am the most hated of all men on Earth, on its ear. The truth is, I never saw or met Mary; she was only a ghost, a whisper, a legend. As I said: I did it for the policy.

Let us pick a beginning spot. I know exactly when my subconscious announced its decision to me and my life turned on its axis. I also know that the subcon had been busy grinding away for months, trying to fit new intelligence, new insights, new relationships into a sort of coherent action plan that I felt I must engineer even before I conceptualized it. Something was wrong in the kingdom, and it would kill the kingdom if it was not stopped, and yet nobody had recognized it, no vocabulary existed by which the issue could be discussed, and when that vocabulary emerged, it would be too late, we'd be gone, we'd be doomed. If you believed, you had to act now; if you didn't act now, you were letting people down, even if they had no framework by which they could comprehend your motives.

Beginning spot: a party in Georgetown, at Win Stoddard's, the crummy west side of Wisconsin Avenue, he and his family in an old, decaying pile of bricks, painted yellow to scare the termites, with a garden straight out of a Tennessee Williams play, all thick and jungly and rancid with moisture and rot. Pathetic fallacy? Dangerously close, I agree, and will not mention the garden again.

It was mid- to late October, the year of our lord 1963, two and a half years into the Kennedy era, Camelot Anno Duo and all that, and what was happening was nothing much: a shop party. That is to say, the glamour Ivies of the Clandestine Services subgroup of the Directorate of Plans met to let their hair down (figure of speech; we wore neat trims in those days) and ease office competitions, grudges, cabal forming, and the like by applying copious quantities of gin or vodka (anthropological note: we did not favor brown drinks) as a lubrication to the competitive friction of the place, as well as a dash of fizz and some citrus wafer in each glass, the martini being entirely too uptown Mad. Ave/gray flannel for us crusaders. It was, I suppose, any staff party, any department party, any unit party, any entity party in any town in any state on Saturday night in America in 1963: cigarettes dangling insouciantly from lax mouths, points made stabbingly, everyone too loud, too close, too drunk, maybe some jazz playing on the hi-fi. (We were the last pre-rock generation.) You know how such things go, and that's how they went: in the early hours, the high officials pay their obligatory visits. Even old man Dulles, though deposed after the Bay of Pigs fiasco, came by for a quick drink with his old boys; and there was an obligatory look-at-me appearance by his successor, McCone, if memory speaks the truth, and to have them both would have been a good nab for Win. Cord came with his youngest boy, Tommy, though I don't think he stayed late and just glowered with tragic nobility while holding a glass of gin in one hand and absently running his other through the boy's thick hair and smiling at the gifts of wit and insight his supplicants brought him. The almost legendary Frenchy Short came and went quickly with a beautiful Chinese girl in tow; an honorary drop-in had to be James Jesus Angleton, a friend of Cord's, even if he was charged with catching theoretical doubles and could destroy any of us with a whisper of suspicion. It was probably better to suck up to him than to ignore him, though it was always a tough call. The dry stick Colby was there briefly, though he had bigger fish to fry that night. Des FitzGerald, who'd run the Bay of Pigs and was, rumor had it, engaged in replacing Fidel, came, got drunk, and left early by cab. Just powerful, secretly famous men behaving with mild sloppi-ness, no harm done, probably better for morale that way anyhow.

By 11 the big shots were gone; by 11:30 most of the wives, all of them luscious and creamy, tans not yet faded from their summers at Bethany, and since most lived in then-safe Georgetown, there were no difficul-ties about leaving. They had been upstairs anyway, my own dear Peggy among them, Smith girls mostly, as we were Yale boys mostly; they'd come down, give the sweet peck on the check, warn us not to drink too much, and remind us that we were due at early Mass or to serve com-munion or something ceremonial the next morning at St. Whatever or First Whatever. Memory speaks: I remember a sea of ragged, baggy tweed jackets, an ocean of blue or white button-downs, maybe a faded madras here or there, dimpled khakis, the more frayed the better, loafers or possibly those suede things that used to be called "dirty bucks." The hair was short, the cheeks clean, the noses straight, the teeth white. We were square yet cool, brazen yet innocent, savage yet mild.

Win demanded the floor. "My brothers," he cried, "I need an ethical finding."

Laughter. We never discussed ethics; to discuss it was not necessary, as it was part of our heritage to know what was and was not allowed. (Hmm, yes, I would say that I would soon push that line a bit.) So that set the key, which was irony, accelerated by gin or vod, and the need to be funny if not coherent.

"Win, you gave up on ethics the night you stole Morison's final in American Classics," and again everyone laughed because the idea of Win stealing from Samuel Eliot Morison was quite amusing, partially be-cause the old admiral was Harvard and Win hated Harvard.

"He never locked his windows, what can I say?" joked Win. "Any-how." He paused, refortified the gin surge to his system, took a puff on cigarette thirty-five or forty, and proceeded dramatically. "Anyhow, you know how Cord encourages us to dip into wire transcripts from the em-bassy teams?"

Everybody groaned. It was a testing ground for newbies, their patience and diligence, but Cord liked to see people seriously busy, and if you found, as the business often produced, an odd spare hour or half hour in the duty day, he encouraged you to wander down to Embassy Wire, pick up typescript of recent interceptions, and peruse. Did anything ever come of this? I don't know. Not until tonight.

"So," said Win, "I'm running through the pages from the Sov Mex City joint, and it's the usual crap, low-grade, beneath action or contempt, mostly 'how come we have to work so much overtime' and 'how come Boris got Paris when I was supposed to get Paris' crap, they're just like us, always whining, and I come across what seems to be some kind of interview with some kind of beatnik defector or something. An American, I mean, southern-fried variety, an ex-marine as far as I can figure out. I track down the actual tapes and run 'em on the reel-to-reel, and over the earphones I hear this guy, Lee Something Something, trying to talk his way into Russia. I should say *back* into Russia, because it seemed he'd already been there for two and a half years, and now and then he'd burst into bad Russian. Well, Igor and Ivan aren't having any of it, even if he was a genuine United States Marine and everything, but he's the asshole type, won't take no for an answer, always looking for a fight or a chance to impress, and he claims, I kid you not, oh, you'll get a kick out of this one, he claims *he's* the guy who took that shot at General Walker!"

Lots of astonished laughter. Shooting General Walker was a much-approved action in our circle. It had taken place on April 10 of that year in Dallas. Someone had winged a bullet at the old beast as he sat at his desk, plotting the next week's atrocities. It missed (typically, I was soon to learn), as the unknown shooter apparently had an uncertain trigger finger.

Major General Edwin Walker (Ret.) was a particular bête noire of Clandestine Services. He was an authentic war hero in both the war we thought of as The War and the thing called Korea. He had prospered, but as with so many of that warrior ilk, hubris destroyed him. His anti-communism became a zealotry, then a psychosis, and finally, a craziness. The commander of the huge 24th Infantry Divison in Germany—

he and his men would face the red tanks pouring through the Fulda Gap if it ever came to that—he lost all perspective. He indoctrinated his men with John Birch Society pamphlets, he gave them voting instructions, he gave speeches in which he declared that all the postwar Democratic leaders, particularly Truman and Acheson, had been "pink," as was, by inference, anyone who followed their steps in the Democratic Party of Treason.

It's not that we were Democrats, although we probably were. Some of us—that would include young Hugh with the soft face and meek eyes and grown-up pipe—were even liberals. It's not that we were in any way pro-com. But he did not meekly disappear into the night, as one would have hoped. When he resigned after refusing McNamara's transfer, all this occurring after a newspaperman exposed his ugliness, he returned to America a kind of hero, like MacArthur, I suppose, though lacking the elegance and poise. He set himself up in his hometown as a speechifying one-man infantry division, riding his notoriety to the max, demanding action from Kennedy, denouncing Kennedy and his minions, supporting segregation, generally raising hell and crowding the administration into postures not sound in the long run. Did he seek power himself and imagine a career in politics? Possibly. At one point he threatened to unify his followers, of whom there were thousands, into a kind of political action force, and that sounded ominous. He was a troubling psychopath with clear fascist tendencies who did not like the Negro or any who supported the Negro's quest for equality, who loathed "diplomacy" as a solution to Soviet expansion as opposed to "battle," who would leap to his feet and start singing tearfully whene'er Old Glory was unfurled. He may have petered out when his gadfly act grew tiresome and reporters no longer bothered to cover his stem-winders, but all through the summer of '63, particularly emboldened by the missed sniper's shot, he seemed to be everywhere, hammering away, not so much a threat in a political or operational sense but more of a malign presence, clouding the policy debate, pushing Kennedy hard to the right even as Kennedy's own instincts may have pushed him hard to the right already.

I particularly loathed him. He made anti-communism, to which I had devoted my life, stupid, coarse, loud, ignorant, rabble-rousing, and suspect to the intelligentsia, a particularly fickle audience with fear of fighting deeply ingrained. He would be one more reason for them to withdraw from duty and strength; a brute, a bully, a screamer, a sprayer of saliva. No one with an IQ over 100 seemed to care for him.

There was a deeper issue. It was pure policy, and here I apply the New Criticism and speak no more of the general's manifold unpleasantries and vulgarities. Stripped of all psycho-historical-stylistic nuances, his sense of anti-communism was inimical to mine, that is, ours. He was macho and wanted to dominate by daring and, if it came, winning a military confrontation. That millions would die in such a conflagration meant nothing to him. His was the iron fist in the iron-glove approach, as it worshipped domination, destruction, and enslavement as the highest, purest form of triumph.

Our gestalt was far different. We feared the big war, the full-theater nuclear exchange, the dark piles of rubble, corpses, and poison air that such a crusade would unleash. We felt that to defeat communism, we had to co-opt the soft left and offer sensible alternatives to the billions of people who yearned for freedom from colonialism, imperialism, and capitalism. We fought surrogate wars, culture wars, if you will. We funded socialist parties all over Europe, we sponsored fashionably lefty lit mags like *Encounter* to woo the intelligentsia to our more reasonable approach, we promoted American jazz and expressionism as a way of winning the hearts and minds of the world population to our gentler persuasions. If we had to resort to force, it would not be the 24th Division's five thousand Patton tanks taking on the T-54s in a new, more tragic Kursk on the plains before the Fulda Gap, and not another iteration of Fat Man and Little Boy providing instant genocide to half the world. It would be a coup here, a labor union strike there, at most an assassin's bullets. We were influencers, nudgers, political engineers, reluctant snipers. We were not soldiers.

"So what's the problem, Win?" somebody shouted.

"Okay," said Win, "here's the problem. Do I A) snitch this guy out to the Dallas police, or B)"—Win let it build, master comedian—"buy him a new box of ammo?"

The place exploded in laughter, as well you might imagine. No one laughed harder than quiet Hugh, leaning against the sofa, nursing a gin and tonic, tamping his pipe, joining heartily in the merriment.

I was aware that I had the answer to Win's dilemma. I would buy Lee Something Something a new box of ammo.

It was all different in those days. The building was new and smelled of paint and fresh spackle and putty. It had yet to acquire the dinge that old bureaucratic sites acquire, the grease spots where generations of sleepy clerks have rested their heads, the scuff marks on the linoleum, the bathrooms leaky and stinky and stained with God knows what, all the caulking having begun to rot, the light uncertain and sure to go bad when most needed. No, the new campus smelled delicious, seemed in synchronization with the spirit of Camelot, and also symbolized the official putting of the Bay of Pigs, our last scandal, behind us. It was all beige with muted carpeting, and we had definitely entered the miracle age of the fluorescent lighting system, so it was always illuminated in the stark light of scientific truth, which was oddly comforting.

You looked out windows still dustless and smearless and saw green trees everywhere, as the Virginia countryside, cascades of leaf, seemed boundless and lush. In memory, at least, it never rained a lot in Camelot. From some high north-oriented windows, you could see a flash of the broad Potomac, and on a sunny day, as I remember most were, that plate of liquid turned blue itself off the sky overhead. Trees, walks, freshness, ripeness everywhere, cheer and high morale, pep and vim and vigor, hope and audacity, the perfect background for my treachery in the most heinous yet most successful intelligence operation in history, the Earth's or any other planet's.

I had to get that transcript and learn who Lee Something Something was. It was not hard to do. A few days into the next work week,

I sent Win Stoddard some kind of meaningless though TOP SECRET/EYES ONLY file with a cover note requesting his input on the proposed project. I cannot remember what it was, and I knew that even with the melodramatic stampings on it, Win would routinely stuff it in his desk drawer for a few days before he got around to considering it. I waited a day, then, timing it perfectly, managed to intercept Win on his way to the elevator at 5:04 on a Wednesday afternoon. I could tell by the speed of his gait—I'm not a spy for nothing, you know!—that he was in a hurry.

"Win, say, sorry to trouble you, that report I sent, did you have a chance to look at it?"

"Not yet, Hugh, sorry. This, that, the other thing."

"I kind of need to get it circulated. Could I have it back and ship it on to the next boy on the list? If Cord calls a meeting on it, I'll brief you."

"Sure, Hugh. First thing tomorrow."

"Damn, I'd like to get it to one of Wisener's people tonight."

"Okay, look, I'm in a rush." He smiled, reached into his pocket, and pulled out his ring of keys. "Here, the little one, it'll open the drawer right away. Help yourself. You can give me the keys back tomorrow. I've got drinks with a senator at the Army-Navy Club, and I'm already behind."

"Good man," I said, and I exchanged with him the one secret I will not violate in this account, the Skull and Bones handshake.

As I said, easy, too easy. Security then was a twenty-two-cent hardware lock on a file drawer made of tin-can alloy. No computers, no magnetic striped cards, no monitoring video cameras, nothing in the beige hallways suggesting war or aggression or intelligence, just a fairly messy if broad office that could have housed an insurance company or a newspaper or a driver's license agency. It had no spy-movie-cliché clubbiness and never did. This was way before the age of computers, and we had not gotten electric typewriters in; everything was on paper, paper was the fuel that we fed into the flames of the Cold War.

Win, being a senior staffer, had a cubicle with three walls of privacy, which made my task somewhat easier, not that it wasn't easy to begin with. Only a few staffers lounged about, none of them paying much attention to a familiar figure such as mine, and I opened his drawer and found my report and removed it, then pivoted slightly, opened two more drawers, and found what I was looking for in the second one, TOP SECRET/ EYES ONLY meaninglessly stamped askew over the title PHONE TRANSCRIPTS/MEX CITY/SOV EMB and a ref to master file RP/K-4556-113M. I slipped this document behind my own legal document, locked everything up, and went back to my desk. I eased it into my briefcase for study at home, but not before seeing for the first time the name that would become so indelible to the lens of history in such a short time. And thus I met LEE HARVEY OSWALD.

My first encounter with him that night, after Peggy and I had enjoyed an old-fashioned and put the boys to bed and she retreated to her boudoir and I to my study, was not compelling. It was, in fact, repellent. I read through the interview transcripts recorded September 27 and 28, 1963, at the Soviet embassy, rm. 305G, at 1130 the first day and 1315 the next.

KGB: And why do you wish a visa?

LHO: Why, sir, I renounce capitalism and wish to raise my family in a society that values the teachings of Marx and the struggles of the workingman.

KGB: But you spent 2 1/2 years with us, Mr. Oswald, and you seemed at a certain point to have your fill of the teachings of Marx and the struggles of the workingman.

LHO: Sir, that was not my fault. I was undone by jealous people who hated me for my intelligence, for marrying the most beautiful woman, for the heroic will they sensed within me, as the great Lenin and Stalin were envied and hated by petty rivals!

I recognized almost everything I despised in a man. He was arrogant, which, combined with his manifest stupidity, made him particularly appalling. He was pugnacious, bellicose, yet quick to retreat and start sucking up aggressively. To watch the crude ploys of his personality over the play of the interview with Boris and Igor (in Agency argot, all Russian operatives, even if their names were known, as these were, went by the noms de guerre of Boris and Igor) was somewhat dispiriting. He'd throw himself at one until he ran into resistance, and then he'd throw himself at the other. On and on it went. They didn't have to play Mutt and Jeff with him, only Mutt and Mutt.

From what I gathered—not having seen our files on him or the FBI's—he was some kind of epic failure, having bungled every job ever handed to him, having offended every boss who ever hired him, having betrayed every friend who ever reached out to him. He had that classic ineffective personality, all front and bluster backed by nothing of substance, bravado for show, cowardice for content, a braggart and a phony, and I guessed that all he claimed for accomplishments would turn out to be lies, as they did. Throw in some other defects: an inability to concentrate, an exaggerated sense of grievance, an IQ that would be classified "dull normal," no outstanding compensatory talent, and the little man's classic resentment of all things in the universe larger than himself. He would be both a bully and a coward, a liar and a cheat, without charm or charisma, prone to true belief in nonsensical goals; in all, a human wreck waiting to happen. That would be my department.

He explained to them that his goal in life was to get to Castro's Cuba, but the Cubans, sensibly, had declined. They had left him with a proviso that if he could get a visa from his good friends the Russians, they would allow him entrance on that document for a limited amount of time. Here he was, giving himself up to the maw of history in order to achieve the greatness he knew as his own and to claim his place in the socialist firmament.

It was a tough sell, particularly on the second day, by which time

Boris and Igor presumably had been in contact with KGB Moscow, had seen synopsized accounts of LHO's unspectacular two and a half years in Minsk and the no doubt unflattering comments on his personality and work ethic from so-called jealous people, and had reached the proper conclusion.

The reds are familiar with this oddity of the American system. It produces men who can move mountains, build industries, win global wars, and break the speed of sound. It can down MiGs over Korea at a six-to-one ratio. At the same time, perhaps inevitably, it produces a small number of malcontents, of ambitious dreamers who lack the skills or the diplomatic grace to achieve anything in life, and rather than face their own inadequacies, they blame some amorphous structure called "the system" and look for its opposite, where they believe they will shine. Then they spend their dream lives imagining themselves as secret agents, destined to bring down the larger apparatus and be rewarded by its opponents, whose conquest they have so wonderfully lubricated.

These odd birds know history superficially and never notice that the first thing a socialist totalitarian state does when it takes over is round up all the secret agents who have worked so hard in its interests, cart them to the Lubyanka by Black Maria at midnight, and plant a bullet behind their ears. Reds cannot tolerate traitors, even traitors who have aided their own cause. Ask the Poumistas of the Spanish revolution, who made that discovery while standing at the execution wall in Barcelona.

Oswald knew or cared for none of this. He was determined to be a traitor, though he had nothing of value to offer his new friends, failing completely to master the nuance that treason was a negotiation and that it takes two to trade, and had failed miserably at his first attempt. Little mongrel. How I loathed him that night, sitting in my study in Georgetown, listening to the midnight crickets and enjoying a splash of vodka.

Then came the key exchange, late on the second afternoon, after they'd already given him their negative decision and before calling in the goons to eject him from the property forcibly when he'd come back to protest.

I gathered that neither Boris nor Igor was there, and this new fellow—we'll call him Ivan—was a little higher in the KGB tree. He seemed wiser, smoother, less awkward in dealing with the screwball American. Ivan tells him, "Mr. Oswald, it is our conclusion that you would not be happy in the Soviet Union a second time any more than the first. My own recommendation is that you could most appropriately serve the revolution from within your own borders, pursuing these activities you have mentioned, such as passing out leaflets for the Fair Play for Cuba Committee and arguing passionately in private with American citizens on the merits of our system versus yours."

LHO: Sir, do you know who you're talking to? I am not some stupid pamphleteer, not by a long shot. I am a soldier of the revolution, I am a man of action.

KGB: Here, now, Mr. Oswald, please settle down, we do not need an incident.

LHO [crying]: No, you listen to me. On April 10, I was the sniper who took the shot at General Walker, fascist, traitor, bully, would-be tyrant, enemy of the left, of socialism, of Cuba, of the USSR. That was me in the dark, with my Eye-tie [?] Mannlicher-Carcano six-five. BANG, I had him dead center, I just didn't see the window frame that deflected the shot. Me, I, me, I went to war for us and for you. I risked prison, the electric chair, I—

KGB: Mr. Oswald, please, get hold of yourself, there's no need—

A few minutes later, he would pull a gun and begin to gesticulate wildly, then break down, sobbing on Mr. Big's desk! It ended with him deposited in the Mexico City gutter. What did he expect? How deep could his self-knowledge have been? He had no awareness that the nakedness of his needs and the tragedy of his incompetence were the signals he broadcast the loudest; he had no idea of the ocean of space between the ideal image of the self he wished and pretended to be and the tragic, limited, feckless little twerp whom he forced the world to see up close and instantly. He was a mess.

The worse he was, the better for me. It took no genius to see the path by which he could be manipulated into anything, and such a ploy was easily within my capabilities. The plan formed perfectly, with no need of revision and only a little required preparation. It would be so simple—like giving candy to a baby.

To make certain of my own intentions, I applied the New Criticism to my plan, laboring intensely to occlude personality, opinion, immaterial knowledge, or rogue or random feeling from consideration and concentrate entirely on the text that was Oswald, understand its dynamics and dimensions without regard to outcome or hope or past indignities or whatever it was that formed the twisted creature he was. I must say, although this sounds egotistical, I felt somewhat like a great white hunter with many tusks in his lodge on the track of a titmouse. I was so overgunned for this safari, it seemed a little obscene, so I made a pledge to myself that though I would use Oswald, even as I loathed and despised him, I would make a tiny effort to see the humanity that lurked underneath, to understand what forces had so warped him, and try to reach somehow the soul in him, and touch it with a gesture that, in whatever larger context of manipulation and betrayal it arrived, had a whisper of authentic human feeling.

I had tasks to be done. First I had to conjure up a fantasy operation and code name so I could liberate black funds to pay for my instantly conceived Oswald-Walker operation, which involved selling Cord on a fiction. Sure, I had enough money from Uncle Colt and his co-uncles Winchester, Smith, Wesson, and Remington, to say nothing of the DuPonts, the five marques of General Motors, and the whole industrial cash box that sustained my portfolio, to pay the limited expenses this thing would cost on my own, but in case it ever came back to me, any investigator would go to finances on the first day and learn that I had spent a hundred grand of my own dough on a mystery project in November 1963. I could swindle the money from the Agency far more easily than I could swindle it from myself, and it would be protected in perpetuity by our Agency's larger mandate to keep all things secret. (It has not been uncovered to this day, nearly fifty years after the fact!) Generations of case officers enjoyed this privilege, some corrupt and for their own benefit, some pure at heart and laboring in the hope that they were helping win the war. As for my pitch, it would not be difficult; I enjoyed high status in Clandestine Services, as the recent removal of Mr. Diem from both presidency of the Republic of South Vietnam and occupancy of Planet Earth was conspicuously viewed as a victory for our side and had found its origins in a classified report I authored entitled "U.S. Interests in RSV: An Assessment for the Future," which made me a star in factions of the Agency far beyond my own. (More on this later.) Second, I had to secure the Oswald master file, as indicated on the transcript, an assignment any third-rate secret-agent-man pretender ought to be able to bring off.

For the record, I will summarize, with apologies to any of you reading this account who haven't a taste for sober explication and prefer the rush of narrative; I cannot, however, let the narrative rush without satisfying myself that I have fulfilled the expositional requisites, if only for the one reader in a hundred who requires such a thing.

As for the fictional operation, I named it PEACOCK and sold it to Cord without a hitch, establishing a hundred-thousand-dollar budget out of the Bank of New York, shielded by accounting ploys so subtle that only a few men, none of whom worked for the government, were capable of penetrating them. PEACOCK, I claimed, was meant to look at the possibilities of identifying young Harvard-Yale-Princeton-Stanford-Brown-UChicago-and-other-elite graduates who had writing talent and seemed headed for the powerful Luce publications or the *New York Times* or the upstart *Post* properties that had just acquired *Newsweek* (Cord's wife's sister was married to a prominent *Newsweek* fellow, to show you how small and cozy the world was in those days), with an idea to nurse them in their careers with secret deposits of information, not money (they would be offended by money), so as to accelerate their climb and at the same time make them indebted to us, although they'd never know who "us" really was. PEACOCK was named for vanity, as I assumed such fools would be morally vain and easily manipulated. I would write Cord a monthly report on what scouts I had befriended in the thickets of academe and what I had offered them and what we could expect from them. It was wonderful, as it was entirely unsubstantiable. No actual journalist would know he was being manipulated by us and could never squeal, and no one could look at a particular piece and say, Yes, the tip came from us or No, it didn't. That's how the old Agency was: it worked on a trust I was only too happy to betray in search of a larger contribution.

As for acquiring the Oswald paperwork, again, not terribly difficult. I memorized the master file number as referred to on the transcript jacket, then went to Records at a particularly busy time—Monday, 1030, when all the girls were overworked with juniors who had been requested to pull files for this or that Invasion of Italy or Nuclear Detonation over Moscow scenario. The place was chaos and anguish, as I expected, the girls overtaxed and bitter because they were too smart for their jobs and too connected to be treated this way by Mrs. Reniger, head of files, in one of her perpetual menstrual flare-ups. The wheels were definitely off the cart, so I pulled Liz Jeffries aside. She was Peggy's older sister's daughter and my niece by marriage. I said, "Liz, Cord's on a tear, I need this fast."

"Oh, Hugh," the wan beauty replied, distress making her more lovable than usual, "we are so behind."

"Liz, it's my tail on the line."

She knew who had gotten her the job, with its glamour opportunity to marry a spy, a much better catch socially than a diplomat or a legislator, so she said, "Look, you know the system, just duck back there and pinch it; don't let Reniger see you."

"Thanks, sweetie," I said, and gave the child—she was a few years younger than I, but she seemed from a different generation—a peck.

It was a common enough thing, so no eyebrows were raised. I slipped back, sliding by a busty young thing in one of the aisles and being careful to make no "accidental" contact with her breasts so that she wouldn't remember me, found the file, opened it—the files were controlled by a series of master locks that old bitch Reniger, an OSS London vet, opened each morning at 9 and closed each evening at 5—and slipped out the Oswald file and the one I had requested, hid Mr. O's inside the covering one, and dropped my file request slip in the box for recording.

That night I made further contact with LHO. I will not bore readers with intricate accounts of one of the most overbiographized men in the world. The details are depressingly familiar. A chaotic childhood ensued upon the too-early death of the father; the strange, domineering, and slightly crazy mother, Marguerite, hauling the family all over America in hopes of finding a place to stay, marrying twice, wrecking both marriages, hauling Lee and the other two boys from school to school, state to state, poverty to prosperity and back to poverty in a single year sometimes. No wonder he was so screwed up: he was always the new kid.

In New York, his growing malfunction was spotted by an alert social worker who wrote perhaps the most penetrating prose ever—little did she know three thousand authors would eventually come into competition with her, yet never best her—and alone in the world seemed to worry about where this sad bean would end up. She was underwhelmed by the narcissist Marguerite as mom and the incoherent wandering as lifestyle, and thought the boy had it in him to do great harm if not put into some kind of treatment quickly. In the whole mad circus that was the life of Lee Harvey Oswald—and I am speaking as his recruiter, his betrayer, and indirectly his murderer—this brave lady alone did a job we can take pride in as Americans. Too bad for LHO and JFK nobody listened; Marguerite snatched him away from the do-gooders and hauled him back to Texas or was it New Orleans before anything official could be done.

Influenced by his older brother, little Lee, like many a small man who dreams of toughness, joined the Marine Corps immediately out of high school (from which he did not graduate). Like everything he attempted, it came to nothing. The marine years were wholly undistinguished, and anyone who trusted him to guide an airplane to its landing strip—his official job—must have had rocks in his head. I saw that the marines didn't let him do much of that sort of thing, as they always had him on noncrucial duty. Somehow he managed to shoot himself in the arm. What a dimwit!

It was in the service where he first proclaimed himself a Communist, to the irritation of all around him in his various postings. You wonder why some fellow PFCs didn't beat the hell out of him and spare the world the tragedy that ensued. It's one of the few times the United States Marine Corps has failed in its duties. It won the Battle of Iwo Jima, but it lost the Battle of Lee Oswald! And once he was out, his first move—another hastily considered crusade—was to defect to the Soviet Union. Our first notice of him came via the State Department after he'd gotten into Russia on a student visa and refused to leave. Sensibly, the Russians didn't want him either—nobody *ever* wanted him!—and for a while State and KGB fought to see who would inherit him as a consolation prize. He spent two and a half years in the Soviet Union, mostly in an electronics plant in Minsk, mastering the intricacies of cheesy transistor-radio assembly. He met and married a young woman who seemed quite attractive in the photo; I wondered in my study that night if the poor gal knew what a damaged package she'd hooked up with.

He burned out in Russia and managed to talk his way back into the United States. I am well aware that some in the conspiracy community—"conspiracy community," God, what an appalling concept! It was both loud and wrong for half a century!—have maintained that the CIA's fingerprints are all over this strange sojourn. Good God! The only fingerprints on it were mine, and I knew paper didn't record fingerprints, so I was safe. What I saw was what real life produces, as opposed to the dark master planning of the spy conspiracy believers: the shaggy, shapeless, pilotless, planless bumble of luck, circumstance, and opportunity, as this weasel of a man tried to get two giant bureaucracies to pay him the slightest bit of attention. Agh, you could feel their lack of enthusiasm in the slow grind of their cogwheels as, eventually, while the long dreary months passed, this nobody was allowed to reclaim citizenship in a country he loudly despised.

From that point on, we got a new narrator, a much beleaguered FBI agent named James Hotsy, who inherited Lee—I will call him Alek from now on, for that is his Russian nickname, and Marina and I both called him that—when the fellow came back to the United States from Russia. He was known to the Bureau as a "suspicious person," given his well-documented love affair with the reds. Poor Hotsy, of the Dallas field office, overworked and underloved, had Alek added to his immense caseload, and it was my privilege to read his reports in photocopy, because at that low level of security, the two agencies happily shared data. Hotsy's picture of him more or less confirmed mine, although the hostility he received after Alek's return added a particularly unpleasant new pathology, the chronic whine. Hotsy could find nothing he'd done that was illegal, only in poor taste, which should be a crime, I've always believed, but who listens to me on these matters? Hotsy's intensity picked up when he discovered that Alek had been to Mexico City in late September and visited the Cuban interest section and the Soviet embassy, and soon he was interviewing Marina, her friend (but never Alek's) Ruth Paine, and anyone else who had knowledge of or insight into Alek. Again, he could come up with nothing substantial, because Oswald himself was not substantial. He was, as they say in Texas, all hat and no cattle. Nobody had any need for him, not even Marina, for Mrs. Paine passed on to Special Agent Hotsy the bad news that Marina frequently displayed bruises on her arms or swelling around the eye. Alek was up to his tricks again.

I do not have one here before me, as I sit in the sunlight on the veranda, scribbling and merrily riding the vodka express to the amazement of the servants, watching the slow progress of shadow across the far meadow, awaiting a call on my satellite phone that will inform me whether my current threat is finished or has grown more complicated, but I do know that at that time I had a photo of Alek.

That face was soon to be burned into the consciousness of the world. I expect it will never be forgotten. At the time, who could know, who could anticipate? What I saw was American working-class *sui generis*, remarkable in its unremarkablity. It was an old shot taken by a newspaper when our self-proclaimed Communist hero (Ma, call the papers!) returned from Russia to proclaim the glories of Marxism but the folly of communism (only a Trot could appreciate the nuances; it's unlikely Alek did). The camera reveals truths, things that Alek did not know about himself and would not learn. The thickness of his nose, his most prominent facial landmark, revealed or at least represented his pugnacity. He had a thickness to him in many respects, both physically and mentally, a kind of fixation on a goal or object from which he could not be stirred. His eyes were beady and small and squinty, and any Hollywood casting director would see him as a Villain No. 2, a minion who administered the beatings or the knifings but had no grasp of Mr. Big's vision and simply took it on trust. He had a small mouth that gave him an unattractive piscean quality, his face somehow "pointed" as it reached its end point in the surly orifice surrounded by thin lips. His receding hairline and overbroad forehead seemed to suggest the same motif, and all of these features together created a typology, as amplified by the perpetual shroud or grimace of annoyance he wore. He looked exactly as he was: surly, obstreperous, self-indulgent, charmless. You knew he would be tricky to deal with, to command; he would be a resenter, a creep (a wife beater!), a natural traitor, an obdurate whiner, a too-quick-to-measure quitter. I don't know if he was a little monster because he looked like a little monster or he looked like a little monster and so he became one. I doubt if any of his three thousand chroniclers do either.

In any event, I stared at that picture, committing its nuances to memory. Sometimes a man in life can look so unlike his photo, you can hardly believe one is the record of the other. I sensed with Alek this would not be a problem and that when I saw him first in the flesh, I would recognize him right away. I can remember lying in bed, listening to Peggy's even breathing, to the night rush of wind, and knowing that my boys were down the hall as secure as possible with futures fixed before them, and thinking of little Alek, pawn and creep, lynchpin and sucker, upon whom the weight of my plan would pivot, and I hoped he was up to it.

That was when I realized, that very night, he wasn't.

It turned on shooting.

Alek was a "trained marine marksman"—whatever that meant, and I suspect, in those dreary peacetime years, not much—yet he had missed a target, according to news reports, who sat at a desk forty feet away, with a rifle that had a telescopic sight! Good God, even I could have made that shot! I realized that shooting wasn't just shooting. He had done his rifle work in the marines with that old warhorse, the M1 Garand rifle, a heavy, steady, accurate semi-automatic that had served from the halls of Montezuma to the shores of Tripoli with distinction. He could not have had a Garand rifle at his disposal in Texas for his try at the general. He'd called his gun "An Eye-Tie [?] Mannlicher-Carcano six-five," a circumlocution so baffling that our poor typist had no idea that "Eye-tie" was argot for "Italian." If it was Italian, it was probably some piece of surplus junk with a squishy trigger and a vino-swilling peasant's intrinsic precision, which is to say none at all, and that would be his weapon of choice, and ours too, as it was linked to him by paperwork, witnesses, and circumstance, for the job I had in mind. Then there was the larger issue of incompetence. He had failed at everything he'd ever tried, and this meant part of him expected failure, and the expectation became the father of the event. Could I trust him? Could I risk my whole career and good name, to say nothing of a long stay in a Texas penitentiary, on this idiot? It had to be clean, smooth, crisp, efficient, professional, not a bumbling, staggering mass of twitches and mistakes.

I don't think I slept a bit that night, or the next either, and I began to doubt the wisdom of a course that depended on first-class work by an idiot.

That's how Lon came into it, and because of Lon's presence, it made a whole universe of other possibilities real and unleashed my imagination in ways that astonished even me.

CHAPTER 14

S wagger summarized his findings for Nick at a meet in a Dallas coffee shop.

"He's not tracking you?" asked Memphis.

"Maybe he hasn't made the leap. Maybe he doesn't know who I am. Maybe I'm off his radar so far."

"Maybe he doesn't exist."

"Then who's trying to kill me?"

"Bob, you've made a lot of enemies. It could be anyone, right? I'm just playing devil's advocate here."

"The same hired killer got James Aptapton."

"Fair enough. You got him, I got a feather in my cap, we took a bad actor off the street forever. Nice transaction all around."

"Any word on this Krulov? The oligarch who's supposedly in with the Izmaylovskaya mob?"

"Yes and no. It turns out that through his many companies, Comrade Krulov has many official contacts with American corporations, such as Ford Motor Company, McDonald's, 3M, Procter and Gamble, and on and on. To investigate, we'd have to get Justice Department approval and convene a task force with subpoena powers and begin a massive effort. Do you think we have enough to take it to Justice?"

Swagger knew the answer. "Of course not. What about, I can never remember the name, Yecksovich?"

"I-x-ovich."

"That guy. Owns a gun company. Weird name, you'd notice that name."

"The name turns out to be a nickname, means nothing. His father was named Aleksandr, and when he was a kid—the father, I mean—his little brother had trouble pronouncing it, so he called big brother 'K-s,' pronounced 'Ix.' Ix stuck, the guy goes through life as Ix, he grows up, has a kid, and since he was a successful goon, he gave his son the patronymic Russian middle name of Ixovich, that's all. Dimitry Ixovich Spazny. Spazny is hard-core KGB, in line when Yeltsin dumps communism and gets all kinds of breaks and becomes a billionaire. I have his businesses, and he's invested all over the world like the rest, and as with Krulov, I'd need a federal task force to begin to make a dent in his affairs."

"That's not going to happen?"

"Afraid not. It's just me, an SAIC on the outs with D.C., and you, a contract undercover. I can finesse some backup and nurse you through the system with as little exposure as possible. I can't fund you. I can't make a major issue of you. If that happens, our wiggle room goes away, and already I'm getting odd looks from my second, who's not sure what's going on. What's your next move?"

"I have to make contact with Richard Monk again. One way or another, he's a sure conduit to whoever's pulling strings. I can play him and see what happens."

"The Swagger investigation method: shake the tree until hired killers come out. Hope you can kill them first. Then learn what they knew. Never fails. Loud, dangerous, but sure."

"I agree with you and my wife and daughter. I am too old for this shit. But I don't seem to have another choice. Except maybe to go away and let old Hugh alone."

"You could never do that. Even if he tries to kill you again."

Richard was just sitting there. His usual breakfast—Egg McMuffin, hash browns, coffee, and OJ—and suddenly, there Jack Brophy was. He slid in next to Richard with a cup of coffee.

"Hey, Richard," he said. "Long time no see, friend." He shook

Richard's hand, and Richard sort of choked, had to swallow, and said, "Jack, I'm glad you're all right. The way you disappeared."

"Oh, that," Bob said. "Family crisis. Had to take care of some unexpected issues."

"Jack," Richard said, "there was a shooting. On the night you left, near the street where you disappeared. A man was killed. Trying to kill someone else, they say. Somehow I worried you were involved."

"Me?" said Swagger. "No sir, I'm a rabbit. I love the guns, but only when I'm shooting at some faraway fuzzy animal or on a nice, safe firing range."

Swagger laid some stuff on Richard about how he'd done some experimenting back in Idaho, and he was convinced that whoever shot JFK used what he called a "hybrid" of some sort, two calibers mulched together, but Richard couldn't stay with it. He didn't see how two bullets could fit in the same, er, bullet. Or two shells in the same bullet, or two cartridges in the same shell. Something like that.

Then Swagger went off on the Dal-Tex Building.

"Still on Dal-Tex?" Richard said. "The angles are right, but it was a huge public building full of people coming and going; it's almost impossible to believe anybody could be brazen enough to get in and get out. Plus, the cops sealed it off within three minutes. You'd need to have a sniper going in the front door and out the front door, unseen, in the middle of a mob scene. I don't see how it could be done."

"You used the right word. Brazen. I figure these boys were top-of-the-line pros, the kind of guys who don't make mistakes and have nerves of steel."

"Mafia hit men!" Richard said. "That ground's been trod over and over again, and nobody's picked up anything but craziness."

"I didn't say Mafia. Fact is, I don't have no theory about who yet. I'm still working out the how. If I get the how, maybe I'll find the who."

The gist of it turned out to be that Jack wanted Richard to help him find some old guys who remembered how Dal-Tex was in the old days. He had to build a case that getting in and out that day was feasible. He swore Richard to secrecy within the community. He declared himself the sole owner of valuable intellectual property.

Richard said he'd look into the possibilities, but discreetly; because of the value of his intellectual property, Jack told Richard he was afraid of a claim jumper or someone beating him to the punch. He'd be the one to contact Richard in a couple of days. He told Richard, "If you don't know where I'm staying and you're captured and tortured, you can't give me up."

Ha, ha. Not very funny, Richard thought, but being a nice guy, he laughed anyhow.

"Okay," said Nick, "initial contact made. Now we've rerun Richard Monk. I was able to slip that one through, and that guy Jeff Neal, the computer genius, I had him do the actual search. He's the best, and if he can't find anything, there's nothing to be found. Or it's been buried by super-pros. At a deep level, we can say once again we come up with nothing. It's the same as it ever was. Brown graduate, twenty years U.S. Army CID, mostly in Europe. Good record."

"He retired as a major," said Bob. "How can that be good? Any fuckups?"

"Jeff got his records. Fabulous fitness reports all the way through, even reading between the lines. The problem is that after 9/11, all the military intel branches clogged up with carcerists who saw it as a fast way up the ladder. By the very fact that was what they did, they made it a slow way up the ladder. Plus, Monk was in Europe, a specialist there, and nobody wanted to move him to Baghdad. He's on record as making many transfer requests. But he was too good to let go. So they fucked him for his excellence."

Bob snorted. "Sounds like typical service shit."

"He stayed in Germany while the connected career boys got to the sandbox and soaked up all the promotions. He was never going to make lieutenant colonel, so he took the out-at-twenty and went to Washington and eventually connected up with that lefty foundation that pays him well and sent him to run their show in Dallas. We can find nothing untoward about him except the Japanese porn collection and the Bangkok vacations."

"Man," said Swagger, "the way this is going, I may head out to Bangkok too."

*This is the hard part. I knew I'd have to get to it some-*time. I suppose it might as well be now. Pardon, a shot of vod. Sometimes I call it Vod the Impaler. Yes, impale me, Vod, impale me!

Ah, that's better. Poor Lon. He is the tragic figure in what happens. It was a shame to watch it happen, it was worse to have made it happen. He was given so much and it was taken so cruelly; he soldiered on heroically, without ill will, doing the best he could. Then I used him and turned him into an official monster. The years passed and he never betrayed me, he never quit on me, he never resented me, he never violated his pledge. He just had to be alone for a while. He was an honorable man, so I used him again, and this time I got him killed. At least he died as he never believed he would or could, with a rifle in his hands, in the intense rapture of a manhunt.

In any event, and for the record: Lon Scott was my cousin on my mother's side, his mother being my mother's sister, the family Dunn, old money, maybe older than mine. She married a man who was far richer than she; Jack Scott, Texas oilman, Connecticut gentleman farmer, big-game hunter, champion rifleman, aviator extraordinary, war hero (fifty missions in a B-24, including the nightmare that was Ploiești), and the father who paralyzed his own son.

Lon was born to be a hero, and he genuinely achieved that status young. At fourteen, he shot and killed a wounded lion as it charged him, his father, and a professional hunter in what was then called British East Africa. His reflexes were the fastest, and when the beast came out of the high grass at fifteen yards, Lon stepped in front of the older men, took the charge, and put two .470 Nitro Express solids into it as it leaped, and when it hit him and knocked him down, the animal was already dead. As for Lon's character, that was a story he never told or wrote (he was a fine writer; see his classic *Hunting Africa in the Fifties*, which I believe has been reprinted recently); it survives only because others told it of him so frequently. It made the later tragedy even more tragic.

Lon was born to wealth and rifles. The former he used modestly, never bragging, never splurging, always generous to family and causes. The latter became his life. I suppose he got it from his father, but there is a genius gene for the firearm that does not respect class or race or economic circumstances, it simply descends and enlightens once every generation or so. I suppose the great gunfighters of the West had it, possibly a few thirties desperadoes (Clyde Barrow, for one, possibly Pretty Boy Floyd), and a few great lawmen. The great snipers have it, a few of the great hunters. Lon had it.

From the time he laid eyes on a rifle, that was his life. In those days—this would be the early thirties—there was no opprobrium attached to such a fixation, and in his circle, it was celebrated and encouraged. His father gave him his first .22 before he was five years old, and by the time he was ten, his skill with the firearm had made him a legend. He spent summers on the Texas ranch, where he became a damned good cowboy, I'm told; by the time he was eighteen and left for Yale, he'd filled a bunkhouse with horned treasures as well as the lion and three rhinos, two Cape buffalo, and a dozen or so antelope species from his adventure in East Africa. That being a randy part of the world, I'm sure his nobility, grace, and courage earned substantial reward between silk sheets during the many evenings in Happy Valley where all the exiled Brit nabobs and their grumpy but beautiful women gathered to smoke, drink, and fornicate in abundance.

His real passion was for thousand-yard shooting. He won his first Wimbledon cup in '50, had an off year, then won again in '52 and '53. It is an extraordinarily demanding discipline that brings all the shooter's skills into play, not only his stamina to hold his position for great lengths of time but his ability to dope the wind and reload ammunition skillfully to get the maximum accuracy for the range, the rifle, and the conditions. He was, at the time, an honors graduate of Yale and unspeakably handsome. It was thought in some circles that he would follow the path of another great shooter, the national prewar skeet champion Robert Stack, and eventually move into movies. His grace with a gun in hand—then a necessity in the American movie industry—spoke well of his chances, and his high IQ, which made flash memorization a trifle (as in scripts), and his intense empathy, which marked him as a charismatic young man, all suggested such an outcome. He was better-looking than Rock Hudson, not a homo, smart as a tack, and could hit a running target offhand at a hundred yards ninety-nine times out of a hundred. He was already famous by '55 and was just waiting for the next big thing to happen to him.

On October 11, 1955, when Lon was thirty, his father shot him in the spine.

He fell to the ground and never walked again.

Characteristically, Lon never made much of it. It happened, that's all, let's get on with it. Of course, the thousand-yard shooting was out, most of the hunting was out, so he devoted himself to the newer sport of benchrest and its application in the fields, varmint hunting, and he spent most of the summer at his place in Wyoming, killing vermin at distances up to a thousand yards off a bench and experimenting with the best ways to get this done. He learned a lot, and it could be said that at one time, he knew more about long-distance shooting than any man on earth. He remained on good terms with his father. The official story: it was an accident. A Model 70 in .30-06, a prime hunting weapon, was dropped and it went off, though the safety was on. Nothing could be done except get Lon to the emergency room fast, which was what his father and other shooters on the line did; Lon's life was saved, but his mobility from the waist down was not. He spent the rest of his life in a wheelchair.

No one ever said a thing. What could be said? The act had no meaning except for the tragic randomness of the universe, its cruel whimsy. What's the line: Whom the gods destroy, they first make interesting? Possibly I made that one up. Or possibly it's Vod speaking. But in outline, anti-Oedipal dynamics are visible. The father, so long thought a great man, sees his usurpation in his young son. He loves the boy, but a serpent of ego whispers into his subconscious: He will replace you. He will steal your memory. You have given him everything, he will take everything. You are soon to become a supernumerary. Thus the gun falls from the hands, thus the safety is perhaps not forcibly off but wedged gently into that no-man's-land between on and off, thus by freak mischance or the weird imposition of evil will on a falling object, the muzzle is lined up for one tenth of a second on Lon's lower spine, and the rifle discharges.

He was lucky, I suppose. It was S4. No quad, no respiratory problems, no iron lung, no electric wheelchair or writing with a paintbrush by mouth. Muscular and athletic, he adapted well. He could drive, he could prepare food, his mind was intact, he could dress, drink, laugh, read, watch, work at his bench. S4, so much more mercy than C2. Still . . .

What is his subconscious making of all this? Perhaps he has felt the hate under the love, perhaps he has heard a whispered resentment in all the lavish praise, perhaps he knows his father a little better than the father knows himself. He suppresses. He conceals his feelings. As I've said, he gets on with it. Who knows what snakes have been released into his mind, what need to strike and kill fathers universally or fathers symbolically or sons who, like him, were created by their fathers and then surpassed them. No one knows any of that, least of all I, but it may explain why, at some level, Lon was okay with the monstrosities I pitched him and kept the faith to the very end. In fact: he died of the faith.

In late October 1963, none of this could be imagined. I told myself I had a question for Lon that needed answering, perhaps denying to myself the inevitability of the course I had set up. I did know that I couldn't be affiliated by record in phone contact from house or office, and I was aware that nobody knew whom that devious busybody James Jesus Angleton was or was not wiretapping. My solution to this was to drive downtown on a Saturday afternoon wearing suit and tie, park around Fifteenth at N, walk up N, and stride boldly into the office building at 1515 upon whose facade the words "The Washington Post" were emblazoned in some sort of ancient Gothic typeface. In those days, newspapers were wide open to the public, especially if the public looked as Official Person as I did, in dark tie, dark suit, white shirt, horn rims, and natty little Princeton haircut, as it was called. I strode in, nodded at the ever-sleepy Negro guard, and took the elevator to the fifth floor, where the newsroom was sited.

It was hardly a tenth full, as a skeleton crew watched teletype machines or took dictation from far-flung correspondents on the rare breaking-news stories. I sat down at Marty Daniels's desk, aware that I looked a little like Marty, who covered the Defense Department for the *Post,* and rifled through the pink stack of messages that had accumulated. I hoped Marty called Mo back, and I hoped he avoided the angry fellow at the West German embassy, and I hoped that Susan didn't call to cancel lunch or anything more interesting, and then, lazily, I picked up the phone. As a senior correspondent, Marty enjoyed direct access to long-distance, and I quickly dialed Lon's number.

I got Monica, she put me through to Lon in the shop, and I said hello.

"Hugh, how's my favorite secret agent? Have you caught Dr. No yet?"

"The slimy bastard changed lairs on us again. He found a new volcano. And how's my favorite cripple?"

"You know, Hugh," said Lon amiably, "I thought I felt a sexual impulse below my waist the other day, but it turned out to be a house falling on my knee."

We both laughed. I had followed his steps to Choate and Yale. He was five years older, and I'd gone down to New Haven my senior year to watch him on the football field, where I took great pleasure in the way he left the Harvard Bambis smashed and bloody in his wake. That was his strength deployed in righteous fury!

"Seriously, how are you doing, Lon?"

"I'm fine except for the ulcers on the leg. They don't hurt, but they're a little annoying. I've got a piece due for the *Rifleman* at the end of the week, and I'm going to a conference on combat-oriented pistol matches next month that looks to be interesting. You?"

"Just spying away like a busy little beaver," I said. "Spy, spy, spy, all day long!"

Soon enough, our jocularity out of the way, I progressed to issues. "Lon, something has come up on the job, and I thought I'd run it by you."

"Good Lord, Hugh, I'd think if anybody'd have experts on this sort of thing, it would be you fellows."

"I'm sure we do, but it's the weekend, nobody spies on weekends. Plus, it will take three days to go through and three days to come back via channels. You probably know more than they do, anyway."

"I'll do my best."

"I've come across a reference to"—I pretended to withdraw it from memory—"something called an 'Eye-tie Mannlicher-Carcano six-five.' Now, I am a professional intelligence officer, so I have been able to determine that 'Eye-tie' probably means 'Italian.'"

"Excellent, Hugh. I feel we are well protected."

"Indeed. But the rest, other than the fact that it's from the firearms world, is gibberish."

"Well," he said, "I don't know too much about it. It could refer to the rifle or the cartridge, depending on context. Or both. Anyhow, the rifle was the Italian service rifle beginning in 1891 and running through the late fifties. It was probably the worst service rifle of its generation, less effective in every respect than the German Mauser, the British Lee-Enfield, our own Springfield, even the French Lebel. But they kept making 'em in various iterations, including a short cavalry or ski troop version."

"I see," I said. "How would an American get one?"

"Very classified. Buy a stamp. That's the secret. When the Italians joined NATO, they converted to our arms—you know, the Garand, the

.30-caliber machine gun, the carbine, the .45 automatic—so they sold off a billion or so of the Mannlicher-Carcano rifles in various formats as surplus, and a great many of them came into this country, where they are being sold as downmarket hunting rifles by mail-order gun houses. I see ads for them all over the place. These guys put a cheesy Jap scope on them and sell them as deer rifles for the workingman who can't afford a Winchester Model 70."

"So it's no sniper rifle?"

"It's basically a piece of junk. Barely accurate, shoddily made, ugly as sin, with a cranky bolt throw. It shows that the Italians never took war seriously, particularly when you compare it to a brilliant piece of engineering like a Mauser. Now, the cartridge it shoots is more interesting and probably deserved a better rifle than the Mannlicher. It's a medium-bore, flat shooting round, meant for battle at more or less longer ranges. The bullet is heavy for its size, with a thick copper coating to hold it together on those rare occasions when Italian marksmanship prevails. It's a viable round for just about any thin-skinned game animal up to and including a whitetail. I'd use it on a man before I'd use it on a bear."

"If you hit a man in the head with it?"

"Good-bye head, assuming a relatively short range, out to two hundred meters."

"Hmm," I said, by which utterance I meant information received but not processed.

"What have you got in mind, Hugh? Is this about some kind of Cuban invasion operation because you have a line on ten thousand Mannlicher-Carcanos real cheap? If so, I'd strongly suggest that you avoid the temptation. There's a lot better rifles available in surplus than pieces of junk manufactured by people who eat spaghetti for lunch and take a nap every afternoon."

"Thanks, Lon. Let me ask you this—what can you do with it?"

"*Do* with it? Kill out to two hundred or so meters, small-game animals, human beings, possibly rabbits if you could hit them, which is doubtful. Shoot targets unsatisfyingly. Grow annoyed at the roughness of its action and the sloppiness of its trigger. Cut it up for firewood. That's about all. But I'm a snob, don't listen to me."

"No, no, that's not what I meant. I suppose I meant could you—uh—counterfeit it?"

"You mean build a fake one? Good God, Hugh, that's ridiculous."

"I'm not explaining myself well, because I don't have the vocabulary. I'm thinking about forensics, about the clues guns leave that identify them. It's not something I know anything about except from *Perry Mason.* Here's what I think I mean. If you knew you had an agent who was going to shoot somebody with a Mannlicher-Carcano, but you didn't trust that person to make the shot, could you do something so that somebody else who was a much better shot could shoot the person with, I don't know, the same bullet or the same kind of rifle at the same time, but it had been fixed so that no investigator would ever figure out that the second gunman with the second rifle and the second bullet was there? Counterfeit in that sense, I mean."

"Is this for your next James Bond novel, Hugh?"

"I wish I were that clever, Lon."

"Well . . . let me think, okay? I'm guessing another requirement would be a silencer. It's really called a suppressor. You know, so the real assassin's shot doesn't draw attention."

"They have such things?" I asked. I was so naive then.

"Yes, it's not just a movie gimmick. Hiram Maxim figured it out over sixty years ago. Any clever machinist can handle it. It's just a tube with baffles and chambers and holes in it. I'll look into it and call you back and—"

"No, no, let me call you back. When, a week, next Saturday, will you be available?"

"Hugh, I live in a wheelchair. I'm *always* available," he said cheerily.

I sold Cord on a scouting trip to Boston for PEACOCK, had Travel book me, moved five thousand dollars from the PEACOCK account to Larry Hudget's FOXCROFT account, knowing he hadn't bothered to master the finances and would never find it, drew a check, and cashed it in a small bank in the Negro section of D.C. where I'd done some business and could trust Mr. Brown to be discreet. The next day I flew to Boston, checked in to the Hilton in Cambridge, then took a cab to the airport and paid cash for a ticket to Dallas, TWA. In my grip was a suit that I had bought in Moscow in 1952, which fit as well as a shirt I'd picked up in Brno a few years ago, and a black tie I'd bought from Brooks Brothers when I had to attend Milt Gold's father's funeral. I figured even a genius like Alek wouldn't notice the difference in tailoring quality between the Brooks tie and the GUM suit, which looked and fit as if assembled by chimpanzees.

I checked in to the Adolphus, rented a car, and put on my Russian monkey suit. It felt odd to walk across the hotel's pretentious old-oak lobby with its Harvard eating-club flourishes, dressed like a kulak afraid he was about to be arrested. Nobody noticed. It was Texas, after all. Nobody notices anything down there.

An hour or so later, I parked my rental car across the street and watched when the downtown bus dropped off its passengers at 5:38 p.m. on the corner of Zane and North Beckley, in the suburb (across the Trinity River aqueduct) called Oak Cliff. It was probably November 5, 1963, maybe the sixth. I had no trouble spotting him. He wasn't cut out for any kind of undercover work, because if any cop or agent were searching for a spy, they'd pick Lee Harvey Oswald out of any crowd. He was more substantial than I expected. I thought he'd be a feral little rat, quick and shifty, ready to pounce on any morsel of cheese. But he was thick, solidly muscled, stumpy rather than fast, solid rather than limber or light on his feet. You couldn't miss him.

He looked miserable. His charmless, uninteresting face was set on grim to the highest number; he looked around sullenly as if waiting for the FBI to arrest him already; and he radiated a leave-me-alone frequency at its highest pitch. About four people got off, and the three others knew each other and were joshing and talking, the way guys do the world over, and Alek just blew through and by them, head down, walking steadily down North Beckley. It wasn't far, because his room-inghouse, at 1026 North Beckley, was just a few houses down from the Zane–N. Beckley intersection. Nevertheless, he passed within five feet of me on the sidewalk, completely oblivious, and I got a good look, not that there was much to see. Head slumped forward, shoulders slouchy, he plodded along in cheap workingman's clothes that probably wouldn't be changed that week. He wore a pair of gray chinos, black Oxford shoes of inferior manufacture, and a green jacket—not a sport coat, a kind of golflike jacket—over a brown shirt, all nondescript. I watched as he turned in to the roominghouse, a run-down dwelling as nondescript as he was.

I moved the car to the next block and, through my rearview mirror, watched and waited. In forty-five minutes he reemerged, his hair wet from a quick standing bath, but otherwise dressed the same. This time he walked more jauntily to the bus stop, climbed aboard, paid his nickel, and sat halfway back. I followed a few car lengths behind, saw where he was dropped, waited until he went into a building, and then parked and moseyed in. It was the Dougan Heights branch of the Dallas Public Library, and I quickly checked the meeting bulletin board and saw that in room 4, the Soviet-American Friendship Society had convened. The prospect of spending a couple of hours with a crowd of American Commies whining about capitalism plus a few bored FBI agents nauseated me, so I drove to a good restaurant, had a steak, and got to bed early.

The next morning either I was early or he was late. But I saw him coming down the street to the bus stop finally, after missing the 8:17 and the 8:33. I was again wearing my GUM suit, and I'd done a little purposely bad buzzing with my electric Remington, giving myself that raw, poorly barbered look seen all through the East bloc, where tonsorial grace had not yet penetrated. Did I think Alek would notice these things? Probably not consciously, but one never knows what the unconscious picks up and how that contributes to frame of mind, receptivity, trust, and malleability. If I had been able to come up with Russian underwear on such short notice, I'd have worn it too.

He paid no attention to me as we passed on the sidewalk, made no eye contact, but as our shoulders almost brushed, I said in Russian, "Good morning, Alek. Kostikov sends his greetings," and continued on.

"Hey," he said in fractured Russian, after having chewed the information over for a few seconds, and processing the information that I knew his Russian nickname, and that I had evoked the name of the KGB who had interviewed him in Mexico City, "Hey! Who am you?"

I turned and watched him eat me up with his ratty eyes, trying to decipher the strange figure before him.

"You should say 'Who *are* you?'" I corrected. "You're still unclear on your transitive verbs, eh, Alek?" Then I smiled and hurried on my way.

I thought he might run after me and knock me down, but he didn't. He came a few steps in my direction, and then I guess the bus rolled in and he was caught in the dilemma and at last decided on the bus. I heard him run to it; when it passed, I felt his eyes on me as I walked along, seemingly uncaring.

I gave him a restless day, a sleepless night, and another restless day—I used the time to recon the area of General Walker's house, to check his public schedule, to visit a gun store in Oak Cliff with the absurdly Texas name Ketchum and Killum on Kleist, and to buy three white boxes of Mannlicher-Carcano 6.5 ammunition and actually hold the thing that some cowboy tried to sell me, telling me it was the best damn rifle on the market for the money. It seemed like a piece of junk to me, though I had been prejudiced by Lon. It was nothing like the fine, sleek rifles that I had seen Lon shoot when we were boys. I thanked him but politely declined.

That evening I watched Alek get off the bus, check around nervously for whatever his imagination had prompted him to suspect, then start walking. I pulled up next to him before he could turn in to the rooming-house. "Comrade Alek," I called in Russian, "come, I'll buy you a vodka for old times' sake."

He looked around nervously, then dashed to the car. "You am might be seen," he said.

(At this point I cease to replicate his horrid Russian. I will recount in standard English as if he spoke in standard Russian, simply because I grow tired of mangling the language to no real effect. You get the picture.)

"No, nobody will see us. Agent Hotsy is watching his son play Little League in Fort Worth tonight. We have the world to ourselves. Direct me to a tavern, please. I don't know Dallas."

He muttered something, and more by body language than words did he guide me to a god-awful Dew Drop Inn or some such, and we invaded the dark, crummy insides. It wasn't crowded and was garishly lit in one corner by a jukebox, which an idiot had primed to play hillbilly music. We found a booth more or less isolated in the rear.

"I don't really like vodka," Alek said in English.

"Good," I answered in Russian. "It was a manner of speaking. I wouldn't order anything out of the way in a place like this, as one of these men might remember us talking in a foreign language, drinking Stolichnaya. I would also speak in English, but I speak it with a New England accent, and that would probably be more remarkable to them than Russian."

A sluggard came over, and we ordered Mexican beer. When he brought the frosty cans, the waiter also brought chips and some kind of tasty red sauce. It was my first experience with Mexican food, and I was surprised by how much I enjoyed it.

"Who are you?" Alek said, leaning forward and fixing his beady, suspicious eyes on me.

"You'll never learn my name. Security."

"But you're from—"

"I'm from your friends."

"You know—"

"I know Hotsy, the police agent who bedevils you. In the Mexico City embassy, I know Kostikov, I know Yatskov. I have talked to the first Russian woman you loved, Ella German. I have spoken to your wife's former lover Anatoly Shpanko. I have talked to your wife's uncle, Ilya Prusakov, the MVD colonel. I have discussed you with your comrades in the Minsk electrical appliance facility. I will say that all of them have one thing in common: they have a very low opinion of you, Comrade."

I took a slow draft of the beer, enjoying it immensely, watching a whole dictionary of emotions flash across Alek's dim little face: anger at being reminded of his mediocrity, his many failures; defensiveness, as he tried to quickly construct his battlements against the truth; fear that someone was here for him; pleasure that he had been noticed at last by what he perceived as the Apparatus; bliss that someone, somewhere, somehow thought he was special.

Finally, he said, "I made mistakes, but only of trying too hard. I believe too hard. It makes some people hate me."

"It seems they *all* hate you."

"They resent me. People always resent me."

"Do you know the term 'projection,' from psychology?"

"No. But I've studied Marx, I've studied—"

"You've studied everything but yourself, which is why nobody cares for you, Alek."

He looked gloomily into the distance. An actual tear may have formed in one of his eyes. He started to speak, but I cut him off.

"In the whole world, nobody believes in you. To all you are negligible, a failure, a man without a past or future. You beat your pregnant wife and terrify your dear little baby daughter, Junie, you are the shame and scandal of the Russian-speaking community in Dallas. You go to the Cuban embassy and they throw you out, and you go to the Soviet embassy, pull a gun, break down sobbing, and they throw you out. No one in the world believes in you, Alek. Oh, wait. I just remembered. There is a man, probably a fool, who thinks you might amount to something, who thinks you can be saved."

"Who?" Alek asked.

"Me," I said.

I had a few more of the chips with the tangy red sauce. Delicious! I loved the crunchiness of the chips, with a vigorous salty aftertaste, subsumed in the fiery yet not unsubtle blast of the sauce, clearly by color tomato-based, yet not sweet, like so many tomato derivatives, the whole thing suddenly going nuclear to the taste when the pepper component detonated, then ameliorated by the tidal thunder of the cold, cold beer. A fellow could get used to such a thing.

I looked back at Alek. "Say, these chips are swell. I don't believe I've ever had Mexican before. Why don't we order some dinner? Go ahead, you're the expert. Call him over and order for us. I think I'd like another beer, please." I held up my empty can. It was called Tecate and had a lime slice wedged into the opener puncture. Why had I never tasted this before? It seemed not to have made it to Georgetown yet. I made up my mind to search out a Mexican restaurant in D.C. and take Peggy and the boys. That would be an adventure.

Alek waved the waiter over and ordered something from memory; as we waited for the food, I made small talk.

"So, tell me, when did you begin to notice that socialism in reality was considerably different than socialism in theory, and that working on an assembly line anywhere in the world is pretty much the same?"

He wouldn't engage for a few seconds but then lurched on sullenly. "It wasn't the work. It wasn't the guys, they were okay guys. Some of them liked me. I just start thinking about reality and lose my concentration."

"You messed up. That's all it was."

"No. I had big thoughts. I just couldn't get them out. But somehow—"

"Your type will always locate a 'somehow.' Somehow this, somehow that, it's never your fault, somehow it's always someone else's fault. Maybe you should for once in your life forget about somehow and concentrate on one thing, do it well, thoroughly, completely, and not give a shit about what happens somehow to you. Then, if you know you did your best, possibly soon enough they will know, and there will be no somehow."

He brought out the Dale Carnegie in me.

"I tried to, I tried to," he protested.

Thankfully, the food came—thinking about it now, I realize it was enchiladas, rice and beans, and a taco on the side—and we were spared more chatter as we put it down with another beer. Again, it was a good meal, and I was happy, for the rest of my life, to enjoy Mexican whenever the chance arose. That much I owe Lee Harvey Oswald.

We finished without much chatter, and I paid, and out we went to the car. It was dark now, and twenty minutes had passed since we had spoken. His face was knit tight, I guessed partly in fear of saying something stupid, partly in confusion. He could not meet my eyes.

When the car doors were closed and I'd pulled out into traffic, I finally said, "Alek, you know how it works, don't you?"

"Sir?" he said in English.

"That is, the organization I represent."

"I suppose so. You find people who—"

"No, no, not the idealized, the propagandized, version. I mean the reality. That reality is that it's a big organization and it has many sub-units, many departments, many cells, all of them driven by ego, fear, ignorance, full of average men attempting to curry favor with supervisors, attempting to *be* supervisors, out of nothing more than petty ambition. Some work at cross-purposes to others, some work at purposes that have no relationship whatsoever to the purposes others work to accomplish, and the communication between them is at all times inefficient, even weak."

"Yes sir," he said.

"Kostikov and Yatskov, for example, they're in a division that is charged with servicing and monitoring our embassies abroad. They watch for spies, they try to recruit spies, they also have responsibilities for vetting defectors, dealing with walk-ins, this and that. Their hope is to get through thirty-five years without making a bad mistake or offending a superior; if they accomplish that, they get a medal, a nice but hardly remunerative stipend, and possibly a small dacha outside Moscow in one of the less fashionable districts. If so, they can consider themselves heroes and successes, you see?"

"I do."

"To them, you are simply a problem they do not care to deal with. Imagination is not their strong suit. Career-wise for them—and there is no other concern—it's best you go away fast and forever and not upset or reroute the Kostikov Express to a dacha."

"Yes sir."

"But I'm in a different department. When news reaches me of the crazy American who says he took a shot at General Walker, I'm not annoyed, I'm fascinated. I have to learn more. My department has use for people like the crazy American; we're charged with actually accomplishing something, not merely maintaining a security perimeter."

Alek nodded.

"We occasionally do what's called 'wet work.' Can you guess the meaning of 'wet'?"

"Underwater," the idiot said.

I sighed. "Try again, Alek."

"Oh. Blood. You kill people."

"Rarely. Sometimes. It's always a tricky decision. It's not like there's a double-oh license or anything and we can go about blasting people with burp guns. But yes, sometimes, when necessary, say a defector, a murderer of one of our people, a particularly loathsome political opponent, then we may kill people."

We reached his neighborhood. I pulled up a few doors down from his roominghouse, because I had no way of knowing if people there knew him and might remember him getting out of a car driven by a stranger.

"Alek," I said, "I have a present for you. It's in the glove compartment. Please reach in and get it."

He opened the glove box and took out a white box of Western Cartridge Co. 6.5 mm Mannlicher-Carcano ammunition. He held it in his hand, jostled it, felt its considerable weight. His eyes lit up.

"Bullets," he said. "For my gun."

"You know Kostikov and Yatskov thought you were making up your story. So did everyone in the apparatus. Except me. I thought: Perhaps this man, who lies about so much and has not finished one thing in his life, nor impressed one person, perhaps he is telling the truth about the shooting. That's why I had to know you, Alek, I had to look into you. That's why the travel, the investigation, all the interviews. But not till now, this second, have I confirmed for myself that yes, you are the rare man who believes in the cause so much that he will do the wet work for it. It's easy to hand out flyers and go to meetings with homos and Negroes and federal agents. It's easy to defect if you get to marry the sexiest Russian babe and begin fucking her right away. It's easy to tell people that you're a red, that you believe in the workingman, and that changes must be made, because you like the attention it gets and the ruckus it causes. The campuses and beatnik cafés are full of such worthless scum. But rare, truly rare, is the man for whom the revolution is worth dying for and worth killing for. He would be the man of action, an ideal. I believe you are such. Now get out, go home, go to bed, and prepare for another day of glory boxing books on the sixth floor. I will contact you again after these matters settle in that tiny little rathole you call a mind."

"But I—"

"GO!" I commanded, and out he scooted.

CHAPTER 15

A week passed before Swagger dropped in on Richard again, this time intercepting him at a pharmacy where he was picking up prescriptions.

"Damn!" said Richard, jumping visibly when his old pal Jack Brophy showed up from nowhere. "You are tricky," he declared.

"I'm paranoid as hell," Swagger said. "I've done some work and have made some progress. Don't want any of those other boys knocking me off."

"You might be better off to relax and let me introduce you to some people who might be able to help you."

"Too shaky for that, Richard. You mean well, but I've got spiders in my mind telling me every-goddamned-body is spying on me."

"I got it, I got it. Well, how about this—I think I could help you, no one else involved."

"How's that?"

Richard laid out his plan. He knew someone in the Dallas Association of Nursing Homes, which put out a weekly bulletin. His idea was to run an ad requesting that anyone who had worked in the Dal-Tex Building in '63 and wanted to share memories with a researcher contact Richard. Then Richard, with Jack along, would interview. That way they could at least get a sense of how likely it was that a brazen penetration like the one Jack envisioned had happened.

Swagger thanked him, thought it over, watched him surreptitiously for a number of days, then okayed the idea.

The next week they visited three homes and talked to three old gadflies, two of whom said it was possible, one who said it wasn't.

"The building was particularly deserted that day," Mrs. Kolodny recalled. "We all rushed down at noon to get good spots to see the president. And afterward, who wanted to go back to work? I didn't go back to work until Monday. It was so sad."

Mr. O'Farrell disagreed, primarily because, it turned out, he was an amateur assassinologist.

"If you look, you'll see that the Houston Street side of the building had a fire escape. And there was a bunch of people sitting there watching the president. Now, if someone fired a rifle shot, they'd be the closest, they'd be the ones who'd hear it and testify that a shot came from just forty or fifty feet above them. Yet there's no testimony to that effect, goddammit. So how could it be?"

Swagger said, "Possibly they used a silencer."

"Silencer, shmilencer," said the old guy. "Hollywood crap! That's what you get from TV and the goddamn movies! No silencer really silences. You can't make a sound that loud and sharp go away. It might be lowered somewhat, but if he was shooting out the window, they'd feel the shock wave and they'd hear something damn suspicious. The only thing any of those folks heard was what everyone else heard, which was three loud cracks from the rifle of no one other than Mr. Lee Harvey Oswald."

Swagger knew this not to be the case absolutely, as the sound itself could be modulated by a variety of techniques, primarily the efficacy of the suppressor and its location in an otherwise sealed room. A savvy shooter would place himself well back from the narrowly opened window, containing much of the sound and much of the shock wave. Unless the people beneath were listening for it and had experience with the vibratory patterns of suppressed weapons, it was unlikely that any lower-floor fire-escape sitters noticed a thing, what with so much else going on simultaneously.

Swagger ambushed Richard at the Palm over his weekly steak and martini.

"Mind if I join you?" Swagger said, appearing from nowhere just as Richard had finished his meat and put in an order for coffee and Key lime pie.

"Man," said Richard, "you were in the spy business. I know you were. You move too silently, you follow too well."

"Ain't true a bit," said Swagger. "I picked up my skills by being worried about Communist guerrillas in the mountains of Ecuador. Had a run-in with the same mob, different race, in Malaysia. Those were men who wanted us exploiters of the wonderful peasants dead. I developed a sixth sense for danger, and I learned how to disappear in plain sight. I was once three feet away from two guerrillas with AK-47s and went so still, they looked right past me, and here I am to tell the tale."

"You could have fooled me."

"Anyway, I wanted to tell you about something I discovered on the Net that's interesting to me. A lot of it is shit, but this gal seems to know a thing or two."

Swagger went on for a few minutes about the discovery. Some researcher had noted that when the FBI expert Robert Frazier had talked about the relative zero of the Hollywood scope on the Oswald rifle, it was clear that Frazier, a distinguished high-power marksman, was unfamiliar with scopes and unaware that if a scope is miszeroed, it will shoot groups in the same spot on the target relative to its miscalculated aiming point, altered only by the geometric progression of the range. If it's an inch low and an inch to the right at fifty yards, it will be two inches low and two inches to the right at a hundred yards, and three inches low and three inches to the right at 150 yards, out until the distance where gravity and falling velocity have a larger influence than the scope misadjustment.

"The point is," said Bob, "how can this guy say the rifle is accurate if he doesn't know the most fundamental thing about the physics of the scope? How can he say a scoped rifle is easy to shoot? He doesn't know enough to make either of those judgments, but those are key factors in the commission's conclusion that Oswald was capable of making the third, longest shot at the smallest and most quickly moving target."

"It's not really my thing," said Richard. "I guess I get it, but it would be helpful if you could show me some of this stuff."

"I will, I will," said Swagger. "When I've got it all put together, I want to fly you out to Boise and take you to my range. You'll see it. In the meantime, please be thinking of ways I could package this or someone I could write it up with."

"Oh, all this on the rifles," Richard said, as if a new thought had kicked its way into his head. "It reminds me. I've been meaning to mention this to you. Ever hear of a guy named Adams? In the gun world, I mean."

"Nah," said Swagger. "Can't say— Oh, wait, there's a guy named Marion Adams, a writer. Does these big fancy picture books on, say, Ruger or Winchester, like corporate histories or historical collections. That the guy?"

Richard handed him a card. "Marion F. Adams," it said. "Firearms Historian and Appraisal Expert." It had a cell number, an e-mail address, and a little picture of a seven-and-a-half-inch Colt Peacemaker.

Richard said, "He came by a couple of weeks ago. He told me some story about his theory of the case—I hear a lot of those, you know. But his was very gun-centric. It was sort of like yours, I thought, having to do with some Winchester gun firing bullets meant for the Carcano at a much faster speed."

"Shit," Swagger said. "Goddammit, that's my theory. It's my intellectual property. You're telling me another guy who—"

"No, no, wait a sec. Here's the deal. He said he was way behind the curve on what did or did not happen in the event, and he could never catch up. The websites gave him a headache. He's not a Net guy. He wanted to shortcut the process. Did I know an investigator who was conversant with the facts of the assassination, the state of the art of assassination research and theory, and firearms. Does that sound like somebody we know?"

Swagger didn't say a thing. His face darkened as if his mood were tanking fast. His eyes narrowed. Finally, he barked, "It took me years to get where I am. I sure don't want to give it away to some fellow with fancy friends who writes the words nobody reads in picture books. It's my intellectual property. It'd be like giving away a piece of land with a mineral claim on it."

"Jack," said Richard, "I see your point. Don't let it upset you. I didn't get the impression he was too organized or anything."

"Did you tell him about me?"

"Not by name. I told him I had a guy in mind who would fit the bill perfectly. And I'll get back to him and tell him you're not—"

"Hold off on that. If he's published, it means he knows publishers, I mean, real New York publishers, like Simon and Schuster and Knopf and Random House, the big guys whose books get noticed by everybody. I had an idea that if I got it together somehow, I'd take it to them, even if they'd probably steal more than the little guys."

"What do you want me to do?"

"Oh," said Swagger, going a little over the top on the angry-proprietor thing, "hold off a bit. Let me look into this guy. I'm not a writer, I'm an engineer. Maybe he could help me, I could help him. But goddammit, don't tell him no more about me!"

Memphis got Agent Neal working again, and the results came back quickly enough. He summed them up for Swagger a few days later, in their weekly coffee-shop meet at a randomly selected Seattle's Best in the suburbs.

"Okay, once again, we get a clean read," he said. "Marion Adams, fifty-nine. Born into gun aristocracy. His father was CEO of a now-defunct Connecticut gun valley company that mainly produced .22

target pistols of very high quality. When target shooting got small in the late sixties, the company folded. But Marty, as he is called, knew everybody, he was, er, connected, and he was able to forge a career as a writer and consultant. He's published nineteen books, many on the big-ticket manufacturers. His connections get him in the doors, he writes whitewashed company histories, he knows everybody, and he produces what many people consider technically beautiful volumes."

"I've seen 'em," said Bob. "May even own a few."

"He seems to service the high-end gun trade. You know, the big-dollar guys who go on safaris with gun-bearers and hunt doves in Argentina with Purdey shotguns and pay fifteen grand for a painting called *Ducks on a Chesapeake Morn.*"

"Got the picture," said Bob, knowing the kind of huntcult gent who was secretly in love with the traditions of thirties big-game hunting, and yearned to tramp the savannah with Hemingway and Philip Percival at his side, and would have cocktails with the mem-sahib under the lanterns before dining on linen every night in camp, while the boys did all the work.

"He makes most of his money advising these guys on what and what not to add to their collections. It's a tricky market, and the main problem is counterfeiting. Turns out that counterfeiting a rare gun is much easier than counterfeiting a thousand-dollar bill or a Rembrandt. Marty works both sides of the trade: he matches collectors to guns, gets a fee from both sides of the deal, and 'validates' the authenticity. You don't want to spend two hundred thousand on a rare early Colt and get it home and hold it to the light and find 'Made in Italy' stamped on it."

"No," said Swagger, "you don't. It does seem like a world where a crook could make a ton of loot."

"That's why someone of Marty's integrity is valued. Now, there have been rumors. It's so psychological. Guy buys a big-dollar piece on Marty's recommendation, but his buddy says, 'Hmm, looks fake to me,' and the guy who was proud and confident is now full of doubts, and he says something and it gets repeated. But nothing substantial that we could find. Like Richard, he seems on the up-and-up, and there's no record of contacts with exotic operators, no hint of criminal malfeasance."

"Got it," said Bob.

"Are you going to meet with the guy?"

"Absolutely."

"I think it's the right decision. I can find no suggestion that anyone here in Dallas is on to you. Those two ex-vice PIs are out to pasture, there's no underworld interest, and our random intercepts never turn up surveillors; everything is looking like Hugh or whoever he is has either lost interest or hasn't picked you up yet."

Swagger nodded, albeit a bit grimly. "That's what every man I ever killed thought one second before the bullet arrived."

I am fully aware that as I write, I am being hunted. I await word from the various agents I have afield, confident that my disguises, my barriers, my fortifications, my confusions are impenetrable. I am sublimely confident. Hmm, then why am I drinking so much Vod?

Anyhow, let us return to the far more interesting past and my courtship of the fool called Lee Harvey Oswald. After our dinner meet, I let him stew a day or so. Let him think it through, get himself ginned up, not force too much on him at once. I spent the next day in West Dallas, trying two more Mexican restaurants, truly enjoying each one. I read the *Times* at lunch, thoroughly, as was my custom, noting yet another White House conference on the Republic of South Vietnam, which was disappointing everyone in its military's lack of improvement in the wake of the coup that killed Diem a few weeks earlier. I don't know what they expected, and it began to make me mad again, not merely that my report had been twisted to nonproductive ends but that another parade seemed to be forming, and I fancied I could hear the drums drum-drum-drumming and the bugles blow-blow-blowing. I had spent six months there, from October '62 through March '63, and I saw little in the place worth dying or killing for. The Southerners weren't a warlike people, and without a great deal of aid, they'd never stand up to a Soviet-fortified and Soviet-advised North Vietnamese army. I was long gone by the time of the coup, which seemed to me a clear doubling-down on an unwinnable bet. But I heard reports and could imagine the look of fiery anger on Captain Nhung's face after he'd shot the Diem brothers in the head, in the back of the armored personnel carrier, on the way to general staff headquarters at Tan Son Nhut. I saw the picture that circulated in Langley: President Diem, a pleasant enough fellow in my dealings with him, with his head blown in at close range.

Anyway, I tried to put my anger aside and pursue my true goal in Dallas, to look around at a cocktail lounge called the Patio a few miles north of downtown, in another dreary suburban neighborhood. The place had little appeal to me, but it was said to be a favorite of General Walker's, where he loved to sit on the outdoor platform and drink margaritas, whatever they were, with his staff. He was slated to give a speech at SMU November 25, and having spent some time with the *Dallas Times Herald,* I knew it was likely that he and his "boys" (a few years later, though I was out of the country at the time, he earned the quotation marks around "boys") would head there for the hooch. It didn't take much time for me to figure where to put Alek so that he couldn't miss, although he would, and where to put whomever was shooting backup so he wouldn't miss. Yes, I had a pretty good idea who that would be, but that lay in the future at least a week.

I made notes to myself, considered angles, heights, and so forth, tracked getaway routes, and although the planning of sniper assassinations wasn't one of my strong points, I satisfied myself that late on a Monday evening, with vehicular and pedestrian traffic low, Alek could easily cut through the alleyway across the street, hide his rifle, then cut through backyards to a pickup spot. Meanwhile, if needed, our real shooter would have undisturbed escape by vehicle; all that would take place in the four minutes that in those days was the norm for Dallas Police Department response, again according to the *Times Herald.* I felt we could probably do it in two with practice, maybe even one. Within a day or so, everything would be back to normal in cowtown, and a certain nasty piece of work would trouble nobody, least of all the United States of America, again.

I think I should say that committing to this murder made the next murder seem not so great a reach. In Clandestine Services, we had a culture of leader killing. We had done it before; we would do it again.

As I have said, a few weeks earlier, the APC had clanked into Tan Son Nhut with its bloody cargo aboard, and everybody was convinced the killer had done the right thing and was willing to assume the mantle of murderer for the sake of his country. There were others, a red puppet in Africa, a series of strongmen in Guatemala, an appalling boss in the ever-troublesome Dominican. Des FitzGerald was, by rumor at least, currently planning the removal by violence of Fidel Castro. That's who we were; that's what we did. There wasn't all this weepy nonsense about the sanctity of life, the preciousness of each human soul. Someone had to do the man's work, and we were the men who did it, took pride in it, felt righteous about it. Orwell never said it, I am told, but whoever did must have worked for Clandestine Services in the fifties and sixties: "People sleep warm in their beds at night because rough men do violence on their behalf." We were the rough men, although we had very smooth manners.

That night he got off the bus and started down North Beckley again, and I pulled up.

"Good evening, Alek," I said. "Possibly some vodka tonight? Agent Hotsy's son has another game."

He looked either way, then jumped in, and off I sped.

He didn't wait for me. "I'll do it. I'll help any way I can. It's my duty, I'll do it."

"Congratulations, Alek," I said, "three complete sentences without a grammatical error. You're learning quickly."

"This time," he said, "there won't be not any mistakes."

"There goes the record," I said.

"Anyhow," I went on, "let us move beyond grammar. I take it you have understood what I have not yet stated but only inferred, and what it is I require of you. I mean not just your heart and mind and body, your faith in revolution and the righteousness of our way, but what in the practical sense it is I want you to do."

"I do."

"I have to hear you say it, Comrade."

He took a big breath, and broke eye contact. He knew he was leaving shore, sailing off again on uncharted waters to what he hoped would be his destiny.

"I will this time succeed. I will shoot and kill General Edwin Walker, for crimes against peace and the revolution. I can do it. I can be the assassin. There won't be any mistakes."

"No, there won't be any mistakes. Because this time I have drawn up a plan, an approach route, an escape route. We will time things to the second, we will measure the distance, we will know that there are no impediments to shooting. Our intelligence will be sound, our preparations thorough. We will do this professionally."

"Yes sir."

"Now, tell me, Alek, why is it we're doing this?"

"What? Why? Because you asked me."

"Forget that part. I mean politically, strategically, morally, what is the purpose? This is murder we're talking here. It's not to be done lightly, on a whim, or for shabby psychological needs."

"He's a bad man. He needs to die. That's all."

"And that's enough for you?"

"It is. It isn't for you?"

"Not for authorization. In my memo to authority, I argued that General Walker applied rightist pressure to President Kennedy, and Kennedy wasn't politically able to stand up to it after failures at the Bay of Pigs, Vienna, and the Cuban Missile Crisis."

"I thought America won that. I was angry."

"Propaganda. Khrushchev traded him Russian missiles in Cuba for American missiles in Turkey. We won, as our missiles were far less valuable than yours. Kennedy knows this and is spoiling for a fight, and General Walker is shoving him into it. Wherever he chooses to fight, it will be a mistake. Possibly the Republic of South Vietnam, possibly Cuba, possibly somewhere in South America, perhaps even Europe. Walker's popularity squeezes Kennedy, and something tragic for both our peoples happens, because of Walker's insanity and Kennedy's weakness. So we take Walker out of the equation. By taking one life, perhaps we save many."

"I agree, I agree," said Alek, his face lit with inner zeal. Again I thought I saw a tear.

Why did I do this? It is odd. I'm not sure I know. Alek was an easy mark; I could have gotten him to wear ladies' clothes in Times Square, shouting "Long live Russia," if I had wanted to. I think I was arguing with myself and using him as a surrogate. I wanted to hear the arguments said out loud, and I thought in some way, I might speak from my subconscious and say something more honest than I intended. I might learn something of my own true motives, as opposed to the policy mumbo jumbo by which I justified the killing, knowing that policy is malleable and that it could be used to justify anything. I suppose I was also preparing for upcoming seductions, knowing I would have to convince the man who would act as backup shooter to do so, and he was far smarter than Alek and might have come up with unexpected counterarguments.

In another sense, I felt I owed it to him. He was the expendable one, the sacrifice. If it happened, he would be left to burn to death in the Texas electric chair, screaming of red agents who'd given him orders straight from SMERSH. I doubted if the officials who executed him could keep a straight face during the operation. I wanted to give him at least an idea of where it fit in in the grand scheme of things and the belief that he had somehow made a contribution. It might help get him through the long night before they turned the switch.

"In a few days, I will contact you again. At that meeting I will present you with a plan and a map. I want you prepared; do not get in any arguments, do not read any papers, do not trouble your mind with new information. I want your mind unagitated. Since you're a fighter and a yapper, I know that's hard for you, but do your best for me. I want you ready to read and commit to memory, do you see? You have to *concentrate* for me, because you cannot possess the plan on paper. If things should go wrong, you cannot be found with a plan written in Russian. It would cause problems. Security, do you see?"

"I do. But what should I do if I'm caught?"

"You won't be caught."

"I know, but plans can backfire. It could happen."

"Then be patient. Say nothing. We will get you out somehow. Possibly a prisoner trade, possibly a breakout, I don't know. We always get our people back, that's our reputation. If it goes sour and you keep the faith, we'll spring you, and you'll spend your life in Havana as a valued citizen who sacrificed for the Revolution. We'll even work out a way for Marina and Junie and the new child to come to you."

"I knew I could count on you, Comrade," he said.

"Okay, now go. I will get you the plan, you will memorize it. You have the ammunition; do you have the rifle?"

"It's with Marina in Fort Worth. She doesn't know I still have it. I can get it anytime."

"Excellent. Leave it there for the time being; concentrate on concentrating. In all likelihood, you will do this thing, get away with it, and in months to come, possibly we will find other wet tasks for you to do. You will help the Revolution. This is what you want, correct?"

"I will show you." He reached into his shirt and pulled out an envelope that he had been careful not to fold. He pulled a photograph out of it. "See," he said, "this is who I really am."

I pulled to the side of the road and turned on the light in the car. The photo later became world-famous when it appeared on the cover of *Life* magazine and a thousand crazed conspiracy books. You've seen it. Alek in black, holding his rifle across his body, his pistol tucked into his belt, and in his other hand copies of the *Daily Worker* and the *Trotskyist International*—he had no idea that these two organs, like the parties they represented, were in blood opposition to each other—staring forthrightly at the camera lens in poor Marina's hand, wearing that eternal smirk of the sucker who thinks he's figured the game as the game is figuring him. I could see that it was a kind of romantic image of the red guerrilla that animated his deepest fantasies, like something out of the 1910s, an assassin, a bomber with a bowling-ball explosive and a long, sparkling fuse, a Gavrilo Princip, a figure out of Conrad. I felt sorry for a man who could be so deluded even as I said, "Yes, Alek. That is it. That's the spirit we need!"

I spent the next few days holed up, working on The Plan. I went back to the operational zone a couple of times, I took public transportation to and from, I walked the distances, I charted the police activity, I noted the mileages to the police stations, I had margaritas at the Patio so I could determine whether Alek's movement on the roof or my shooter in the car where I would place him would be particularly visible. I even climbed up on the roof in old blue jeans and boat shoes, Yale poof playing Jedburgh commando! I got a good look at Alek's shooting position and tried to imagine his actions.

I knew certain things. First, that the immediate result of the shot would be a frozen moment of fear followed by absolute chaos. As I saw it, my shooter would have the general zeroed and be well prepared for Alek's shot. If Alek missed, he would fire a silenced shot (I took on faith that Lon would solve all problems), finishing the issue. But witnesses would remember it differently; some would say there came a shot and the general's head exploded, and others would say there was a shot and the general's head exploded a full second later. What if Alek missed and the bullet was recovered? That would be dicey, yes, but it would be so confusing to everybody that no one would get it. There would be—assuming Lon had worked it out—no record of a second bullet existing. Since the Patio was brick, the building behind it stone, there was a good chance that a miss by Alek would shatter on a hard surface. In any event, the worst-case scenario seemed to amount to confusion, conflicting theories, an eternal mystery, a suspicion that there was more to know—but nothing substantial leading to our plot, except a theoretically captured Alek's crazed insistence that the reds had made him do it.

The difficult part wasn't the plan itself but reducing it to easily remembered components. I tried to find a mnemonic device that would help Alek's pea brain retain the information. I came up with APPLE: approach, position, patience, liquidation, escape. I knew that "liquidation" was weak, but I had to get a known word out of the puzzle. Since it was a word associated in the popular imagination with old NKVD practices and employed frequently by the patron saint of agents, Ian Fleming, in his Bond books (which Alek had read devotedly), it was okay but not optimal. I thought that authorities would consider it the kind of hokey nonsense a fantasist like Alek would come up with.

Each letter had further information associated with it. APPROACH had a set of numbers, 830 15-33-15, which meant 8:30 bus no. 15 to Thirty-third Street, fifteen-minute walk down Thirty-third to target area.

And so forth and so on, very secret agent–like. I thought Alek would enjoy the primitive spycraft, and if I got his imagination fired up, maybe he'd apply himself.

I sent him a postcard, knowing in those days of postal efficiency, it would be delivered the next day. It simply said, "Texas Theatre, 8 p.m. show." That was the movie house a mile or so from his roominghouse, where, ironically, he would be arrested on November 22.

That night he showed up. The movie was absurd, something about teenagers on a beach, and I could not stand it. I'd noted him when he came in. I went, sat next to him for a second, and dropped the plan (in an envelope) in his hands.

I whispered, "Take it home, commit it to memory, and copy it in your own hand. Do not destroy it. It must be returned to me when next I make contact. Every night study it until you know it by heart. Run through it one night and be sure you can make all the connections. I will be back in contact in ten days or so, the week of the eighteenth. Our target date is November twenty-fifth, that Monday night."

Then I left. You must remember, in those days there were no easily accessible copying machines. Xerox had yet to take over the world, there was no fax, and the only "copiers" were extremely expensive photocopiers of the sort that produced negative imagery, to which Alek, in his reduced circumstances, would be unlikely to have access. I knew that making a copy of it was beyond him.

I left him in the Texas Theatre, while silly California girls did the frug and the monkey on-screen, and disappeared into the night. I had become an expert on Dallas transportation, so I walked a few blocks west and caught a bus downtown. The next day I flew back to Boston and then back to D.C. My next mission was to see what Lon had come up with.

It took most of the day to get back from Dallas. I had to pay cash for the flight to Boston, take a cab to Cambridge, sneak upstairs, come down and check out of the hotel, take another cab back to Logan, then the flight to National. The only problem was the checkout, where the clerk said, "Was everything all right, sir? We noticed you didn't seem to sleep in the bed."

I said, "Yes, it was fine. Look, if anyone should ever ask, it'll be my wife's private detectives. So take *this*"—I winked and handed him two twenties, after having considered the whole flight back to Boston how much to pay, twenty being too little and apt to annoy him and fifty being too generous and apt to prove memorable—"and remember to forget that I never mussed the sheets."

"Yes sir," he said with a smile. "And I bet the housekeeping reports disappear too!" In those days, all us "wolves" hung together; manhood was a national adultery culture, possibly under the influence of *Playboy* magazine, which made such activities hep, like jazz and hi-fi. I never once cheated on Peggy, but many was the time I used the pretense of such a thing to help me out of a tight one.

I called Peggy from National and told her I was back, I'd be home, but first I wanted to run to the office. It made sense, because once I was on the GW Memorial Parkway, it was just a few exits beyond the Key Bridge, and I was at our big shiny new campus.

I went to my office—it was more than half empty because I arrived around 5—and quickly typed up a fictional report on my PEACOCK adventures, what young writing stars I had talked to, which of them were likely to go into journalism, which would waste their lives writing movies or potboilers or even, God help them, television. I should say as an aside that after Dallas, I moved PEACOCK from its fictional guise to an actual existence, and it was one of the Agency's enduring successes. I made friends through PEACOCK who served me the remainder of my years at Langley, particularly in Vietnam, when I ran Phoenix and wanted to get the Agency's side of the story told in the right papers; it exists, in slightly different form, to this day.

I also checked on three operations I was in charge of that seemed to require no immediate influence and whose details will only bore the reader, as they would bore the writer; I sent inter-office notes to a few colleagues with updates, questions, requests, to get back into the flow of things and make sure my absence hadn't been noted.

Then it was home by 9; Peggy had a highball waiting, and before I had a sip, I visited each of the boys to find that the pattern was the same. Jack had missed me and showed it and gave me a big hug; Peter, my middle boy, never had much use for me and more or less communicated his indifference (yet I am told he gave the most passionate oration at my "funeral" in 1993); and Will hadn't really noticed, as he'd had games or practice on all the days when I was gone. Peggy and I had a late supper, and she went to bed and I poured another highball and told her I'd be up in a bit, I just wanted to check the mail.

I'm glad I did. Mostly, it was bills, but there was one strange, rather large envelope without a return address. Hefting it, I suspected it contained some kind of tabular matter; it had the weight of heavy paper. I noted that it was postmarked Roanoke, near Lon's place in southwestern Virginia.

I opened it up. It was a copy of a magazine called *Guns & Ammo,* and it was full of pictures of various firearms and articles on such things as "Remington's New 700: A Challenger to the Model 70?" and "Llama's Big .44 Mag Makes Its Point Loud and Clear," whatever those things meant.

Flipping through it once, I noted nothing. Flipping through it a second time, I noted that one of the center pages seemed heavier or less flimsy than the others. I looked closely and realized that pages 42 and 43 had been glued together. I peeled them apart, and a letter fell out on the floor. I had to laugh; Lon was playing cloak-and-dagger tricks on me, to his own merriment.

I picked it up and read the salutation:

To: Commander Bond 007
From: Technical Department
Re: The Assassination of Dr. No
Disposition: Burn After Reading

Good old Lon. Ever the cheerful gamesman, and it was in that vein he began.

Commander Bond, I have given much thought and some experimentation to your requirements and believe I have just found a solution. Put a pot of coffee on because you've got a long night or afternoon ahead of you, much of it boring, unless you're like me and find the arcana of firearms and ballistics fascinating in and of their own. But since that's about .0001 percent of the population, I wish you luck.

I should hereby give the same admonition to the reader. Henry James's explication of the prose narrative—"Dramatize, dramatize, dramatize!"—will hereby be put aside and replaced by "explain, explain, explain." For you to understand how we managed to fool the world for half a century, you must steel yourself to the assault of the details. After reading Lon's letter, I burned it in the fireplace. Probably a week hasn't gone by in the fifty years since that I haven't thought of it, for it made, as I knew it would, what happened possible. It was the fulcrum of the event. I think I remember it pretty well, so I will now give it to you as I got it from my great and tragic cousin Lon:

Let me begin by narrowly defining the technical requirements. You, James Bond, have been assigned to eliminate one Dr. No for his multifarious crimes. Yet you cannot be caught, and there can be no evidence of your involvement or the British Secret Service's involvement. Fortunately, you have a handy patsy, Felix Leiter of the American CIA, that dunderheaded American would-be intelligence service. Poor Felix: you can manipulate him into almost anything because he so wants to be like the debonair, suave, bunny-bagging Commander Bond. So you have easily conned him into taking a sniper shot at Dr. No. Alas, he has only one weapon available, and that is a surplus war rifle of Italian vintage, namely a Model 38 6.5 mm Mannlicher-Carcano carbine with a dreary Japanese telescopic sight of questionable utility. You worry that Felix is incapable of making the shot, so you have arranged for a backup shooter of much higher ability to be present at the moment of the killing. If Felix, as is probable, misses, the agile backup shooter will take the kill in the next second or so. But all ballistic evidence must point at Felix; he is the Judas goat in the operation.

I will not worry here about firing angles, getaways, placement, any of that stuff. That is your department. I will not worry about the disposition of poor Felix; that is yours as well. Mine is simply the technical: how can backup Shooter X put a bullet into Dr. No's cerebellum and leave no trace of his existence so that the apprehended Felix Leiter is held responsible for the shot, as proved by the ballistic forensics scientifically applied by experts. It's the case of the bullet that never was.

This is what I would do. First, I would provide Felix with the ammunition he is to use, having previously secured an example of it myself [this I had already done, basically on instinct, so I was ahead of the game]. So we give Felix a box of 6.5 mm Mannlicher-Carcano ammunition manufactured by the Western Cartridge Company under contract from the Italian government, declared surplus by the Italians, resold to American wholesalers, and packaged in a nice white box. The bullet Shooter X fires is basically identical to Felix's and off the same cartridge-manufacturing line at Western's St. Louis manufacturing facility.

We have before us one of those cartridges. Let us examine it. It is blunt-tipped with a copper-coated bullet protruding from its brass case that has an unusually exaggerated length given the overall size of the cartridge. It doesn't look like a missile so much as a cartridge case with a cigar stuck in it. It is a heavy, dense item for its size, speaking eloquently of its seriousness of purpose.

You are aware, Commander Bond, that firearms and ammunition are not the stolid, imperturbable things they seem? They are plastic; they may be altered, customized, improved, their tasks changed, their performance envelope shifted, all kinds of magical tweaking and petting may be applied to them. That is what we are going to do with our 6.5 mm Mannlicher-Carcano cartridge.

(If you've forgotten or never knew: a cartridge is composed of several units. It contains a bullet, which is propelled down the barrel to terminal effect. The bullet is powered by rapidly burning—not exploding—powder, which is contained in a brass vessel often called a shell or a case. The rear of the shell, called the head, contains a rim which is machined to fit tightly, held in perfect alignment by cleverly machined grooves on the bolt, thus locking it into the chamber of the rifle. The head also contains, wedged tightly into its center, a magic gizmo called the primer, a chemically potent nubbin of specific materials that becomes a spear of flame when struck by the hammer, lighting the powder and producing the expanding gas that propels the bullet down the barrel and into history. Not that it matters, but the cartridge is an extraordinary device, so efficient and well designed that it has not been replaced in over a hundred years and will not be for another hundred years. But back to our cartridge, our 6.5 M-C.)

The first thing we do is pull the bullet from the shell, easily done with a common reloading implement. We throw out the cartridge case, full of powder, with its primer. Don't need 'em. This is about bullets, not cartridges. Now let us examine (as I have done at length) what is before us. It is 1.25 inches long. It weighs 162 grains. It is copper-covered, and its copper covering is somewhat thick, thicker than normal, as it is designed to be a hard object that does not deform when it strikes flesh but penetrates deeply. The copper is wrapped around a lead core, which can be seen by looking at the base of the bullet, observing the lead interior where the copper hasn't covered.

We put this bullet in a vise, upside down. Or we put it on a lathe, horizontally. Any advanced hobbyist's shop has one or the other. We drill a .200-inch tunnel through the latitudinal (lengthwise) center of the bullet, that is, through the lead from the base, up toward the nose of the bullet, though we stop at 1 inch depth, leaving the nose of the bullet intact.

Now what have we got? We have a bullet that weighs probably 20 grains less than it did originally but has been substantially altered in terms of its performance, without sacrificing any of its accuracy.

Next we return the bullet to the vise and we carefully saw or file off about an eighth of an inch of its blunt nose, removing enough copper to open up the lead (which is much softer) to the impact point of the bullet.

It is now substantially more volatile than it was, and instead of being counted upon, by virtue of its structural integrity—its hardness—to penetrate and stay more or less together on penetration, it may be counted upon to disintegrate when it strikes a living target, particularly if it strikes the skull or other bone structure. That is because of two dynamics: first, the nose of the bullet, which is now soft lead, will rupture on impact, peeling backward, almost blooming like a flower. Second, from within, the bored-out center has left the whole far more fragile; it will atomize in the violence of the explosion. Expect massive brain damage if the round hits the brain.

Next we take that doctored bullet and reload it in a case for shooting at Dr. No. But wait! We threw out the Mannlicher-Carcano case and its powder. Why, we have a dressed-up bullet with no place to go. Or do we?

Here's the key: *we reload that bullet into the case of a cartridge called the .264 Winchester Magnum!*

How is such a thing possible? Stop and think, Commander Bond. The 6.5 mm Italian cartridge is simply measured in metric-system terminology: 6.5 mm *equals* .264 inches diameter, or close enough for government work, like assassinations. The Carcano bullet fits neatly into the .264 Win Mag case and produces a new cartridge, the hybrid .264/Carcano, which slides neatly into the chamber of a .264 Winchester Magnum rifle. In the interest of making this less boring, I simplify. You might have to make slight adjustments to the hybrid cartridge or the rifle to get it to fit. The actual diameter of the 6.5 is .267, three thousandths of an inch larger than the barrel diameter of the .264 rifle. That might make a difference in the cartridge fit to the chamber, but it doesn't require surgery to fix, only minor altera-tions. For example, you might turn the Carcano bullet on a lathe against a hard blade held at a precision measurement and whittle it down three thousandths of an inch. Or you might "neck turn" the cartridge casing, meaning you mount the shell in a fixture and rotate it by hand against a blade set to a particular depth. Benchrest shooters do this all the time, because manufactured cartridge shells are frequently inconsistent in their neck thickness, and in that game, regularity—ZZZZZZZZ! Wake up, Bond! More coffee, damn you!—is the key to accuracy.

What have you accomplished?

First of all, you've made the bullet, now explosive, much more lethal. So what? It was lethal to begin with, as any object that strikes a human skull at over 3,000 feet per second will result in death.

The subject, I assure you, won't notice the difference. He won't be deader with one round than the other. There is no deader than dead.

More important, you've made the bullet more accurate. Not in itself, but now it can be fired in the Model 70 Winchester with, as mine has, a Unertl 10X Vulture scope, one of the best, if not the best, rifles currently manufactured in the United States (of course the idiots are changing it next year!). And absolutely the best scope. The reasons a rifle is accurate have to do with a variety of factors, all of which the Model 70 enjoys and the Mannlicher Model 38 does not: the precision fit of metal to metal and metal to wood; the crispness of trigger pull; the fit of the rifle to the human body; the precision with which the scope has been mounted to the receiver; the quality of the rifling in the barrel and the kind and grade of metal used in the barrel; the quality of the glass in the optical system. Maybe there are others that I have forgotten, but you get the picture: the shooter with the Model 70 has extraordinary technical advantages over the shooter with the 38, and this is before the quality of the shooters, their experience, their natural levels of talent, their strength, health, stamina, and mental preparedness, are factored in.

You've made the bullet invisible. You say, do you not, Commander Bond, sir, You're mad! I am not at all.

Here is another key point: by making sure the bullet explodes upon striking the skull and renders itself into fragments and powder eviscerating the cerebral vault, *you guarantee that it cannot be read for rifle signature!* That is, no piece will be recovered that will bear any marks from the lands and grooves on the interior of the barrel it was fired through. It cannot reveal its fraudulence. It cannot be linked to Felix Leiter's barrel, but *it cannot be linked to any other barrel either.* From the physical evidence available, there is no suggestion or inference that you, Commander Bond, were firing your fine Model 70 at almost the same time poor Leiter was firing his Eye-tie eyesore.

Don't the witnesses hear two shots when there was only one?

Not at all. You've seen—good God, Bond, you've starred in!—movies with silencers, no? Of all the Hollywood gun gimmicks, those devices are the most accurately portrayed. No, they do not work on revolvers, and no, they do not sound like a midget sneezing. But a suppressor—the real name—can blunt and diffuse the sound of the report considerably, so that people around it are unable to associate it with a gunshot and equally unable to say from what direction it emanated. Your Yank colleagues in the war, the OSS, fixed them on High Standard .22s and Thompson and Sten submachine guns and used them creatively; you Brits had a gizmo called the Welrod pistol, same thing. I'll spare you the long description, since I know you're drifting, drifting, drifting, but a bolt-action rifle is admirably suited for such a device, which consists of a tube attached to the muzzle. That tube contains a series of baffles or waffles within it, a series of chambers and holes so that the expanding gas is slowed down as it wends its way through the thing, until it escapes with a fizzle rather than a pop. Any competent machinist can put one together for you in a day; or you can obtain a professionally manufactured item, as they've been available to certain markets for a long time. It so happens that in my collection, I have a *Schalldaempher* Type 3, the 8 mm silencer the Luftwaffe paratroopers used during the war. They're pretty rare, but a friend of a friend wanted to move one he'd brought back and . . . you can guess the rest of the story. Out of curiosity and enthusiasm, I went ahead and machined a steel application to fit it to my Model 70 so that affixing the German device was a snap, even with supersonic ammunition, which emits a crack downrange but not at the shooting site.

Oh, I sense your suspicion. It all turns, does it not, the deception, the getaway, the mission itself, on that bullet. How do you know the bullet will explode? In gun events, something always goes wrong, something anomalous or untoward happens, nothing can be predicted with 100 percent confidence, it's too big a risk, and on and on and on.

I left the best for last. This .264 Winchester Magnum isn't just any cartridge. It's brand-new from New Haven, a cartridge designed specifically for western plains game shooting—that is, long-distance shots at antelope and mulie way out beyond the briar patch, possibly in the next county. It shoots flat, it shoots fast. It shoots faster—I'm talking about bullet velocity—than any bullet known to man. The metallurgy of the Model 70 is such that, unlike the 38, it can stand up to the highest pressures of modern chemistry that the geniuses at Olin can conjure. That means our doctored bullet will strike Dr. No not at the velocity of a Mannlicher Carcano, which is just under 2,000 feet per second, but at the full vel of the .264, which is over 3,000 feet per second. It will explode! It is guaranteed by the laws not of man but of God: that is, the laws of physics.

And still more. If it leaves any trace amounts of metal in the destroyed head of Dr. No, and the autopsy doctor manages to salvage them, the only possible test will be metallurgical. By looking with an electronic device, they will be able to determine by comparison with other metallic samples what kind of bullet felled Dr. No. It will prove undisputedly that Dr. No was shot with a 6.5 Mannlicher-Carcano bullet manufactured by the Western Cartridge Company and no other.

I've appended a drawing to chart these developments.

I want a nightful of martinis for all this labor, Bond, and the sooner the better.

There was no signature, of course. I read it over and over, then burned it and its envelope in the fireplace, having committed the salient points to mind. I had trouble sleeping, I was so excited, but eventually, the long day of travel caught up with me and I drifted off.

The next morning at breakfast, I said to Peggy, "Sweetie, I think we should take a weekend in Virginia. I haven't seen Lon in several years, and I'm feeling bad about it."

Peggy said, "But Will's team is playing Gilman in Baltimore on Saturday. He'll be so disappointed if we miss it."

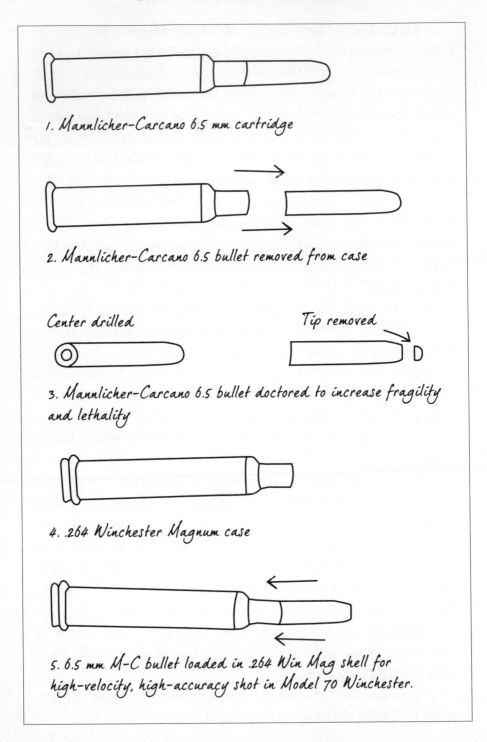

1. Mannlicher-Carcano 6.5 mm cartridge

2. Mannlicher-Carcano 6.5 bullet removed from case

Center drilled   Tip removed

3. Mannlicher-Carcano 6.5 bullet doctored to increase fragility and lethality

4. .264 Winchester Magnum case

5. 6.5 mm M-C bullet loaded in .264 Win Mag shell for high-velocity, high-accuracy shot in Model 70 Winchester.

"Oh, gosh," I said. "Oh, I hate to disappoint him. On the other hand, Lon is family also, and I feel that we haven't seen him in too long. It'll be okay with Will; he'll understand?"

Peggy knew when I had my mind set on something, and she also knew my defying her was so rare that when I did so, it was for a purpose. She relented. Such was the rarely deployed but nevertheless uncontested power of the husband, father, and provider in those days. I called Lon that afternoon—it was an easy call from cousin to cousin, sure not to rouse any suspicion from Mr. Angleton's theoretical eavesdroppers, so no subterfuge was required—and told him we'd be down for a visit and dinner on Saturday. That night I had a man-to-man with Will. He was never a rebellious or resentful son. He understood, and by that time, the boys were old enough to be left alone, so there were no difficulties with last-minute babysitters.

I had one last task other than convincing Lon to join my little crusade. That was to recruit a third member to the team. If Lon was to handle the shooting and I the driving and logistics as well as running Alek, I needed an action guy who could navigate us out of trouble's way and handle with aplomb any unseen difficulties or tough stuff that could come up (though I had planned assiduously to avoid that) while Lon and I concentrated on our task. I needed someone who was a field agent's field agent, slick, quick-thinking, tough, with a burglar's guts. Naturally, I chose a burglar.

I will call him Jimmy Costello, not his real name, because he has sons alive in the Washington, D.C., area, all, like mine, prosperous and well-regarded members of the community. I want no shame affixed to them on account of their father's deeds. Years later, I wrote the middle one a letter that got him in to Yale; it was the least I could do for Jimmy Costello.

Jimmy was in his forties by this time and well known in the intelligence trade. Though we assumed he had learned the trade on the far side of the law, he had somehow turned to the side of us angels and now worked strictly for the Agency or the Agency's friends, some other agencies, and a number of divorce lawyers. He may have been the best burglar in Washington. He could get into any place because he had a natural genius for locks. I'm guessing he was raised in the locksmith's trade, as no one could pick up so much any other way. He simply looked at a lock and understood how it worked, and carried with him always a set of picks and, in a matter of seconds, could spring any secured door. Safes took a little longer, but not much. He had no fear of heights or of walking at midnight along the precipice of an embassy roof, gymnastically lowering himself to a window under the eaves, hanging by one hand from a gutter and with the other popping the lock, then propelling himself through the open orifice. Our embassy section used him to plant microphones and wire, and with his nimble fingers, he could loot an inner sanctum of its secrets in a matter of minutes, then be gone and leave no trace of having been there, and from that night on, we were a third party to any discussions between Igor and Boris and their supervisor just in from Ye Olde Country. I don't know if we used the intelligence cleverly or not, but we got it cleverly. The FBI used him against both Sov agents and the Italian mafia; divorce lawyers against wealthy philanderers, so that after the proceedings, they were not so wealthy. He could have stolen the recipe to Coca-Cola for the Pepsi people if it had come to that, and he could have gotten us the bomb diagrams if we hadn't beaten the reds to it.

The best thing about Jimmy was his loyalty. He could be counted on. He was a stand-up guy; all you have to do is look at the history of the Irish to understand how that attribute ran in his veins. He would have kept mum to the point of torture; it was bred into him by long centuries on the bog plotting against my ancestors, and leaving them dead more often than not, and never snitching when caught, out of fear of facing the eternal hell of the traitor. That he would never be; that he never was.

His other skill—it goes with his profile—was his charming brazenness or possibly his brazen charm. He had that Irish gift of conviction, and when the sneak wouldn't do, bullshit would. He could talk you out of your underpants and send you home happy. I suppose he was a complete psychopath, but he was our psychopath, and that was exactly what the proposition demanded.

I met him in the bar of the Willard, where he hung out every night when he wasn't working.

"Jimmy, me boy," I said in my phoniest movie brogue, a joke between us.

"I am," he said, affecting his own version of a brogue, which he'd probably learned from Bing Crosby movies, "and how's his eminence Mr. Meachum?" He always called me Mr. Meachum, as if I were of the castle and he of the cottage, and no amount of argument could convince him to do differently.

"Don't know about his eminence," I said, "but I'm fine." It was an old line, but he pretended otherwise and laughed.

We exchanged banal chitchat for a few minutes, each consciously eyeing the room to see that no known adversaries happened to be there. When we were satisfied that we were publicly in private, we proceeded to business.

"Might you have a few days toward the end of the month for your old pal Meachum?"

"I might, though I am busy this time of year. Is there any flexibility?"

"Alas, no. My sales plan is cued to something I cannot control. It would require your presence in the city of Dallas, Texas—our expense, of course—from the nineteenth to the twenty-fifth. We'll stay at the Adolphus—"

"A first-class joint."

"Indeed, it is. I need a trusted fellow at my side while I deal with problems as they may come up. Someone smart, tough, fast. He's not available, so I thought of you."

He laughed. "They do keep James Bond busy these days, do they not?" James Bond was on everybody's mind then.

"Never have trusted the Brits, Jimmy," I said. "Wouldn't take him if I could have him. Give me a son of the auld sod, with a twinkle in his eye and steel in his fists."

He liked the compliment, even if we both seemed to be playing movie roles. "So, Dallas?" he said. "Not your usual sales area, Mr. Meachum."

He was drinking Glenlivet on the rocks, myself Pinch and soda.

"Duty takes us where it takes us, Jimmy. I'd rather it were Paris myself. I do pay well, and if there's hardship involved and some schedule shuffling, then I'll pay for that; a kind of schedule-rearrangement bonus, as it were."

"Well, Mr. Meachum, yours is my own favorite firm, and continuing in their favor is definitely in my interest, so aside from travel expenses, I'll not charge more, and I will see you where you want me in Dallas at any time on the nineteenth."

Simple as that, I got Jimmy, and as with Lon's genius and talent for rifles, what happened could not have happened without his contribution. He was always a rogue and hero, the bravest of the brave, the truest of the true. You see, we weren't monsters. I suppose that's the lesson. You've been taught that if we existed, we were the vilest of the vile, snatching greatness from the young prince and sending our nation on its way to hell. But to us, we were professionals, patriots, and men of honor. We weren't in it for the money, or to sell more Bell helicopters and McDonnell-Douglas fighter jets, but to save lives and lead the nation through the swamp to the hilltop. Besides, we were only going to kill a screwball right-wing general.

CHAPTER 16

A s I said, Sergeant," said Harry Gardner, "Dad was a man of literature, really. So his books, his private books, were all fiction."

Swagger once again stood at the threshold of Niles Gardner's office, that book-lined cave where the CIA's famous Boswell had tried for thirty years to write novels and failed. He could see the Red Nine lying undisturbed on the desk and the four ceramic bluebirds and the illustration of the six green elm trees on the shelves.

"Well," said Swagger, "as I say, it's a long shot. But I noted that beside the pistol, which is sometimes called a Red Nine, there's that collection of bluebirds, four of 'em, and that picture of elm trees, six of 'em. It occurred to me that somehow the phrases 'Red Nine,' 'Blue Four,' or 'Green Six' might have had some meaning to him, like in some private way he was commemorating them."

"Wow," said Harry, "you know, that's remarkable. I noted those things too, and I thought them strange, but it never occurred to me to put them in a pattern. They were so unlike Dad. He was not a sentimentalist, and those bluebirds in particular are so kitsch that I can't understand why they're there. Let's look at the picture." He took it down from the wall, handed it to Swagger, then took it back. "Dime-store frame. Let's see what the picture is."

He turned it over, unfolded four soft copper flaps securing the mounting board, and shook the board free of the frame. The picture fluttered to the floor. Bob picked it up and discovered that it was folded in such a way to display the six trees, but it was actually an illustration from a *Redbook* short story entitled "Passion's Golden

Tresses." Unfolded, it showed a handsome young man chastely embracing a beautiful young blonde against a forest backdrop. The subtitle on the story was "Her Hair Was Beautiful, But Was That All David Loved?" The author was Agnes Stanton Phillips.

"Good Lord," said Harry. "Now, there's your classic fifties kitsch!" He turned to Swagger. "You've introduced a strangeness to my father that not even *I* knew existed! What on earth does this mean?"

"It connects with nothing of your father, or his mind, or anything that you can think of?"

"Nothing. I'm astonished. Where's this going?"

"I found the pistol odd too, in its way. I noted those other things, all with the numbers attached to colors. I thought: Radio call signs, agent names, map coordinates, some kind of color code, all of which could have some connection to intelligence work and might have some bearing somehow on the fake name he cooked up for Hugh Meachum."

"In other words, if you can decipher the pattern, maybe it's the same pattern that connects to Hugh. Or the same principle of pattern, is that it?"

"Something like that. I know it's thin, believe me."

"Thin or not, it's fascinating but way beyond me, Sergeant."

"It could also be nothing. He liked bluebirds. He liked trees. He liked Mausers."

"But he didn't like trees. He didn't like Mausers. He most certainly didn't like bluebirds, that I can guarantee you, particularly ceramic ones. So maybe you are on to something."

"If so, I ain't smart enough to figure it out."

"I'll tell you what. You feel free to dig around here. As I say, I've been over it all, and I can guarantee you: no porn, no hidden notes from mistresses, no decoded instructions from his secret masters in the Kremlin, no movie scripts, nothing that anyone but a son would find interesting, and even his son didn't find it that interesting. I am going to leave you alone with Niles Gardner, and if you find anything, more power to you. Do you need coffee, beer, bourbon, wine, a sandwich, anything like that?"

"No sir."

"The bathroom is down the hall. Feel free to use it."

"Thank you, Mr. Gardner."

Bob turned and faced the mind, or at least a portion of it, of Niles Gardner. He found it intimidating. It was all books, and most of them Bob had never heard of. But starting at the top left-hand corner of the top left-hand bookshelf—the book was *A Death in the Family* by James Agee—he began to methodically pull each one out, flip the pages for inserts, bookmarks, underlines, whatever, and work his way through the shelves, going from the As to, finally, the Zs.

It took over three hours, and from the well-thumbed, well-worn condition of the volumes, Swagger could tell that Niles Gardner was a man who loved his novels. Hemingway, Faulkner, Dostoyevsky, Tolstoy, Orwell, Dickens, Wolfe, Wells, Bellow, Friedman, Golding, Brautigan, Pynchon, Fitzgerald, Crane, Flaubert, Camus, Proust, Wharton, Spillane, Tolkien, Robbins, Wallant, he read passionately and catholically. A classic in a Modern Library edition was apt to be found next to something by Jim Thompson. Kurt Vonnegut and James Gould Cozzens and Lloyd C. Douglas and Herman Wouk and Bernard Malamud and Robert A. Heinlein and Norman Mailer and Anton Myrer and Nicholas Monsarrat and John le Carré and Howard Fast and Irwin Shaw and Robert Ruark and Franz Kafka, all were equally displayed and beloved on the long feet of floor-to-ceiling shelves. On and on it went, and there was no relief from the weary task of unshelving, flipping the pages, reading the comments, then replacing. Occasionally, something would fall to the floor, some kind of long-ago bookmark, like a dry cleaner's slip or a folded index card or someone's business card or whatever, and each would indicate a stopping place or a passage of brilliance that Niles had awarded an exclamation point.

Finally, Bob was done. He had come across no oddities, no irregularities, no anomalies. It was just a serious reader's collection of the best his species had done at the ridiculous effort of telling a long story in prose.

"How're you coming?" asked Harry, leaning in the doorway.

"I suppose it was a game try, but I didn't learn a damned thing I didn't already know, except that the world is sadly full of books I'll never read."

"This room makes me feel the same way. I—" He paused. "This probably has nothing to do with anything," he went on, "but I did find one book hidden away when I was searching. It was nonfiction, old, a first edition. It was strange for Dad to have, and he'd hidden it in the bedroom, in his nightstand, under a pile of magazines. What did I do with it?"

Swagger waited as the internal drama played out in Harry's head.

"I thought it might be valuable, so I set it aside for an appraisal and then never—" He snapped alert. "Wait here. I put it in the attic, where I have some of Dad's old suits that I've been meaning to give away."

He turned, and Swagger heard the echoes in the old house as the man bounded up the stairs two flights, then bounded back.

He walked in with his trophy.

"Some kind of obscure Victorian science book, though the author's name is slightly familiar; I can't remember from where."

He handed the heavy volume to Bob. It was *The Visions of Sane Persons* by Francis Galton. It weighed about three tons.

Swagger turned to the title page and saw that it had been published in 1884.

"It's got a bookmark," said Harry.

Swagger cracked the old volume to the page that, sometime in the distant past, Niles Gardner had designated as of special meaning, and found himself at the intersection of pages 730 and 731, where he began to read Frances Galton's comments on numbers and colors.

I'll spare you details on the weekend and the pitch I made to Lon and his eventual acceptance. As you may have gathered, I would make a later, tougher pitch to Lon, and that was the dramatic one. I'll detail it at the proper time.

To sum up, Peggy and I got there around 5, had cocktails, and took him to dinner at his country club, where all knew and loved him. The food was excellent, and he was in good spirits. I could tell the intellectual exercise of solving the problem had energized him. The next morning, he and I went out to his range, and he showed me the rifle he had prepared and the ammunition, and convinced me that it was fine, that it would work. I suppose he knew what would come next. He displayed no surprise at the course the conversation took.

Lon was a big man. That's why he played fullback; ask the Harvard pansies, they know him well. He watched his weight and worked out his upper body with dumbbells regularly, but he was always fighting the pounds; they seemed to creep on him like fog and cling like putty. He had a square American face, wore wire-rimmed glasses, and kept his hair short, like all of us did without question in 1963. He favored corduroys, chinos, and crewneck sweaters, all well worn, so that he looked like an English professor—again, like we all did in those days. You were an English professor in a rumpled sport coat or an IBM salesman in a sharp dark suit and black tie. That was all there was.

His face was so lively and intelligent that people oftentimes didn't realize he was moored in that hateful steel chair, S4 forever. He'd gotten awfully good with it over the years, and he may have been the one who invented the wheel ring of smaller circumference than the rubber tire he used to propel himself. He could probably climb a mountain in the thing, or rob a bank, or go up or down stairs. But it got to him, I know it did. His vitality crushed into that metal framework, his liveliness anchored by the great dead wastage of his lower body, his talent frustrated by his immobility.

It took a bit, as it always does when you recruit a solid citizen to go against all that he's been taught, but I had advantages. I knew he read Lippman in the *Post* and admired Murrow on CBS and had what might be called "enlightened" social ideas about Negroes and Jews, and while he wanted to destroy communism, he didn't particularly want to kill anyone doing it, especially not millions of innocent Russian peasants. We all felt that way. And he hated, as did most Ivy League people, General Walker, who seemed part of a long tradition of recent American troglodytes, from Martin Dies to Joe McCarthy to Richard Nixon to the John Birch Society and the Ku Klux Klan, men who saw Commies everywhere and made it much tougher on those of us charged with fighting real Commies, men who hated Negroes and wished them to stay backward and pathetic and never equal under law or in opportunity, men who still hated Jews and thought they secretly controlled everything, men who just hated because that was all they had been taught to do.

When I explained my fears that Walker's right-wing pressure might force the callow and decadent JFK into doing another stupid thing, this time a stupid *tragic* thing, and assured Lon there was no chance whatsoever of being caught and laid the plan out for him, he finally agreed. Let it be known here and now that he never asked for a cent, he never got a cent, he never discussed a cent. He did it because I convinced him that it was the right thing to do, and he believed in me.

There was some logistics planning to be done, but that's always a task at which I excel. I got a big chunk of operating funds out of the black budget by my usual means, bought each of the tickets at a different travel agency, paying cash, booked rooms for us from the nineteenth to the twenty-sixth at the Adolphus under fake names—easily done in those precomputer days—used a fellow in the gray economy who did a lot of intelligence trade work to put together fake driver's licenses for the three of us, and made sure everything was delivered and nothing was written.

I had my own career to tend to, so I worked extra-hard in the meetings and at appending notes to reports and keeping Cord up-to-date on PEACOCK and the like. I was busy, or at least I gave the impression of being busy. My one worry was that Kennedy would make another mistake and we'd find ourselves on crisis footing and stuck in weeks of eighteen-hour days while the grown-ups at State worked out ways to prevent him from ending the world in fire. I guess those midweeks in November, he was busy screwing Cord's ex-wife, Marilyn, Angie, and everybody except poor forlorn Jackie, when he wasn't plotting his next campaign. He didn't seem to do much except think about his career and wait for things to happen. It was that hunger that killed him: the trip to Dallas was strictly politics and had nothing to do with his actual job as president.

In any case, I sold Cord, who had seemed hazier and more morose of late and perhaps was drinking more than he should, as his nose was turning into a big red blob, on another PEACOCK trip—this time, to make it easier on myself, to the south. The idea was to hit the prestige North Carolina schools, like Duke and Wake Forest and the University of NC, and spend a week trolling for talent down there. For some reason, North Carolinians always did well in prestige journalism circles, possibly because, although they were Southern, they weren't *too* Southern. From my point of view, the hop to Dallas from Raleigh and back was much easier and less exhausting or time-consuming than the one to Dallas via Cambridge.

The night came when Lon, Jimmy, and I met as a team for the first time. It was November 19, 1963. I had rented a Jeep Wagoneer, and the three of us drove from the Adolphus, a grand hotel that bathed in the red glow of the neon pegasus atop the Magnolia Petroleum Company next door, out to the Patio and got acquainted, first with one another and second with the field upon which our operation would transpire.

It was a good trip. Jimmy and Lon bonded instantly, and it was understood, without having to be explained, that Jimmy would be the action guy, the assister, Lon's special friend. Lon would shoot; he was the artist, the special talent, who made the thing work. I would supervise, though discreetly, more by studiously considered suggestion than direct order; I would also handle everything organizational, logistically and strategically. It was a good healthy dynamic. There is no I in "team," or so they say, and for the three of us, it was true.

I drove, Lon was in the back where he'd be a week hence, and Jimmy sat next to me. We had not much trouble negotiating the Dallas traffic. I can remember only a little about the drive over to the neighborhood: the colors of the early 1960s. Somehow, in the soft air of that time and place and season, they were lighter. I can't put my finger on it, and no words may exist, at least within my reach, to describe it, but everything was less urgent, less hard-edged, and more light filled the air. The great Nabokov could probably conjure it in two or three words, but I grope and babble. It was as if America was too comfortable for primary colors; they would come later, after the event I engineered, during Vietnam, during the huge change in demographics as the ignorant generation whose fathers had won the war took over. But not then, not yet. Everything was softer, lighter, quieter. I don't know how else to make you feel it.

Speak, memory. Now I remember pulling into a parking space about forty yards down from the Patio and sitting there for a bit, letting it soak in.

"This is where we'll be?" said Lon. "Suppose we can't find parking."

"The two nights I visited, there were ample spaces," I said. "I can't imagine we'll have trouble late on a Monday night."

"Where'll the other guy be, Mr. Meachum?" Jimmy asked.

"See the alley directly across from the restaurant? I've told him to take up a position, entering from the rear. We'll place some wooden crates there so he can get a good braced position. We'll have to walk the range, but I'm guessing it'll be about seventy yards."

"And you want me there?"

"This guy is such a jerk, I'm not sure how he'll do. If someone confronts him, if he gets confused, if he loses confidence—in all those circumstances, you may have to intercede. You've got a slapper?"

That was a cop's blackjack, a flat, flexible piece of leather with about a pound of buckshot sewn into it; a master could whack a man to unconsciousness with one quick blow.

"I do, and it's saved my bacon more times than I can remember," Jimmy said.

"That would be your move. It's messy, but we can't kill any private citizen; we just have to get Alek out of there cleanly. Do you see any problems, Lon?"

Lon grunted. "This is sort of like *The Man Who Shot Liberty Valance.* I'm John Wayne. I do the real killing. I must say, Hugh, I never thought I'd get a chance to play the John Wayne role."

We laughed. We were all John Wayne fans.

"Technically, it's an easy shot off a rest. I am worried about a deflection. It appears I'll be shooting through some bushes."

"If you want, Mr. Scott, I can visit some night late and discreetly trim what needs to be trimmed. We'll take that worry off you."

"Great idea," I said. It was. I hadn't thought of it. I'm glad Jimmy, ever practical, had.

"Then our patsy falls back through the alley, cuts between two houses, turns right, hides the rifle under the Forty-fifth Street Bridge, takes off his galoshes, climbs up to Forty-fifth Street, and takes a bus home. Can he do that?"

"That's why I want you with him at a discreet distance. It's possible he'll get scared in the dark. If he turns the wrong way at the river, he'll be miles from a bus stop. It'll all be different in the dark. He was supposed to do it in the dark to familiarize himself, but he's such a disorganized twit, I don't know."

"I'll lead him by the nose if I have to."

"Good man, Jimmy. Now let's go into the Patio, get a table, and try their margaritas."

So we did, three merry murderers having a good time on the patio of the Patio, which would soon be the scene of our crime. Since the duty day was done and we were on to the bonding aspect of the operation, I passed on the tequila drink and knocked back three vodka martinis, and Lon kept up with me, though he was a bourbon guy, and Jimmy sipped beer, regaling us with stories of his youthful run-ins with a Sergeant O'Bannon of Boston's Fifth Precinct in the North End of town, where it was still more a suburb of Dublin than Beacon Hill. He told a funny story in perfect dialect. There was hardly anything Jimmy wasn't good at.

I arose early, took the Wagoneer to Alek's neighborhood, parked well down from his roominghouse, and waited for him to emerge. He was late, as usual. (The idiot was on time for only one thing in his life, the murder of JFK.) I let him turn the corner on the way to the bus stop, then pulled up to him. No one was close enough to hear us in Russian.

"Good morning, Alek. Hop in, I'll run you downtown."

He got in, and I took a U-turn to avoid driving by the bus stop where a few commuters waited, in case any of them happened to notice the highly unusual spectacle of the grumpy Lee Harvey Oswald being picked up in a large American vehicle.

"Tell me what you've been up to, Alek," I said.

"I memorized the plan. I went to the Patio twice, walking it, getting used to the lighting. I will make a good shot."

"Excellent," I said. "Earlier that night, we'll move in some old wooden crates. You can use them for support so you don't have to try any fancy positions."

"I'm a Marine Sharpshooter."

I knew that Sharpshooter was a relatively easy distinction to attain in the Marines; he had not made Expert.

"I have complete faith in you. And you have walked your escape route? You won't get lost in the dark? I worry about you being arrested, going the wrong way home, and singing like a canary."

"I will die before talking, Comrade," he said fiercely. "You can count on my love of socialism and the working fellow to get me through any ordeal the fascists have in mind!"

"Well said," I replied. "That's the kind of spirit we need."

There was nothing particularly memorable about the discussion. He had a kind of morose personality and didn't seem agitated about what lay ahead. We just went through the details rather dully, without much sparkle at all.

"Any more visits from the FBI?"

"Nah. Maybe Agent Hotsy is bored with me."

"How's Marina?"

"She's fine. I'll see her this weekend and Junie and new baby Audrey. Also, I'll get the rifle."

"Any problems getting it out of the house?"

"No sir."

"You know she'll look for it when the news comes, and not seeing it, she'll conclude you went back on your word and murdered him."

"She won't talk," he said. He held up a fist. "I am the king of my house, and the wench"—he used a cruel Russian word, *devushka*—"knows better than to betray me."

He guided me through traffic, which thickened as we drew near to Dealey Plaza along Houston Street, after crossing the river. In a block or so, we were there, and I had my first look at Alek's place of employment, with its Hertz sign set on the diagonal above. I cannot say I paid it much attention, because at that point Dealey Plaza and the Texas Book Depository were utterly meaningless to me. I had no revelation, no surge of heartbeat, no epiphany. The structure was a big, ugly building on the edge of a municipal park of no particular charm, brick, six or seven stories tall, completely without character. The cars whizzed by it, all the other buildings were equally uninteresting, even the triangle of grass that constituted the plaza lacked feature or interest. I regret many things I did over the next few days, and among them—not the first but up there nonetheless—was that I made the Book Depository eyesore a historical shrine, never, ever to be demolished.

"That's it," he said.

"Okay, I'll turn here so nobody sees you get out of this car. Oh, I wanted to get the diagram from you."

He reached into his jacket and pulled it out, the only article except for the box of cartridges I'd given him that both of us had touched. I knew I'd burn it at the first opportunity.

I dropped him at the corner of Main and Elm, then turned left on Elm, passing under the shadow of the Book Depository as I headed down the slight slope of Elm to the triple overpass a hundred yards ahead. I came within sixty or seventy feet of the even more famous grassy knoll on the right. In all the years that followed, I always had a smile—perhaps the only one the operation ever produced on my face—at the expense of the lunatics who believed that the little green lump explained everything.

I found a way to reverse my direction, got back to Commerce, and in ten blocks or so reached the Adolphus. There, I made phone calls to Jimmy and Lon to set up a real-time run-through that night, as we would do for the next six nights, to get used to the routes, the patterns of the shadows, the rhythm of the traffic, the different hues of darkness as the conditions altered the nighttime weather.

That night after dinner, I had a moment of happiness and calm. I was doing something big that I thought would help my country at the cost of one small, worthless, ugly man. It did not feel wrong at all to me, and I had no doubts, no qualms, no reservations. I was going to make a difference. I was going to change history.

The next morning, Wednesday, November 20, 1963, I woke, ambled groggily to my door, opened it, and grabbed the newspaper, the *Morning News* I think it was, and before I sat down, I saw the headline: "JFK Motorcade Route Announced." I had not known Jack Kennedy was coming to Dallas on the twenty-second. But as my eyes ran down the story, I saw the names of streets I had driven the morning before: "... Houston to Elm, Elm under the triple overpass ... ," and I knew in an instant that I had been given a chance few men have. Circumstance had bent itself to offer me an opportunity that was not only the logical outcome to my ruminations, but almost a moral obligation. Who could say no to such a possibility? Not Hugh.

Ah, Vod. So dependable. Such a friend, an ally. Vod
always has my back, my best interests at heart, my happiness paramount
in its fermented little potato brain. With Vod at my side as well as in my
blood, I launch into the final act, which would leave me, theoretically
at least, history's most abominable man. I slew the prince who was the
king. I widowed the goddess of all our dreams; I made Ari Onassis possible. (There's one I know I'll never be forgiven for!) Oh, and I orphaned
those two little so-cute-it-hurts-even-now kids. Bad Hugh. Hugh, you
bastard. Vod, a little help here, please.

I knew I had to convince three people to help me tilt Operation LIB-
ERTY VALANCE a little bit, so that instead of shooting General Edwin
Walker on November 25, 1963, we would shoot John Fitzgerald Ken-
nedy on November 22, 1963, two and a half days hence.

The three people were Lon Scott, Jimmy Costello, and myself. As for
Alek—Lee Harvey Oswald—I knew the glory pig would take zero convincing. The idiot would be like a rabid dog pulling on a leash. He might
have come up with it himself if he'd read the paper. It was everything
his fetid little sewer-Commie mind demanded and had dreamed about
for years. His eagerness would surely get him killed and everyone else
electrocuted. But I felt I could control him and improvise a new plan so
brilliant that even he couldn't screw it up too badly. I would see him tonight at the bus stop.

As for me: Did I believe in what I was about to do? And if I didn't,
how could I convince the others? I tried to apply the dictates of the New
Criticism to the ethical issue, as if it were a poem demanding the most

rigorous attention to detail, untarnished by the excesses of biography, assumption, sentimentality, lugubrious emotionalism. Read the text, I told myself: read the text alone.

Here was the text I read, trying to ignore the young president's glamour, his vitality, his beautiful children, his strangely beautiful but beautifully strange wife, his brood of brothers, cousins, sisters, parents, whatever. No room for sailboats, touch football, movie stars, no thought of parochial politics (we were both Democrats), all that out. Lyndon Johnson, whoever he was, out.

My clinical reading of the text that was JFK demanded only one answer: what were his intentions in the Republic of South Vietnam? I didn't give a damn about Castro or Cuba, I didn't see much that could be done in Europe except minor maneuvering for minor leverage, a missile base exchanged here or there, a spy betrayed, a minister blackmailed, all of it, in the long haul, meaningless.

But what of that steamy glade, with its ravishing jungle and mountain landscape, its little yellow people who wanted nothing in life except to be left alone to raise their rice plants ankle-deep in water and shit? The issue was: would JFK get us into a big shooting war there? If so, who would fight it? The tiny yellows he cared nothing about—they would die in the hundreds of thousands, for sure—or a generation of college kids unlikely to care to risk a war to save a country so far away, whose rise or fall meant so little to them and would not be worth dying for. Left to their own devices, neither of these demographics would vote to let slip the dogs. It wasn't like the Vietcong had bombed Pearl Harbor, much less Winnetka. No, it would happen only if JFK willed it to happen by inventing reasons to send our troops over there. He'd already begun, and I'd seen them, tan, lean young men with the close haircuts and narrow eyes of highly trained professional military, the so-called Green Berets, yearning for a war they thought would be quick and glorious, with a nice sniff of powder to it. I knew there were a lot more of them there than the *Times* had reported, and I knew also that despite my report and Cord's passionately earned and argued reluctance, there were those in the Agency who'd smelled the treasure of career enhancement hunting Pajama Charlie for a year already.

To me it was shit. The place was infinitely more complex than anybody in Washington suspected, and it had the kind of suction that could drag us down to ruin in its whirlpools of deceit and danger, its anthropological conundrums and village traditions, its cruelty; our enemies would degrade us, but not as much as we would degrade ourselves in fighting them.

I took, as I said, the recent murder, under our auspices, of Diem as doubling down on a bad bet. We knew Diem was so corrupt that his military was incapable of winning a war, and that the reigning tactical concern for field and general-grade officers, much less administrators and bureaucrats in Saigon, would be filling their own secret bank accounts in Paris. We had decided to wipe that corruption off the face of the earth, to encourage new, younger, American-trained (and American-allied) officers who would win the war. If they proved unable, we would begin to send more than "advisers": we'd send divisions, we'd send our new helicopter-borne army, and the general slaughter—as well as Eisenhower's feared "land war in Asia"—would be on. There was no telling how many would die, theirs, ours, the unfortunate peasants caught in the middle, and for what? One piece on the board, said to be a domino but maybe just a piece on the board.

That JFK was a philanderer, that he was screwing Cord's wife (among the many), that he came from a family as narrow and clannish and narcissistic as any Tudor or Hanoverian, all these I tried to discount. That his heroism in the Pacific was greatly exaggerated, that he received the Pulitzer for another man's work, that his father bought him every election he ever won, all that I tried to push aside. I don't know if I did. But in the end I made up my mind, and once I'd done that, it was on to the others.

I called Lon.

"No, Hugh," he said. "Not a chance."

"Lon, please—"

"I will be on a flight to Richmond by three if you say one more word, Hugh."

I let the conversation simmer off into silence for a bit. Finally, I came back with what I knew was the weakest of propositions. "Just let me make the argument."

"My mind is made up. As soon as I saw the paper, I knew how that devious little insect that you call a brain would set its antennae to twitching, its mandibles to grinding, its pincers to snapping, and I knew exactly where you'd go. I know you better than you know yourself, Hugh. Anyhow, what's the point of listening to the argument? There's only one argument, really. You believe you can pull off the biggest coup in history. You would call it an 'operation' in your spy-novel lingo, so as to distance yourself from it, as if it's scientific or medical. It's hubris, Hugh. It's just hubris."

"Lon, you are—"

"I know you, Hugh. I know you."

"If you've made up your mind, how can it hurt to hear my argument? I assure you, it has nothing to do with me, my needs, any of that. The psychology involved is yours, Lon. I will make you see how it has to do with *your* needs, and you will see your duty clearly."

"Oh, right. Oh, that's rich. Hugh, you are a bastard."

"That's what they pay me for. The things I've authorized, you wouldn't believe, the things I've seen. Please, Lon, meet me in the lobby in ten. We'll go for a little walk."

"Agghh." He snorted, signifying surrender.

I pushed him in silence across the street from the hotel. I didn't head south, down Commerce toward Dealey, but north, and then I turned east down a street I don't remember. It was November 20, 1963. The sun was out, and true fall, as we New Englanders would recognize it, had yet to begin. The leaves were still green. In late November! We arrived after a block or two at a small park that seemed to be dedicated to some glorious Texan or other who had triumphed at the Battle of Squashing Mexicans or some such. That's what we did in the Agency—if not Mexicans, some other little brown tribe, anyone who got in our way. That's what I helped us do. We were in the empire business, after all, and I was paid to make sure that empire stayed strong and lasted forever, and anyone who opposed us got squashed. If the empire was to fall, it wouldn't be on my watch.

We sat in the sun. Should I say birds sang, the wind blew gently, the sun was bright, the world seemed full of hope? Maybe all that is true. I have no idea.

"Get on with it, goddammit," Lon said. "I don't have all day."

"I just have one question," I said. "Request, actually. Then I'll shut up."

He waited.

Finally, I said, "Lon, tell me about the chair."

"The what?"

"The chair. The one you're sitting in. It's made of steel. I can see a label; I think it was manufactured by Ridgeway Medical Equipment Company, Rahway, New Jersey."

"Don't be ridiculous. I don't talk about such things."

"No, tell me. You're a goddamn noble Roman, Lon. I know you too. You're sick with honor. You'll never complain, you'll never cease to maintain the code. Stoic, dignified, without complaint to the end, a study in Protestant rectitude and Western heroism. You're braver than John Wayne, Gary Cooper, or—"

"They're actors," said Lon.

"Audie Murphy, Neville Brand, I don't know, the boys who raised the flag on Iwo, Robert C. Scott, Cord Meyer, Bill Morgan, Joe McConnell, Major Darby."

"It's nothing to do with courage. It's the practicality of acceptance and resignation. It's doing the best you can with what you've got."

"Tell me, Lon. You've never told anyone, probably not even yourself. Tell me."

Lon waited a bit. Then he said, "All right. S4 is lousy. It stinks. It's no fun. It's better than S3, it's better than any of the Ts, it's much better than any of the Cs. But still: it's lousy. I get sores on my legs, and I don't even feel them. But the pants are smeared with blood and pus and have to be thrown away because no dry cleaning gets it out. I shit in my diapers and don't know I've done it, and I have to somehow deal with the diapers on my own, in my room at night, a truly repulsive job. I worry that there'll be a leak, that I'll offend, that something humiliating will happen. I get bruises on my spine, and sometimes they climb above S-4 and I get tremendous pains. I sometimes remember my legs in my dreams, remember walking, feel the experience, and almost believe that, by some miracle, I've— But then I wake up, dead from the waist down. Psychologically, that's hard to take, particularly the seven hundredth time or so. I have nightmares about Dad. He had a look on his face for a split second, before the horror came over him as he saw what had happened. I saw it as I twisted around to see what the hell had happened and saw him standing there with the rifle on the ground before him. I think about that look. Was it a smile? It could have been a smile! I— I don't know. There was something there, a kind of, I don't know, satisfaction or something. Dad was great, considering. Until he died, he did everything he could to make my life livable. He spent a fortune, he was with me nearly every single day. I know that he hated himself for the accident, and that it took twenty-five years off his life, but still . . . That look. A father's worries about usurpation. His inability to get totally behind somebody who will replace him."

He was silent for a while, gathering wind. He had never spoken of such things.

"The women," he said. "I don't know if it was better to have had a decent amount of intimacy before or to lose your sexuality as a virgin, because then you'd never remember, never know what you were missing. I have no policy position here. But I smell women's perfume, I see the crease between their breasts, I see the tops of their stockings. It happens all the time, because around me they're not so guarded in their body movements; they know I'm out of the game. They're not being cruel, it's just their nature. They love to put out the sniff of sex, but they hold it back until the wedding night to make sure he shows up at church. That whole ritual guardedness, the flash, the tease, the lean-over, the crossed legs, that's all missing around me, because, absent a working penis, I'm one of the gals. That's what happens to us S4s. So I see breasts and even thighs all the time. And I remember, and it makes me crazy, and I have to get through it on what I suppose is Yankee grit or something. But I hate it. I hate them, yet I yearn to be around them, to smell them, to see them smile, to make them laugh, to know that except for the one thing, I would be with them. Instead, I'm the witty eunuch in the chair, the gelded stallion, so charming yet so unable to satisfy and give to them what they desire, children and dick. So yes, Hugh, the chair is no fun. I'm guessing you probably already deduced that with your spy's keen powers of observation. What the hell does this have to do with anything?"

"Lon," I said, "Kennedy is going to send thousands of young Americans off to a war we cannot win. He's going to do that because he wants the reelection, and he can't be called soft on communism. We were going to correct that problem by eliminating a fellow who called him soft on communism the loudest. Now I see it. We have a chance not to 'correct' but to 'eliminate.' To erase totally.

"I directed you to the chair you ride in all day long because thousands of boys will come back from the war in those chairs. At some point or other, all of them will wish they had been killed. Because they won't have your strength, your heroism, your 'Yankee grit,' as you call it. They'll have nothing and they'll get nothing. You command the gun world with your shooting skills, you have extraordinary resources of intelligence, charm, and will, to say nothing of a considerable personal fortune. These poor boys will have none of that. They'll just have the chair. You hate the chair, but you have managed to transcend it. They won't have that chance, Lon, and you know it. The chair will turn their lives into daily torture. Forever and ever and ever, which is how long they'll feel their lives lasting. So that is why I ask you to do this, Lon. Not for my hubris but for yours. Keep those boys out of their metal chairs.

Endure, publically if you get caught or privately if you don't, the mantle of regicide, the man who killed the king. If you can bear the chair, you can bear that easily enough."

He laughed.

"Ever hear of an Argentine writer called Jorge Luis Borges?" I said.

"No. Hemingway's as far as I go."

"He writes stories in the form of fictional essays. Conjectures on this or that, always astonishing in their brevity and their insight. In one, he postulates that the true son of God was Judas, not Christ. Anybody could be Christ, suffering and becoming immortal. But it took a strength of character that only the son of God could muster to make the crucifixion possible, by the betrayal. That was the true heroism, the true sacrifice, for without it, there was nothing. He didn't bear the pain of the cross for a day, he bore the pain of hatred, exile, universal loathing, all that, forever. *That* was strength."

"Sounds crazy to me," he said. "Your Bor-haze, or whatever, carries no weight with me. How do you know you'll prevent this war? Maybe this Texan, Johnson, maybe he'll wage the same war."

"He won't. He's a New Deal Democrat forged in the crucible of thirties Washington. He has no interest in military adventurism, nothing to prove, because he's an older man with plenty of mistresses and an ugly wife. He'll use his time in office to siphon money off to Texas and his cronies in the party; he'll give a lot to Negroes so Lippmann will write well of him; he'll build dams and highways and buildings with his name on them. Like all of them, he'll screw everything in heels. He has no interest in foreign affairs. I've looked at it carefully. Internationally, he's as sober as Eisenhower; domestically, he wants to be the next FDR. He's FDR with ants in his pants. The last thing he wants is to go off on a crazy crusade in a foreign swamp. It's way too expensive."

"This thing, this ambush? You don't even know if it's possible."

I suppose I knew I had him then. He'd gone in a single breath from the strategic to the tactical. He didn't realize it, but he'd surrendered on the strategic. Now it was a matter of details.

"We're so close, Lon. We've solved the ballistic issue, we have the best rifle shot in the world, we have a silenced rifle, the most advanced assassination tool in the world, we have a prime patsy who will, I say again, *will* take the blame for us, the poor dummy, and we have the best breaking-and-entering man in America. And we have JFK in an open-top limousine parading by at twelve thirty p.m. the day after tomorrow. We have one thing yet to do, and it's something that should be within any case officer's reach. We have to find a place to shoot in reasonable proximity to Oswald's at about the same moment, and while everybody is going after him, I will push you away in your wheelchair, and we'll have martinis and steaks that night."

"It's not a joke, Hugh. Killing a man, a young beautiful man, no matter the reason, it's not a joke."

He was right. My foolish attempt at levity had sabotaged the moment.

"I overplayed that hand, I know. It was stupid. I apologize to you, Lon; you deserve better from me. No, we won't celebrate, we'll mourn along with the rest of America, and we'll never boast or tell. But we will save thousands, maybe hundreds of thousands, of lives."

"Damn you again, Hugh. You are so willful, so convincing."

"Let me sell Jimmy and see what he comes up with. If he comes up with something that's workable, *then* make up your mind. If you still don't want to do it, fine. I suppose I did my best. We'll go back to the Walker thing, as we originally planned."

That was how we left it. I pushed him back, and he retired to his room for a nap. I called Jimmy. There was no answer.

I saw him get aboard the bus near the depository, and I followed it across the long aqueduct over the Trinity River all the way back to Oak Cliff, through the late-afternoon Dallas traffic. I wasn't interested in the bus so much as in who else was interested in it. I looked for black Ford coupes, maybe with antennas, G-man cars. Neither the Bureau nor the Secret Service was there or shared any interest in Comrade Oswald; they were, as usual, profoundly asleep on the job. I could almost hear them snoring. Zzzzzz-zzzzzz.

In Alek's neighborhood, I watched from across North Beckley as he got out; again, no other cars were parked on the street, and the two other men who got out at the same stop disappeared in another direction. Alek walked by me, oblivious to all in the fading light, his details hard to make out.

Even from the few lines the declining sun revealed, you could read him: he was like a figure out of Walt Kelly or Al Capp, a caricature of grumpy hostility, a stumping, glaring, shabby figure, all lines in face and body pulled down as if by overwhelming gravity, broadcasting the message DO NOT APPROACH OR YOU WILL BE FIRED UPON. No wonder the idiot was friendless, always getting in fights or bitter arguments, a trial to those few who had decided to let him into their lives, a wife beater, a jerk. Yet he became the ball bearing of history. How utterly strange and unpredictable.

I flashed my lights. He looked up, startled, recognized the Wagoneer by shape, and came over and got in.

I pulled away. "Good evening, Alek," I said.

"Good evening, Comrade," he said, "I'm set," or something similar in his garbled Russian. "On Friday evening, I will go to Fort Worth and return Monday morning with the rifle for—"

"Alek," I said, "I take it you haven't read today's paper. Or talked to coworkers in the plant?"

"I read papers a day late. It's cheaper, I get them from the garbage. As for coworkers, they are not worth—"

"All right, all right. Time is short, the stakes are high. Now listen to me carefully. Don't say a thing. Don't react or have a bowel movement or begin to hip-hooray. The situation has changed radically."

I felt him turn. "The ears are all of me," he said, his clumsy literal translation, I'm guessing, of "I'm all ears," for which there was no Russian equivalent.

Idiot! Agh. Anyway, I went ahead. "On Friday, at around twelve thirty, a motorcade will pass in front of your building on Elm Street. In an open limousine will be the president of the United States. Alek, can you alter history for us with one shot of your rifle? It is a great opportunity, so great that one must suspect the laws of the universe are turning in favor of our moral insistence on progress. Alek, can you do this thing for us? Are you the man who has been sent to do this thing?"

I heard his breath being swallowed, I heard him gulping. I couldn't bear to look at his face, for I knew I would see a cavalcade of madness, narcissism, greed, and ambition and that his beady little vermin eyes would burn hot and fierce. The worst are full of murderous intensity, I thought.

"Comrade," he finally said, and then he blurted off into English, "Jesus Christ, yes, goddammit, I have waited my whole life for this, oh, I will in one strike change the course of history, I will show the world the magnificence—"

"Settle down, you fool," I said. "You're carrying on like a schoolgirl. Get ahold of yourself and listen to me, all right?"

"Yeah, yeah, sure," he said, still in English.

"In Russian. I insist, all discussions of this matter must be held in Russian."

"Yes sir."

"This is the sort of thing we do reluctantly, but we do not want this young man sending troops off to invade Cuba or anywhere, and he shows signs of instability, poor judgment, downright imbecility. He is too easily influenced, too desperately ambitious. He has no moral character. He is the kind of sparkler who could start an atomic war. He must be stopped, and a responsible leader put in charge of your nation. Alek, you must understand, in pulling that trigger, you are not destroying, you are building."

"Yeah, yeah, I get it," he said.

He didn't, of course, and I was fooling myself, really, throwing a last grenade into my own lingering defenses; I was arguing with myself.

"Alek, if you are to do this thing, you must do it under our absolute discipline. We will provide you with an escape route. We will get you to a safe house, we will get you out of the country, we will get you to your glory in Havana and your rightful place among the revolutionary fighters. In a year or so, we will get your wife and children to you. But this can be guaranteed only if you submit and trust absolutely our rules, do you understand?"

"I agree, I agree. I hear what you're saying. If it comes to it, I won't let them take me alive. I'll have my pistol with me, I'll go down shooting, as I am willing to die for—"

"No, no, no," I said, fearing this idiot on a shooting rampage in downtown Dallas, "you must *not* bring your pistol. Believe me"—I struggled for the appropriate fiction to disabuse him—"if you kill the president on a policy issue and because of your own sense of idealism, however warped they may think it, you will be reviled but respected. You will have a legacy of courage and dignity. If you also shoot some postman or some housewife, you become another punk Negro murderer, and your electrocution will be cheered by your own children, and you do not want that. Believe me, leave the pistol at home; swear to me you will harm no one except your target. That is the discipline we demand. We are not butchers, we are scientific Marxists."

"Yes sir," he said.

"Tell me how you would proceed."

He laid out the obvious. He'd have to go home tomorrow night—Thursday—to get the rifle; he would break it down so it could be disguised and carry it into the building in a brown paper bag. Nobody would challenge him. He would go to the sixth floor, which was largely deserted, as it was pure stock storage area. He would situate himself overlooking Elm as it passed by Dealey Plaza on the way to the triple overpass, and he would shoot the president as he passed by.

"Which window will you shoot from?" I asked.

"What?"

"Which window? You have your choice of any; which window do you chose?"

"Uh, I guess the one in the middle."

"Why?"

"It's in the middle."

"Excellent reasoning. You are a genius. Where on Elm will you shoot the president? That's the determining factor on the window. You cannot make these things up on the spot. You of all people cannot make things up on the spot, because you will do it stupidly."

"Where should I shoot?"

"You know the building at the street."

"I— I don't know. It doesn't seem to make any—"

"Idiot. You want him where he's closest and slowest. Any map should give you the answer. Where will he be closest and slowest? This is why you're such a failure, Alek. You don't think. You just make things up!"

His face knitted in shame. Then I saw a bulb go on behind that dull face, those dim eyes. Bingo! Eureka!

"When he's turning the corner. He has to turn the corner from Houston to Elm. It's very sharp."

"Excellent. It's a hundred and twenty degrees. The car is big, it will pivot slowly. For all intents and purposes, he will be standing still. His chest will be open to you at a range of about seventy-five feet. An idiot could make the shot."

"I'm not an idiot," he said. "Sure, I make mistakes, but everybody—"

"Which window, Alek?"

"The corner window. The closest window to him. If I planned to shoot later, as he went down Elm, then I would move to another window down Elm."

"Excellent," I said, glad that he had figured out this elementary riddle (though no conspiracy theorists did, I might add) so that I could praise him and raise his spirits. "You shoot him when he's closest, when he's stillest. One shot, center chest, easy to make."

"Fish in a barrel," he said in English with that dreadful smirk.

"After shooting," I instructed, "you will have little time to make your escape. The police will be in the building within minutes. Drop the rifle, walk, do not run, downstairs, being careful not to acquire oxygen debt so you are swallowing for air. Look no one in the eye, but do not shirk either. Your face is neutral. Exit the building and slip off into the mob. It will be chaos outside. Proceed down Houston Street one block to the corner of Houston and Pacific. You will see this car, though I might not be driving, and it could be anyone, a couple, an old lady, a Mexican, a hepcat. Climb in the back and lie down on the floor. Commit yourself to a long, boring drive. In a few hours we will have you at a safe house, and at that point, you can relax, eat, drink. The next day, or really the next night, we will move you out of the country. These will be an arduous few days demanding stamina, commitment, attention to detail, and obedience. Trust us, Alek, will you? Can you?"

He said yes.

"I wish we had time for run-throughs, for rehearsals, for shooting practice, for all of that. Can you hit that easy, almost stationary target under seventy-five feet away?"

"I'm a good shot. I won't miss," he said.

"All right. We must make do with what has been given us. For some reason, history has chosen you. You have to justify that choice. I believe in you, Alek, as no one else has. You owe me, you owe your true motherland, you owe history. You must not fail."

"Comrade, I swear to you—"

I cut him off, as we were a few doors down from his house, and I gave him a Russian hug, smelling the body odor of a man who seldom bothered with hygiene, fastidious New England priss that I am and always will be.

"Now go, little Alek, and become a hero."

He stepped out of the door, and I pulled out, leaving him behind.

You're thinking: Okay, Hugh. Call your friend Jack Ruby and set the second part of the plan in operation. Tell us about Jack, how you manipulated him, how far back you old buddies went, your underworld ties, the implicit sponsorship of the Mob, particularly the Trafficante connection, running through the attempts on Castro that your own section, Clandestine Services under the great Cord Meyer, had set up.

Hah. The joke's on you, friend. You shouldn't be thinking about Jack Ruby, unless you sloppily missed the Warren Commission detail that he'd sent a Western Union moneygram to one of his strippers a full forty minutes *after* the announced transfer time of Alek to a more secure locale; he didn't show up at the station basement until a full hour after that designated time, so he could have had no idea that Alek was in the building. Though that is the sort of thing the conspiracy hucksters always fail to mention, it destroys any possibility of Ruby as anything but a random mote of dust adrift on the currents of history, being blown this way and that.

For the record, I never heard of Jack Ruby until shortly after he finished poor Alek and took over the story himself. I suppose this may be counted as several of the immense strokes of good fortune that Operation LIBERTY VALANCE enjoyed, though perhaps it was meaningless in the end. The truth is, I planned to betray Oswald to the police; I expected him to be picked up and eventually electrocuted.

I didn't think it mattered. His personality—I am no psychiatrist, but I'd studied him enough and been around him enough—had the smell of disintegration. He was a crackpot to begin with, with enormous mental disorders that had afflicted him his whole life. The outward manifestations were hotheadedness, empathy with outré causes and policies, lack of attention to details, sloppiness in all manners of being. He was a man at war, though primarily with himself. I suppose, inside, he hated his absent father and his overbearing, vulgar, disorganized mother; he hated himself for his continual incompetence and his total inability to engage people at any level; for his utter intellectual mediocrity. He worshipped the god of communism, knowing little about it. He had a streak of melodramatic vainglory—more than a streak, it was perhaps the largest part of his identity. I do think that he genuinely didn't care if he lived or died; he was willing to risk his own life in an attempt to fulfill his most urgent need, which was to matter and no longer be a marginal loser detested by all. Loved or hated, it made no difference to him; that his name would be on the world's lips with this opportunity, it was an aphrodisiac that his dull-normal mind and undisciplined lunacy could not have resisted. I believe he would have taken those shots whether or not we existed.

Most important, I believed if he was captured, he'd find the pressures too much, and in time his mind would fall apart. He wouldn't be able to recall his own truth. First he'd claim he alone authored the deed and cling to that for months because he wanted the glory, the notoriety, the fame. Finally, he'd tell them the "truth," as he imagined it, that he'd been picked up by a Soviet agent, coached and prepped for a mission against General Walker, and at the last moment diverted to the president as target when that opportunity revealed itself. Dutifully, the FBI would check out the tale and find no evidence of it. No one would remember seeing Alek in the presence of this agent; someone at a desk near mine in Langley—maybe it would even be me!—would be given the mission of discovering if there had been any remote possibility of Soviet involvement and, using sources, networks, leverage, penetration, and analysis, would produce a report in a year that, aside from the idiot's attempts to secure a visa from the Russian embassy in Mexico City in September, there had been no record, no rumors, no traces of Soviet contact with Oswald.

If Oswald went through photo albums of known agents in order to ID his mysterious mentor, he'd come up with nothing, for in truth I looked far more like Dave Guard of the Kingston Trio than I did Vassily Psycholosky, KGB killer and goon.

If all went well, there would be no physical evidence—no fingerprints, no footprints, no jimmied locks, nothing slightly out of the ordinary, nothing ambiguous in meaning; the clincher would be the ballistics, which, as I have explained, would suggest his rifle and his rifle alone.

As I drove away, he receded into the shadows. I would see him only one more time—the closest our plot would come to discovery. I quickly headed downtown to the Adolphus, where I still had to talk to Jimmy, to convince him, and where we had a great deal of planning to do.

When I got back to the hotel, I was not surprised to see Jimmy waiting for me in the lobby.

"Hi, Mr. Meachum," he said, rising, smiling in that Irish way, "how about letting me buy you a drink."

"Sure," I said, and like two cronies from an Oklahoma vacuum-cleaner manufacturer, we trundled off to the dark Men's Bar, not the Adolphus's famous Century Room, where a Rosemary or a Gigi or a Maryanne was singing. We found a table well away from the few other drinkers left, ordered up our poison, and waited for the girl to bring it and then to depart. For the record, in those days Texas had insane drinking laws, and we'd had to "join" the club in order to receive our own private bottles.

"So, Jimmy," I said, "I've been trying to reach you. Have you spoken to Lon yet?"

"No, I haven't. I thought I'd let the two of you work things out between you today. It seemed like a good time to take a little break."

"Actually, it was. From what you're saying, I guess you've figured it all out. That I want to change the nature but not the purpose of the mission. Same operational principles, different target. Lon, to be fair, is not so sure. He didn't sign up for what I'm proposing. Neither did you. Neither, come to think of it, did I. But it's here, it won't go away; I believe it can be done. I also believe it *should* be done. It's really just a continuation of the original idea. Do you want the full nine-ninety-five sales pitch or the bargain-basement four-ninety-five version? It's getting late and I haven't eaten yet, so I suppose the five-buck version will have to do."

"Mr. Meachum, you don't have to break a sweat. I get it. If you say it needs doing, then I'm the one to do it. Loyalty. You boys in your outfit, you got me out of prison and got me a new life doing what I do best and doing some good in the world. Never thought I'd have a shot at a house in the suburbs and two boys in private school, which is what I have today. I'll sail with you to hell or the edge of the world, whichever comes first."

"You're a good man, Jimmy."

"Plus, I hate them Castle Irish. Always putting on the airs, always carrying on like they weren't bog-slogging peat burners like the rest of us. My father hated them, his father before him hated 'em more than the English. You're doing me old dad a favor, and he's smiling in heaven."

"You're a great man, Jimmy. Knowing I have you along means I know we can do this thing."

"That we can. Do you know what I did today?"

"Of course not."

"I was all over a joint called the Dal-Tex Building. 'Dal-Tex,' know what that stands for?"

"Dallas, Texas?"

"Dallas Textiles. It's the heart of what passes as the garment trade in Dallas. Office building, a warren of offices, you'll find fifty of 'em in every city in America. Full of rooms with desks and telephones and secretaries. What else do you need to make a buck in America? That and a good case of business smarts. This one is worth exploring because it's located behind the Texas Book Depository on Elm Street. It has at least twenty offices that give a good look down Elm Street from almost the same angle as the Book Depository."

"You're way ahead of me, Jimmy."

"You know me. I've got a natural talent for mischief of all sorts. There's a fair number of buildings on the plaza that would give Mr. Scott an angle, but the only one that's a few degrees off from the Book Depository is the Dal-Tex Building. I don't see where else we could run the operation from without running the risk—too big, in my mind—of leaving an obvious clue that some other birds, that is, us, were involved. They're going to investigate this one up the ass, with all the national experts and the best techs the Bureau has. If anything's wrong, they'll sniff it out. Something you never heard of, like arterial spray pattern or skin stretch marks or powder dispersal pattern or something subatomic that not even Dick Tracy has thought of. We have to minimize everything that differentiates our shooter from the little red nuthead. It's a much higher threshold than with General Walker. That's what makes it a puzzle and, frankly, for this boyo, great fun. I love to match wits with the best, that's for sure."

"Glad you're so excited," I said.

"We have to get in and out of that building, find a shooting position, all within a few minutes, and over the last part, it'll be screaming and panic. It's no easy thing."

"I suppose it's too late to rent an office. We don't know if one's available, but it would attract a great deal of attention if we contacted the management and put down a deposit tomorrow."

"No, they'd tumble to that right away."

"Are there any bathrooms or deserted offices where we might set up?"

"No bathrooms, boss. They always put bathrooms on the interior side of the corridor, because they get more rental dough for a window. One or two of the offices I saw looked empty, but there's no way of telling how they'll be the day after tomorrow. It's a tough one."

"We're two bright boys. And I see a gleam in your eye. I think you've already found a way."

"That I have, boss," he said with his total-mischief smile.

And then he told me his plan.

CHAPTER 17

M arion Adams, gun expert and official lounge lizard to the monied collector set, had an insidious charm. It was easy to see that he was one of those gifted enablers who helps the big tall rich get what they think they want with a minimum of fuss. He was tall, fair, rather flitty, serious only about himself, hiding behind square black glasses and a suit so dowdy that it had to be expensive. He could have been an embalmer, and in a sense he was, masterminding the transfers of dead guns soaked in formaldehyde for a profit.

He insisted on high end all the way, no casual tamale and beer joint for him, and so the three men met in the French Room at the Adolphus, a Texas fantasy of high Louis XV dining, where every item on the menu boasted its own apostrophe and some two or three.

Marty, as he was called by all who knew and could afford him, held the floor, as he always did. It was the divine right of blowhards. It turned out he knew a great deal about apostrophes, French dishes, wines, art, politics, just about everything, and even Richard yielded to the torrent of knowledge; meanwhile, Swagger picked at the morsels of overprepared food, wished he'd ordered the chicken, and worked at keeping a look of polite interest on his face. Finally, Marty turned to business, over coffee.

"I am not a conspiracy 'nut,'" he said. "In fact, like millions of others, I accepted without question the Warren Commission report and was willing to let it go at that. But I do make my living telling gun stories. I was born into the business, really at its high-water mark. My father was a manufacturer and his father before him. Connecticut gun people. I had the gene too, but from a slightly different angle. I had the hunger to know and chronicle, not manufacture, not shoot, not hunt. I'm the amanuensis of the American gun culture. I've written books on all the major manufacturers, I consult at the country's finest auction houses, I am a registered appraiser in thirty-nine states, and I advise many of the nation's most distinguished collectors on the guns they are about to purchase. I assume you have checked my background and found it satisfactory."

"Nobody has a discouraging word about you, Mr. Adams," said Swagger.

"Nor you, Mr. Brophy. I've checked too. You seem to be a man who's handled crises all over the world."

"I seem to have come out okay. I am a lucky son of a gun."

"May I ask you, respectfully, for a brief account of your life?"

"Sure," said Swagger, launching easily into a colorful spin on the mining engineer's life, the risks, the near-misses, and the long nights alone with books.

He finished on Brophy's fictional JFK obsession. "Some years ago, I got hooked on JFK's death. More I read, more I questioned. Read some conspiracy crap and was not impressed. Read Warren, and it seemed ragged. Started thinking hard about it, using my engineer's brain. Realized a couple of years ago, I had enough money to last several lifetimes and two or three more wives, so I decided I was tired of sleeping bags and would prefer to spend the rest of my life going into this thing in eighth gear and seeing where it would take me. Always loved guns, so that was a start, and I guess 'cause I'm mechanical by nature, my approach has always been through the guns. Interesting. Somehow I came up with some ideas that I don't believe nobody has, and I'm trying to push forward from them. Not for money, not for fame, just because of a goddamned stubborn streak. If I dig a shaft, I like to have something to show for it. Is that enough for you, Mr. Adams?"

"Excellent account, Mr. Brophy. I'm going to make the first move here and divulge a portion of what I've found out. You see if it squares with what you know, and we'll see where we are at the end."

"Go to work, sir," Swagger said.

"All right, here's my story. I am always looking for subjects for the next book. Some months ago I got interested, quite innocently, in the life and career of a great but tragic American shooter named Lon Scott—"

Swagger's eyes stayed modestly interested, his breathing smooth, his lips unlicked. He gave away nothing and made certain not to choose this moment to break off eye contact and take a sip of coffee.

"Lon Scott. Interesting fellow," Adams continued. Then he went ahead to issue the specifics on Lon Scott, the bright youth, the safari heroics, the football stardom at New Haven, the extraordinary run of national match successes in the years after World War II, the tragic accident in '55 at the hands of his father, his father's suicide, his reemergence as a writer and experimenter in the late fifties, and then his own death in 1964.

"Sad story," said Bob as at last Marty had to take a breath and left a gap in the noise. "I hate it when someone so talented gets cut down young. Fella had a lot more to contribute."

"Yes, it does seem so," Adams said. "Then I made another interesting discovery."

He went on to tell how, in the early seventies, a fellow named John Thomas Albright emerged as a gun writer and ballistics authority and soon became a revered if mysterious figure in gun culture. He had an excellent career until he was killed in a hunting accident in 1993, at the age of sixty-eight. "I learned by accident that he was also disabled, wheelchair-bound. You'd never know it from his writing. I checked for pictures, and none existed that I could find. I went to Albright's home in rural North Carolina and learned that he was a mystery there as well. I began to wonder: could Albright and Scott be the same fellow? If so, why would Lon contrive his own fraudulent death in 1964 and reemerge as John Thomas Albright? What was he hiding or hoping to distance himself from?"

The question hung unanswered for a moment or two, and Bob

glanced at the grim countenance of Richard, the third member of the group, and then answered. "I suppose you're referring to our point of common interest, a certain event in November 1963."

Adams, versed in upping the dramatic ante on his tale, paused an artful second or so, then nodded. He waited another second.

"Of course. So I decided to look into the life of these two men more carefully. I discovered that while, obviously, Lon Scott never published an article after 1964, John Thomas Albright never published one before 1964. I acquired copies of all their articles and first by myself and then with the help of an academic who specializes in forensic reading, we made a line-by-line comparison and found deep organizational similarities as well as dozens of turns of phrase that were similar. I found three cases where Albright made reference to discoveries that Scott had made as if they were his own. I discovered that the documentation on Scott's death was very, very thin, as if contrived by an amateur. I could go on with the irregularities, but the point is obvious: Lon became John. The question is, why?"

"You're in areas I haven't even gotten to yet," said Swagger. "You're coming at it from a different angle. See, I'm on the *how*. The way an engineer's mind works, there's no point in proceeding until the how is answered. But you've started on, or you've advanced to, the who."

"You can see what I need," said Adams. "I need that *how*. Just like you need the *who*. So what I'm looking for, basically, is a theory. It's one thing to put together a biography full of mysterious elements that might circumspectly suggest that Lon Scott, a great rifleman and ballistic experimenter, was involved in the Kennedy assassination to some degree. But a lot of people, if the data is manipulated and selected carefully enough, could fit in a similar template. What I need is somebody of extreme capability to put together a coherent narrative, based on what I can uncover about Lon Scott in 1963, as to the *how* part of his engagement. Where would he shoot from? What would he use? How would he get in and out? Who helped him? Remember, he's in a wheelchair, so he needed allies. Here's a provocative fact: I learned that he had a first cousin named Hugh Meachum who was some kind of CIA star at the time. He too died in 1993. But the connection of Lon and Hugh in 1963, if it can be documented, is titillating. But see, it's all meaningless without that first part. How did they do it?"

"You don't have any idea?"

"Well," said Marty smugly, "I can't reveal how I know this yet, but there is some suggestion that another rifle is involved, and it was a Model 70 Winchester. It's more than Lon's engagement over the years with Winchester. I'm talking about a specific Model 70, caliber as yet unknown. I got to thinking: what could you do to either a Model 70 Winchester or a Mannlicher-Carcano to make them compatible? Somehow interchange parts? Take the barrel off one and—"

"Trust me," said Bob, "you are now in my pea patch, and there is a way of doing just that. That's where my thinking is taking me. I'm looking at some kind of deal where a .264-caliber bullet from a Carcano shell was fired from a .264-caliber casing, say .264 Win Mag, 6.5 Swede, maybe a wildcat like a .30-06/6.5, in order to get enough velocity so the brain-shot bullet self-destructed."

"Excellent," said Marty. "Oh, this is so exciting."

"There's an issue of timing, but the reloading angle is interesting. And you say you can link it to a Model 70? That would really tie the bow on it."

"That's it," Adams said. "I'm hoping the answers are in sync with the Warren Commission, not crazily opposed to it. You have to know the hard facts of the Warren Commission. And it all has to fit in that time frame. Nobody has ever come close to that."

Swagger went all engineer on him, hard and practical. "I can see this might work. But what's your pitch?" he asked. "What is it you want from me?"

Adams said, "Well, I'd like to hear your ideas, though, please understand, I'm not forcing you. Your theory is your intellectual property. I am not trying to pry it from you. You decide if you care to share somewhere along the line. What I am suggesting is that we explore working together. I'd get a lawyer to draw up a contract so that each of us is protected. I know you're a cautious man. When you're satisfied, we should have a working session and a frank exchange of evidence. I should also tell you—I alluded to this earlier—I may have a piece of evidence that could nail this absolutely. I won't tell you what it is or where I got it, but it could astound the world if it's what I think it is."

"Is it this mystery Model 70?"

"When I explain it to you, you'll understand what I'm talking about. I can't say more until we've signed contractually. I should add that I have a very good agent in New York, and we are talking about a book as the end product, are we not? I will write it, you will vet it. We may have to bring in another, better writer at some point, properly vetted and legally obligated by contract to us. Is this satisfactory?"

Swagger squinted hard. "I never move fast on anything. You have your lawyer draw up that contract, I'll have mine look at it, and we will see where we are then."

"That works for me," said Adams.

"If that happens, I will settle down and write—I ain't no writer, so 'scratch out' is a better term—all the stuff that comes out when I have a late-night thinking session. I think that will do better than any yakkity-yak session. You'll see that it's taking you where you think it should. We'll proceed from there."

"Absolutely," said Adams. "I don't want to apply pressure, but I think we should have as our goal, going public, by either book or other media, by or on November 22, 2013. The fiftieth anniversary. There's going to be a groundswell of attention then, so we might as well cash in on it. It never hurts to think about marketing."

The next day, Swagger issued his report over expensive coffee, amid prosperous moms and boho kids and various cino-machines, to Memphis.

"Blew me away when he pulled Lon Scott out of the hat."

"It is possible that he came up with Scott independently, without knowledge before of Hugh or 1993. I mean, Lon was real, he left tracks, traces, and that is the area in which Marty Adams is known to be an expert researcher."

"It is. I ain't saying it ain't."

"He seems to be clean. We've looked hard at him. I will direct Neal to look hard again."

"Appreciated. Even a paranoid like me has to admit, though, there ain't no signs of a game."

"Before you go anywhere with Marty, I will have everything on him except his colon X-rays."

"If you get them, I don't want to see them."

"I don't want to see them either. I'll have an intern go over them. That's what interns are for. Meanwhile, where are you? Investigation-wise, I mean. Still having fun?"

"I'm tussling with Red Nine. It's got me up nights. And then when I get real depressed over that, I think about the other riddle I have made no progress on, the deal on the timing. How they did it so fast, how they got Oswald into play when nobody knew until three days before that, by fluke, JFK was going to be driven under his window. Man, they were good."

"Or lucky."

"Or even worse: both."

In this business, bad days are an occupational hazard. I spent several under intense artillery fire at a forward operating base in Vietnam when I was running Phoenix. An Israeli rocket buried me in rubble for six hours in Beirut, ruining a perfectly fine suit. I was detained in 1991 by some obnoxious Chinese border guards for what seemed like years but was only hours. I thought they were going to beat me up because I was Russian, although I wasn't, and if I'd told them who I really was, they would have beaten me up twice as hard, plus allowed me to rot in their prison system for half a century. It was frightening, coming close to melting my phony sangfroid and tarnishing my Yalie style. *Incroyable!*

But no day of my life has been as bad as November 21, 1963. It seemed to last forever, and at the same time it seemed to be over in split seconds, and the next one, although we all had fierce doubts, was upon us so quickly, we couldn't believe it.

We were a grim-faced bunch. I don't think any of us had come to terms with what we were about to do. Some doubts you never put away, and those haunt you—all of us, I mean—for years and years. Now is not the time for the postmortem; I can say only that I plunged ahead on the faith that the change would be for the better, that it would save lives in the hundreds of thousands, white, yellow, north, south, theirs, ours, that it would forestall the anarchy and chaos that I quite rightly had predicted, that I was and we were reluctant assassins, that we believed ourselves to be moral assassins.

Nevertheless, the day was spent in a kind of existential dread, a clammy dryness of breath and persistent wetness of body. Food had no taste or appeal, liquor had too much taste and appeal (and was therefore avoided), and to quote a line from, I think, James Jones in *The Thin Red Line,* "numbly [we] did the necessary." (I trust my posthumous editor will have the energy to run the quote down.)

Alek was out of my control, if he'd ever been in it. There was nothing that could be done at this point. He would do what was required of him well enough to enjoy the success that had eluded him in life, or he would not. I suppose it was possible, and I confess it never occurred to me, that he could have called his "friend" Agent Hotsy of the FBI and turned me in, as part of a scenario by which the red spy (he thought) was nabbed and JFK's life was spared. He'd be a hero then, and money and fame would come of it. In retrospect, I'm glad I didn't concern myself with such nonsense. In the first place, he didn't have the imagination. In the second, truly, he didn't have the disposition: he was a born Dostoyevskian or Conradian subversive, a hard-core assassin or mad bomber. In another century, he'd have carried a bowling-ball bomb with a fizzing fuse under his cape. He wanted to destroy; it was his destiny. He wanted to reach out and atomize the world that had relegated him to bug status, cursed him with reading difficulties, attention difficulties, a sluggish mind, an obsessive streak. It never occurred to me that such a figure would betray me. I was his only hope, his true believer.

My fears about Alek, instead, were practical. Would he remember the rifle? Could he sneak it out of Mrs. Paine's house without either her or Marina seeing it? Could he sneak it into the Book Depository the next day without dropping it in the lunchroom with a clatter, sending its removed screws all over the place? Could he reassemble it, or reassemble it correctly? A black comic vision came to me of him having done everything perfectly, the sight exactly on the target, the perfect trigger squeeze achieved, and SNAP!, nothing, because somehow he'd dropped the bolt and hadn't noticed the firing pin fall out on the floor. Or maybe his ride into work on Friday morning would catch a glimpse of the front sight, and the fellow would say, "Lee, what the hell is that?" and Lee would panic and jump out of the car. With an idiot like him, any number of screwups were possible, and I have to agree with a number of anti-conspiracy commentators who, after the fact, said that no intelligence agency would trust such a moron for an important assignment. They were right, but for the fact that operational necessity sometimes compels gambling on a disreputable character.

I tried to put aside my doubts on poor Alek and proceed with business that I could control.

We met that morning after room-service breakfast in my room. Not a bunch of happy fellows, as I say. Jimmy had things to do: he had to get business cards printed, he had to figure out and fabricate some way to smuggle Lon's silenced rifle into the building, which, among other things, would involve buying a voluminous overcoat whose sleeves would have to be tailored so they didn't hang down ridiculously beyond his fingertips, like a clown's. He wanted to go through the Dal-Tex Building again, to reaffirm his impressions, to memorize all the stairwells and floors and sequences of offices, to check out the locks, to conjure escape routes and hiding places, though if it came to hiding, the jig was already up. Basically, he wanted to apply his professional expertise and mind against the site of the crime again, so there'd be no surprises during the operation. I sensed he had to be alone for that, and also that he wanted to be alone. He was always the lone-wolf type, God bless him.

Off he went. Lon and I decided we should get a good look at Dealey Plaza. I pushed him over to Main, and we traced what would be the president's route, turning right down Houston, flanking the plaza, then halting at Houston and Elm for a good look at Dal-Tex and its big windows with their excellent vantage over the plaza. We then crossed Houston and headed down the gentle slope and curve of Elm in front of the Book Depository. It was all pretty empty, for the plaza wasn't a tourist attraction; why would it be? It offered no grace or beauty, as a Boston or Connecticut or Washington, D.C., park would, no grand leafy trees, just a few stunted oaks, no brilliant gardens, no ponds with swans and ducks. It was basically banal, a greensward plopped absurdly into the middle of nowhere, a rough triangle of grass between three streets, with, for some bizarre reason, a little annex to the north where the civic fathers, in their infinite wisdom, had thrown up some mock Roman Coliseum–style pillars in a semicircle atop a little rise, as grotesque and misguided attempt as any I'd seen at classical grace. Sure, it was *Texas*, but why didn't they hire an architect, for God's sake, not the mayor's wife's drunken brother or whoever perpetrated Dealey upon the world. It was less a park or a plaza than an abandoned field.

We didn't say much, and I didn't want to linger. I was being careful; maybe someone would recall the strange Ivy League prince and his wheelchair-imprisoned pal and report that to the feds, and who knew where that would lead. Or maybe Alek himself, taking fantasy shots from the sixth floor, would catch a glimpse of me, though would he recognize me in a gnarly Brooks Brothers tweed jacket and dark slacks with a pipe in my mouth and my horn-rims firmly in place when all he knew was a fellow in a lumpy GUM suit with sleeves of mismatched length because Natasha had been asleep at her sewing machine in hour fifteen of her sixteen-hour shift back in '55 when she sewed the suit parts together on a Soviet sewing machine the size of a Buick. Then I relaxed. Today Alek would be in Pretendville, riding down the Malecón in Havana in the rear of a well-waxed '47 Caddy next to his god Fidel, waving at the adoring crowds.

I pushed Lon down the street.

We followed the Elm sidewalk down the slope, and I had to pull against the wheelchair to keep it from getting away in gravity's grasp. Lon saw a chance for a joke. "Don't let me slip away, James Bond, and get creamed in traffic. You'll be one pathetic Danger Man tomorrow."

I was glad to hear the humor in his voice, even if it was sardonic. "Pip-pip, old man, I shall do my duty, as Yale instructed me," I said in priss-soprano, kidding the blueblood-agent stereotype of which I was almost a pitch-perfect example.

I didn't get Lon killed, and we passed the Book Depository off on the right, got down the incline, and I stopped us about halfway to the overpass, just past the idiotic Roman folly on the right, and turned Lon 180 degrees back so that he could see Elm Street, the rise of the hill, the two buildings that commanded the angles, the depository and the one from which he'd be shooting—we hoped—the Dal-Tex Building a little behind it across Houston. We were alone on the sidewalk, with the traffic whizzing by us.

"I make it about a hundred yards," I said.

"To which building?" Lon asked.

"The one in the rear. The one we'll probably be in."

From that angle, you couldn't see all of Dal-Tex, only the wall along Elm, though at an extreme angle, and a stretch of the Houston Street facade. Another completely ugly, graceless building. I think it was trying to be "modern." Ugh. It changed personalities after floor two and went to soaring archways encompassing the windows, a flourish that registered as completely idiotic to me. What did they think that did for them? These Texans!

"Suppose we don't get in?" Lon said.

It was as yet unsettled, and it worried me too. I couldn't let that show to Lon. Cousin or not, I had leadership responsibility and had to represent clear-voiced optimism.

"Oh, he'll do it. Jimmy's the best. He's very clever. And if he doesn't, you've had a nice trip to Dallas at government expense and gained a story so fascinating, it's a shame you'll never be able to tell it."

"I can't believe I'm here, looking at this, talking about this," he said.

"I can't believe it either. But here we are. Do you see any difficulties in making the shot?"

"No. At that range, with a velocity a little over three thousand feet per second, it won't drop an inch. The downward angle won't play because it isn't far enough, and the buildings as well as the dip will cancel any wind effects. Fish in a barrel. It's technically point-blank, except you don't know what 'point-blank' really means, and I don't have much interest in explaining it now. Trust me. The bullet will hit what it's aimed at, and it will destroy what it's aimed at, even as it destroys itself. And then we enter the Lyndon Johnston era, God help us."

"Johnson. Not Johnston."

"Is this a quiz?"

"No, I'm being a jerk because I'm nervous."

"Let's get out of here. I've seen enough. Can you push me up the hill, or shall we wait for a cab here?"

"I'm fine."

I pushed him up the hill. November 21, 1963, sunny but breezy, in the fifties, two men in jackets and ties, one pushing the other up a slight hill in a wheelchair. And that was that for recon, planning, rehearsal, and psychological preparation. We dealt with the issues as they came up, that was all, and improvised our way past any obstacles.

That night we had a final meeting in my room. Both Lon and I were eager to hear what Jimmy had been up to.

"I got this overcoat"—he held up a tan gabardine model, single-breasted, light, perfect for the weather and so banal that it would fit in anywhere in America—"and had a Chinese lady shorten the sleeves. Here, look."

He threw the thing on. It hung well, even if the shoulder seams were a little off the shoulder, a few inches down the arm. Who would notice? More important, you could hide a tank in its folds.

"Okay," he said, "here's the interesting part. Question: how do we get a forty-inch, eight-pound rifle with scope and silencer into a building without anyone noticing it?"

"Something more sophisticated and more secure, please, than wrapping it in a paper bag," I said.

"You're going to have to break it down, obviously," said Lon. "And I'm going to have to show you how to reassemble it. It isn't just screwing in screws. You've got to set the three screws at a starting point, then tighten them three turns apiece in order, to a certain total for each hole. You've got to line up the slots with a piece of tape. That way, you preserve my zero."

"He's good at doing things," I told Lon, nodding to Jimmy. "If you show him how to do it, he'll do it exactly that way."

"Mr. Scott," said Jimmy, "I think I can manage. I'm not as stupid as I look."

"It's okay, Jimmy," Lon said. "I didn't mean anything snotty. I'm just nervous."

"Me too," said Jimmy, who looked as nervous as a stainless-steel rat trap, and we both had a tension-breaking laugh over such a ridiculous concept. Jimmy could talk his way into the Kremlin if he had to. "I also had the Chinese lady make me this," he said.

He took a roll of material out of the coat pocket and unfurled it on the bed. It was about six feet long, four inches wide, and the woman had sewn pockets at either end, with crude but robust stitching meant to support weight.

"I throw it around my neck like a scarf," Jimmy said. He did that so each end hung down the side of his body. "Now, in the left pocket, I slide in the rifle stock, with trigger guard and screws Scotch-taped in place and also the silencer. In the right pocket, I slide in the action, barrel, and scope. The pieces are hanging down my sides, halfway down my thighs, the metal parts a bit heavier than the wood, the whole thing awkward but secure. The lady was a good seamstress. Then I throw the coat on, and the coat being much longer than the ends of the scarf are, to my knees, it covers both completely. It's so voluminous that nothing shows through the material. I just look like a businessman about his job on a coolish fall day in the great downtown trading center of Dallas, Texas. As long as I don't run, squat, bump up against anybody or anything, I'm all right. Remember, my exposure will be short. Just the walk over from the car, the elevator upstairs, the walk down the hall, and one second to get in. I can get the rifle together in thirty seconds, you boys arrive, we open the window. Then we leave and go home and watch the rumpus on the television."

"You must have brass balls, Irishman," said Lon.

"Learned in the bog, sir," said Jimmy.

"Tell me the rest, will you?" Lon said. "I don't get it. I need to believe in it, and bloody Hugh here was so gung-ho and excited, I couldn't follow him. I'm jumpy. I have to hear it from its author and know it's going to work."

"Yes sir, Mr. Scott," said Jimmy.

"It's a very good plan," I said. "But we do need input. We need to know what to look for."

Lon shook his head sadly.

"Tomorrow morning," explained Jimmy, "around ten, I'll show up at the Dal-Tex Building dressed in my best suit, my hair all pomaded fine-like, my eyes twinkly, my demeanor all charming Irish boyo. I will go into six offices on each of the fourth, fifth, and sixth floors of the Dal-Tex Building, those that front Elm as it nears Houston, and those on Houston as it looks down Elm. From any of those offices, Elm, as it passes the Book Depository and Dealey on its way to the triple overpass, is easily reached from the angle we need.

"In each office—I know what they are, I'll spare you the details, but they're garment wholesalers who move goods to Texas retailers in and around Dallas, some ladies' lingerie, some men's haberdashery, a tie specialist, two shoe lines, the rag trade, in short—and I'll introduce myself to the girl and present her with my card."

He reached into his pocket and pulled out a stack of cards.

JAMES DELAHANTY O'NEILL

"JIMMY"

REPRESENTING

PREMIERE FASHIONS, BOSTON, MASS. 02102

DA9-3090

TELEX 759615 PREMIERE

"Then I hit her with my patter. Jimmy O'Neill, down from Boston, representing Premiere Fashions, purveyors of fine suitings, ladies' wear and lingerie, and gents' haberdashery. There is such a place, all will know it, but it's not in this market. My pitch: we're thinking of expanding, going national with the fine economy we're experiencing, and I'm on a look-see tour to gauge the interest and was wondering if I could get a minute with the boss man to see if he'd be likely to take on a new line. In all instances, the answer should be no, not today. The reason is that the president's coming to town, and we're closing down the office from noon till two to go out and wave at the great young fellow. Darn, I say laughingly, my luck! I've seen him a thousand times in Boston, even in bars and restaurants, but I pick a day to come to Dallas, where nobody's seen him, when he himself is here. She laughs and ushers me out.

"Of course, I'm scouting. First, will the office be closed? Second, how good is the angle to the street, particularly since we're guessing the idiot will find some way to miss his first shot at the corner and Mr. Scott will have to pick it up as the limo goes down Elm and that little hill. Third, how big is the staff, in case there are any Republicans who might stay behind because they're not about to admit a Democrat Irishman has become president. Fourth, what kind of lock's on the door, and will it be easy to pop if I come back. Fifth— What's fifth, you tell me. That's what I need to know."

"The windows," said Lon. "We couldn't tell from the street how they opened. We need an old-fashioned sliding window, up and down. No foldouts, because their hinges don't let them fall low enough to be out of the line of fire."

"Very good, sir," said Jimmy.

"Books," said Lon. "I've got to stabilize the rifle on something other than my lap. A heavy board that slides across and is supported on the arms of the chair would be best, but I can't ask for that, I know. You'd never get it in. The best thing would be some heavy books to pack onto my lap. I'll rest my elbows on them. That's a request, not a demand. If it comes to it, we can secure the chair, and I can make that shot offhand. I still shoot offhand, sitting offhand, and I'm damned good, but the books would be helpful."

"Books it'll be, then," said Jimmy.

"Finally, you said fourth, fifth, and sixth floors?"

"I did."

"I'm thinking fifth is the preferable by far. I need as little angle downward as possible. Not for the shooting but for my placement in the room. If I'm on the sixth floor, I'll have to be close to the window and maybe projecting the muzzle of the rifle beyond it in order to get the low angle. Not good, especially as it lets the muzzle of the suppressor out into the air, and the sonic boom won't be contained in the room."

"Is that it, Lon?" I asked.

"I can't think of anything else," Lon said.

"All right," said Jimmy, "let me sum up how I see it happening. I find the most suitable of the offices that matches everything or nearly everything. I tell you by telephone which it is. Then I go back to the hotel, and around noon, I slip the rifle in its straps about my neck and cover it with the overcoat. I amble back through the crowds heading to the plaza to see the young president, head down Elm, and casually dip into the Dal-Tex Building. Should get there around twelve ten. No problem, though there is a busy sheriff's station to the right of the lobby, but it's a fine public building of commerce, with constant, unmonitored, in-out. I take the elevator to the proper floor. I'm guessing the place is largely deserted. I get to the office, pop the lock, slip inside. Quickly, I break out the rifle parts and assemble the rifle as Mr. Scott has shown me.

"You fellows hit the building at about twelve twenty. By that time most of the crowd has gathered and is awaiting His Highness. Mr. Meachum pulls Mr. Scott's chair up the three steps and into the lobby, and again takes the elevator to the proper floor. Down the hall to the office. It's open, and you slip in, time about twelve twenty-five. No need to rush, but we all know what's got to happen. I'll have cleared a space near the window and the rifle, loaded and assembled, will be there."

"By the way," said Lon, "the cartridge is too long to feed up through the magazine. You'll have to carefully thread the rim into the bolt, then slide it forward. Only one. No need or time for a second. I'll show you later."

"Got that, sir. Then Mr. Meachum pushes Mr. Scott to the shooting position, and I pile and arrange the books in his lap. We hear the roar of the crowd as the motorcade comes down Main a block over, turns down Houston, then turns again down Elm. Mr. Meachum raises the window—"

"Say," I said, "maybe it would be better if you opened the window first thing. That way, there's no chance of somebody across the street being attracted to the moving window and then seeing evidence of the shot. I'm guessing even with the silencer, there'll be some burst of gas."

"That's good," said Lon. "It won't be much, and it'll be so light that I doubt it'll be observable, but why take the chance?"

"So be it," said Jimmy. "The second the job is done, down comes the window."

"Shouldn't he do that last?" Lon asked. "Anybody who hears a trace of the noise might have oriented to Dal-Tex and could catch the motion."

"That's good, sir," said Jimmy. "Consider it done. Anyhow, I remove rifle and books from Mr. Scott, and Mr. Meachum wheels him out, down the corridor, and I'm guessing out of the building within two minutes, well before the police can have gotten over to seal it or investigate, though I'm sure they'll be concentrating on our friend in the next building who's making all the noise. In any event, it's a man in a wheelchair and his attendant, who'd suspect them of mischief? Off you go, in whichever direction seems feasible, until you're well clear of the mess. Possibly you stop off for lunch. Then back to the hotel.

"As for me, I break down the rifle, repack it in the whatever-you-want-to-call-it, throw on the coat, replace the books, close that pesky window as mentioned, and slip out, using my toys to lock the door. I'm out of the building a few minutes after you."

"I thought of one more thing," said Lon. "It just occurred to me. I don't think it matters in the hallways, because there's a lot of traffic, but if you can, the office has to have linoleum or bare wood. See, I'm a heavy guy, and the wheelchair leaves tracks. If they get back tomorrow and someone notices these mysterious wheelchair tracks on the floor, again, questions may be raised, maybe, I don't know how investigations work, maybe—"

"It's good," I said. "The tracks, that's very good. Jimmy, also try to find an office with thirteen-year-old Glenlivet Gold. Not the Glenlivet Red, but the Gold. I might want a highball during the—"

Everybody laughed, and so for the first time, I felt slightly optimistic.

I didn't feel like breakfast that morning, but after a sleepless night, I had to get some air. Around 8 a.m. I left the hotel and took a little walk around downtown. It was dowdy, even shabby, since the miracle of Dallas with its steel and chrome skyline was years off. Absent the glow of the flying red neon horse fifteen or so stories up the Magnolia Oil Company building, it just looked crummy. The sky threatened rain, but the fresh air felt good to my lungs. The temperature would rise a bit, into the high fifties or low sixties, and these trees, at least, had lost most of their leaves, which blew about in the skittish wind. In those days, everyone raked their leaves, then piled them at the curb and burned them, so the odor of burning leaves was ever-present during the autumn; I tasted it as well, enough to give the air texture and remind me of boyhood days before I got myself into the president-killing business. (Remember the coup in Saigon? I'd killed other presidents.)

I stopped at the Walgreens soda fountain, read the *Dallas Morning News* over a cup of coffee, and listened as the Texans all about me gibbered excitedly about the president's upcoming visit. The main thrust seemed to be whether or not to go to the parade route and see the handsome young man and his beautiful wife. There was also some annoyance at an ad that had appeared in the morning paper, in which someone accused the president of being soft on communism. The Texans in this corner of Dallas found the ad in poor taste, and more than a few of them groused about it.

I kept to myself, engaging no one, even if my tweed sport coat and red tie made me stand out a bit from them. They were so excited, they didn't notice. I thought I had a white shirt left in my room and decided to change into it, and to a duller tie. I wished I'd brought a dark Brooks Brothers suit, but I'd not given much thought to wardrobe when I packed for the trip.

I walked back to the hotel, though chance took me by a hatter's, on Main, a few blocks over. I went inside. I looked around, and a fellow came to wait on me. We had a pleasant chat, and I bought a mild little cowboy hat, gray for fall, with more brim than I was used to and with slightly more dramatic curl. I knew I would feel foolish in it, but the trick to wearing a hat is to pretend that you are not wearing a hat. The idea was to lower my profile and fit into the hat-rich Dallas culture, where a short-brim fedora, as I usually wore, would be far more noticeable than the demure cowpoke's lid I now capped my head with.

Feeling more camouflaged, I walked back to the hotel and went upstairs and lay down for a bit. There'd been no calls. I was assuming Jimmy had already left and was doing his jobs, and that Lon was resting. I also assumed that our pigeon, Alek, had managed to get out to Mrs. Paine's, retrieved his bag of "curtain rods," gotten back to Dallas without spilling them all over the highway, and was on his way to work. I was never a praying type of fellow, and it seemed wrong to invoke celestial support for a deed so foul, but I couldn't help myself from looking skyward and muttering a little something in case someone was listening on the upper floors.

At 10:45, I showered (again!), changed into my white shirt and dull brown tie, and sat and waited. And waited. And waited. At 11:18, the phone rang.

I picked it up.

It was Jimmy.

"Got it!" he said. "A little high, but everything else is perfect. Office 712, the seventh floor, right turn from the elevator, take the only left, and it's on the right. Great lines down Elm."

"Got it," I said, and headed downstairs, pipe in mouth, horn-rims on, junior-cowpoke headgear firmly mounted. Lon was waiting, and I nodded at him.

"Nice hat," he said.

It turned out we had little to say to each other beyond that exchange. If I looked as bad as he did, we were in trouble, hat or no hat. Then again, I had the normal Lon to use as baseline, the ruddy, vivid, sometimes outrageous paragon of stoicism and mordant humor, not this pale, solemn corpse. I could feel myself in the same colorless shroud of skin, with the same dryness of breath, the same sense of dread and doom all about, the presentiment of failure, tragedy, utter destruction of self, and all the self-love he had built. Plus, I was wearing a stupid hat! I was so damned heroic, I made myself sick! I pressed on, noble Yale champ that I am.

I had decided to spare myself the agony of pushing Lon to the site, a twelve-or-so block ordeal made more difficult in those unenlightened days by the absence of ramps or rails for the disabled. But getting Lon into the cab was never easy. You had to sort of roll-push him from his chair to the seat and wait until he squirmed and pulled himself upward; then you folded the wheelchair, slid it into the front seat, and went around to the other rear seat. For some reason, he seemed especially heavy that morning; perhaps he was involuntarily resisting me, willing himself into sheer deadweight, above the waist as well as below it.

"Where to, gentlemen?" asked the cabbie when, huffing and puffing, I finally got in.

I gave him the address of a medical building on Poydras, just beyond Main.

"You know, there'll be traffic there," he said. "JFK's in town, he's coming down Main in a motorcade, and it'll all be jammed up with viewers."

Damn! I hadn't thought of that! Fool, jerk, dolt! Agh! What a ludicrous end to the operation if the assassins got stuck in traffic.

"I realize that," I said. "That's why we're early. Jim's appointment isn't until one."

"One-*thirty*," said Lon, picking up on the game.

"Off we go, then," sang the cabbie. "No problem."

The cab whizzed along, did seem to slow almost to a stop on a main stem, but the driver cleverly plotted a new course and got us to Poydras well in advance of our time. I never even breathed hard during the trip.

He pulled up outside the building, and I got out to unload the wheelchair and Lon. The driver called, "Need any help, sir? Glad to pitch in." They are so polite in Texas.

"Thanks, I'm used to it," I said.

Indeed, Lon somehow willed himself to be lighter. I don't know how he managed to vanquish the laws of physics, but it seemed he had obliterated a good twenty pounds of matter from the universe, and I fairly tossed him into the chair. Then I paid the driver, $1.75 plus a quarter tip, and turned to wheel Lon up the steps to the North Dallas Medical Arts Building. Damn, the driver seemed to linger, waiting for me to call for help to pull Lon up the steps, but then another fare slipped into the cab, and off they went.

I wheeled Lon the half block down Poydras and turned him left—that is, west, if it matters—and slowly down Elm a block to the Dal-Tex Building. Meanwhile, the threat of rain had cleared itself up; a broad, cloudless Texas sky vaulted overhead, full of brightness. In the opening between Dal-Tex and the County Records Building on our side of the street, I could see the crowd gathered in front of the Book Depository; it seemed like they were three or four deep already, and there were batches of people across the street, on the grass of the plaza. I wonder if it was as merry as it seemed or if that's my memory playing tricks, filtering through the knowledge of the event that I knew was about to occur.

I suppose that was one America there, gathered gaily in the sunlight. You could hear indistinct crowd noises, a kind of purr or mutter from the breast of the mob, somehow fueled by happiness, glamour, hope, good thoughts of self and president and country. I knew I was about to take all that away and didn't feel particularly great about it, but I felt—I say this over and over, do you think I'm overcompensating a bit?—I felt that in the long run, when things settled down, even if we never healed our wounds over the young man slain, our collective future would be brighter and fewer boys would come home in boxes or wheelchairs.

"Hugh," Lon said, "I've got a great idea. Let's not do this. Let's take a cab to the airport and fly to Tijuana. We'll spend the next six weeks drinking margaritas and screwing whores, even if I can't screw anything. How does that sound?"

"You can't screw whores because of a tragedy called paraplegia, and I can't screw whores because of a tragedy called marriage," I said. "Even if we both dream of whores, that's the end of that."

"You're right. I guess we ought to go ahead."

"Besides," I said, "we can't find any cabs. This isn't Manhattan, you know."

At Elm and Houston, we got a good look at the celebration. More and more people seemed to be gathering and spreading across the grass of the plaza as if it were some racecourse infield or county fair. The sun was bright, and I could see hats, cameras, and sunglasses and feel those positive feelings in the air. From pop music: "good vibrations." It felt more like a circus or ball game than a political event, but I suppose that had to do with the unique identities of Jack and Jackie, who were more like movie stars than politicians.

When the light changed, I pushed Lon across Elm, then we turned up the street, to the entrance of the Dal-Tex Building. I checked my watch. It was 12:07 and felt a little early. But it wasn't easy going up Elm, with the crowd continuing to rush down to get a good place to view the Kennedys, and a few times I had to pull back or turn sharply to avoid colliding with anybody.

When I got to the three broad steps that led to the entrance of the Dal-Tex Building, it was 12:15. I turned Lon outward and pulled him up the steps, then, evading this fellow and that, pivoted him and steered him to the main entrance. Luckily there were no revolving doors, a royal ordeal for anyone in a wheelchair. Someone held the door for us, and I slid into the dark lobby. To the right, behind a thick window and illuminated from within by fluorescent lighting, full of bustle, was an office of the sheriff of Dallas County. I could see a few uniformed deputies inside, but mainly, it was women at desks with typewriters, talking on phones or fill-

ing out official documents. There was a receiving counter, and a few people stood in line to be waited on by a sergeant. No one in there showed
the slightest awareness that in a few minutes, the president of the United
States would come by in a Lincoln limo, waving happily to the folks,
breathing the sweet air, and enjoying the lush sunshine one last time.

I got to the elevators, punched up, and waited till a door opened.
A few late stragglers were there, and I pulled Lon to the side to let
them out, as they straightened hats or pulled ties tighter or shrugged
into jackets against the slight chill in the air. When the car was empty,
I backed Lon in, and the doors were just about shut when a woman
ducked in. She smiled, punched—ah—three, and turned and asked me
for a floor. "Six," I said, because lying was natural to my state of being.
Again: overcaution, a sign of paranoia, fear, lack of confidence.

The three of us rose in silence, and she got out at three, smiling,
turning to say politely (as usual), "Good afternoon," and I think we both
muttered something. Then I quickly hit seven to make sure the elevator
continued its ascent after the stop on six.

At seven, I pushed Lon out. The hall was darkish, empty, with no
sign of human buzz or hum anywhere. Most people had gone to the
plaza to see President Kennedy.

I pushed Lon down the hall, watching the signs on or at the door-
ways slide by, watching the numbers climb, until at last we came to an
intersection and turned to the left, down another, better-lit corridor (the
offices to the right, behind opaque glass, had exterior windows).

FUNTASTIC FASHIONS
MARY JANE JUNIORS
712

I pushed the door and stepped into the two-room office suite that
was the headquarters of Funtastic Fashions, apparently, from the idealized pictures on the wall, some kind of line for naive young women
whom you might find in the farm belt, all wholesome gingham and

flower-patterned jumpers and dresses in heavy patterns, as worn, in the artist's sketches, by pictograms representing the perfect, happy, well-adjusted junior miss. Odd how some details stick in mind: in one, Our Heroine was running with a dog, and the dog reminded me of a neighbor's dog from some distant past. I could remember the dog, though not the neighbor or the city or the year. But the dog rang a bell.

I pulled the door softly shut, hearing it click locked, and pushed Lon across wood flooring beyond the secretary's desk. The name on the door to the boss's office was simple: Mr. Goldberg. It meant nothing to me; nor did the pictures on the wall of a middle-aged fellow who looked to be Jewish, with a wife and three children, all five beaming at the success Mr. Goldberg had made in Dallas, Texas. I slid Lon into the boss's office, a square, high-ceilinged wood-floored room full of light, with an overhead fan rotating sluggishly with a slight hum. It was dominated by two large windows, and immediately across the way, I could see the upper floor of the Texas Book Depository. I pushed Lon to the window, and as we approached, the angles widened and revealed, in all its detail and seething mass of witnesses along both curbs, the spectacle of Elm Street trending left as it descended the gentlest of inclines, shielded at our end by the canopy of a few oak trees, yielding to the broadness of the plaza, green in bright sun, dotted with last-minute scurriers trying to get into at least the third rank along the curb for maximum proximity to the glamour couple. From our vantage, we could not see the grassy knoll, we could not see the amphitheater, the pillars, the marble benches, all the flourishes of Athens on a good day in 300 B.C., that the Texan city fathers had constructed there. But we could see every square inch of Elm Street once it emerged from the trees.

Jimmy had assembled the rifle, raised the window a few inches, and laid out a few large swatch books on Mr. Goldberg's desk for Lon's lap. I glanced at my watch. It was 12:24.

When I pushed Lon to the place where he'd determined to shoot from, we had our inevitable crisis. What do they say—no plan survives contact with the enemy?

The issue was height. In order to assure that minimum noise would escape from the room, Lon told us we had to be as far back from the window as possible, even with the German suppressor jerry-rigged to the muzzle. If it extended beyond the window, it would admit the report to the outer atmosphere and might attract attention, or at least curious eyes. The point was to contain as much of the attenuated report as possible within the confines of the room, where it would be deadened by the noise-absorption qualities of the walls and furnishings and by the buzz of the ceiling fan swishing away overhead. Lon would shoot from his chair but as far back from the window as possible while still having vantage on the target. The problem: at no place in the room would Lon be high enough to get the necessary angle over the sill!

We stood stupidly. Brilliant Hugh had fouled up again! It never occurred to me, nor had it occurred to Jimmy, why the fifth floor was preferable. It was too late to get down a floor or two, where the angles would have been more welcoming.

"Can we get you standing, Lon?" I asked.

"Not without my knee braces, which are in Roanoke."

"We have to raise him," I concluded.

It was Jimmy who remembered the swatch books originally destined for Lon's lap. At least three inches deep, they contained fabric samples. He brought four of them over. "We can lift him up on these," he said.

He set two down, and we labored to lift the wheelchair's right tire, not an easy task, though Lon helped by shifting his weight accordingly. Then the other one. Lon plus chair was really heavy, and this lift was no picnic. I could feel my veins bulging with blood as I gave it all my strength, but it was probably Jimmy who did the bulk of the work. Lon was up high enough.

"Yeah," he said, "good angle. But it's crooked. The left one is higher than the right one. I can compensate, but—"

"I got it," said Jimmy.

Quickly, he peeled off his nice new overcoat, folded it into quarters, and bent to the wheel. I did my part, again using all of my muscles, and

Jimmy got the coat wedged between the rubber and the book. I saw that the tire had left a black mark where it pressed into the gabardine.

"Dry cleaning's on me!" I said.

"Much better," Lon said. It brought him to the level where he had the angle above the sill but beneath the bottom of the window. "Lock the brakes."

As I bent to do so, we heard a rise in sound; it seemed that the motorcade had hit lower Main a block away, and when the magic Lincoln passed, it unleashed a roar of inchoate human energy, cheers and yells, yes, but also the collective sighs and deep breaths of the enchanted. Their prince had come. I knew that Kennedy was but a minute or so away.

"Here," said Jimmy, handing Lon the rifle. It was a long, sleek thing, not like Alek's piece of battered military junk, not like the dangerous army guns, the carbines and BARs and tommy guns I'd seen in Vietnam, not like the red burp guns, with their ugly, ventilated cooling housings and their Mob-style drums featured in every statue in Russia. I had to say that the rifle had an aristocratic grace, and in some odd way, it seemed appropriate to the young prince's demise. Lon had told me it was a Winchester Model 70, and I knew that he and his late father had enjoyed a long and mutually satisfying relationship with the company. At one point, Lon's father had been presented with a rifle called the Tenth Black King, in some awesome caliber, called that because the American walnut of the stock was so bloodred that it looked black in certain lights, and when Winchester wanted to give "Presentation Guns" to some who were prominent in the gun world, they had their custom shop build an edition of ten, all called Black Kings. Both Lon's father and Lon used that rifle—which turned out to have unusual powers of accuracy— to win or place highly in national rifle competitions.

This one was not customized, at least not by Winchester. Lon had done some work on it, lightening the trigger, "bedding" the action, which I understand to be coating the interior, where the metal of the action sits in the inlay of the stock, with a kind of fiberglass or epoxy so that the contact between the surfaces is 100 percent even, and no odd stress from irregularities is transferred to the rifle, affecting the accuracy. On the whole, the thing was beautiful, a graceful orchestration of tubes supported in a slice of burnished wood, with a slight streamline that seemed to have it leaning forward, like a thoroughbred at full extension, muscles cut and the entire beast captured in a kind of forward bound.

A long tube, black and shiny, was secured to the action above the bolt by two stout metal rings, and at a point on the scope's length between the rings lay an administrative housing, the site of a vertical and a horizontal turret by which the scope could be tuned for maximum accuracy. I was close; I happened to note the white lettering above the horizontal turret, and it read simply J. UNERTL. What distinguished this rifle from any other I'd seen was the German suppressor, the *Schall-daempfer* Type 3, as Lon called it. It too was tubular, and locked over the muzzle by means of a pivoting lever cranked to the closed position. The genius of German engineering! It was surprisingly stubby, under a foot long, looking like a steel water bottle screwed to the muzzle, and much discolored and tarnished from military use.

Lon handled the gun with extraordinary ease, I must say. His face deadpan, he accepted it and mounted it to his shoulder, one hand at the comb, the index finger suspended on the stock above the trigger, not touching the trigger. His other flew to the the end of the stock, which he acquired and used as leverage, thrusting the rifle back hard to shoulder, now supported by two elbows. This was the holding position. Because we'd used the swatch books to elevate him, they were not available for lap duty. He'd have to shoot offhand. I thought, For want of a nail, the shoe is lost, for want of a shoe, the horse is lost, for want of a horse, the battle is lost, and imagined the chain of catastrophe that could undo us.

Nevertheless, he was an elegant construction, slightly canted, the rifle and man solid, immutable, bent forward a bit under muscular tension as if in sprinter's blocks, the slight vibration of his slow and easy breaths the only sign of life. The rifle was locked in his arms, which were resting on his elbows on his dead legs.

I positioned myself at the window, immediately adjacent to the opening. Craning to the left, I could see the Houston-Elm intersection as I heard the roar rolling toward us like a wave. I saw a Dallas police sedan and then . . . nothing. I guessed he was some sort of advance car a half mile or so out. It seemed a minute passed, and then a white sedan came down the street, leading the parade. Three motorcycles followed, then five more in some kind of formation, then another white sedan, and finally, the large black Lincoln, with its cargo of imminent tragedy open to the crowd. It was flanked by motorcycle policemen, and we watched as it pulled wholly into view. It looked more like a black lifeboat than a car, a huge thing, with a driver and guard in the front seat, then behind them, though considerably lower, as if squatting, a male-female couple I took to be Governor and Mrs. Connally, and then Jack Kennedy himself, and next to him, in a pink pillbox hat, his wife.

His reddish hair glinted in the sunlight. Even from almost eighty yards and without binoculars, I could make out the ruddiness of his skin and could tell that all the lines of his face were pulling his mouth up into a smile, and at that moment it incongruously struck me that he was quite a handsome man. He was waving with one hand but only intermittently, and if I read his body posture in that split second, it was one of relaxation. The man was campaigning and happy.

The limo reached the hard left turn onto Elm from Houston just below me. At that point, it was out of sight to Lon, but I leaned forward and pressed my forehead against the pane. I watched as the car slowed almost to a halt and began its slow, majestic pivot toward its new direction. I could not breathe. This was Alek's shot, his moment to enter history and send us all home absolved of any guilt.

Nothing happened.

I don't know what the idiot was doing up there, but it wasn't shooting. Silence. Obviously, some kind of failure, as per all anticipation. That put us right back on the fulcrum of events, the little creep with his cowardice, his incompetence, his stupidity. Agh!

The great car turned slowly left and began its descent down Elm, sliding down the slight undulation that led to the triple overpass, which moved it left in Lon's sights, but gently, not radically. The public feet away on either side, all madly waving and cheering, you could see the excitement, the sparkle or glitter of crowd passion that you see at key moments of big ball games. The car was fully oriented toward Elm but just feet beyond the axis of the turn when Alek managed to fire his first shot.

We heard the *crack!* In my peripheral, I saw Lon react, not a jerk or a spasm but a tight, controlled lurch. He kept his discipline, though, and didn't lose his hold on the rifle, which was still. He seemed calm. I knew he would fire at a specific point, in seconds, waiting for the target to climb into his crosshairs, and would make final mini-corrections before coordinating his shot with Kennedy's arrival at the point of impact designator.

I locked my eyes on Kennedy and the car. Nothing stirred, no reaction, no sudden dive for cover, nothing. Had they noticed? I thought: Maybe it's not Alek, maybe it's a backfire or firecracker.

Then a second *crack!* rang out, and though the car had traveled a good twenty-five yards or so in the interval between shots, I could make out no reaction this time either. Possibly some movement, but nothing radical or reflexive as a bullet impact might have unleashed.

The fool missed twice. Of course! Idiot! Idiot! A burst of rage knifed through me. The little moron! God, what a fool he was; never did anything right in his life. He was struggling to catch up from the blown easy shot, was rushing, shooting poorly.

"He missed. Lon—" I said.

Again I pivoted instinctively, enough to see the fluid grace with which Lon raised the rifle, right elbow locked up for maximum support, canting the living part of his body slightly against the dead part, his head utterly still and locked on the opening in the telescopic sight. He was a portrait of stillness in motion, a discipline acquired over a hundred thousand rifle shots, the ball of his finger exquisitely balanced against the blade of the trigger. The next two, three seconds seemed to hang in eternity, although possibly that's a conceit I impose from memory, for dramatic purposes, to make the tale more compelling, even if the only soul I've ever told it to is myself.

Feu.

The rifle leaped, but only slightly, in his hand, while his head stayed immobile to the scope and his trigger finger followed through to pin that lever to the back of the guard. It produced an oddly attenuated report, something like a book being dropped on a wood floor with weird tones of vibration, maybe a poke and a buzz to the inner ear but nothing sharp and percussive like a gunshot. You would expect more, would you not? It was a phenomenon of vibration, this key moment in history, a thrum or cello note extended by a master bowman. Yet in the instantaneous aftermath, I thought I heard Alek's third shot. Could they have been simultaneous? No, because then I wouldn't have heard both. It was as if Alek had fired a few hundredths of a second after Lon. We didn't realize then, but it was the biggest break we were going to get that day.

Jimmy, unperturbed, was in charge in another second. "All right, fellows," he crooned, "out you go now, while I tidy up here."

Lon, stone-faced, handed the rifle to Jimmy as I knelt and raised the two brakes. It took another second for Jimmy to single-handedly ease Lon's chair from the swatch books and pull the coat off, and then I had him turned around and was beelining to the door.

"Don't rush, sir," called Jimmy. "You've nothing to hide, remember."

I took a quick peek back and saw that Jimmy already had the rifle half disassembled and was working on the third screw. Then the door closed, and I was in the outer office. I sped to that door, and it locked behind me with a click and we were in the hallway. I pushed down it, trying to control my breathing. Finally, I had to ask. "Good hit?"

"Don't ask me what I saw through the scope, Hugh. Ever."

We reached the elevator, I punched the down button and waited an eternity for it to arrive and the doors to open. I shoved Lon in, hit 1, and listened as the doors closed behind me.

When the elevator doors opened and I pushed Lon into the lobby of the Dal-Tex Building, it was as if we'd entered a new America. I say that knowing how trite it sounds, and then I worry again that my memory is playing tricks on me and has added a drama that wasn't there.

Maybe. I still say it was like a massive change in the weather. I'll argue till death that the color had been drained from the day and the atmosphere had turned sepia. I'll claim that all the human specimens we observed were in a state of stunned shock, mouths and faces slack, posture discipline unhinged, a tone of disbelief bleeding toward numbness and shutdown everywhere. It was only about ninety seconds after Lon's shot, and no one had processed what happened yet, although all knew, almost instantaneously, that something, something horrible, had transpired.

Then, as we watched, it transformed instantly into panic, buzz, dread, gibbering, stupidity. People couldn't shut up. An insistent yammer began, a mutter with high notes, inflections, voices piping or breaking or losing steam in a flood of phlegm. The lobby was not crowded, but everyone began yapping at each other, along the lines of "He was shot?"

"In the head?"

"Oh my God, is he dead?"

"Who the hell could have done it?"

"Was it the Russians? Did the Commies get JFK?"

"Where did the shots come from?"

"The Book Depository? Are you kidding? *The Book Depository!*"

"Who would do such a terrible thing?"

Nobody paid the two of us any attention, and I pushed Lon to the door, rotated 180 degrees to back out and pull him through, got that done, and emerged into sunlight, heat, panic, incredible motion, pandemonium everywhere, random, brain-dead movement, and people talking insanely among themselves.

I saw only one man moving with purpose, a Dallas policeman who raced to the building, almost knocking me down getting by, and bulled his way inside. He was quick, that man, and I don't know if it was by official directive or his own decision, but he'd understood that if the Book Depository was the probable origin point for the shooting, other buildings with access to Elm Street should be sealed for investigation.

He'd missed us, or perhaps scanned us from afar and dismissed us because of Lon's disability. As for Jimmy, still inside, I felt confident that he could outthink and outmaneuver a Dallas policeman any day of his life.

I gingerly pushed Lon to the edge of the steps and began the ordeal of easing him down into the roiling crowd, which, drawn to tragedy exactly as had been the thousands who'd lined up to see the bullet-riddled corpses of Bonnie and Clyde, surged toward the plaza to see, to know, to feel, to bear witness, to be a part of what all felt was a calamitous day for our country.

I was trying to figure which way to go, as fighting the crowd with Lon wouldn't be easy. I'd pretty much decided to get across Elm, divert to Houston, hit Main, and head up until the crowds had thinned, then cut to Commerce to get us back to the hotel.

Then the left wheelchair tire caught on something on the middle step. I bent awkwardly to see what it was (a chunk of loosened cement that had worked out of the joinery between the stone slabs) and was readjusting the chair by pulling it back a couple of inches when, in my peripheral vision, I saw Alek.

I happened to be tilted away from him; I was looking down and hunched and twisted to jigger the chair free, and perhaps that is why he didn't see me. Was that luck? I suppose. The other truth is, he probably wouldn't have recognized me under the cowboy hat I wore and under the pall of doom he wore.

He was the betrayed man. For an instant, but only an instant, I felt a mote of sympathy for him. He'd been looking through the scope, trying to get on target for his third shot, when he'd seen what only Lon had seen—though within months, thanks to Mr. Zapruder, the world would see it. Alek, with his low, weaselly cunning, would know in that instant he was tricked and abandoned. Stupendous fury must have overcome him, replaced in seconds with abject, sickening panic. Along with thoughts along the line of: Fucked again, failed again, now I'm really cooked. Or maybe there'd been a twinge of ego gratification in what had to be his impending destruction: at last he was important enough to betray. His paranoid fantasy had at last come true. He was that crazy. Somehow he'd gotten downstairs and out of the building before it was sealed. Now he had no place to go, he had no escape plan, he knew the Wagoneer wouldn't be waiting at Houston and Pacific, that it wouldn't be long before a canvass was taken at the depository and his absence was discovered, a few minutes beyond that when his FBI record was connected to his name. He knew he was about to become the most hunted man on earth.

He already looked it. He knew he was the patsy. He was grim, hunched, angry, churning ahead with menace and dread in his beady eyes. His skin was ashen, his hair was all messed up, his cheeks were hollow, his jowls set hard, as if he were grinding his teeth. Though muscular, he had his hands jammed into his pockets, which narrowed his shoulders and gave him an almost negligible slenderness. He was the quintessential man of the fringes, aware that the bright glare of the world's attention was to be focused on him. No trained clandestine operative would have presented such an obvious profile to the world, but nobody else was paying much attention either. He fought against the human current that gushed toward Dealey and the scraps and fragments of hope that filled the air. I heard them too.

"Maybe he's okay. Head wounds bleed a lot."

"They got him to the hospital in minutes, maybe seconds. These days, docs can do anything."

"Maybe it was a grazing wound, you know, splashed some blood but didn't do any real harm. That happened more'n you'd think in the war."

"A guy that vigorous, he'll be up and about and playing touch football in a few days!"

Impervious, head down, clothes ever grubby and attitude ever surly, Alek bucked ahead, ducking, stutter-stepping, evading, and soon I lost sight of him. His destiny lay elsewhere.

I got Lon all the way down to the sidewalk and joined the human tide. Everywhere I looked, small scenes of grief played out: a Negro woman had collapsed and was shrieking violently, there seemed to be cops everywhere, children cried, women wept, the men had that grave, glaring war face that I'd seen and would see again in Vietnam. The pedestrian masses overspilled the streets, and traffic was at a standstill. We could see more and more police cars converging on the scene, though trapped in the amber of people and vehicles, going nowhere. Guns had come out, and I think federal agents had arrived with their tommy guns, or maybe it was Dallas Homicide with all the firepower. I don't know who they thought they were going to fight; maybe some red sniper nest defended by machine guns on the sixth floor of the Book Depository.

That was the focus of the attention. It was surrounded by policemen and cars and earnest federal agents who'd taken out their badges and pinned them on the lapels of their dark suits. Many had pistols out too. At the same time, the television trucks—remember, TV news was in its infancy then, and the camera equipment was cumbersome—had somehow bulled their way through, gotten their cameras out, and set up shots. I could see, every which way, earnest reporters addressing the tripod-mounted eyes of the networks and the locals. (I think Dan Rather was there somewhere.) Farther down the hill, I could see armed officers on the grassy knoll that would become such a feature, and all across the green emptiness of Dealey, small groups of people stood, many pointing, first at the looming Book Depository, then at the grassy knoll. Nobody pointed at Dal-Tex.

And the noise. I can't quite describe it, but it was as if, involuntarily, every one of the thousands of folks there had started to moan or snort or breathe too heavily. A persistent murmur filled the air, not the surge of joy I'd heard from Dal-Tex 712 but something guttural and low, animalistic. No one person contributed that much, but it was the voice of the collective unconscious expressing its horror and grief and regret. I'd never heard before and would never again hear anything like that.

I got Lon across Elm and we began to push our way up Houston toward Main. People stormed by us, late to the party but intent on joining. Nobody gave a damn about us except for one cop at the corner of Main and Elm, who noted me waiting for the solid stream of traffic to break to get across, and when I was about to give up and go up Main, he took command of the traffic, whistle and attitude at full blast, and cleared a space for us to get across. I nodded thanks to him, and he nodded back; that was my only encounter with law enforcement that day, and I'll bet in ten seconds the officer had forgotten all about it.

I continued down Houston until I reached Commerce and started up it. The Adolphus was ten or so blocks away. Then, miraculously, I was able to flag a cab. I gave him the hotel and got Lon in. The driver couldn't stop jabbering.

"Did you see it?"

"No," I said, which should have been sufficient, but like any guilty man, I overexplained. "We were at the doctor's for my brother's checkup."

He didn't notice. His mind was obsessed with what had happened ten minutes ago. "Man, I can't believe it. Can you, mister? Holy cow, it's such a tragedy. He was such a handsome young man. And that wife. God, what a dish. She was Jean Simmons and Dana Wynter combined with a little Audrey Hepburn. Oh, Lord, what she must be going through. I heard on the cop channel, they drilled him square in the head and there wasn't anything left and—"

"Is it official? Is he dead?"

"I don't know. God, what a mess."

It took some time to fight our way up Commerce—it was as if the city had shut down everywhere except Dealey Plaza—but eventually, we arrived at the Adolphus. The doorman, solemn as was everybody, helped me get Lon out of the cab seat and into his chair. I could see he had been crying.

The crying continued inside, where a few old ladies of the flowery Southern-gentlewoman sort sat in a corner of the lobby, two of them in tears, the other two ministering to them with white hankies. I heard someone ask if the show at the Century Room would be canceled that night.

"I need a drink," said Lon.

"Good idea," I said.

I wheeled us through the lobby, past the Grand Staircase and the elevators, and into the dark Men's Bar, surprisingly crowded, surprisingly quiet, dominated by a large black-and-white TV above the mirror at the center. We found a table with a good view of it, requested that the waiter turn it up, and went through the Texan idiocy of the bottle club.

"Jenkins," I said, giving my official cover name, under which I was registered. "I have a bottle of bourbon, J.B.; could I have a shot straight and a glass of ice water?"

Lon remembered his own nom de guerre, laid claim to his bottle of Southern Comfort, and ordered his own straight shot, with ice on the side.

"Bring both bottles, sirs?" the waiter asked.

"Yes," I said, "I think we're going to need them."

I checked my watch. By now it was 1:39. Evidently, Walter Cronkite had just announced, then taken off his glasses and pinched his nose, that JFK was gone. Someone said something wise, and someone else closed him down fast Texas-style with "Shut up, Charlie Tait, or dadgum, I will shut you up myself."

We sat there all afternoon in the dark silence, watching the images float across the screen. We watched the discovery of Alek's rifle and the three cartridge cases, we heard of the swearing in of Lyndon Johnson, all without comment. The news came shortly thereafter that a cop had been shot to death in the Oak Cliff section of Dallas, but nobody knew whether it was related to the president's death except me. Alek's roominghouse was in Oak Cliff; it had to be him, and the description of the assailant—young white man, five-ten or so, muscular build, under thirty—had to be him. At the time, I thought, Damn, I *told* him not to bring a gun, and the bastard disobeyed me! I knew I never should have counted on him and cursed myself doubly for springing such a dangerous incompetent on the snoozing world. Later, I realized he'd gone all the way back across town to retrieve the pistol, so he had at least stayed under discipline until he understood that he'd been betrayed. That was all I could have asked of him.

I said a prayer for the policeman. Hypocritical, no? But hypocrisy is one sin I cannot evade; it is, after all, the core of my profession, a demure churchgoing dad and Yalie by weekend who plots murder by weekday. I was quick to come to terms with it. I concluded in the end that I had done all that was possible to ensure such an outcome would not happen. It did anyway because of the intractability of the piteous Alek. It is a misfortune but not a tragedy. All operations of force—we were to learn this in spades in the coming decade—involve risk of collateral damage. The policeman, like the president, made his career decision based on a cost-benefit analysis, took his chances, and his number came up. That is the wicked way of the real world, morally justifiable if the ends themselves are morally justifiable. So it goes.

"I don't think I can take any more of this," Lon finally said.

"You okay?" I said.

"I've felt better," he replied.

"Remember," I said. "The long view."

"Easy to say," he said. "Not so easy to do."

"I'll push you," I said, and started to get up.

"Hugh, I've had enough of you for one day, all right?"

He wheeled himself out of the bar, and I watched him propel himself across the lobby to the elevator, where another guest had to punch his floor. He rolled into the car, the brass doors closed behind him, and off he went.

I went back to the bourbon and the television. I watched *Air Force One* take off with the new president, the body of the old president, and that poor crushed rose of a woman who was, just two hours ago, the glamour center of the world.

At about 3:20, it came. It signified the beginning of a new phase, one in which I was extremely vulnerable, as was the agency for which I worked (and which I loved), whose reputation and possible ruin I had risked.

This from Dallas. The police department arrested a twenty-four-year-old man, Lee H. Oswald, in connection with the slaying of a Dallas policeman shortly after President Kennedy was assassinated. He also is being questioned to see if he had any connection with the slaying of the president. Oswald was pulled yelling and screaming from the Texas Theatre in the Oak Cliff section of Dallas . . .

It didn't take long for them to round him up, did it? About two hours, and in that time he'd managed to kill a policeman. What a complete fool he was. Again it made me sick, and I took another bolt of the hooch, which hit like a mallet, driving me further into blur. I think I phased out after that, as the bourbon took over, and I fell into a stupor. I was not behaving well. This was not in the "Pip-pip, onward and upward" tradition of the agency and all its Skull and Bonesers. The event had reduced me to alcoholic stupor.

I don't remember going upstairs to my room or taking a shower. Or climbing into my pajamas. I don't remember going facedown on the bed.

I do remember waking up around midnight. And I remember the panic I felt.

Where was Jimmy Costello?

CHAPTER 18

T hese strange 'visions,' for such they must be called, are extremely vivid in some cases but are almost incredible to the vast majority of mankind, who would set them down as fantastic nonsense. Nevertheless they are familiar parts of the mental furniture of the rest, whose imaginations they have unconsciously framed and where they remain, unmodified or unmodifiable, by teaching."

Bob squinted, feeling his brow crunch in pain. So wrote Francis Galton in the late nineteenth century, and Bob thought: What the fuck?

If he understood it, and he wasn't sure he did, Niles Gardner had been fascinated by whatever thing it was that Sir Francis had noted 120 or so years earlier, some "fantastic vision" disease or condition. It had to do with colors showing up when cued by encounters with nothing of color. A letter could have a color to it or, in this case, a number.

He seemed to be saying or acknowledging or somehow having fun with—there was an unidentifiable sense of lightness to it, humor, almost a joke—how he saw certain things in color. He would always see the number four as blue, which was why he had four junky ceramic bluebirds on his shelf, and the number six as green, which was why he had a magazine illustration from the fifties that incidentally displayed six green elm trees. Most provocatively, he saw the number nine as red, which was why he had a Mauser 96 pistol lying around, one of the few Mausers designated by the numeral 9 engraved in the grip, then painted red, and known forever after as Red Nines.

Swagger sat in the business office of the Adolphus, where he was again staying in Dallas, and banged his head against the enigma at a computer monitor that the hotel provided its guests. Outside the door, prosperous men seemed to push to and fro; by extreme happenstance, the hotel was that weekend the site of some sort of JFK Assassination Research meeting.

Swagger had ridden down in the elevator with a batch of them, mostly heavyset white guys in sport shirts who hung together.

"Y'all interested in the assassination?" he asked one.

"Mmm," said the man, looking off, as if he had some big secrets cooking and couldn't share them with an outsider. Maybe he was the guy who realized that the Commies had not one or two but *three* Oswald clones in play on November 22.

Swagger looked back at his notepad, where, in childish script, in an attempt to keep it straight and orderly, he had inscribed some notes that anyone else might see as insane.

"Blue = 4, Green = 6, Red = 9," read one line.

"Maybe numbers not as significant as colors?"

"Maybe sequence isn't important?"

"Maybe it's not a code, it's just what he sees?"

"Why would Hugh have anything to do with 4, 6, or 9, or blue, green, or red?"

That was a stumper. He was, he realized, on the second step, but only on the basis of fragile assumption. That assumption: that Hugh's last, best, lost work name was a reflection of Niles and Hugh's love of Nabokov, and that it involved a pun, possibly cross-lingual, that could be noted only by someone who knew it existed.

So: what linked them?

But: there was no direct link between the three numbers, the three colors, and Hugh.

Except: the pistol, as his son noted, stood for espionage. It had to. It was exactly the implement any spy in the twenties or thirties might have carried if he didn't have a Luger. What were its advantages over a Luger?

More firepower, ten rounds to seven.

Longer barrel, meaning more accuracy.

More ergonomic, because its weight was ahead of the trigger, not above it, as in a Luger.

More psychologically threatening to an opponent.

More flexible, as it could be mounted to a shoulder stock and used for longer-range shooting.

It did have disadvantages.

Bigger, heavier.

A little harder to load, with a stripper clip that demanded fine motor control to mate with the interior magazine lips, rather than a magazine, which, by gross motor movement, could just be shoved into the Luger's grip.

Harder to conceal, maybe very difficult to conceal, because it was bigger.

Yet these were the sort of things a Bob Lee Swagger would consider, not a Niles Gardner. Niles, after all, was a lit guy, not a gun guy. He wouldn't be thinking tactically but symbolically, and in his brain, the glamour and the romance and the vividness of classical prewar espionage, back when it was called the Great Game, was just as easily conveyed by the Mauser as by the Luger.

Maybe the meaning of the gun as tool was of less importance to Niles than the meaning of it as symbol. In his mind, it could and probably would be his image of his friend the heroic (three tours in 'Nam!) Hugh Meachum. After all, Hugh was the man Niles could never be but would always want to be. The gun, solid steel, precise, deadly, able to destroy at long distance, concealable under a Burberry trench coat, the indispensable leverage that enabled its possessor to control any dangerous transaction, was a perfect projection into objective reality that expressed all the Hugh traits that Niles didn't have.

As Niles's mind had to work, Hugh *was* the Red Nine. It had to be that way. Maybe the assumption wasn't so small after all. The "Red" association was another buttress in the argument, for it conjured up

Russia, which, after all, had been Hugh's primary target, the Vietnam tours being mere diversions. It all fit together.

But it went nowhere. It didn't connect to Nabokov, it didn't connect to the Agency. It just sat there, an old pistol on a dead man's desk, its secrets locked away, only a glow of hopes or fantasies about it, its sole uniqueness the Red Nine on its grip.

I wish I had a drink. I wish I had a cigarette. I wish I had a whore. I wish I had a mansion by the sea.

No, he didn't. He didn't wish he had any of those.

I wish I had an answer.

He thought that maybe that answer lay somewhere within the work of Sir Francis Galton, cousin to Darwin, Victorian polymath (Bob had to look up the new word).

He Googled Sir Francis.

The Wikipedia entry came up first, and he absorbed the info quickly.

Eugenicist. Another word to look up.

Hmm, seems to believe smart people should breed and dumb ones shouldn't.

Fingerprints.

Hmm, noted the uniqueness of fingerprints, classified them, and thus invented the forensic discipline of fingerprint index, and thus, in one sense, was the father of scientific crime investigation.

Heredity.

Believed passionately in the power of genes (obviously, eugenics and fingerprints) and that talent clusters could be associated with certain families, i.e., those of the "superior" English upper class, into which he was born.

Synesthesia. It was something he had been the first in the world to note clinically.

But it was another new word.

Bob Googled it.

Synesthesia.

Alek's grubby face stared at me from the screen. Same surly demeanor, same anger, same radiant negativity and self-pity, undercut with toxic defiance. It made me sick.

I staggered to the TV set and changed channels, but no matter where I turned, there was Alek, with some demented commentator spewing out the sordid details of his life. Russia, Marine Corps, attempts to defect, poor employment record, marriage to a beautiful Russian girl, father of two baby daughters, known for temper and abusive, explosive behavior. There was a fuzzy film of him handing out pro-Cuba pamphlets in New Orleans: really, what did he think *that* would accomplish?

Now and then they'd cut to film of his wife as she carried the two babies to a car amid a swarm of reporters and cameramen. I remember being struck with how pretty she seemed, but also how confused and vulnerable. I hoped she had somebody good to take care of her and was later gratified to discover the ministrations of the angelic Ruth Paine on Marina's behalf. Thank God for the good people of the world, to somewhat ameliorate the pain caused by teams like Alek and Hugh.

It took a while, but I was more or less sober when I got around to assessing my position. Of Alek, even in police custody, I had little fear. What could he tell them, and when would he tell it? Listening carefully to the reports, I concluded he'd not yet made any wild charges about Russian agents guiding him. Rather, he'd been indicted only on the murder of Officer Tippit, for which he had no alibi and no defense and for which there were plenty of witnesses hungering to send him to fry in the chair. He was probably enjoying the attention and plotting how to spin it out for years and years and years. That he would die at the end was at this point meaningless; he was having too much fun being famous at last.

Every time the coverage shifted to Washington, to tracking the grief and shock of the capital city, to images of a weary LBJ arriving home, of Jackie returning alone to the White House, I changed channels, and by one had turned the damn thing off. I knew it was the beginning and that it would go on and on, and we'd have to get the reaction of each family member, each intimate, each acquaintance, we'd attend the funeral and the burial and the . . . It was too much. So much for tough guy Hugh, the New Critic of politics and policy, not letting emotion or sentimentality get in his way.

When the tube was dark, that left me alone with my biggest fears, concerning Jimmy Costello. I checked my watch again. I stole down the hallway to knock on his door softly and got no answer. (I paused at Lon's too and heard the regular breathing of merciful sleep, though now and again he'd stir uncomfortably.)

Back in my room, I tried to think things through. Suppose they'd nabbed Jimmy and the rifle? Suppose they'd offered him a deal, no execution if he rolled over fast. Though it was against his principles, maybe he'd seen that taking the rap alone was no bargain, so he'd talked.

It went on. Maybe even now, police raiders were assembling to swoop us up, men with tommy guns and shotguns, hell-bent on justice and retribution. I wished I'd brought my .45 with me. The best thing, under those circumstances—though tantamount to an admission of guilt—would have been the swift application of 230 grains of hardball suicide to the head. But that would leave Peggy and the boys and poor Lon to face alone the mess I'd made. I knew I couldn't do that. If caught, I'd also have to absolve the Agency of any blame, make certain all knew it was my ploy and my ploy alone, that I'd coerced Lon into it against his will, that I had done it for what I believed were sound moral policy reasons, confess, take my sentence, and face my executioners with dignity and grace, leaving a legacy for my sons and the Agency.

There was nothing to be done. I called the desk to see if the bar was still open, and it was not, and inquired if I could have a bottle sent to my room and was told it was too late. So I just sat there, waiting for— Godot, I suppose. The knock on the door. The explosive entry of the raid team. Mr. Dulles, so disappointed? Cord, even more disappointed. I saw myself saying, "But Cord, it was your wife he was screwing," and Cord answering, "He was the president of the United States, you fool!"

Then there was a knock on the door, soft but firm.

Oh, Jesus, I thought, for it was the climax to the day. Live or die would be decided upon the opening of the door. I glanced at my watch. Good Christ, it was nearly five.

I walked over.

Smiling sheepishly, Jimmy Costello, with something wrapped and bundled in his suit coat, was standing there. "Sorry I'm late, Mr. Meachum," he said. "Hope you wasn't worried."

"I only had three heart attacks and finished my bottle and tried to order another."

"Very sorry."

"No, no, God, man, not your fault, mine. I should have been tougher. The leader hangs together in the bleak moments, and I didn't. Thank God for that Irish rascal Jimmy Costello. Bet you've got a story to tell."

"No heroics. Just me sitting in the dark for twelve hours until the night became wee and I was able to make a dash."

"Tell me."

"Sure, but can I go to my own room first and get myself my own bottle?"

"Absolutely. Enough for a glass for the boss?"

"Count on it, Mr. Meachum."

He laid the bundle down on the bed, where it fell open. I was happy to see the rifle, in parts, still in its odd canvas holster straps. The man himself returned in a few seconds, undid his tie, poured us each a couple of fingers, and commenced with the tale. I can't capture the trace of Irish brogue that underlay his account because it was more a thing of rhythms and lightly alternative syllabic emphasis, so I won't even try. It would be blarney. But here's the gist of it, as I recall.

"You leave, I get the gun disassembled and holstered, I snatch up the coat and I'm out the door maybe thirty seconds after you. I hear it click and head down the hall when I remember the damned window. The window. I give it a second. Maybe the old man won't notice his window open where it was closed before. But he's a Jew, smart as a tack, with a gift for details if he's in the garment trade, because that's the biggest of big business games, so I duck back, pop the lock, flee across the outer office to the inner, and get the window down as it was. So I'm maybe a minute and a half behind you as I hit the hallway, and lo and behold, ahead of me, the elevators open and a couple of birds pop out. They's all concerned about the president, but more so about not being able to leave the office because of that damn cop. What, did he think a haberdasher gunned down the president? They were so taken with it, I know they didn't pay a hair's attention to me, so I figured I was okay.

"But when I get to the elevator and push down, the doors didn't open. I figure there's been another call and check the indicator above the doors and see both cars are downstairs in the lobby and ain't budging. I figure that means the cops have put the kibosh on them for a bit while they check out the real estate.

"I go to the stairwell and can hear commotion on the flights below. Not sure if it's cops coming up or citizens going down, whatever, but it's not good. I slip off my shoes and, in my stocking feet, head up a flight to the top, me with the death rifle hanging around my neck, heart beating like a drum."

He took a pull of his bourbon, and I joined him.

"I make it up and then run out of building. I'm hard against the roof. Fortunately, the stairway does lead up to a door set horizontal in the roof. Using my picks, I pop the door in a second, roll to the roof, and let the door slip shut behind me, hearing it lock. I look about. The roof is empty, and no building stands taller to give vantage. The only structure would be the elevator machinery house twenty-five yards away. I ease my way to it, feeling naked as a jaybird and worried about helicopters or low-flying planes, but the sky is empty too. I've got my jimmy keys and I'm in in a flash. I squint and can see there's not much but space for the greasy lifting and lowering machines. I get past the machinery to the far end of the house, where some quirk in design has left a platform in the wall so it forms a shelf or space or something.

"Fortunately, Jimmy's a strong boy, and he gets himself up there and wedges himself way back to the wall, so he's not visible to flashlight beam from the doorway. A searcher'd have to come by the motor works, go to the rear, and shine a beam directly in.

"I squeeze this way and have to do some squirming to get more or less comfortable, pushing my coat this way, fixing it so I'm not lying on the gunstock, or got a lump of coat under my ass, because I've decided my best bet is to stay still till the middle of the night, then ease out. I committed myself to the long haul in the dark.

"A few hours later, I hear noises, and sure enough, the door into the machine room is opened, lights are turned on, and I hear a couple of detectives and a janitor. The janitor is saying, 'See, nobody's been up here since the last inspection in July. Besides, you got the guy.' The cop answers, 'We have to check everything, bud.'

"I hear them poking around, and some light beams shoot around the machinery. Nobody wants to go in any farther. They dip out in a second, and that's that for another twelve hours."

"Very good," I said. My Jimmy! I knew he could outsmart a couple of buckram Texas detectives.

"Well, not so good," he said. "I haven't told you of my problem."

"How can it be a problem, Jimmy? You're here, poor Alek has been nabbed, and everything's as it should be."

"I'm hoping so. Anyway, here's what happened. I lay flat after that and let the time pass. After a bit, they okay the elevator, and so I'm close to the huffing and humming of that motor and can hear the cables winding and unwinding, the whole elevator cycle, the doors opening and closing, the cars going up and down and on and on. By ten it's settled, and by eleven it's gone away. I figure a few more hours. But around two, I'm suddenly smelling something, and I don't recognize it. Acrid-like, industrial, for some reason I'd say it smells brown, if that makes any sense, smells of machines and such, and here's the funny thing, I know I've smelled it before, but I don't know where or when.

"The smell continues, and I realize it's rising out of my own clothes. I feel around with my fingers and come across a spot on my overcoat upon which the rifle has lain, and it's damp, and I bring it to my nose, and that smell nearly knocks me out. I've got the picture. Somehow I arranged myself in a certain position, and the rifle action had slid out of its pouch a bit. It laid on its side over a long time, and whatever Mr. Scott used in cleaning and lubricating it—"

"Hoppe's 9," I said. "It's a bore solvent and lubricant. He uses it to clean, then he lightly coats everything with it as a lube. Yeah, it's pungent."

"That's it, then. Anyhow, this stuff has to obey gravity. It begins to seep downward, and it starts dripping out. This happens over and over as I'm lying there, and a stain is spreading. Fortunately, from the way I've got my things arranged, it's all on the overcoat and none on the suit coat, which I'd pushed back so it didn't get lumpy on me.

"Now I've got a problem. It's not just the stain but it's the smell. Suppose, as I'm heading back to the car, I'm stopped. The cops are sure to be about. I can talk my way out of anything, and I've got my James Delahanty O'Neill card and Massachusetts license to get me out. But that stain's standing out like a bull's-eye on my chest, and maybe these Texas coppers know guns and can ID the smell. Not good.

"After I climb down, I take the coat off and fold it. It turns out they used that shelf to store carpeting, so I slide the coat into the carpeting so that it's covered by a lot of weight. I smooth the carpeting over it. You can't tell from looking at it that the old carpeting pile contains a coat, and it's so heavy that I'm thinking it'll contain that smell forever, at least until it evaporates.

"That leaves me with only my suit coat to hide the strap with the rifle parts, and it's not long enough. I figure I can make it out of the building unseen, and then I'll dump the rifle behind some garbage cans. I'll go to the car, come back, drive around a bit to make sure no cop car is patrolling, and jump out and secure the rifle. That's my plan, and that's what I did, and I didn't have no problem. It seems there's lots of folks out, they keep going down to the depository, which is all lit up, and they're placing wreaths and bunches of flowers on the hill. Anyway, sir, that's the story."

"I think we're okay," I said. "They're so convinced it's Alek and only Alek, and he's probably beginning to think that way himself, they'll never do the kind of search that would uncover the coat."

"Possibly in a year, when all this settles down, you'd want me to return and revisit and remove that piece of evidence."

"I wouldn't do it too soon, Jimmy. I'd wait to see how the trial goes, I'd wait to see if the investigation stays with Alek or they tire of him and branch out. If the government commits to Alek and history commits to Alek, nobody'll ever look any further. It could lie there for fifty years and never be seen and never tell its story. In the meantime, get some sleep, and I will too, and there's nothing left for us to do here except make a low-profile exit from Dallas and return to our lives. You've done great, Jimmy."

I shook his hand. For the first time in twenty-four hours, I felt the weight of dread come off my shoulders, and the air tasted clean on the way down. I took a last sip of the bourbon and this time enjoyed the mallet. It amplified the feeling. I realized then: we'd done it.

And that's the way it happened. I have to laugh anytime I encounter the "deep plot" theory with various government (ours, theirs, anybody's) manipulating forces, making exquisite plans based on surgical precision and split-second timing (the clandestine operation on JFK's body on the tarmac at Andrews being the most hilarious). It happened the way everything happens; it was part of the world, not an exception to it. We had a plan for something else, and from that basic text we improvised, we adapted, we bluffed and lied and risked, and we brought it off. We were given an opportunity and maximized it, but we couldn't have done it if we weren't already there, on the ground, in midoperation, on another mission. It changed its essence and the scope of its ambition, seizing on the one-in-a-billion happenstance that put JFK seventy-five feet outside the Book Depository, and even that opportunity Alek the Idiot blew. Still, we prevailed. It was, like everything, ramshackle, clumsy, full of mistakes, and unconscionably lucky. We threw it together, that's all, because it seemed right and moral, at least to me, and because it was, I believed, my duty.

I won't argue the morality and I won't—can't—argue the strategic outcome in the next years. I will say this: as espionage, it was a masterpiece.

CHAPTER 19

The lawyers—Adams's in Hartford, Connecticut, and Bob's, actually a recruited FBI surrogate in Boise, Idaho—dickered for a couple of weeks on issues that lawyers find fascinating: share of profits (equal), share of expenses (equal), no first-class travel (a major concession for Marty), equal exposure in the case of lawsuits for libel, misrepresentation, the expropriation of intellectual property, and so forth.

Meanwhile, Swagger heard from Kathy Reilly in Moscow that his friend and ally Stronski had been released from the hospital, with no charges filed, and had promptly disappeared, figuring he was on an Izzy hit list. A day later, Stronski himself checked in: "Am fine, brother. You saved my life. One second later on that shot, Stronski is dead. I owe all. See you soon."

Then word came from the "lawyer" that the contract, basically boilerplate with a filigree or two, was okay. Swagger arranged to have it sent to him at the Adolphus, where he stayed in the open as Jack Brophy. Richard was witness to his signing, and it was sent off to Marty for countersigning along with Bob's hastily written notebook, recording all his late-night ideas, for Marty's perusal.

The word came back quickly, via an e-mail.

"This is brilliant. Much more than I expected, and it seems to dovetail exactly with what I have suspected but was unable to articulate. I especially like your focus on Oswald's behavior in the two hours of freedom he had left. It seems you've noticed things nobody else has, and all point to a conspiracy of the sort that could easily involve our friends, the happy cousins Hugh and Lon and maybe a few others. Let me come to Dallas and meet with you, and I will tell you what my contribution to our cause is to be. I think you'll be impressed. French Room again. On me! No need to split expenses on this one, I'm so happy!"

They met in the French Room three days later, ate more sliced carrots, filigreed celery, thigh of rabbit marinated for three weeks in squid broth, and plum-banana tart under a glaze of honey and strawberry, all to Marty's narration, which was complete to all apostrophes and something he called an aperçu. There wasn't even a Richard Monk along to absorb some of Marty's excess attention and keep the conversation from becoming too Marty to bear.

Finally, Marty relented and got to his tale over the last morsel of bunny.

"Suppose," he started, "Lon Scott—after all, not a sociopath or natural-born killer by any means—returned to his home in Virginia on November 24, 1963, with two pieces of luggage. One contained clothes. The other contained a Model 70 Winchester rifle that he had used to put an exploding bullet into the head of John F. Kennedy.

"Like any man who's never killed, Lon feels contrition, regret, doubt, self-loathing. This can but double, triple, multiply grotesquely as the week wears on, and after it the months and the years, and the man he's killed is declared in the popular culture a secular saint, a martyred king—Camelot!—and, finally, a demigod. Lon cannot bear to confront the instrument by which the deed was done, for that is to acknowledge that he was the one who did it; and so he commands a servant to stuff it in a closet somewhere. There it sits and sits and sits.

"Let us consider such an object, the case in which the rifle is stored. It's leather, possibly from Abercrombie and Fitch, about a yard long and half a yard wide, able to contain the two parts of the rifle, stock and action/scope, plus the tube of the suppressor, in parallel on velvet cushion. There's plenty of room for the bolt, for the screws, maybe a two- or three-piece cleaning rod, a pack of patches, a brush, a small container of Hoppe's 9, a small bottle of lubricating oil, and a rag or chamois for mopping up.

"Maybe in the case as well are two or three extra rounds, that is, of the counterfeit iteration on which you have such provocative insights. Suppose, further, a metallic residue could be removed carefully from the uncleaned barrel, and that residue, by neutron-activation hocus-pocus, would link it to only one kind of bullet at the exclusion of all others, the Mannlicher-Carcano 6.5 manufactured by Western Cartridge Company in the mid-fifties. That's the point, if I understand it, right, Jack?"

"That's right, Marty."

"Let us further allow that in those days they always put a luggage destination tag on every suitcase, which one can fairly guess bore the initials of the ultimate destination—in his case, Richmond—and wrapped it around the handle, and there was some kind of adhesive or stickum by which the two ends were joined. And suppose they were always dated. And Lon's name and address would have been validated by another tag.

"We have this object, linked by dated tags to Dallas, November 22, 1963, never opened, because Lon never again used or touched the rifle. It is physical proof that Lon was in Dallas that weekend; Lon, one of the greatest shots in the world. We have physical proof that he had a rifle capable of firing a bullet into the president. We have several samples of the cartridge, possibly with Lon's fingerprints. We have the rifle itself with his fingerprints or DNA traces on it. The barrel of the rifle will contain metallic traces that can be linked metallurgically to the bullet that assassinated the president. Your Honor, I rest my case: whoever has possession of that case has physical proof of the conspiracy to murder the thirty-fifth president of the United States and, by fair inference, the identity of the man who pulled the trigger. Such a discovery would force a reopening of the case, and reopened, the case would lead straight to wherever it would lead, perhaps to the CIA cousin Hugh Meachum. The jig, as they say, would be up. Do I have your interest yet, Jack?"

Swagger stared at Marty intently. His mind was abuzz. Was this bullshit, a setup, or had the silly fool stumbled on exactly what he'd said and had the key to the whole goddamn thing?

"It's very interesting," said Swagger. "Are you saying—"

"Let's continue. As I've said, Lon doesn't like to look at it, so it's stuffed away somewhere, in a closet or a storage room. In a few years, his paranoia gets the best of him, and he does some research and then clumsily fakes his own death and takes up a new persona. He's not a professional, and that's why it will be easy for anyone to learn that 'John Thomas Albright' is Lon Scott, cousin to the mysterious Hugh.

"After he 'dies,' a lot of Lon Scott's shooting material—his beautiful rifles, his notebooks, the drafts of the articles he wrote for the gun press, his reloading and experimental records, all that is left to the National Rifle Association, and some of it is displayed in the National Firearms Museum, first in D.C. and later in Fairfax, Virginia.

"As for the gun case, it is incriminating, so he wouldn't give it to the NRA. When he 'died' and became Albright, he took that with him, unopened. It was at his new very fine home in North Carolina when he died for real, this time as Albright, in 1993.

"To whom would he leave the case? He had no living relatives, no children, there were no women in his life; maybe Hugh? Maybe a faithful servant? A loyal lawyer? Another shooter? Another shooter's son?

"Hmmm. Let's go with that one. Maybe this son dumped it in an attic, having no interest in it but unwilling to dispose of it. Some years later, he was contacted by a writer. Not a real writer but one of those fellows whose obsession with the arcana of firearms impels him to pen volumes like *Winchester, An American Tradition* and *The Guns of Ruger* and so forth, and they are such beautiful volumes and he has such great connections in New York that he can get big firms to publish them. Maybe this writer has tumbled to the fact that famous shooter Lon Scott, mysteriously dead in 1964, became John Thomas Albright, famous shooter, who lived another thirty years before dying in a hunting accident in Arkansas. What an interesting life the fellow had, even absent the minor detail of November 22, 1963, in Dallas, Texas. He's decided to write the biography.

"As I say, this writer contacts the son of another shooter who has unwittingly inherited all the John Thomas Albright material, and he sells the young man on his project. The young man agrees to turn over all the stuff—the gun case, a few other rifles, the Albright manuscripts, whatever is left, everything for and by and of John Thomas Albright—for research purposes. The deal is that when the book is published, the stuff will be returned to the son, he will donate the papers to the NRA, and sell whatever other goods remain at auction, and the provenance of ownership by Albright/Scott will make the stuff very valuable. Everybody wins: the writer gets his book, the son gets the profits of the sale, John Thomas Albright/Lon Scott gets his place in history.

"The writer is in receipt of the material at his domicile, and the first thing he does is make a catalog. That's when he discovers the gun case, unopened, and he's about to tear into it when he sees the date on the tag and the originating city. Ding-dong! Something goes off in his head. He puts it down, his own mind racing.

"He thinks and he thinks and he thinks. He sees how Lon Scott, later known as John Thomas Albright, could have been the Kennedy triggerman. That would explain the otherwise baffling, clumsy midlife identity change. He's sitting on the scoop of the century. But he doesn't know enough. He reads books, he tries to master the gears and flywheels of the event, he tries to figure angles and so forth. He realizes he needs help. So he goes to Dallas and discreetly looks around. He locates Richard Monk, who is, after all, a responsible figure in the assassination community, and after they bond, the writer tells him his story and admits he can't handle it himself, he needs a better investigator, someone he can trust, someone with practical ballistics knowledge and experience, etc., etc. And that is where we are right now."

Swagger said, "Wow. That's a lot for one bite."

"Oh, there's more," said Marty. He reached under the table to remove a briefcase, opened it, and produced two items. The first, unrolled, was an X-ray. It clearly delineated a Model 70 broken down into action and Monte Carlo stock, a tube that had to be a Maxim silencer, a disassembled cleaning rod, a few spare brushes, two small bottles, and three cartridges of oddly blunt configuration. The second was a photograph that displayed the sealed travel tag in close-up, with its inscription dated November 24, 1963, and its Braniff DFW-RIC route indicator and Lon's name and signature and phone number, MOuntaincrest 6-0427.

Swagger's response was explicit. "Do not open it. Do NOT open it."

"Of course not," said Marty.

"Is it secure?"

"It's in my gun vault in Connecticut. In the country house."

Swagger thought, feeling overwhelmed: Is this it? Does this idiot actually have it? He could only come up with security-arrangement questions. "Is the house guarded professionally?"

"No, but it's locked in a vault that guarded my mother's diamonds and my father's rare guns for sixty years without a problem."

"Okay," he said. "This could be big. This could be it. We have to proceed carefully now."

"I agree."

"I think you should hire a security company to patrol your house. Or move it to some highly protected site."

"Jack, I'm in the middle of nowhere. And nobody knows a thing except the two of us. No one is going to steal it, I guarantee."

Swagger nodded. "You're right. I do get paranoid."

"Understandable. This is exciting."

"I have to see it. I just have to look at it, to have a sense of it, so it's settled in my own mind that it's there. Oh, wait. Let's get a handle on all this. Have you examined the provenance? Can we determine that the gun itself is linked to Lon outside of the case?"

"Doesn't his name on the case make that point rather eloquently?"

"Yes, but if we could link the gun going to Lon, Lon possessing it, via an outside confirmation, the argument is so much stronger. Any idea where Lon got it?"

"This is the sort of practical detail I never think of. No, it didn't occur to me. I've just kept it, trying to figure out my next step."

"Aren't the Winchester records all at the Cody Firearms Museum?" asked Bob.

"Yes, but no. There was a fire in the Winchester plant, and all the modern records were burned—among the casualties, all those on the Model 70. But Lon didn't get his rifles directly from Winchester. He got them from the Abercrombie and Fitch gun room on Madison Avenue in New York City, where all the American swells got theirs. Teddy Roosevelt and his sons, Richard Byrd, Charles Lindbergh, Ernest Hemingway, Clark Gable, Gary Cooper, probably through Lyndon Johnson, all the fancy big game hunters who went to Africa for short happy lives in the fifties. Abercrombie was purveyor to the aristocrats, the celebs, the nabobs, the millionaires for nearly a century. They went bankrupt in '77, and the current outfit just has the brand name." Marty snorted. "Now it's a mall clothing company for twenty-year-olds with actual abdominals."

"But the firearms records?" asked Bob. "Were they destroyed?"

"No," said Marty. "Now that you mention it, they're in a warehouse in Rutherford, New Jersey. Too valuable to throw out, I suppose, yet not valuable enough to catalog, index, and display."

"Can we get in?"

"I do happen to know Tom Browner, who was the last manager of the room. Though he's old and retired, I know he has some sway still. But Jack, it's not like you can give a name to a clerk and he comes back with the files ten minutes later. It's a bloody mess, years dumped into other years, shipping documents spread everywhere, correspondence half there and half not. Finding Lon in that mess would be like cleaning the stables."

"I have cleaned some stables in my time," said Swagger.

"I see it would make you happier to try. Maybe you'll succeed. All right, I'll call Tom Browner tomorrow and see what he has to say. When will you go?"

"Ah, better leave it open. Sometime soon. Early next week, say. Rutherford, New Jersey. Anyhow, when I get back, I'll call you."

"Do you want to make it one trip and go from—"

"No, New Jersey will wreck me for a week. I'll need recovery, believe me. So we should set up a date for me to see the case in a couple of weeks."

"Excellent," said Marty.

"It was your idea to go to New Jersey?" asked Nick, in Seattle's Best number eight, this one in Oak Cliff.

"Yeah," said Swagger. "But it could easily be anticipated. It would have to be done sooner or later. You'd think Marty, with his connections up there already, would want to do it. But he let me come up with it and volunteer to do it, because he wants me to believe in the authenticity of the thing on my own. If I find anything in the Abercrombie files, that nails it."

"On the other hand, it commits you to a known place and time, and if this is a setup, that's where it could go down. Jack Brophy walks out of the warehouse into four guns, and that's the end of Jack Brophy."

"Sure. But my call is that neither Marty nor Richard have the stone cojones to get involved in a hit. Not their part of the forest. I don't think they could hold it together mentally, setting something like that up. There'd be tells all the way through. Marty'd be sweating like a pig, and Richard couldn't stop swallowing, licking his lips, avoiding eye contact. They're not suited for the violent end of the game."

"Maybe they don't know. Maybe whoever's pulling the string is lying to them, telling them it's some other kind of scam; maybe they're expendable to this guy, who, after all, is fighting for his life, his legacy, his family name, if he's who you think he is and has done what you think he's done."

"But how can I *not* go? If I'm who I say I am, I have to go, or the whole deception falls apart and we're left with nothing and I have to sit around and wait for Hugh to find me."

"You tell me what to do."

"I have no suggestions. Pray for luck, how's that?"

"Okay, then I'll make a suggestion. You set up your appointment. On that day, I'll have a team from New York in the parking lot. No big deal, plainclothes, but with enough signs of serious operators on-site. Overcoats concealing long guns, vests under the coats, snail-cord earpieces, tactical shades, bloused boots, that sort of thing. If Hugh has people, the last thing he'll want is a gunfight in the parking lot. They'll take a powder fast, and there won't be any action."

"Okay," said Bob. "It sounds good. You can pay for that?"

"It's under the James Aptapton investigation and the Sergei Bodonski investigation. Capping Bodonski wasn't enough; we have to find out who let the contract. It's legit law enforcement initiative."

"Great," said Swagger. "I'm appreciative."

"If we can take down the contract taker and he's someone big, maybe even a once-dead Hugh Meachum, then we don't have to go to JFK up front. And once we bag him, we can work for proof, and eventually, it gets out."

"Not bad," said Swagger. "There would be your career finisher. Your—what do they call it? Your capstone."

"Just," said Nick, "so it's not your—what do they call it? Oh, yeah. Your tombstone."

Like many Americans, I'm not sure if I saw Alek get his in real time, live on the network, or if I saw it a few minutes later, when the other networks ran the tape. I suppose it doesn't matter.

I'd missed his brief encounter with the press Friday night, since I'd been ingloriously passed out. But I'd seen it on tape, as they had to fill the time when nothing was happening, and what I'd seen had seemed classical Alek. He was scruffy, as usual, hair a mess, and the shiner from the punch in the eye he'd taken earlier that day from a Dallas cop hadn't subsided. He was surly, squint-eyed, radiating animus. The cops shoved him up on a riser, and immediately, a surge of newspeople surrounded him, shoving mikes in his face, yelling questions. Bulbs flashed; he winced and got to speak only a few words before the cops hauled him up to Homicide.

"I didn't kill anybody," he said, or words to that effect, and I suppose to him, it made perfect sense. He had to know he hadn't fired the fatal shot. It would be a while before I worked out what had happened to him up there, but he must have seen the president's head take its hit, and he knew in his feral way that there was a game going on, that he'd been played for a sucker and was now somebody's prey, and off he went.

That's why his cry of "I didn't kill anybody" as he was taken away haunted me. What you heard in that plaintive tone was self-belief. He *knew* he hadn't murdered anybody—it follows that if he was a setup, he had concluded that his shooting of the Dallas police officer was pure self-defense—and you hear it in that yell.

The next morning, after an alcohol-free, somewhat redemptive sleep,

I returned to the television. It seemed all the TV people were grouchy too; they'd been working long hours without sleep, chasing witnesses and rumors, dealing with bureaucratic recalcitrance and ass-covering, shoved this way and that by defiantly unempathetic Dallas cops, being screamed at for being slow by network headquarters and screamed at louder for getting things wrong. What a life. I wouldn't give it to a dog.

As I fought for clarity with my first cup of room-service coffee, I could sense the irritation everywhere. We were now in the basement of the police station, to witness Alek's transfer from the supposedly vulnerable jail to one that offered more protection. To that order, an armored car had been arranged, so that only a bazooka rocketeer could kill Alek, and not even in Texas were bazookas legal.

But the transfer had fallen behind schedule. Things almost always do, don't they? The reporters had been milling around listlessly for about an hour, and when anyone "reported," it was time-filling banality, updates on the timing of the transfer or explanations on why it was late. Occasionally, they'd cut to Washington, where again, nothing was happening. They might run some old tape, to remind us what this was all about, not that we'd ever forget. Nobody did or could distinguish themselves under those circumstances, and I stayed with it only because it occupied all the channels. I'd decided to take a shower, get up, go for a walk, find a nice restaurant, head back, maybe watch some football—the NFL had decided, amid much controversy, not to cancel its slate of games. Tomorrow I'd fly back to somewhere under my fake identity, then to Washington under my real one, and rejoin the human race and my family.

Suddenly, on the television, it was as if a wave of energy had crackled through the black-and-white image of lolling, sullen reporters. Our correspondent—I have no idea who it was—informed us that Lee Harvey Oswald, indicted for the murder of Officer J. D. Tippit and the only suspect in the murder of John F. Kennedy, was on his way.

Why do I relive this incident? Surely any who read these pages will have seen it for himself. There's no suspense; it turns out the same each time the tape is run, and as movie special effects have gotten almost too realistic, so the almost chaste, bloodless death by gunshot of this appalling man is of little consequence to anybody. That is the view from a comfortable perch in our present. Then it was all different: nobody knew what the next big twist in our giant American narrative would be. Nobody could have predicted it, not even I, who had made the unpredictable happen two days earlier. Nobody had any idea that Mr. Deus Ex Machina was about to introduce himself.

I saw the surly Alek emerge from a door at the rear of the crowded room. He was shackled to a cartoon figure out of the old west, some sort of gigantic cowpoke in a smallish Stetson—it was like mine, though light where mine was gray—and what had to be called a westerner's suit, apparently khaki. It was Captain Fritz of the Dallas Homicide Squad, but he looked to our uneducated eyes like a foursquare avatar of Texas Ranger justice. He stood out in a sea of dark suits and snap-brim hats, as if intent on representing the best of Texas to a shocked world. Next to him, Alek jauntily, perhaps even smugly, set the pace. He'd been allowed to clean up and change clothes and wore a black sweater over some kind of sport shirt. He grasped his hands at his waist and, for some reason, projected a "Mr. DeMille, I'm ready for my close-up" sense of self-possession.

I have to say that the quality of the broadcast was exceedingly fine. Every detail stood out, almost as if iridescent; the lines were bold and sharp; the depth of the image was startling. I don't think I ever saw anything so clearly in my life.

Alek never knew what hit him. Deus ex machina hit him. Fate hit him. Retribution hit him. The fellow Ruby stepped from nowhere and jammed the pistol—a gangster's snub-nose, so appropriate to a strip club owner—into his side. I don't think there was a flash, but the report was enough to carry the news.

The famous photo almost does the scene a disservice. It freezes and therefore distorts. You can see Captain Fritz bending backward in surprise, Ruby hunched like a boxer who's delivered a solid gut hit, and

Alek, mouth open in pain, eyes wincing. In reality, it was so damned fast, like a man slipping under the waves in the grasp of an undertow; he's there and then he's gone in the flashing of a nerve synapse.

Then chaos, disbelief, the whirls of spinning figures, as people fled the shot, Alek pulled Captain Fritz down with him, and various officers leaped on Ruby and shoved him to the ground. If the famous cry "Jack, you son of a bitch" was uttered, I missed it in my disbelief. I sat back and watched the melancholy play end. Alek, uncuffed, slid onto a stretcher and wheeled out, fast. Ruby pulled away. The reporters tried to make sense of it, interviewing each other to make certain the gigantic plot twist they'd just seen had actually happened.

I got a glimpse of Alek's colorless, expressionless, perhaps breathless face as they wheeled him out and knew he was a goner. You don't come back from that one, for I'd gotten a good fix on the bullet's diagonal trajectory through innards, and I knew the violence it would do to the sweetbread of mysterious but crucial organs that the middle of the body conceals.

Perhaps you'll think better of me for it, but my first thought was sadness at his death. Another man dead of violence in America, as if I hadn't been the one who killed the last man dead of violence in America. It seemed like a contagion. You sow the wind, you reap the whirlwind, and I had to wonder when my whirlwind would come.

I'd known him and loathed him, as all did, while at the same time understanding that he was nevertheless human, like the rest of us. Did he "deserve" it? I suppose so; Jack Ruby thought so, and a few days later, I'd hear my oldest son say, "I'm glad they got him."

Alek was a jerk, he was a fool, he was utterly incapable of doing a single thing right, but he was human and died as all too many humans do, alone, in pain, abruptly.

It wasn't until that night that it occurred to me, amid the hysterical news reporting, that again we'd caught another gigantic break. Luck does favor the bold, no question of it. Now that Alek's lips were forever closed, there'd be no crazed stories of manipulations by cynical red spies who set him up and played him as a sucker. A myth wouldn't spring forth—others did, of course, all patently incorrect—to tantalize the imaginative for decades to come. Books wouldn't be written, not about the Red Master at least, nor movies made, nor TV series commissioned. All Alek's secrets would be buried with him, and the narrative would shift its focus to this apparition out of *Chicago Confidential,* this fireplug-like gunman with his titillating connection to the demimonde and women with improbably large hair and breasts and arcs of eye shadow. I thought, You know what? I don't have to learn a goddamn thing about Mr. Jack Ruby, and that's okay with me.

I viewed the end of Alek in solitude, because Lon and Jimmy had already left, both of them early on Sunday the twenty-fourth.

I saw Lon before he was gone. I gave him Jimmy's report and delivered the rifle. I watched him put the parts in the gun case. He seemed dolorous and depressed; I got little out of him. Jimmy awakened and came by, and the two embraced. Then Lon was gone, and Jimmy was off to pack for his later flight, and I was enmeshed in the Oswald denouement.

Jimmy always got it more than Lon did, and he was too professional to let it affect him. I couldn't have known then that within six months Jimmy would be dead. Another Clandestine Services colleague enlisted him to do a routine wiretap insertion on an East-bloc embassy in Canada. It was a low-level, routine thing. But somehow he was spotted—a first—and a Mountie, of all people, saw his shadow in the alley and drew. Jimmy knew he couldn't surrender and testify; it would embarrass too many people. He turned, and the Mountie fired one shot and Jimmy fell dead on the streets of Ottawa, the death addressed as "mysterious," as in "Why was an American businessman messing about in the alleys behind the Czechoslovakian embassy, and why did he flee the Mountie?" *Requiescat in pace*, good friend, loyal operative, hero.

As for Lon, I knew I wouldn't hear from him for a long time, until he worked some things out. If you are thinking, Danger Man, he was the only one who knew, why didn't you have him eliminated?, you've seen too many movies. The answer is, I don't eliminate. I don't even like the euphemism "eliminate" for "kill"; it sounds like cheap fiction. I am a

373

moral murderer. I can kill only for policy. I cannot kill for personal reasons, such as to deter threat or to earn money or for the pleasure of removing one of the world's annoyances. What will come will come, and I will accept it. If Lon went mad with guilt and decided to confess, then I would accept that decision and ride the horse where it took me. But the world wasn't worth living in if you didn't trust the people you loved, so I let it go at that, and that is what happened; I didn't see him again until 1993, when he had a different name and a different identity.

I stayed in the hotel until Monday the twenty-fifth, ironically, the day we'd planned the General Walker job. I stayed even though I was anxious to get home to Peg and the boys and help them through the emotional crisis that they couldn't have suspected was my invention. But I couldn't hurry, because I didn't want anyone associating my coming and going with events in Dallas, the overcaution of an overcautious mind. I returned, took a day off, then went back to work in an effort to impose workaday normality on the inchoate grief that was everywhere.

Since this is memoir and not autobiography, allow me to skip details of the healing of the family, the stunned disbelief in Clandestine, the sorrow of even Cord Meyer, the lugubrious mourning of Washington, D.C., that seemed to last through winter and into spring. You're familiar with the iconic images of the period, no doubt, the lasting one for me being the prancing of the riderless horse, Black Jack, with its single boot mounted backward in the stirrup. If I suggest, horribly, that I felt grief for the man I had murdered, it's still the truth. Never did I feel joy except that one moment when Jimmy showed up and I knew we had done it, and that was a professional's pride in craft, not a hunter's exhortation of bloodlust after the kill.

I should not have been surprised, moreover, at the way in which Kennedy, a mild failure of a president who had shown a little promise and the barest possibility of intellectual growth, immediately became a symbol of greatness and his time in office christened "Camelot" and held up to the popular imagination as a bright and shining moment of moral excellence, star glamour, vivid beauty, and so forth. Yet I was not sickened. It happens that way, and in my mid-thirties, I was barely mature enough to get it. Nothing makes the heart grow fonder than a nice bloody martyr's death, real or imagined.

Dully, I soldiered on. I lost myself in the Agency and began working the terrible hours that I later became famous for. I wasn't escaping guilt or voices in my head or the sad faces of my family upon my return or anything like that. I didn't feel that I owed anything or that redemption was in order. It just seemed the way to go, and if I wasn't already the section star, I shortly became one, and in time a legend. It's amazing what a little hard work can do.

God love Peggy, who stayed true as an arrow's flight through it all, the travel, the intensity of the effort, the distraction. She was the real soldier. She raised three fine boys through difficult American teenage years almost on her own, though when around, I did try to get to the football and lacrosse games. I owe a great debt of gratitude to my forebears, who had the perspicuity to invest wisely so that we were always comfortable, which helps immensely when the father figure is absent. Nobody ever wanted for anything, and I also hope and believe I taught by example that dedication to task is its own reward, even at some personal cost. I'm happy to say that each son surfed through the horrors of the sixties without a major wipeout—no drugs, no binges, no criminal misdemeanors, no bombs planted in police stations—and each has prospered off the work-ethic lesson that was their real inheritance from me. My deepest regret is that in my present circumstances, I'm not able to enjoy the pleasures of grandfatherhood.

It would be a time yet before we realized the obvious: that my attempt to game history was an utter and inglorious failure. You might say the patient died, but the operation wasn't a success. Who on earth would have guessed that the pea-brained egomaniac Lyndon Johnson would have wanted, as I'd predicted, his domestic revolution *at the same time*, as I had *not* predicted, that he decided to win a major land war in Asia? No one could be so foolish, but he—egged on by the slippery, weaselly opportunings of the Kennedy hotshots he inherited (until they deserted him, as was easily foretold)—proved himself equal to the task. No vain murderous folly has ever been more obvious and more unstoppable. Many is the time I wished I knew where Lon was and that Jimmy was alive so the old unit could go into action on LIBERTY VALANCE II.

It was madness, and by '66, at least, it was obvious that the American future in Vietnam was bleak and bloody, that countless boys would die or come home in that dreadful steel chair for nothing beyond the vainglory of a stubborn old man hellbent on proving he was right. The more the Kennedy slime deserted him, the more stubborn he became. The pusillanimous Robert McNamara was the worst, in my book, later stating that he stayed long after he had quit believing, thus sending men to their death for no other reason than his own reputation in a cause he cared nothing about. When it was over and he grew tired of not being invited to the good parties on the Vineyard, he mea culpa'ed his way back into the good graces of the liberals who'd abandoned old LBJ years earlier. It was truly scoundrel time in America, and with my peculiar burdens of guilt and responsibility, I found the going difficult.

My answer was to offer myself up to the war gods. It was to taunt irony, which those gods do seem to enjoy a good deal, and let them kill me in the war I had committed blasphemy to stop. I suppose I felt I owed it to my sons, and that better I go and die than one of them, though by the time the eldest was fodder for the draft, Nixon had ended it, the one thing I thank him for.

As for me: three tours, each of a year's length, the first running agents and supervising operations, 1966–'67; the second, 1970–'71, overseeing psywar ops against the North from a bunker inside Tan Son Nhut; and, as I have stated, the third as head of the murder program, Operation Phoenix, 1972–'73. I tried hard to get myself killed, and the North Vietnamese tried hard to kill me, even putting a reward on my head and coming damned close enough times to turn my hair gray, but even they, clever little devils, were never able to bring it off. I am proud to say that within Langley, I was known as the coldest of the cold warriors and the hottest of the hot warriors. Though I was a murderer, I made it clear to any who cared, and that would probably be only myself, that I was not a coward.

Here I leave off personal narrative only to say that after Vietnam, I was able to return to Soviet affairs, my true calling, and again I prospered. I grew a reputation for ruthless rationality—applying the precepts of the New Criticism again—and developed keen judgment; a vast network of sources inside Russia; savvy, superb reflexes; and a taste for vodka in the Russian style, neat in a peasant's glass. I could drink that stuff all night, until Peggy finally objected, at which point I quit cold and didn't take another drop until after her death, when, you might say, I made up for lost time. I'm still making up.

In September 1964, after employing hundreds and working eighteen-hour days, the Warren Commission released its report. You might think I'd gobble it up, but I didn't. I read the news coverage in the *Times* and the *Post* and realized that no matter how diligent the eight hundred investigators had been, they still hadn't a clue what happened. I left it at that and continued my total immersion in Agency affairs.

I can't say I was surprised, but at the same time, I was annoyed when the first of the anti-commission books came out in '65, Mark Lane's *Rush to Judgment*. My annoyance had more to do with the temerity of Lane: how easy it is to sit back and carp and bitch at the efforts of people who work so hard under a mission mandate to find out the truth and allay national fears; how easy to make a fortune out of nitpicking. It seemed likely that the report contained errors, as anything run by the government on so large a scale and compiled at such breakneck speed is bound to. What was called for was a second edition with a few corrections, not the initiation of a culture that would swell grotesquely and display its leftist tendencies and true agenda, which was to protect the left from any involvement in spite of the fact that Alek was created solely in the hothouse culture of screwball Commie crackpotism, and to sow general distrust of a government bent on winning its war in Asia, damn the cost in treasure and lives.

I watched from Washington and even abroad as the conspiracy theories metastasized into a huge tumor on the body politic, all of the conspiracies shamefully absurd and manufactured out of nothing more than occasional coincidence or good-faith errors in the rush, all of them driven by animus and the profit motive. I detested them: lefty scavengers picking at the bones to make political points and dough. Did I read them? No, but I read the reviews assiduously to see if anyone came close. I did see the Dal-Tex Building mentioned here and there, usually as a shooting site in either the four-rifle theory or the seven-rifle theory. I noted that the police did apprehend a fellow there, though they let him go the next day. Still, it was clear that we'd pulled it off, as all the theories and speculations remained comically off the mark. They seemed to think it was a "big" conspiracy, because only a huge governmental agency would have the wherewithal to make such an event happen, which included secretly influencing the Secret Service and the White House and poor Alek in a concerto of such exquisite timing and psychological acuity that it resembled a Swiss watch set to music by Mozart.

I suppose I should temper my contempt with a little understanding. After all, I knew things that no investigator did. For example, it was possible that the down-range sonic boom caused by Lon's shot, obeying some unpredictable acoustical logic, rebounded weirdly in the echo chamber that was Dealey Plaza and caused a pressure spike or a reverberation or even a report-like sound, which would strike many ears as coming from the grassy knoll. Perhaps it was that confusion that spawned the thousand-odd theories.

As well, I knew that the extreme velocity of the bullet Lon fired could have easily unleashed a fragment that would travel another three hundred feet and draw blood from James Tague, situated at the triple overpass. Mr. Tague's facial wound has long baffled and tantalized theorists because the Mannlicher-Carcano, grievously underpowered and slow-moving, wouldn't have had the oomph to reach out and touch a person so far away. The detonation of Lon's bullet, moving at close to three thousand feet per second, could have easily accomplished such a trick.

Anyhow, we succeeded exactly because we *weren't* a government operation, despite my connections. It was my op, and the team was bound in blood and loyalty, working without pay, risking all for a belief system. It was the kind of highly professional, small-scale enterprise that is the only hope of success, that needed no documentation, no vetting committees, no senior supervisors, no cliques with their concomitant resenters and traitors, no office politics, no budget, nothing. It could be betrayed only from the inside; no detective could unravel it because there wasn't one clever enough to read the signs in the dust, which were too subtle. We were too smart for them, for at least fifty years. The next few days? We'll see.

Anyhow, back from my first tour in Vietnam as a kind of hero, with a few empty weeks to fill before a tour in Moscow, I decided it was time to read the damned report and see what they had learned. By that time, my own internal turmoil had settled and I felt I'd be able to confront the findings in a more or less rational manner. My conclusions were mainly that the operation had succeeded brilliantly, particularly Lon's solution of the ballistics issue. If you recall, our problem was to shoot a man with a bullet that would leave no trace of itself except in tiny metallic residue that could be traced only to a specific bullet identified by category and lot but not to any particular rifle. (I suppose if Lon's rifle were located, traces of the same metal might be found within its barrel. But Lon— though we never discussed this, I'm sure it's so—would have destroyed the rifle so that no such discovery was possible.)

That is exactly what Lon managed: the head-shot bullet exploded dynamically when it hit the skull, leaving no fragment large enough to be tracked to Alek's rifle and therefore no fragment that could be ID'd as *not* from Alek's rifle. The investigators did locate two fragments in the limousine large enough to examine under the electron microscope, but clearly, they were not from the head shot. They were both pristine, without any contamination by blood or brain tissue, as the FBI expert explained in detail during his testimony. He also testified that, although fragments are generally hard to relate to a particular rifle, these two, one twenty-one grains, the other forty-four grains, did bear marks that related them to Alek's rifle. The only explanation for their presence is that they were fragments from Alek's first missed shot.

As I see it, he fired wretchedly, coming off a mistake that I will describe shortly, and the bullet (other testimony buttresses this argument) hit the curb immediately behind or adjacent to the limousine. Since the angle of refraction is always less than the angle of reflection, when the bullet tore itself to pieces against the hard stone, its "cloud" of fragments was projected in a conelike shape that almost perfectly intercepted the vehicle a few feet away, all of this in micro-time. Some think that one fragment hit the president in the scalp, stinging him. Maybe so, maybe not, but one hit the windshield from the inside, cracking it, and that fragment bounced downward and to the left, where it was found the next day by FBI searchers. Another fragment also landed there, but no one can identify the trajectory, other than to say that the energies released by explosions are madly random.

We know the two frags found in the car couldn't have come from Lon's rifle, because of the rifling marks already mentioned, but also because of the geometry of the head shot. It is not particularly enjoyable to focus on such a morbid topic, but in the interest of truth, I shall go onward. The detonation took place in the upper right-hand quadrant of the president's skull, above his ear (suggesting, among other things, the left-to-right axis of Lon's shot, given our position to the left of the sniper's-nest corner; LHO's theoretical shot would have created a necessarily right-to-left axis, which would have exploded out of JFK's left-hand quadrant, maybe above his left eye). The salient point is that, given the physics of the "explosion," all those fragments would have spewed at high energy from the right-hand upper quadrant of the skull along that axis, carrying metallic debris and brain tissue to the right, out of the car; there's no way the widely documented head shot, as witnessed eventually by the whole world, would have deposited fragments radically twenty full feet to the left, and downward, no less, to the carpet near the pedals, where those two pieces were found.

My one criticism of the report is that its investigators quickly came to believe in the single-gunman theory. Lane was right about one thing: it was a rush to judgment. Though they worked hard and honorably, that precept framed their findings, shaping them, perhaps only at the unknowable subconscious level. Had they remained open to theories outside their own invented box, they might have seen indications, subtle but persistent, in Alek's behavior that suggested strongly there were other players on the field.

Therefore, I shall walk you through Alek's last hour or so of freedom. There were developments that baffled the commission's investigators and continue to baffle the amateur assassinationologists, so let me lay out, for the sake of history, exactly what I think happened between 12:30 p.m., when Alek fired the first bullet, and 2:17 p.m., when he was nabbed in the Texas Theatre.

I doubt he was nervous. He was too exuberant, too happy, too coursing with energy. I can see him, crouched and hiding behind the fortress of boxes he'd arranged on the sixth floor of the Book Depository, his eyes beady, his face tight with the characteristic smugness that so exiled him from his fellow man, presidential assassin or no, thinking not What if I miss? but Hurry up, hurry up! He must have been hungry for his destiny, for his entry into history. He wasn't giving escape or survival a thought, but concentrating entirely on getting the job done to the best of his meager abilities. Consider his mind at the moment: he was about to strike a blow not merely at the United States, which he claimed to loathe, but at all those who'd seen him as he was—a fringe man clearly unable to hold a job, much less have a career, a life of normalcy and contribution—and insisted on reporting the bad news: You are nobody. You are not equipped to compete. Your destiny is nothingness. So this was his moment: to all of them, he was saying *I exist!* in thunder. But do not abjure the political for the psychological: he was a true believer, so true that he could and would kill for his principles. That puts him at the very end of the spectrum of political behavior, though it does not push him off it. In some fashion that he probably could not articulate, he thought he was birthing a new socialist world, and his idealism loaned him the self-esteem nothing else had provided for him. Then there was greed, the treasure at the end of the rainbow. That was the idealized image of himself as hero of Havana, in the '53 Cadillac convertible with Dr. Castro on the Malacón, waving to the throng. That was a risk worth dying for. He must have been, all taken into account, one of the world's happiest men in the split second before he pulled the trigger.

As we were, he was alerted to the approach of the killing moment not by his watch but by the roar of the crowd as its crescendo followed the motorcade down Main like a human wave. He saw it emerge, the long boatlike vehicle, with its bounty of politicians and wives, as it turned for its one-block run down Houston. I'm guessing it was here that the rifle flew to his shoulder and he edged closer to the window, not caring if he was seen (several witnesses noted him all but hanging out of the frame). The car reached its 120-degree turn at Elm, rotating slowly to the left. Question: why didn't he fire then? Car hardly moving, Kennedy as close as he would be, probably under seventy-five feet, head-on, pivoting slightly as the automobile pivoted; plus, instructions from his Russian control that this was the moment. Why would he go against his own instincts as well as orders from a superior whom he feared and loved? Again speculation: the safety? He pulls, ugh, nothing happens, so he breaks his line of vision through the scope, unshoulders the rifle, finds the safety—a poorly placed button half under the protruding rear of the firing pin assembly—and struggles to get it off. Perhaps his heavy sweating occluded the scope, and he saw nothing and had to quickly clean it with his shirt collar. Whatever, it was already going wrong for him, one tenth of a second in.

Desperately, he frees the mechanism, throws it to his shoulder, and fires the first shot in haste. True to form, a clean, clear, almost comical miss. I hold with many that the bullet, sailing along at that leisurely two-thousand-feet-per-second velocity, broke apart on the curb, depositing only its wan spray of fragments into the limo. He rushed, his trigger squeeze was a mess, the target was lost in the single tree that stood between him and his quarry, and the first shot, the closest shot, was a complete failure.

The man is haunted by folly. Now he's in a panic, having missed pitifully, given up his position, fair game for counter-snipers (there weren't any that day, though there would be evermore), and he hasn't even hit the car!

He labors through the cocking motion, the rifle jerked from his shoulder by the raggedness of the manipulation, and he comes back "on target." His finger lunges against the coarse grind of the pull, and my guess is that the crosshairs weren't anywhere near the target when he fired, for the simple reason that he hit it.

Or did he? Yes, according to the commission, he did, with the famed magic bullet that drilled through the president's upper back and exited his throat, its angle adjusted slightly by the muscle tissue through which it had traveled, which also cost it enormous velocity; then, spinning sideways, it hit Governor Connally in the back (its impression recorded indelibly in scar tissue), sliced through his body, exited much damaged (despite claims to the contrary), and drilled his wrist and his thigh. Then it tumbled, spent, hot, mangled, to rest in the folds of his jacket, to be discovered by a technician that afternoon at the hospital on the governor's gurney after the governor was removed. Oh, what a bad boy that bullet was! The mischief it unleashed! What grist for the mills of the ignorant, the malicious, the embittered lefty proletariat-intellectuals! Yet I knew then and I know now that the bullet did what Arlen Specter said it did. It is beyond dispute.

What isn't much thought about is the next issue. *Alek thought he missed!* I have seen a fair number of men shot. It's not usually like the movies, which instruct us to the theory of the instant, spastic reaction, the firing of all nerves simultaneously and the twitchy-legged death tumble to Earth. It can happen that way. It happens other ways too. Often men don't even know they've been hit. They think it's a punch or they've bumped into a door or they notice nothing at all, and not until they look and see blood welling (and sometimes it doesn't even well!) do they comprehend after putting two and two together that they've been shot. It cannot be predicted. Each wound is different, based on a thousand or so factors from velocity, bullet shape, angle of strike, muscles and/or bones encountered, vitality of target, blood pressure, speed of target, target's relationship to solidity on Earth (standing, sitting, moving, whatever), weather, barometric pressure, and on and on and on. There is no knowing, so anybody who tells you what should have happened—and infers, from the fact that it didn't happen, something is amiss—is a bald-faced liar.

Let us not concentrate on what was happening. Let us concentrate on what Alek *thought* was happening. What he saw through the fuzzy optics of his Hollywood—the brand, not the town—Japanese scope was . . . nothing. Look at Zapruder's film. We don't see the hit because the president is behind the sign, but when he emerges, the only thing that's happened is that he's begun to lean forward a bit, and his hands have come up, which are probably not visible to Alek, if he's looking at all, and he's probably not because he's lost in the drama of cocking the rifle for the second time. When Alek returns to the scope, Kennedy's head and posture may be incrementally degraded, but that's too subtle for Alek to note.

In his mind: utter panic, complete self-loathing. Physiology: fingers bloated with blood, oxygen debt, woozy vision, yips coursing through his arms and trunk, sweat sliding down his face and flanks, presentiment of doom. Target: small, getting smaller as the vehicle pulls away (though it doesn't speed up), slight left-to-right movement produced by the angle of the street relative to the position of the shooter.

Our boy is not in a good spot to make the next shot.

He tries to steer the scope crosshairs onto—where? Having missed twice—from his point of view—he has no idea where to hold for a killing shot. He has no idea of the index between point of aim and point of impact, he's in a shooter's no-man's-land, even as he's taken the slack out of the trigger and sustains it right at the tipping point between shot and no shot.

Suddenly, the president's head explodes.

Alek is so startled that his own trigger jerks and he fires his third bullet, but his jump at the sight of the destruction of the skull is so intense that his third bullet goes sailing off to the general southwest, presumably landing in some distant Oz beyond the triple overpass, never to be noted or found. It was an awesome break for us; it meant that witnesses saw him fire his third shot, it squared all accounting of bullets, shells, and wounds, it forever connected Alek to the event, lacking any tangible, empirical evidence of our existence, and it cemented all investigative effort to the Book Depository and to Alek. Cops are predictable; they want to put things in a box, and the sooner and tighter it fits, the happier they are, and the more outsiders tug and pull and poke at the contents of the box, the more stubborn and angry they become. It's all personal to them.

Back to Alek, for whom the world has just changed mightily.

Given to paranoia anyway, he sees in that second that a conspiracy against him does exist, that he is a patsy, he is a chump, a fool. He's been set up to take the fall, and that reality becomes instantly clear. (Let us also postulate that his narcissism is secretly pleased; he is important enough to destroy!)

He realizes that all he believed in was false, that there was no Russian agent, he is not working for KGB, there's no escape car awaiting him, he will not be hustled away and secreted to Havana and the loving ministrations of Dr. Castro. Instead, he's the sucker at the center of every James M. Cain novel, every film noir, lost in a nightmare city as forces so vast he cannot imagine them grind into position to crush him.

It occurs to him that his life might be in danger. He knows the sixth floor is empty only because it always has been empty, but that wisdom is no longer operative; it is from a different world. It occurs to him that his death is absolutely necessary for the new narrative. It may be that a detective, a security guard, an armed citizen in the know might already be there, hiding behind his own clump of boxes, ready to step out and issue the coup de grâce and become both the hero of America and the secret lynchpin of the plot against Alek.

He does what any man in such circumstances would do.

He cocks the rifle, throwing another shell into the chamber, finger to trigger, slack removed, weapon at the ready, and like a patrolling infantryman in an ambush area, he hastens the ninety-five feet diagonally across the empty space to the one stairway down, ready to respond to any emerging attackers. Nobody's there. And no bullet comes crashing through the windows to snipe him as he sought to snipe the president.

He pauses at the head of the stairs, hating to relinquish his weapon. But he knows that he can't emerge into society at the site of a presidential assassination with a rifle in his hands. So he stuffs the rifle between two book crates at the top of the stairs, where it will be found an hour later by a detective. That is why it wasn't found abandoned in the sniper's nest; that is why it was loaded and cocked.

He heads downstairs, and his adventures in the building, back in society, have been well chronicled. He slides into a chair in the lunchroom, is accosted by a policeman and identified by a coworker, and once the policeman heads upstairs, Alek zips out the front door.

Now what? He knows there'll be no pickup awaiting him at the corner of Houston and Pacific, and there may be ambushers. Instead of heading north up Houston, where we were nominally waiting to pick him up, he turns east and heads up Elm, past the Dal-Tex Building. That is where I see him as I am pulling Lon out of the lobby while we beat our own hasty retreat from the seventh floor.

Alek continues to surge up Elm for another four blocks. Let us assume it is in this period that he more or less returns to his rational mind. He knows it's a matter of time before they locate the sniper's nest and the rifle, take a canvass of employees at TBD and note that he's the only one missing, though he's been noted earlier as present, so they'll know he left right after the shooting. Possibly that's not paramount in his mind. He thinks he's being hunted by his own co-conspirators, and he remembers my warning him against bringing the handgun, because I was gaming him into being the easy prey that would be the exclamation point on our operation.

I don't believe he thinks he can get away, as in escape to a new life. Impossible. He wasn't stupid, just incompetent. But at that point in his life, I think the one possibility of victory he saw, the one glimmer of hope, was to defend himself against his murderers, not the police or FBI. If he could shoot one of them and bring the bag to the cops, it would be proof of sorts that he'd been manipulated, though he hadn't worked out the allegiance issues and didn't know who had used him.

Again, as for any man on the run, his first impulse would have been to get a gun, which explains why, after walking away from the site of the assassination, he climbed aboard a bus headed down Elm Street back to the site of the assassination. No one has bothered to work out the destination of that bus: it was to the Oak Cliff section of Dallas. He wasn't fleeing crazily, as so many have stated; he was going to get the gun.

Soon enough, the bus is moored in traffic a block east of the assassination site. Time is ticking by, he knows that the police effort is grinding along, possibilities are being examined, questions asked and answered, the winnowing process begun, and that it will cast him up quickly.

He vaults from the bus at the corner of Elm and Lamar and heads south down Lamar for two blocks and goes to . . . *the bus station!* Does it occur to him to buy a ticket on the next bus out of town, to put distance between self and pursuers? He has seventeen dollars with him, which can get him as far as San Antonio or Lubbock or Midland or Austin. But his brain is not working that way; he is thinking, Get the gun. He hails what will be known as the only cab he took in his life. He's in the cab at 12:45, in Oak Cliff, a block or two past his house so that the cabbie won't associate his passenger with the soon-to-be-announced address of the suspect. He dashes into his house, goes straight to wherever he's hidden it, snatches up his revolver, stuffs it into his waistband, throws on a jacket— to cover it, which shows he's thinking tactically—and is gone in seconds.

Consider how dangerous a move he's come up with. He knows they'll know who he is and where he lives. He risks capture in a daring attempt to get back to the roominghouse because that's where he left his S&W .38 snub-nose. The gun is more important to him than his life, and he takes an awesome chance to get it, because he knows that without the gun, he has no chance against his pursuers, who aren't the cops but the members of the conspiracy who've betrayed him. He does this rather than, say, take the cab to a suburban bus station or train station and try to catch a ride or hop a freight out of town before the authorities can throw out their manhunters' net. Time isn't of the essence; the gun is of the essence.

Alek heads back down Beckley in the direction he's come, diverts at Crawford to take a diagonal going nowhere, turns down Tenth, again seemingly arbitrarily, reaches the intersection of Patton and Tenth, and notices in horror that a black Dallas police car has just pulled over. The officer beckons him.

Now comes the tragedy of Officer Tippit. Had I known that the monster I created was capable of such violence, I would have put a .45 into him and walked away. That said, I must also say that I should have put a .45 into my own head as punishment for the mayhem that was about to transpire, which was entirely my own invention. What is the point of claiming responsibility if you don't act on it? There is no point. I tried to use my sin as a motive for redemption and, over the years, gave my life in toto to Agency and country, knowing that I hadn't the guts to punish myself as I should be punished. Perhaps my punishment lies ahead.

Poor Tippit. By accounts no genius, but a decent ex-GI who loved his job and did it well, content to be a patrolman forever, he was on the cusp of the biggest bust of the century when it all went bad on him. Moved from a farther patrol area into Oak Cliff as a precautionary measure and to stand by for orders, he had been alerted three times on his radio of the age, weight, height, and hair color of the suspect. He spies such a man walking down Tenth Street in Oak Cliff. Who knows what other tells Alek the idiot was broadcasting: walking too fast with his face screwed up in anguish, almost running, radiating the don't-tread-on-me animosity that was his stock in trade, refusing eye contact while looking cautiously over his shoulder now and then. It could have been any or all of them.

No identification of Alek by name has yet been given over the radio, and none has linked him to Oak Cliff and the Beckley Avenue area. It's just that his appearance is so right. That's why Tippit tails him for a block or two and then pulls over. Yeats: "It's old and it's sad and it's sad and it's feary." Yes, it was, especially "feary," that is, fearful, horrifying, tragic. Had I but known. But I didn't. Guilty, guilty, guilty.

Alek sees the black vehicle slow up and pull over. He realizes he's been nabbed. He ambles off the sidewalk to the vehicle, where the officer, window rolled down, awaits him.

What could they have said? It's pointless to imagine, and it was probably a banality, a cliché, nothing memorable. Witnesses—there were several, some close—report no hostility, no harsh words, no threats; it wasn't an altercation, it was an exchange, and Alek may have gotten away with it for a second, for then he broke contact with the seated officer and turned to go on his way.

Tippit isn't done with him but at the same time hasn't made up his mind to make the pinch. He climbs from his squad car, gun definitely not in hand, and possibly calls to Alek.

Alek turns, walks around the car to place himself in range, draws, and fires three times point-blank. All three hits from close range are solid mortal blows, careening through center mass, upper body, blood-bearing organs, and as soon as he is hit, Tippit is down, bleeding out if not already dead.

Why?

After all, Alek is not without his verbal faculties; he's a debater, an arguer from way back, a guy who's always got an answer. That's how he defines himself, part guerrilla warrior, part dialectical soldier. Why doesn't he at least try to con his way out? The performance isn't beyond him, and his intellectual vanity that he's smarter than some cop would surely be in play.

From Alek's point of view, the fact that the cop is already there—it's only forty-five minutes after the shooting, and chaos and confusion reign—is proof that the man is part of the conspiracy. Whoever set Alek up either informed the authorities of his address or hired a professional killer dressed as a cop to ambush him when he returned home. Perhaps Dallas is full of professional killers in search of Alek, already equipped with his name, address, description, and likely whereabouts. That would be an easy intellectual leap for a man with Alek's tendencies toward paranoia and conspiracy.

So Alek thinks the cop is a hit man. His rage, his paranoia, his violent nature, his fear, his self-hatred, and his other hatred were in full bloom in that single instant, and that and that alone can explain his next move, which utterly violates any principle of self-preservation.

If Alek has just shot a cop to escape, his next move has to be to turn and flee, race down alleyways, cut across yards, throw off any followers, catch a bus, get out of the area, fast.

Instead, he walks over to the downed Tippit and shoots him in the temple. From the autopsy: "[The bullet] is found to enter the right temporal lobe, coursed through the brain transecting the brain stem, severing the cerebral peduncles surrounded by extensive hemorrhage and found to exit from the brain substance in the calcarine gyrus to the left of the midline." Of course he wasn't shooting Officer Tippit; he was shooting me.

His vengeance expressed, Alek mutters, "Poor damn cop," as he empties the shells from his cylinder and quickly reloads, then turns and heads up Patton, down Jefferson, cuts through a yard and dumps his jacket, then cuts back to Jefferson, which, in a half mile or so, will take him to the Texas Theatre. His absurd incompetence comes to the fore again. So lame is his attempt at escape and so ignorant is he of what's going on around him, he is followed by a number of citizens. One of them has called the murder in to headquarters on Tippit's radio. Two men snatch up Tippit's revolver and begin to hunt Alek on their own.

In a brief while, a matter of several blocks down Jefferson, trailing trackers, Alek comes to a small commercial district. He's consumed with evading his killers (even though he hasn't bothered to look behind him), and his main thought is to get off the street. To the logic of his twisted brain, he seeks refuge by dodging into the Texas Theatre on that street. I suppose he thinks his killers will eventually be driven off the streets by the excess of Dallas policemen who will flood the zone in hours if not minutes. Perhaps he imagines a surrender, the revelation that the "cop" was a Mafia hit man, and some sort of redemption as he proves he never killed the president and he was manipulated by shadowy "others" of indeterminate origin. He might see himself as a hero, the subject of an admiring movie. In those ten minutes in the movie theater's private darkness, he must have comforted himself by self-delusion. Facing the reality, for a man whose resources were so fragile, would have been too much.

And then the lights came on. His vacation had lasted ten minutes, and cops were closing in from both sides.

I first heard the name sometime in '74 or '75. I was in Moscow, working undercover in one of several well-documented Soviet identities. I was in and out of Moscow in those years under a variety of guises, and I have to say they were great years, maybe the best of my life. We knew we were getting somewhere and doing some good, and the economics and the demographics were breaking in our direction, so we were filled with hope and optimism. Moreover, Vietnam was managing to wind down without killing me or any of my sons, for which I was eternally grateful.

We were under pressure from Langley—or from the Defense Department by way of Langley—to come up with a gun. It was a new Soviet-issue semi-auto sniper rifle that bore the seemingly but not actually melodramatic name of Dragunov. It sounded like the SovMil had gotten all Hollywoody and called the thing the Dragon. No such luck. Soviet military nomenclature has always featured the name of the designer, which is why Sergeant Kalashnikov became world-famous, as did, in an earlier age, Comrade Tokarev, whose stubby little pistol snuffed out so many lives in the cellars of Lubyanka during the Great Purges of the thirties. In any event, although it seemed absurd in a world where giant rockets carrying nukes could obliterate millions in minutes, everyone in American military culture was in a frenzy over this Dragunov, and it went without saying that he who obtained either plans or working copies of the thing would be awarded a gigantic feather to be stuffed into his cap. I meant to get myself that feather. Petty ambition; I am diminished by the memory.

But Bob Lee Swagger beat me to it.

Can you imagine a name like that? What a moniker to conjure with. He was every Ole Miss quarterback, every NASCAR driver, every tiny-town police chief or state trooper rolled into one. He was actually a gunnery sergeant in the United States Marine Corps, with an intelligence background, as he'd worked with another Agency jamboree, called the Studies and Observation Group, on an earlier tour. That was particularly dangerous duty; it consisted of leading indigenous troops up near the Laotian border to run interdiction missions against the North Viet supply line. Lots and lots of combat, lots of shooting. The talent pool consisted of aggressive senior NCOs from either army special forces or marine infantry outfits, and they had themselves a dandy war amid the mountains and swamps of the Laotian border.

It was his third tour as a sniper in which he snatched up Comrade Dragunov. At a forlorn fire base somewhere in the jungle, he and his spotter worked a ruse, with an Agency team and the marines in full co-op mode, that resulted in our acquisition of the first Dragunov in Western hands. That rifle today is at the Agency museum on the first floor of the main building in Langley. Before it was put on display, I had a good hands-on experience with it at the Langley technical directorate's shop. The very same one!

His twenty years after Vietnam were the most banal of hells. It seems sad that a man of such gifts should suffer so basely, but what are you going to do? Men of such dark fury and skill frequently turn it on themselves, as Pilgrim Swagger did, and the record is beyond melancholy and well into squalor. Alcoholism, business failure, brushes with the law, car wrecks, a failed marriage, a whole litany of messages to God requesting annihilation, since reality was too painful. God must have been busy that day, or perhaps he was saving Swagger to punish a real sinner, such as *moi*; somehow the sniper retreated to the woods, acquired a trailer, and rebuilt himself. Despite his many feats of arms, this was probably his greatest, bravest accomplishment. He became a reader, curious as to what had caused Vietnam and, beyond that, what had caused so much pain, from his traumatic wound and from the losses he suffered, his first Vietnamese wife and then his spotter. Swagger, I tried to save you from all that. I knew as early as '63 that it would come to no good end and your story would be written in blood and pain a million times. Kill me if you can, goddamn you, Swagger, but I committed the crime of the century to save you. You should love me as you press the trigger, if that's what is in store.

Alone in Arkansas except for a dog and a brace of rifles, he gave himself over to the history of the Vietnam War and then the history of war itself, which after all is paradoxically the history of civilization. He educated himself in the ways of a world he served but never knew. His mind refined itself, shed itself of childish notions like pride and bravado and domination, and became wise. He stopped talking, he started listening. He shot and shot and shot and turned his grade-A talent into something almost beyond knowing. He retrained himself for a mission, and at last one came along. I should know. It was my mission.

In '93, I was sixty-three years old. I was a hoary old éminence grise, beloved by the younger men, known for steady advice, unquenchable rationality—I had never abandoned the New Criticism—and superb technical skills, especially at planning and funding black ops. I was Mr. Black in Agency lore. I was in high demand. Though I spent much of my time on Russia—it was I who put together the money train that enabled Yeltsin to take over after Gorbachev, and I don't think he or anybody else ever knew I was an American, much less an American agent—I oversaw or advised on projects in other spheres as well.

That was how El Salvador came into my life. God-awful place, never want to go back. It reminded me of Vietnam, though the food was all mealy and saucy, nowhere near the level of the Mexican that Alek had introduced me to.

This need not be a long tale, and I will spare you details and dramatization. I begin with a personal note, although my memoir is by design professional, not personal. But the personal intrudes on the professional. In 1992 Peggy died of breast cancer after a six-week ordeal. It was a terrible thing to see, a woman so vital, so intelligent, so beautiful, so loyal, so terrific, the best of all her peers and the source of whatever strength I had, as well as an extraordinary mother to the boys, eaten alive by the crab. The boys and I were at her side when she passed, and she lived long enough to see them through college and through their own well-established careers and families. It was a devastation for me, one that hurt and hurt and hurt. I am not making excuses; I am merely explaining why I was not at my best in what followed. I made bad judgments, mistakes, my concentration slipped; it was far from my proudest hour. I was lucky to escape alive, even if I didn't.

Let's speed this up. Time may not be on our side, thanks to Mr. Swagger. It became necessary to eliminate a man, and it occurred to me to replicate Operation LIBERTY VALANCE. Same method: a patsy sniper, a real sniper, a ballistic deceit, the patsy caught during the op and eliminated, the home team getting away clean. The details are forever sealed in Langley's files, but again I cast Lon as the real shooter; it turned out he was hungry for the adventure, having become bored stiff by his self-decreed "retirement." I cast Swagger as Oswald.

Bad career move, as they say.

Swagger, unlike poor, stupid Alek, escaped, and it became a race and a chase. We had to get to Swagger before the FBI did. This was Shreck, my main operative's, task, and Swagger outsmarted, outfought, and outshot him at every turn. My first mistake: not realizing he would have made a better shooter than patsy. Neither Shreck nor I saw until too late that the plot we had engineered for him generated not his death but his rebirth. He reentered the world he had abandoned stronger, smarter, more guileful, more cunning, and braver. All along, we weren't hunting him, he was hunting us.

A final ambush was painstakingly set. I urged Lon to be the shooter, and I do think he enjoyed the whole thing. It was better than rotting away in a wheelchair in a secluded estate in the North Carolina countryside. For his heroism, his effort, his high morale, he was awarded a bullet in the head. I should regret this more than I do, but after all, given his tragedy, Lon enjoyed an interesting life because of my importuning. Better he passed that way than via decay. Shreck, for his part, was unhappy to discover that a shotgun slug could penetrate a bulletproof vest. He wasn't as unhappy as his number two, a stumpy little ex-NCO of extremely violent tendencies named Jack Payne, who made the same discovery, but not until Swagger had blown off his arm with the same shotgun. Swagger: the best man I ever heard of in a gunfight, bar none.

Even then he had surprises. He was captured, and our deeper trap seemed to still be in place, by which he would swing for murder.

Oops, I say! He'd outthought even the great Hugh Meachum. He'd subtly disabled his rifle before the whole thing happened, so it was impossible for it to have fired the fatal shot. As far as I know, they're still looking for the person who did, but it was at this point that Hugh Meachum decided to die.

Again I pull the screen of discretion between the reader and the details. Let me say that it should be beyond the ken of no professional intelligence operative—and I was one of the world's best—to arrange a convincing fiction for his own death. I was, after all, a superb planner, a manipulator of documents and secret funding, and had long since made the necessary preparations for such a contingency. It helped that I lived alone and there was no spousal difficulty to contend with. It helped also that I was still under discipline, and I knew that once I made the break, I made it permanently: there could be no going back, no farewells, not a minute crack in the facade.

I put the operation into action on a Wednesday, and by Friday I was gone. I left without saying good-bye to the boys and their children. That hurt. That still hurts. But I knew them to be secure both financially and emotionally and that the lessons of labor and loyalty, as well as the dividends that Colt, Winchester (now FN), Smith & Wesson, and so forth and so on provided, would continue to comfort them against the rude buffeting of circumstance.

I enacted a certain computer code meant to eat all my files in the Agency database. I suppose that was overkill, but one can never be certain. It was doubtful that anyone would go trolling that deep in the distant past, particularly in a world that was changing as rapidly as this one, but safer is always to be preferred over sorrier.

And thus Hugh Meachum shuffled off this mortal coil.

As for the real me, he went where he went and became what he became. I prospered. I had been quietly looting money from the Agency for some years—if an old spy doesn't look out for himself, who will?—and the ample fund in a Swiss bank account made my new life one of comfort. I had some contacts, I knew some things, I had some documents: in time, I improved my station, for my mind was still sharp. In time, I did more than improve; I became wealthy, even filthy wealthy. I lived in splendor.

In my new life, I developed a taste for flavors of decadence. I reacquainted myself with the nuances of delight that alcohol provided. I discovered the pleasures of sex with younger women, especially when amplified beyond the power of the man himself by drugs in all their variations. I found I excelled in business manipulations that produced munificence for me and all who sailed with me. I had fought so hard for capitalism, it seemed appropriate to enjoy its fruits. I became an entrepreneur, a builder, an investor; I devised layers and further layers of supernumeraries between myself and reality.

It has come to this: I live in a mansion hidden behind a thirty-foot steel wall off of Ulysse Nardin drive, in an area patrolled by a special battalion. I sit out on my veranda in the warm weather, and all I see is mine to the river a mile away. I am totally secure. I have mistresses and masseuses and chefs and sommeliers. The world has been kind to me, which I take as proper recompense for the efforts I put into my crusade to secure freedom and peace for the largest number of people, and which, despite some setbacks, I believe I accomplished.

What could possibly go wrong?

The answer came one night deep in sleep, when I was feeling most safe. I don't know why it chose that moment to announce itself, but it did, and while I can't say it changed my life (at least not yet), I will say it gave me a lesson in paranoia from which I've never recovered, and that is why my security arrangements are the most impenetrable in the world.

The coat.

The goddamned coat.

I hadn't thought of those days in the ten years I'd been building my new life. It was so far behind, and all the players were dead. But I awakened in the middle of the night in a cold sweat, remembering.

Jimmy Costello had hidden in the elevator machinery house on the roof of the Dal-Tex Building for a long sixteen hours, and during that time, the bore solvent from Lon's Winchester collected and migrated and ultimately seeped into the garment, soaking its breast from the inside, forever cursing it with the smell of the murder weapon. Even before that, it had been placed on the stack of swatch books we used to elevate Lon to the proper height, leaving a tire tread on the back.

Jimmy had wisely decided not to get it out of the building, in case he was stopped by a policeman who'd recognize the penetrative odor. He'd left it there, folded, as I recall, inside a pile of carpet remnants on a dark and deserted shelf in that little-visited area.

It seemed unimportant at the time, and Jimmy had said he'd come back at some point, reenter the building, and destroy it. But he had been killed prematurely, and in my grief over his passing, my mourning for Lon's exit from my life, the press of my career, and whatever residue of subconscious guilt and regret remained from LIBERTY VALANCE, I had forgotten until that moment.

The next morning I dealt with the problem. My first thought was that I buy the damned building and tear it down and throw in a parking lot. It was well within my means. But I realized such a radical decision might attract more attention than necessary, the building having been declared officially "interesting" by too many who thought they knew something about architecture, and that a prudent first move was to determine the situation on the ground. Through the various levels of administrative anonymity I had arranged, I ordered a discreet Texas private investigator to penetrate the building and examine the room in question. In a week or so, the answer came back: the elevators had been completely modernized in 1995, and that machinery room demolished, and a new one constructed on its spot. All well and good. But also all sick and bad.

I had no idea of the coat's disposition before the demolition. Perhaps some workers simply dumped the pile of carpeting remnants down a chute, and they'd gone into a Dumpster and thence to the landfill or the enviro-chummy reclamation plant. Yes, that was probably it.

But . . . what if? What if someone had discovered it and remarked upon the oddity of such a coat with such a bounty of evidence being found in a building overlooking Dealey Plaza, and moreover, dating from sometime in a past easily as ancient 1963? Suppose this nugget of info, by some whimsical path, had drifted laterally and entered assassination lore? Given the hunger of the conspiracy theorists for new theories, new provocations, new possibilities, new evidence, such a tidbit could easily inspire a new area of research, a new book, a new focus.

Maybe with this new framing theory—a gunman in Dal-Tex—a brilliant investigator could rearrange the old evidence, find some new evidence, engage in brilliant speculation, and see into the heart of the thing. Could I be located? Highly unlikely. After all, I had disconnected myself from that possibility by conveniently dying in 1993.

But suppose someone got as far as Hugh Meachum? That would be far enough. My legacy would be destroyed, my memory in the minds of children and grandchildren, family members from mine, Peggy's, and Lon's family, even Jimmy's. That presented a possibility I could not live with happily.

I arranged—through supernumeraries, layers of buffeting, clever financial manipulation so that the source of the funding could never be tracked back to my address—for a man to relocate to Dallas and join the "assassination community." His announced career was to "solve" the Kennedy assassination mystery, so he had to be studious, highly intelligent, labor-intensive. He also needed delicate social skills, for I wanted his penetration to be aggressive enough that he could acquire a network of informants, all of whom had no idea they were informing, to keep him apprised of the latest in the theory and practice of the ongoing investigations.

To fit in with the culture down there, he needed one more salient attribute: he had to be insane. Despite his evident intelligence and charm, he would be seen as harmless. His "theory" would harm no one because it was so manifestly absurd. He had to put together a scenario that sounded rational until it reached a point and then twisted off crazily into the ether of the impossible, and he had to sell it with earnestness and passion, not estranging his allies.

I feel we did well in recruiting and am satisfied, even gratified, by his employment and performance and creativity. His name is Richard Monk, and he is a former major in army intelligence who retired honorably after his twenty with no sign of disgrace. His assignment: if anyone on the Net or anyone in Dallas shows an undue interest in the Dal-Tex theory of assassination, that subject is to be engaged at a deep level, his theories, his evidence, his capabilities all assessed for further monitoring. Ultimately, after reports are filed and analyzed and passed along, the information will arrive to me, and I will make a judgment as to disposition. Subtle methods will be explored as a means of dissuading the subject, but if it comes to that place, I will authorize, and have set up a structure to execute, a kill order.

I do not kill for money, I do not kill for anger, I do not kill for pleasure. I kill to preserve my legacy and the legacy of the institutions and people I served. That is enough. People have killed for a lot less, for pennies, or, more worthless, for pride.

The first victim was an amiable writer whose specialty was guns and the men who use them. I assume it was his analysis of the firearms issues that brought him to Dallas. As he explained to Richard Monk, he had come up with a theory that was suspiciously like the actual one Lon created all those years ago. And he had picked the Dal-Tex Building as his shooting site. Those two developments alone doomed him. Nothing personal.

Some months later, real trouble started.

CHAPTER 20

The records of the great Abercrombie & Fitch seventh-floor gun room were a mess, a disgrace, a disaster. Evidently, when the new owners acquired the corporation after its 1977 bankruptcy, they knew the future lay in jeans for kids, not Westley Richards .577 Nitro Expresses for Nobel Prize–winning writers. This trove was part of the property they acquired, along with the long-term lease on the warehouse facility in suburban Jersey. That lease had ten years to run, so no idea toward disposition was necessary until that time.

The vast room of ruin and confusion afforded one pleasure to Swagger, and that was escape from the enigma that was synesthesia, which he had learned was a freakish affliction—ability? gift? curse?—in the brain by which cues mix and produce something called "responses in differing modalities." Most commonly, it meant that a letter or a number, for some odd reason, appeared not as it was objectively but in a peculiar color. So to Niles Gardner, the number 9 was red, the number 4 was blue, the number 6 was green. If he saw a headline in a newspaper, "Most pro careers last 9 years, study finds," he would see the numeral in the color his mind told him was there, not the smudgy black of newsrag ink.

Swagger had made one further connection, but not to Hugh; it went down in the chain of linkages, not up, and anyway, what the fuck did this have to do with anything? No idea. Not even a whisper. It seemed another dead end, and the discomfort of it, like an undigested clot of food in his stomach, created great anxiety.

So the files, in their chaos, represented relief from that anguish.

They were real, occupied space, could be manipulated, and were on a medium with which he was familiar, that is, paper. He happily confronted them.

Many other researchers had already pillaged the room, notably, Hemingway and Roosevelt biographers. That perhaps was why Bob found no documents for the great writer or president: all filched, sitting in files in Princeton or the University of Illinois or someplace. There were few pickings for other great men, though Bob did find an invoice for the .38 Colt Detective Special that Charles Lindbergh carried through every day of the Bruno Hauptmann trial. But that was a random, rare find.

As Marty had promised, the files had more or less imploded, collapsing into themselves like one of those buildings brought down with a minimum of strategically planted explosives so that it seems to disappear into a hole full of rubble. The bound books of firearms sales, required by the ATF since 1938, were casually distributed through the mess. Some of the shipping invoices were filed in boxes, some of which were labeled by years, some of which weren't; other clumps of invoices lay here and there on the damp cement floor of the corrugated tin structure that from the outside was just another cottage-industry headquarters and manufacturing joint in a seemingly endless complex out by I-95. No one was on-site; Swagger had to pick the keys up at the real estate management company in downtown Rutherford after instructions and permission from corporate headquarters in Oklahoma City, under Marty's good auspices through the intervention of Tom Browner, whoever he was. Swagger had been smart enough to bring a can of Kroil to lube locks that had grown stiff and unaccustomed to the penetration of keys. Now he crouched on sore knees, trolling in the disaster under bad light, in the acrid odor of metal that corrugated tin gives off.

It unfolded before him, a cavalcade of American high-end sporting rifle and shotgun life. Big-game guns, elegant British shotguns for upland birds, the occasional accidental invoice for a rare, expensive sort of fishing tackle (fishing tackle had dominated the firm's eighth floor, a floor above the guns, and on the roof there was an artificial casting pond for the trout-fishing swells to try out their technique). That it was a vanished world meant little to Swagger by this time, though at the early going, he felt a twinge of something when he came across a shipping order for three boxes of Kynoch .470 Nitro Express to an "R. Ruark" of "Honey Badger Farm," RR 32, Kingston, S.C. Mostly, it was long-forgotten members of the bourgeois money-eyed set ordering ammunition, mundane guns for domestic hunting, and the like. Despite the gun room's fancy clientele and worldwide fame—that was marketing—its bread and butter lay in servicing the nonfamous dentists, lawyers, doctors, auto-dealership owners, and cotter-pin and plastic glass manufacturers of the unphotographed, unsentimentalized American small-town elite, many from the South and the West.

There was no other way to proceed than this straight-ahead plunge through stuff. Chronology, compartmentalization, geography, brand-name, all the retail categories by which a large mass of documents could be organized were pretty much shot. So many had gone through, grabbed their treasure, and left without repacking the boxes, much less resetting them on the shelves, that methodology seemed useless. He'd spent three hours going through the boxes tipped sideways on the floor, to no effect. He'd examined clumps aisle by aisle, trying to find such elemental regulators as year, manufacturer, destination. No effect. It was a maze of random paperwork, abandoned, most of it facedown, goddammit, on the cold concrete floor. He'd moved on to the boxes on the shelves. So far, to no effect. Just to make it more unendurable, the fluorescent light in this sector of the warehouse flickered on and off, making visibility more difficult. Why hadn't he brought a flashlight? Or better yet, to free up both hands, one of those lights you wore on your head, so he could see clearly what was before him.

It bothered him immensely that outside, four really good FBI operators lounged, going on coffee and doughnut energy, as his body-guard team in the crowded parking lot, putting out the message to all observers, Do not fuck around here. Didn't these highly trained guys have better things to do than guard him and suck down caffeine and calories? Shouldn't they be busting cribs in lower Manhattan, freeing sex slaves in Chinatown brothels, or serving high-risk warrants on button men on the Lower East Side? Nah. They just lounged in their Cherokee, joking and smoking and talking sports.

Finally, he was finished, six hours and two bruised knees and an oncoming cold later. Nothing. Not a goddamn thing. It was like syn-esthesia all over again. Under better circumstances, he could have brought a team, they could have indexed and sorted as they went along, and when they were finished, they would have bucked up the mess considerably and restored some sense of coherency to the chaos. Not this time, which had represented a once-over-lightly approach, in hopes that something would turn up on the surface. It hadn't. Time to let the feds get back to busting chops and him to his life on the assassination beat.

It wasn't the last unit of shelving, but nearly so. Three boxes lay on their sides, placed knee-high on the second-to-last unit. They'd been ripped open, some material removed, some stuffed back in, some left on the floor. He bent and brought his eyes up close to examine the labels on the boxes.

Whoa, mama.

What have we here?

One read:

MANAGER'S CORRESPONDENCE
June 1958–August 1969 (Harris)

He moved the box to the best light, pulled the lid off, and found himself looking at approximately three hundred carbons, stuffed in indiscriminately, clearly having been looted for Hemingwayania and restored haphazardly. They were roughly chronological, though when a clump had been pulled out, it had been stuffed back in at the easiest point, which was toward the end of the carton. It was so tight, each piece had to be pulled out delicately one at a time.

He glanced at his watch—4:15. Too much time already wasted.

Do it, he ordered himself.

He found it at 5:18.

July 23, 1960

Lon Scott
Scott's Run
RR 224
Clintonsburg, Va.

Dear Lon,

Hope this finds you in good health. The last time I saw you, you still looked like you could crack the Harvard line for a first down just about any time you wanted. Hope you're as chipper now.

Anyhow, you'll be getting three packages from us in the upcoming weeks. Or if not from us, at least under our power of suggestion. You've probably heard that New Haven is introducing a new model in a new caliber in the fall. The rifle is called "The Westerner," and it's in the new belted .264 Winchester Magnum. The cartridge was developed with a lot of conversation from retail—rare for New Haven, I know!—and has terrific potential. It's designed as a flat-shooting plains cartridge, perfect antelope or mulie medicine, meant for those long tries over the flat prairies or across the valley. It delivers about 1,680 pounds of muzzle energy at 300 yards, off an estimated drop of only 7 inches (200-yard zero). Muzzle velocity, in the factory load, will be about 3,000 feet per second. We heard from too many hunters who failed to connect at over 250 yards because they underestimated the drop in their .270 or .30-06s and hit nothing but dirt 50 feet in front of the target. Dirt, as you know, makes a pretty poor trophy.

Put a nice Unertl or Bausch & Lomb tube up top, and you've got a super hunting machine! To us, at least, it looks like a real winner, and believe me, the industry needs a winner! It fills a definite niche.

You'll get one of the first .264 Westerners off the production line. I've asked them to select a nice piece of wood. Hard to believe anything coming from Big W with figure in the wood, but miracles do happen! Play with it as long as you want. If you want to return it, no problem; if you want to keep it, I'll get you a wholesale invoice, and you can send a check at your leisure.

That's the first surprise. The second two are also as per our suggestion, with New Haven's heavy hand behind the tiller, so to speak. Roy Huntington will be sending you a set of his new .264 Winchester Magnum dies, and Bruce Hodgdon will be sending you a five-pound canister of their H4831, which looks like it should get even more range, velocity, and muzzle energy and less falloff when fully developed.

Naturally, what we're looking for somewhere down the road is a column in your *Guns & Ammo* "Reloading" column, on finding the full potential in the new offering. I think if you play with loads and the Sierra or Nosler Partition .264 140-grain bullet, you'll be impressed with what can be done.

By the way, Lon, this is a definite exclusive. We're not sending similar kits to Warren or Jack. It's yours and yours alone, because we know that Lon Scott has the market clout to launch a major success, where the others don't. You can't get Jack to shut up about his pet .270 anyway!

Sorry to send you off to the railway station for so many pickups, but I think you'll find it was worth the effort.

Best,

      Charlie
      Charles Harris
      Manager, Gun Department

Abercrombie & Fitch
Madison Avenue
New York, N.Y.
CWH: mlb

"Maybe we ought to switch to Starbucks," said Nick. "This stuff is beginning to taste like swamp water."

"I think I saw a snake in mine," said Bob, putting down his cup of Seattle's Best. Around them hummed suburban Dallas mall life, all of it at hyper-speed and lubricated by smiles, unction, and beauty in the paneled English Department milieu of the joint, with its fancy frappo, cappo, and whatever-else-cino machines, its pastry cabinets groaning with frilly sugared bombs. Mainly, it was moms in here, with the odd lonely salesguy on break; the servers all looked about twelve.

"Okay," said Nick. "Let's get to it. First off, I got a good team into Richard's while he was having his Friday-night steak. They did the house top to bottom, came up with nothing. These guys can find anything. Plus, I've had a wire team on Richard, not every second of every day but enough to get a fair picture. Van parked down the way, different camouflage. Again, goddammit, nothing. No microwave transmissions to satellites, nothing. A little suspicious, if you ask me. He's too clean."

"Absence of evidence is not evidence," Bob said.

"Hmm, where have I heard that before? Okay, that's from my end. Now tell me about yours."

Bob didn't mention synesthesia, Sir Francis Galton, or colored numbers. He didn't have enough. "I found a letter in New Jersey. It establishes that, yeah, Lon was sent a .264 Win Mag in 1960, first year of production. So the gun in the case could be his. No serial numbers, unfortunately, but it checks out as far as it can."

"You think it's legit?"

"That's my feeling," said Bob. "I spent another hour there. Obviously, I'm not a scientific document expert. But the paper was the same weight and shade as the others in the file, even accounting for aging. Typewriter was the same font, perfect to the slight darkness in the center of the small 'e.' The format was in accordance with other letters from Charlie Harris, including those to Jack O'Connor at *Outdoor Life* and Warren Page at *Field & Stream*. The diction felt right for about 1960. The shipping reference is right; he said 'trips to the railway station.' That's because guns and powder couldn't be shipped by common carrier in those days, meaning they couldn't be delivered. You had to go to the Railway Express office at the train station and sign for the packages. And, Charlie Harris *was* the manager of the gun room. I found references to him all through the literature of the time. He sold Hemingway a batch of guns."

Nick considered. "I don't like it. All that may be true, but it's within the reach of professional high-end forgers."

"Maybe, but because that's so it doesn't mean this is forged."

"Too bad you didn't bring it with you."

"I wanted to preserve the box, for comparison purposes. And I thought to go the lab route would take too much time. If and when, we can subpoena for it. I stashed it carefully in that mess."

"I don't like it, Bob. If it means you go alone to that estate, out of our swift-response zone, you could be dead and buried before we get choppers in. Help is minutes away when you need it in seconds."

"I don't like it either. But it seems to me we have to keep going on this line or cut bait."

"What about we bust Marty and Richard for attempted fraud and third-degree 'em. As you say, they're not tough guys; you know they'll fold. Meanwhile, we give that letter the full nine yards in our doc lab. Marty and Richard roll over, we go to the next link up the chain, and he rolls over. If the letter's forged, our forgery guys will know who did it, and we round him up and bang his head against the bars. He squeals. That's how you bring a crime lord down."

"Yeah, but a crime lord has property, a place in the community, investments, family, all of which make him more or less stuck in place. If Hugh's alive, he has none of that, that we can find. We have no idea where in the world he is. He can disengage in a second, and he's clever enough to have designed break-offs in his network so he can disappear from our reach instantly. We pick up Marty and Richard, he's gone for good. Then next year or the year after, I catch a .338 Lapua in the ear while I'm riding spring fence, and that's the end of that. We're close. I know we're close. Nobody has been this close. I feel him."

"What are you getting?"

"It has to be Hugh. He's old, cagey, smart. He's been in the game a long time. He knows what he's doing. He's no psycho; everything is rational, objective-driven. He's subtle, he's witty; in a funny way, he's honorable. We left his kids alone, he's left my family alone. I don't know why, but I trust him for that. Like his cousin Lon, he's a decent man, except for the few seconds when he killed the thirty-fifth president of the United States."

"It's your ass, so it's your call."

"Then I go."

"I'll have people close by, chopper teams, observation—"

"No, uh-uh. If Hugh has people, they'll see it and hit eject hard, and that means he'll hit eject. It only works if I go in alone, unobserved, no teams, no air cover, no radio nets, no backup. If I need help, I'll call the state cops."

"Swagger, still crazy after all these years."

"I'm not saying I'm not scared or that I think this is wise. I am, it's not. I just don't see any other way."

"That's what they said about Iwo Jima."

"We won Iwo Jima. Look, here's my plan. I'll call Richard, tell him about the letter, have him contact Marty, and set up a date for next week. Then . . . I go on vacation."

"Do you have a time-share or something? A condo in Florida?"

"No. But I have to get away. By myself, somewhere quiet. I'll pick it at the airport. I have a lot to think about."

"You seem to have done a lot of thinking already."

"Not enough. I have crap in my head that I can't figure. There's something called synesthesia involved, which reflects a mind glitch that sees certain letters or numbers in color. Niles was a synesthete, as they're called."

"What does that have to do with anything?"

"So was Nabokov. He saw letters in color. Niles had a connection to Nabokov through synesthesia, and I think that's why he used it to construct his bogus ID for Hugh. It was an expression of his and Hugh's love of Nabokov, and it represented the kind of cleverness Nabokov used. Niles saw nine as red. I'm guessing the fake name that Niles gave Hugh all those years ago reflects a color or a number, probably a variation on red or nine. I'm trying to work that angle."

"It's thin," said Nick. "I mean, even knowing that it's a color or a number, a red or a nine for some reason, what use is that without a suspect pool?"

"Oh, I've got a suspect pool," said Bob. "It includes everyone currently alive on the planet Earth."

"Good," said Nick. "That's encouraging."

"Then there's something about the Charlie Harris letter. Don't know, but I'm getting a buzz. Everything's perfect, as I told you, but I get this buzz. Got to figure that."

"The Swagger buzz. Admissible in all state courts. I have complete confidence that you'll get your man."

"I'm sure I will too. After all, Humbert got Clare Quilty at the end."

"What the hell are you talking about?"

"Another manhunt story. I'll tell you later."

Swagger!

It clawed me from unconsciousness. I awoke, as before, in a cold sweat, enfeebled, aged, overmatched. I tried to sort it out before my heart exploded and aneurism did finish me. I had directed Richard to work with a police artist to prepare a likeness of the "Jack Brophy" who had shown, possibly killed my driver, then disappeared in Dallas, and it took until that night, but . . . could it be Swagger? No. Impossible. The odds were too distant. But I'd seen long odds cash in enough times not to see it as a possibility. I grabbed the drawing from my desk and bore down on it.

I had seen him, of course—that day in 1993 at the preliminary court hearing in New Orleans. I had sat behind the prosecutor's table in gray herringbone and red bow tie. I looked like ol' Perfesser Flibberty-Gibberty out of a Frank Capra movie, very much the Ivy paragon of diffident and eccentric genius. That was my style then, hopelessly tweedy of appearance, of mind.

I remembered: lanky, jeans, boots, some sort of cowboy jacket. For all my efforts, I couldn't get a face. I had impressions, not images. I saw that stretched-out body, not accustomed to sitting, unsure how to arrange those legs. Wary—the word "wary" keeps coming to mind. He seemed to be watching everything evenly, without remarking, holding his cards tight to his chest, always calm, a kind of easy grace to his actions. It was easy to project that temper into a sniper, who'd need wariness, a gift for observation, patience, and could have nothing of the showy, boastful, immodest, or psychopathic about him. The work was too dangerous for show; it demanded contradictory gifts, the precision for equipment maintenance and the patience for detailed preparation, but also the imagination to project into space an enemy's movement and predict where he might be; and beneath it all, the stubbornness to keep the imagination from inventing demons and letting panic take hold. Many men can be brave in batches, where sacrifice and support are the group norms; being brave on your own, out in Indian country, for hours and hours—that's a trick.

So now, at 4:19 a.m., I looked at the likeness and racked my memory. Were they the same man?

I felt like Laurence Olivier's Crassus in *Spartacus,* who learns with amazement that he's seen Spartacus fight but can't remember the details. I stared frantically at the rendering, trying to resolve it. Finally, I faxed it back through the layers of administration between me and the facilitators of my orders and required that the artist do his best to render the same face minus the twenty-odd years. I thought that might help. I also ordered the issue expedited.

The new version came the next day, and it did the trick.

There was no doubt: Bob Lee Swagger was hunting me, and if history was any guide, I wouldn't survive that distinction.

Now I tried to imagine the fantastical circumstances that would bring him back in quest of me. How had it happened? What were the links, the whimsies, the chance connections that put him on my trail again, twenty years later, when I thought I was out of it? I couldn't run an investigation for the simple reason that it would soon reveal itself to him, he would then know I knew, and the game would become infinitely more complicated. The first rule of my war against him was to prevent him from knowing I knew his identity. I did resolve that when it was over and I had him dead and buried, I would solve the mystery. It was that fascinating to me.

The first step was hard thinking: what could he know? Not what *did* he know, but what *could* he know, as a maximum? That would be our parameter for action. I had to apply the tenets of the New Criticism to my interpretation of his mind, to ruthlessly obliterate wishful thinking, daydreams, sentimentality about his nobility and heroics, his capacity for Hemingway's classic grace under pressure, and think of him purely as an enemy who needed to be destroyed. I realized that he would come upon the "dead" Hugh Meachum sooner or later. He'd track me through Hugh.

Was there much on Hugh Meachum available? No; I'd been smart. No family pix, no glory wall, that Washington vanity, behind my desk, nothing written for the record. Moreover, the Buddings Institute of Foreign Policy, the feeble cover for me and many of my colleagues in Clandestine, was long gone and had left no records. A genius might tease out some information by tracking through real estate records to determine that the funding that staffed (if barely) the suite in the National Press Building for many years originated in Agency coffers, but I didn't think that was the sort of work Swagger was capable of.

Then there was Agency culture; would he try to find survivors of Clandestine, men like me in their eighties, in hopes of turning up a memory of Hugh Meachum, poor old long-dead Hugh? Possibly they'd talk after a lifetime of being coached not to.

All that didn't matter in the long run. Even if he discovered that Hugh had survived his own funeral, my new identity was secure; he would never know, and he could never locate me, while it was a matter of time before I located him. I had to like my odds in this fight.

I made decisions. Richard in Dallas had to stay put. It was probable that "Brophy" would try to contact him again, since he was the one possible link to me, whom he presumed was still alive. Brophy/Swagger wouldn't be sure whether our man was an agent or simply someone we kept under observation and piggybacked our ops off of, so he'd be sly about it. But when it happened, the Dallas operative was to notify us immediately. He would be given a special number by which he would directly contact the unit I meant to set up. They would be able to hit the ground running, the object being to kill Swagger.

I knew I'd have to put together a first-rate kill team, preferably men with special-ops experience, SWAT or Delta, that level, at any rate, and I'd have to equip them with the latest toys, because those boys would as soon work with cool toys as make millions of dollars. I'd have to put a jet at their disposal, have all documents at the ready, so that they could be anywhere in the world in twenty-four hours.

The same unit would have an intelligence component too, the best people, well experienced, savvy manhunters; my mind turned to the Israelis, the world's best at this sort of thing. They would be charged with running as discreet an investigation as possible into Swagger: what had he done the past twenty years, where did he live, how did he support himself, what were his operating patterns, his preferred methods of travel and communication, his ties to a logistics base (did he have access to sophisticated documents, photos, forgeries?), what were his technical capacities, who were his allies, his relatives, his children, how was he vulnerable, whom would he die for, whom would he kill for? If possible, I wanted to leave family out of it; if he was married and had kids, I hoped I had the strength of character to keep them off the board. After all, he had not come after mine and was not interested, as far as I had any knowledge, in my three sons or their wives and children. That was how I hoped to keep it.

I went back to bed, humming with excitement. I have to say, it was good to be back in the game. Retirement, even in a style of haute billionaire decadence, didn't appeal to me that much. This was going to be fun.

Within a month, I was set up. My intelligence team was headed by Colonel ———, formerly of Mossad, with a reputation for prying Arab terrorists out of the gutters of casbahs all over the Middle East. He was assisted by Captain ——— and Sergeant ———, also Israeli manhunters, specialists in seeing tracks where there were none, reading signs, making brilliant deductions, and with the patience of hawks high in the air, planning and executing the best in assassinations. Their specialty was the helicopter-wire-driven missile hit, and they could put a bird through any window in the world if they had to. It took a pretty penny to dissuade them from their duty stations in the Tel Aviv defense complex and relocate them to a command bunker I had prepared. Fortunately, I had several pretty pennies at my disposal.

I secured a landing site and training ground in New Mexico and there located my kill team. These were magnificent men. Two were ex-SEALs, one ex–Special Forces. All had survived, even flourished, during much time in both war zones. They were under the leadership of a major from 42 Commando Royal Marines, where he'd run a close-combat troop. He had more combat time than the others combined. The Brit was one of those tough guys who, by reputation, would not stop coming; he had been shot in the head, laughed it off, and killed the fanatic who shot him. Who was the real fanatic? I leave it to you. All commanded another pretty penny, but all—I personally vetted them—had sterling reputations. They spent their mornings in brutal physical workouts to keep themselves in top shape, and in the afternoon, they worked on devious tactical live-fire exercises. They were probably the best close-quarter battle unit in the world, and they loved the unlimited ammunition budget even more than the ample pennies I deposited into their accounts on a regular basis.

Close by them, in a rather too nice condo in Albuquerque, I had my forgery unit. This was basically a man-wife team who had provided product to all the major Western intelligence agencies. They cost a fortune too, and I must say, they were the only ones I resented, because while the killers were shooting and practicing jiujitsu or Bruce Lee kung fu or whatever, and the hunters were locked in cyberspace, penetrating databases, monitoring police reports, and accessing satellite data, Mr. and Mrs. Jones, as I called them, spent their time on the golf course or in the malls, living a grand old life at my expense. Such loafers! That's the price of talent. I knew that I could send them a BlackBerry alert, and within eight hours, they could produce identification documents, passports, top-secret clearances, the whole gamut of access media that would get my killers in anywhere in the world, except perhaps North Korea, and I bet they could do North Korea in sixteen hours. Meanwhile, they shopped and golfed.

We waited, we waited, we waited, life went on, pleasant but more expensive than before; I encouraged the government to up the budget for and the manpower of the special battalion responsible for security in my neck of the woods, and still we waited and waited. I spent five thousand dollars a day on ammunition, I lived at the end of an umbilical cord to my communications, and finally . . .

Moscow!

Do you need details? I am too weary to note them now, and besides, what difference does it make? Final score: S&S: 5, the Izzie boys: 0.

But I knew: the real hunt was just beginning.

CHAPTER 21

J ean Marquez" was how she answered her phone.

"Jean, it's Bob Swagger."

"Oh, you!" she said. "I'm so happy to hear from you. I thought you'd disappeared."

"I can be hard to find at times. My old crank's suspicion."

He was calling from his cell in the arrival terminal at Baltimore/ Washington International. Vacation in Baltimore? In the real world, it's been known to happen, but in this case, he was on duty, as it were. It wasn't exactly Marquez he wanted to see; nor did he want to rent her inherited tommy gun—yet. He had another purpose.

"I heard about some Russian driver-murderer killed in Dallas," she said. "I know I can't ask you questions, but—"

"That was part of the deal. He was the wheel man. He tried his trick on somebody who was waiting for him. It was part of an FBI sting."

"You—"

"I had a little to do with it. But the job ain't finished. Have you got time to talk?"

"I'm a newspaper reporter. I chat, that's what I do. Go ahead."

"Ah, this is sort of hard to explain, but some evidence has come up that suggests a puzzle of some sort, many years old, might be involved and has to be solved. I know, it sounds goofy. It is goofy. But that's how they worked back then."

"I'm listening."

"Did your husband ever make a connection to the Russian writer Vladimir Nabokov?"

"I must say, the last two words I ever expected to come from your mouth are 'Vladimir' and 'Nabokov.'"

"They were the last two words I ever expected to say, believe me."

"The answer would be no. Jimmy's literary period was long past. He read about guns and he read history and politics. I don't think I ever saw him read a novel."

"Long shot here: did he ever show any interest in a gun called a Red Nine, an old German automatic pistol?"

"You know, it was always one gun or another, but they didn't stick in my mind. I could check his books, I suppose. He was forever buying gun books from Amazon. The one-click shopping was his financial ruin."

"That would be a help. I have one other question. This one is strange. It's so strange, I can't believe I'm asking it."

"Wow, I can't wait," she said.

"It's about literature."

"Not exactly a small topic. I'll try."

"This puzzle, which involves both Nabokov and Red Nine, was put together by a guy who loved literature. His office was crammed with fiction books, up, down, everywhere, with underlines and commentary on what he was reading, all of them alphabetized, all of them in good shape, which I take to mean that they were of great value to him. He knew, loved, dreamed, and breathed literature. Fiction stories, anyway. So the puzzle might reflect that, and guess who's stupid about it? Me."

"I doubt you're stupid about anything, but go on."

"My question is, do you know somebody who really knows literature? I have to find a principle to uncork the message in the bottle, and I don't even know what the cork would be, much less the bottle. I thought if I could talk to someone who knows and loves it, maybe that person would see something I never could or would say something that might organize my thinking in a helpful way."

She paused. "There's a creative writing department at Johns Hopkins that's supposed to— No, no, wait, I have another idea. There's a nice woman in town named Susan Beckham. She's published a series of novels that have been extremely well received. She sent me a wonderful note when Jimmy died. She doesn't talk to the press. She doesn't want to 'give too much away,' she says. She's the only writer left in the world who doesn't court publicity. I could call her. This is exactly the kind of intriguing question that she might like. And as I say, she's nice."

She was nice.

They met at three the next afternoon in a coffee shop in a utopian village in Baltimore called Cross Keys, where it was possible to forget the ugliness of the rat- and crime-infested city just beyond the fence.

She was willowy, her reddish hair shot with gray, her freckles still visible into her fifties. Well-turned-out in pantsuit and glasses and low heels, she could have been a mom, a vice president, a lawyer, a teacher.

"Hi," he said. "I'm Swagger. Miss Beckham?"

"Mr. Swagger," she said, rising, offering a hand, "it's nice to meet you. Jean told me you were an extraordinary man, a real hero in the old-fashioned sense."

"She got the 'old' part right, anyway. All that was a million years ago. Even then I was lucky. The real heroes came back in boxes. Only us fakes came back on two legs."

"I saw a limp as you walked in."

"Okay, a leg and a half, then."

That got him a smile. He sat down across from her.

"I've never solved a puzzle in my life," she said, "so I don't know how I can help you. But I'll give it a try."

"Thank you, ma'am. Here it is. There was an old CIA fellow whose job was making up phony biographies for agents overseas. He was good at it, because he had a creative mind and he knew a whole lot of stuff. He may have made up a name for someone, and I'm trying to find that man. Here is what I've found out so far."

Swagger told her of the office full of novels, the special love of Nabokov and his puns and gamesmanship, and finally, the synesthesia that Niles and Vlad shared. "I know it's hard to believe, but—"

"Mr. Swagger, I happen to be an expert on the tricks the mind can play on people. I believe it completely."

"So that's it. I'm thinking you'll see a pattern or come up with a question I should ask, or might have an idea that—"

"Tell me what writers he had in his library."

"Some I knew, many I didn't. A few years back I read a lot of post–World War II novels. So I recognized *The Big War* by Anton Myrer, *Catch-22* by Joseph Heller, *Away All Boats* by Kenneth Dodson, and *The War Lover* by John Hersey. And famous important writers, Hemingway, Faulkner, Fitzgerald, Updike, all the famous foreigners, Tolstoy, Dostoyevsky, Trollope, Woolf, le Carré, a lot of those Modern Library classics."

"He had refined tastes."

"Not quite. There was also a lot of what you might call junk. Crime stuff, thrillers, that sort of thing. A couple of books by James Aptapton. Lots of paperbacks, people like Hammond Innes, Jim Thompson, Nevil Shute, James M. Cain, Dashiell Hammett, someone called Richard S. Prather, John D. MacDonald, another Mac— Ross Macdonald—books that, from their title or their cover, seemed to be about crime or murder. It was all mixed up. He wasn't a snob, I'm guessing. If it had a good story, he'd learn from it. All the books felt read—you know, all the spines were limber, most were marked up, he had one of those ex libris labels in each one with his name. He was a hard, serious reader of stories. Nabokov, he had every Nabokov thing, some in Russian, even. Are you getting anything?"

She sighed. "No, not really. Only this, and I don't see how it would be any help at all. It has nothing to do with synesthesia, colors, Russian lit, Nabokov, anything."

422 • STEPHEN HUNTER

"Please, who knows, maybe it's the key."

"One thing he would have learned over a lifetime of reading assiduously in both serious and pop literature is the difference between the clichéd and the authentic."

"Yes ma'am," Swagger said. "Clichéd and authentic."

Without humiliating him by asking if he knew what that meant, she went ahead, after a sip of her coffee. "Clichéd. Meaning written to a formula, familiar from a hundred other stories, with certain expectations. If you've read it before, it's a cliché, but clichés are so insidious that many fine professional writers don't notice them. And they're comforting, like the furniture in an old house. They're prominent in some of the pop writers you mentioned. Examples: the rescue in the nick of time. The hero and heroine falling in love at first glance. The hero winning the fight every time and never getting shot."

"You do get shot in gunfights," Bob said.

"Exactly. You know that, but many of these writers don't. They just know that for the formula to pay off, the hero has to survive."

"I get you."

"On the other side—and please understand it has its own pitfalls—is what I'm calling the authentic. By that I mean the normal, the undramatic, the small. The world is never at risk. No one ever mentions a sum of a million dollars. People misbehave, get angry, forget things, come down with colds, lose the grocery list. The hero has terrible flaws that cripple him. No plan ever works right. The universe is largely indifferent to the fate of the characters. But life counts, love is important, pain is real. You have to find a way to dramatize that."

"I understand," he said. "Could you give me more clichés? Somehow that idea, what you've identified, I have a feeling it's something Niles would have enjoyed thinking about."

"It's not just plot elements. It's also language. Words that have been put together so many times, they're as comfortable as an old bar of soap. 'Dark as night.' 'Sky blue.' 'Wine-dark sea.' 'Raven-haired beauty.' All those are familiar, so their meanings have eroded. They don't carry any electricity. They remind you of a movie."

"What about 'Passion's Golden Tresses'?"

"Perfect. Good God, where'd you get that?"

"It's from an old magazine. Anyhow, I think I'm getting it."

"Characters can be clichés too. Compare, say, Chandler's detective Philip Marlowe with Nabokov's Humbert Humbert. Marlowe is incorruptible, smart, and brave, and he sees through everything, every motive, every feint, every lie. He's too good to be true. Humbert, though he's super-intelligent, makes every possible mistake, is in the grip of a pathetic obsession, can't control his own behavior. Even when he shoots Quilty at the end, it's not some terrific, highly choreographed gun battle but a pathetic transaction, where, shooting wildly, he runs after a begging, crying man. So Marlowe is the cliché, Humbert the authentic. Nabokov wouldn't write about a cliché, except maybe to joke about it, to turn it on its nose, to make a game out of it."

"I see," said Bob. "Would Niles, after Nabokov, make a game of a cliché?"

"Well," she said, "as you know, Nabokov loved games, so I suppose Niles had to pick up on that. He might have. His 'code' may involve a spirit of play. You know him better than I do."

"Can you give me some other plot clichés? Nick of time was one, the hero never getting shot was another."

"The most famous would be 'The butler did it.' That's from a type of English crime novel in the twenties, when murder was considered an upper-class occurrence and the books were pure puzzle. The temptation of the butler was too delicious to resist: he was invisible, he was discreet, he was loyal, he knew the house and grounds perfectly."

"There were a lot of books with a guilty butler, then?"

"Dozens. Hundreds. Then they reversed the cliché. Since everyone expected that the butler did it, it turned out the butler *didn't* do it, even if he was the chief suspect. That became just as much of a cliché."

But if you wanted to do that today, the real joke would be a game on the game. That is, the butler really *did* do it."

"I see," Swagger said.

"Here's another one. It's prevalent in a modern thriller: nothing is what it seems. The hero's in a situation, and he continually interprets the signs for guidance. What he doesn't know is that some evil genius has purposely constructed false signs to lead him astray. It never happens in real life, but it's a great, if cheap, device. Most such books or movies dramatize the process by which the hero sees behind the manipulations and figures out what's going on."

"Got it. And if Nabokov, or even Niles Gardner, were to do a game on that, his version would make you think that nothing is as it seems, but actually—"

"—*everything* is exactly as it seems," she said. "I see, by the light in your eyes, I might have scored a point."

"Yes ma'am. I'm realizing that was the principle of the Red Nine. I thought it stood for something or labeled something or meant something else—say, a code name for an agent, a radio call sign, a chess move, something like that. In the end, it turned out to mean nothing else. It simply was what it was. He saw nine as red. He saw *all* nines as red, that's all."

"It was literal, not metaphorical. So it was the subtlest of codes, yes. The code was that there was no code. Who would ever figure that out except maybe a Bob Lee Swagger? No college professor would figure it out, because no college professor would be capable of thinking that clearly."

"I'm thinking that maybe he used the same principle on the next step. Something seems like a code, but it's not. It just is what it is, in plain sight, but you could look at it all day and not get that. The code is that there is no code. The secret is that there is no secret."

"It's too clever," she said. "I could never use it in a book. Real life is never like that."

It is all right to fail if you learn from your failure. Here is what I learned from the Moscow debacle. Swagger, at sixty-seven, was still very, very good. He could not be taken by run-of-the-mill criminal gunmen. He was too smart, too swift, too calm in action, too determined. Moscow had hardened him while confirming his suspicions, and he would move more directly to the target, which was, alas, me.

The second thing I learned (I have had to learn this lesson over and over again; maybe it will stick by the time I reach ninety!) is that you can't rush things. They will happen at their own pace, at their own place in time. The more you rush, the more you cut corners, the more damage you do to yourself. I should have flown in my kill team at first notice and not tried to make do with a crew of uncertain talents and dubious motivations. To take professionals, you need to have professionals, so that issues of pride are involved, not just greed and the will to violence. My world-class killers wouldn't have panicked, would have planned better, would have shot better, would have had more contingencies in play, would not have been thrown off their game when their sitting ducks proved to be armed.

The third thing I learned (I knew this too, but I forgot it also!) was to prepare the ground. Our team took Stronski at a place he, Stronski, knew best. He knew all the shooting angles, the paths through the bushes, the locations of the bench pedestals, which would stop incoming, and the trash cans, which would not.

I resolved to do better next time. For one thing, it would be the full focus of my attention. There would be no tending to empire and plea-

425

sure and turning to tactics in spare minutes between soirees. No, I had to go to war footing to win the war, which meant it had to be a 24/7 operation. I had to put aside my decadence and find my war brain again, and become the hard and ruthless Hugh of Clandestine Service, that old legend who'd killed a president and hundreds more in his time.

My first resolution was: take the fight to the enemy.

I knew I could not back off and let him find a new angle of attack to which I would react, because in the reaction would be encoded my failure. I was not going to live in anticipation of a move against me by this genius operator at the time and place of his choosing and pray for the luck of my guards. No, I had to go to him, I had to net him, I had to lure him to prepared ground where we knew the locations of the trees and benches and all the escape routes were predetermined, the sights zeroed, the weapons tested. It had to be done not just professionally but at the highest levels of professionalism.

I did have one advantage: I knew where he had to go. He had to go to Texas.

The only sure link to me was through the man who'd been his mentor in Dallas, and he suspected that man was an agent of mine. He'd have to reengage and infer from that a way to me. Who paid him, what were the arrangements, how did he report, how could he be played? He'd have to confront those questions.

In Texas I'd put something before him. Something so seductive, he could not resist its temptation. He would have to go after it; it would be his grail. He would study the approach, sniff a dozen times, seem to go, then back off. He'd circle around, he'd look for signs, for disturbances, for indicators of preparation and ambush, and I'd have to prepare carefully enough to survive that scrutiny. And finally—weeks down the long and winding path before me—he'd make his approach, and then we'd have him.

Since he was by nature a gunman, and since guns were in a way his Yoknapatawpha, I understood instinctively that he'd come at me through the guns. He would have no choice. They were what he knew, his terrain; he was the master navigator of that small world, and he would feel the most confidence in that arena. But there was more. I could feel it as if it were just beyond a screen or covered by a sheet, its outlines barely visible, no details yet to be seen. It had to do with guns. Guns were at the heart of it. Alek's junky little war-surplus Italian clunker, Lon's sleek, excellent Winchester, the whizz of the bullet to the target, the extraordinary damage such a small piece of matter could engineer within flesh if propelled at the proper speed and—

Then I had it. The breakthrough. Quite a moment, when it feels as if God is whispering in your ear. No, He is otherwise busy, I'm sure. The rapping at your chamber door is from your subconscious, which has been engaged with the issue full-time, trying facts against possibilities, seeing if parts fit or must be discarded, testing, testing, testing all the time until that moment when, miraculously, it all comes together in perfect, stunning clarity.

What I needed was a physical object, a file, a confession, something tangible and palpable, which would prove the existence of our plot against Kennedy. I needed something Swagger would kill to get and, at the same time, risk death to get. To make it real, I needed a plausible narrative to sustain it. I had to invent documents to validate it, I had to have unimpeachable witnesses to verify it, I needed a realistic chain of events that would account for its whereabouts since 1963 and that put it within Swagger's reach today. This is what my imagination created in one gushing rush of fact and detail.

I came up with a gun case containing Hugh's Model 70, the suppressor, and some of the hybrid .264/Carcano ammunition, locked and sealed with shipping tags proving it was shipped from Dallas to Richmond on the night of November 24, 1963, by Braniff. I imagined a backstory by which it was lost and then found by a writer doing a bio on Lon/John who would need the help of someone with practical ballistic experience. I imagined Richard bringing them together.

The one thing I could not imagine would be Swagger's refusal.

I must say that, though they cost me a fortune, the Joneses turned out to be worth every pretty penny. The profusion of old documents they produced was amazing. It turned out that Mr. Jones was some sort of paper expert who knew about thread counts, finishes, manufacturing processes, the effects of aging, and all the minutiae of what I suppose could be called the paper game. His true expertise was chemical; using a variety of magic potions out of little brown bottles that produced vapors, he could give a routine sheet of papyrus the brittle yellowness of age so accurately that it was laboratory-proof as to time of origin.

That product was dispensed to various nimble professional criminal figures under contract to people who were under contract to various other people who were under contract to me, and in a bit of time we'd inserted a document in the necessary file, which appeared to be the files of the Madison Avenue seventh-floor gun room of Abercrombie & Fitch, a legendary place that shipped Lon most of the rifles he decided he couldn't live without.

The Joneses had access to a whole range of criminal fabricators I had no idea even existed. They were able to hire a contractor who built an exquisite replica of a 1958 Abercrombie gun case and had it suitably aged; they came up with a Model 70 of the appropriate vintage, a Unertl scope, aged bottles of Hoppe's gun oil, and an ancient .264 brass brush. No luck on the German *Schalldaempfer*, so they settled on an ancient Maxim silencer that at least was time-frame-appropriate. They used a noted arms expert to fabricate the cartridges, and he did so on brass of the proper historical pedigree, loaded on dies of the proper historical pedigree, and the bullets loaded into the shells were authentically from the rare lot 6003 of the Western Cartridge Co. 6.5 Mannlicher-Carcano white-box ammo. Don't ask what it cost. I'd rather not know.

Then there was the man who'd play the "writer" in whose care the gun case would be left. I couldn't hire a con man or a real actor for this tricky role. It had to be an authentic firearms expert with great knowledge and a list of published volumes with whose work Swagger would be familiar. He had to be able to talk guns with Swagger, while Swagger was secretly monitoring the conversation, looking for telltale signs of a fraud. It had to be someone who was known to others in this field, so Swagger could get personal recommendations. Nobodies need not apply. Hmm, how would we settle this? I chose the expensive course, and the mission was given to my Israeli manhunters, those bird dogs of deceit and human weakness. In time they produced. They came up with a fellow named Marion "Marty" Adams, who, helpfully, had a character defect: a tendency toward larceny. As a known expert, he became a broker on many fine gun sales, the man who assured the buyer that it was indeed a rare first-model Henry rifle he was spending his $150,000 on and not a counterfeit. But there was so much more money in the counterfeits. Marty, it seems, was in the process of being sued by one enraged buyer, and if that became known, his reputation would be shattered, his career destroyed, and his bridge to the high end of the gun biz forever burned. Marty was approached; the offer was one he couldn't refuse. He would quietly settle out of court with the plaintiff, paying an exorbitant punitive fine, and the case would disappear before causing damage to Marty's reputation. Since Marty was an idiot with no money, cash and legal guidance would be our contribution. In return, he would be prepped to play a part in a larger deception, the point of which would never be clear to him.

There was one more figure, the lynchpin. That is, Our Man in Dallas, Richard Monk.

I decided to run him myself. I would do so by encrypted satellite phone, the most secure form of verbal communication in the world. I arranged for him to be given the implement, already dedicated to my number alone, so he couldn't dial up sex talk from Vegas or make anonymous dirty calls to teenage girls in Tennessee at my expense. He would be the one man in the world who could reach me instantly and directly when the situation demanded it.

I knew I could not tell him he was tasked with leading Jack Brophy to his death in a violent commando ambush in which he might himself be winged or even terminated. He would flee to the moon by tomorrow noon. Or if he didn't, Swagger would read the sick anxiety on his face like a road map. I told him a little fib as part of the briefing.

"I represent a venture group that has its eye on a nice collection of corporations. Alas, the sole owner of this group, a discreet, elderly WASP, cares not to discuss selling them to us at a reasonable price. Since we don't kill, we have targeted the crown jewel of his collection for ruin, and when it collapses, it will drag down the stock prices of his other holdings. We will pounce, and he will wake up the next day a minority stockholder. We will buy him out for pennies on the dollar."

"I see, but—"

"The crown jewel is an old and prestigious New York publishing house. We will swindle it, through your good efforts, into paying an outrageous sum for a book that 'solves' the Kennedy assassination, with the physical proof to make the case stick. That is why everything is arranged so carefully, as if we were the CIA. This is a deep deception. When the book is published to much huzzah, we will prove, through friendly journalists, that it is a hoax and that the publishing house has been deceived and is selling a fraudulent product that must be recalled. And thus falls the house of cards. Do you understand?"

"So it has nothing to do with the Kennedy assassination? Just some big-dough guys trying to outhustle each other?"

"No Q-and-A, Richard."

"Yes sir."

"Let us return to business. We expect in some time the man you know as Jack Brophy will make contact with you. Your job is to steer him, very carefully, to the man called Marty Adams. This should all be familiar to you."

"It's been pounded into my head."

"You will brief me before and after every meet with Brophy."

"Yes sir."

"You will take *extreme* security precautions. He must never see this communications device, never suspect you are in real-time communication with me. He will penetrate your house, he will go through your underwear, your collection of dirties, he will read all the squalid details of your failed marriages, Richard. Where is the phone secured?"

"It's in a book safe in the basement shop. It's in Bugliosi's *Reclaiming History,* which was the only thing big enough to conceal it. But there are thirteen thousand other books down there."

"That's the guy, Richard. You make me so proud."

We started getting responses from the operation almost immediately. Pings, blips, echoes, readings, whatever you want to call them. Swagger was on my trail, and it was impressive. It wasn't just his courage and his skill with a rifle that made him a standout. By some queer mutation, he had been given a superb mind for analysis and deduction. It is strange how genius occasionally shows up in a single generation, then vanishes. Yet as impressive as his skill and determination turned out to be, they didn't answer the one question that most intrigued me. Why?

I suppose he needed a mission, and this was the one that came along. He was the type who couldn't live without a mission. There was also the issue of grief: he had lots, beginning with his father, then moving on to his spotter, Donnie Fenn (he was married to Donnie's widow, Jen), and finally, an Agency officer named Susan Okada, killed in his most recent foray into our world, which ended with a missile detonating in the Rose Garden. Was grief driving him?

Or was it something else? Could it be a love of Kennedy? Was he a JFK groupie whose world had been shattered at Lon's shot heard 'round the world? Was he in love with Jackie, with Camelot, with the children,

John-John and Caroline? Did he see himself as their avenger? It seemed unlikely to me that a man so relentlessly pragmatic would have a soft core, particularly in devotion to something he had never experienced himself but only read about and saw on TV as an American teenager. I remained baffled.

Nevertheless, he was a formidable opponent. And he was getting closer and closer. Could he win? I honestly didn't see how, as I knew who he was, and there was an impenetrable wall between who I had been and who I was now. Even if he determined, as he was sure to do, that Hugh's death was fiction, I had removed all traces from my records of who I might become. Anybody who knew me then was dead; only their children survived, and we of the Agency did not, as a rule, share with our children.

I knew this: he had to return to Texas.

The satellite phone rang at 5:55 p.m. my time.

"Yes?"

"He's back in Dallas."

"Richard, he approached you?"

"Out of nowhere. Like nothing had happened. I was sitting in Mc-Donald's a few minutes ago, eating my usual Egg McMuffin, and sud-denly—there he was."

Richard continued with his report, the upshot being that Swagger was back in town, as I had anticipated, and was playing Richard again.

"How did you leave it?" I asked after hearing the nuts and bolts of what had happened to Brophy, where his researches had taken him, where he wanted to go now.

"I'm going to look into the possibilities he's interested in. He wants me to be discreet, because of the value of his 'intellectual property.' He's afraid of a claim jumper or someone beating him to the punch. So he'll contact me in a couple of days."

"Do you know where he's staying?"

"No. He made a joke about that. If I don't know where he's staying and I'm captured and tortured, I can't give him up. Ha, ha. Not funny, in my opinion, but I laughed anyhow. He said it's better if he finds me than the other way around. Just protecting his intellectual property."

"Excellent, Richard. Do go ahead and help him. Don't mention Marty Adams until you've gotten him what he wants. Don't force it; it's an afterthought, not a main point. If he doesn't respond, don't mention it again. He's paying attention, even if he pretends he's not. He's mentally recording everything you say and will spend hours going over it. He'll look into Marty, sniff, paw, howl a little, head up one trail, come back, circle around, and return. If he senses you're trying to force him in a direction, he'll be suspicious of you."

"Sir, are you the type who kills people if they fail?"

"No, Richard. You will be tortured exhaustively, but not killed."

"Thank you, sir."

I will spare us all the tedium of close reporting on the game. I will say only that its one amusement was the image of Richard, a fat lake trout with two hooks in his jaw, being played by two expert anglers. Poor Richard, trying to please me and trying to please the mysterious, slippery Brophy, with his far-seeing eye and almost supernatural gift for anticipation.

On the fourth meet, I felt that Richard was confident enough to work the Adams angle and authorized him to do so. He reported that Swagger reacted with indignity, even anger, but in the end seemed to warm to the idea of a collaboration. His final instructions: "Hold off a bit. Let me look into this guy. I'm not a writer, I'm an engineer. Maybe he could help me, I could help him. But goddammit, don't tell him no more about me!"

He checked into Marty through the auspices of the FBI. Our computer wizards determined that another deep data search was done on Marty Adams, and circumspect inquiries were made in the publishing world and the high-end gun-sales world and so forth and so on, and we knew that they'd come back positive, since we had interceded before any stain on Marty's honor could be recorded (just barely; he'd left many unsatisfied customers, so it was only a matter of time).

In week four, we got the news: our two fictions would meet. Jack Brophy and Marty Adams, each not who they said they were, each with a different agenda, but each eager to continue the charade.

It seemed to go well. Marty, as anticipated and confirmed by Richard, was a blowhard autodidact, and he bored both Richard and Swagger out of their socks with his various pontifications. In the end, Swagger/Brophy was intrigued enough to agree to another meeting. Clearly, his interest had been snagged, particularly by the mysterious "thing" that Marty had promised would tie a ribbon around the case.

The wait. I am required to show that my craft discipline hasn't eroded over the years. It wasn't easy, but enough was happening to keep me busy, and for nights, I had Viagra, Shizuka, and forties musicals and melodrama. The Israelis, monitoring through their various cyber-penetrations, reported a more thorough hunt for Marty Adams particulars and now a network of field interviews by anonymous young men. Even Marty Adams's agent was interviewed, seemingly on another matter, but the well-trained investigator managed to divert focus to Marty and spent most of the time unearthing details on him.

I realized the time was appropriate to initiate the tactical phase. The famous Meachum luck provided that Marty's inheritance included an estate in western Connecticut, the last remaining relic of the fortune that his father lost trying to sell high-quality .22 target pistols to a country gone mad on fast draw and mock combat shooting in the fifties and sixties. The place, about a hundred miles outside Hartford, was hard against a scut of mountains in the low northeastern configuration, hills with trees to anybody who's seen real mountains. On the property was a decaying house, and Marty's taxes were in arrears, so we paid them off (ouch!) to preclude municipal interest. It wasn't gated or fenced or up to modern security requirements, but it was remote from neighbors, and Marty retired there to write and shoot often enough that gunshots didn't necessarily cause the police to drop by. It was also nice that he had a Class III license, so the sound of full automatic weapons, if heard, was not another police signal.

I had an engineering firm discreetly map the place, as I had an aerial photographer record its nuances from his Cessna. This documentation I provided my shooters in New Mexico. I asked them to prepare a plan from the documents, then to journey up there one at a time, infiltrate the property, and spend a few days exploring it and learning the land. They were all equipped with digital cameras for close-ups on the cover-versus-concealment issue, for the angles of fire, for whatever other tactical concerns came up.

The plan was sound. The goal was to get him under all four guns, run them hard to empty, and take him out in one decisive assault. Marty and Richard, if there, might fall in the fusillade. I decided that was an acceptable price to pay, although I never told them that, as I never told Marty about the incursions on his property and my plans for the final moments. He would survive or not, depending on his luck. But he was strictly collateral.

There was some debate as to timing. I ultimately decided on hitting him after he'd had his conversation with Marty and examined the un-opened case and was on the road out of the place. The reason was that coming in, he'd be wary, he'd have a tiny worry that it was an ambush, and all his senses would be extra-sharp. He'd be volatile, prickly, at high combat readiness. He might be armed. If Richard was with him, that could tangle things as well. So we'd let him come in, and once he saw the package and realized its significance and gamed out what it explained and what it made possible and examined it closely (without opening), and looked at Marty's X-rays of it, once he'd swallowed that, he'd be far more relaxed and at the same time distracted. His mind would be going a hundred miles an hour; he'd be in a mode of triumph because he'd found the leverage at last to prove the conspiracy, get the case reopened, and loose the dogs of law enforcement on Hugh Meachum and begin the international manhunt that would shake that villain out of the trees, no matter where the trees were.

The hit would go down a quarter of a mile out of Marty's rambling wreck of a house, on a dirt road with a 33-degree angle and no maneuverability due to the dense trees and sharp angles on either side. If he should escape—doubtful, given the firepower—there was only one way to run, and that was up a low Connecticut foothill where the trees gave out. He'd find himself on Robert Jordan's hilltop in Spain—no, Jordan was at the bridge, not the hilltop, who was at the hilltop?—anyway, that person's hilltop in Spain, unarmed, with only a few low stones as the four best operators in the world moved in. El Sordo, by the way, was the fellow on the hilltop. El Sordo didn't make it off of his, and neither would Swagger.

The firepower and accessories (someone, possibly Anna Wintour, said: "It's all about the accessories"): the boys had decided to go with deep ghillie camouflage and to infiltrate the property two days in advance. There'd be no movement on the place the day before, and to any observer, casual or professional, no sign, no trace, no indication of penetration. If they had to move quickly, the boys would shuck the ghillies and revert to digital-camouflage battle tunics and trousers. Faces would be blackened or painted green-brown (for some reason, these commando types love the touch of the painted face!). Hatwear: either the ubiquitous black wool watch cap or a suitably dappled boonie cap. Fashion is so important to high-end commandos, and I wanted mine to be up to Ms. Wintour's standards.

As for the guns, the boys would each have as primary ambush weapon the MK48 light machine gun that had happily mowed its way across Iraq. This superb piece of combat engineering was ultra-reliable, even in the sand, and spat out its deliveries at a rate of about seven hundred rounds a minute of 7.62 mm ammunition. It was beloved by high-speed operators. The ammo, slung underneath the gun body in a hundred-round belt rolled into a canvas-wrapped container, would be standard military ball, for penetrating the body of the auto. Anybody inside that vehicle would be Bonnie-and-Clyded in the first few seconds. If, by some odd trick, Swagger survived the initial hose-down and headed up the hill, the fellows would dump their MK48s and default to the latest AR platform, the M-6 IC from LWRC on the Eastern Shore of Maryland, accessorized with Eotech hologram sights, LaRue flexible 3X magnifiers, and at least ten H-K mags with twenty-nine rounds of Black Hills 77-grain hollow-point. And of course—nothing is too good for my boys—each would carry a Wilson CQB .45 ACP and a Randall knife. I know all this because I saw the invoices, and it added up to Pretty Penny no. 2,318,314. Too bad these fellows couldn't have been deployed against a meaningful national target instead of my need to get another hundred or so blow jobs from Shizuka before the reaper came calling on me, but there you have it.

As far as the extract was concerned, I would have a helicopter in orbit on the outskirts of the estate. One of the pilot's duties was to monitor law enforcement channels, to see if the gunfire attracted any undue attention. If squad cars were dispatched from the state police barracks, he'd notify the ground team, swoop in, and evac. If not, he'd wait until they'd policed the killing ground, removing and disposing of the brass and the body and that load. Finally, I'd made disposition that he had FLIR aboard, forward-looking infrared technology, so that if, by a one-in-a-million chance, Swagger got into the brush, the chopper could nose him out via his heat signature and direct the kill team to him, again in a few minutes.

Meanwhile, back in the real world, the process ground slowly on. Swagger leaped at the rifle lure, as I anticipated, but insisted that he first establish the provenance, and Marty skillfully guided him to the Abercrombie & Fitch records in Rutherford, which we had penetrated and into which we had inserted a superb forgery establishing owner-ship. When Swagger saw that, he would be hooked through the gills! He would insist on being allowed to examine it, and a date would be set for his trip to Connecticut. That was it. No big deal. Swagger was so pro-voked by the rifle case that all other precautions were irrelevant. That was the whole point of the multimillion-dollar operation, and it was ac-complished in a split second, as an afterthought.

I had him.

PART IV

Connecticut

"Telling me I got to beware"

CHAPTER 22

Richard made all the arrangements. Bob met him at Dallas/ Fort Worth International a week later, and the two flew direct to Boston, then caught an American Eagle puddle jumper to Hartford, where Richard had booked two rooms in the airport Marriott. Dinner in a local steak house.

At eight the next morning, Richard picked Bob up in a blue rental Ford Focus, and they set out for the two-hour drive west through the rolling Connecticut countryside for the arrival at Marty's estate in Litchfield County, west of Warren.

"Beautiful country," said Richard. "Reminds me of the Cotswolds, in England."

"Never been there," said Bob. "But beautiful it is. And you don't see any shacks or rusted-out cars on cement blocks or run-down places like you do in the South. The American South or any south."

The trees, the houses, the farms, the towns: all mature. Mostly white, wooden clapboard, impeccably serviced, shutters boldly painted a primary color, all well scrubbed by people for whom maintenance was an obsession. They took care of stuff, these people. Flowers beautiful, hedges trimmed, all towns, big or small, boasting a civic hall, a hotel, a park, a church. It felt like some kind of ancient land as imagined by Disney. Every other building seemed to have been built in some far-off place called the eighteenth century, and laws of Enlightenment rationality were still in control.

Swagger ate it up. It was in his genes, it lit his imagination, it was the way things should be, a military duty ethos fused seamlessly with daily life. He was also scanning for air cover—a shadowing chopper or some other sign that Nick had violated the agreement and laid in backup too close; he'd wondered if the next little Revolutionary War burg would conceal gunmen with body armor and RPGs.

"You seem tense, Jack."

"I can't stop looking over my shoulder. I told you, I've had a price on my head, and once you've been hunted, you never fully relax."

"Jack, it's a beautiful day in a beautiful part of America, and you are part of one of the most exciting historical-intellectual developments of our time, which, I should add, will probably have a tremendous financial upside. You should just enjoy the ride in."

"You are so right, Richard. Man, I wish I had it in me to click the off switch and go to take-it-easy. I just want to look at this rifle case, get the business deal set, and get to work."

Onward they went, passing through Warren, passing more rich Yankee farmland and forest, finding the hills on the rise, and feeling the gentle slope as the car climbed several hundred feet into the hills.

"There it is," said Richard. A rusty green sign at a rusty gate sunk in faded concrete abutments with pretensions of grace announced "Adams Glen," and Richard slowed and took the turn.

The road ran through thick trees on hillside, with slope above and below the dirt of the track. Dust flew in two tire contrails behind them, smearing the pristine beauty of the azure, windless, cloudless day, but on either side, the world seemed green, dense, and hushed. Bending over, looking through the windshield, Swagger could see the hill rising, buried in forest the whole way, to a rounded peak another four hundred or so feet up. Cubed limestone boulders, like fallen ceremonial heads, showed here and there among the trees, which were heavier or lighter in density depending on nature's whimsy.

They rounded a last gentle turn and the hillside opened up to permit a spacious house against its flank, on the same theme as all those before: a huge clapboard mansion, built with an eye toward symmetry and precision in an age when those things were beauty. This one was beyond mature and had eased almost into senility. The landscaping had grown ragged, with lawn unkempt, weeds annoyingly clotting the beds, hedges out of square and in some places out of hedge, just jumbles of bush.

Richard eased the car to a halt and Bob got out, noting how badly the house could use some saving paint, having faded from white to something near pewter, with more than a few of the slats corrupted by rot, the shutters flaky and mottled. It was a million-dollar house a million dollars away from restoration.

"Hello, hello," said the chubby Marty, beaming, stepping from a lesser door. He wore baggy blue jeans and a blue button-down shirt and a shawl-collar cardigan, as sloppy as the decaying house from which he had emerged. "Right on time. You engineer everything just right, don't you, Jack?"

Swagger smiled, taking the soft, plump hand and shaking it. "Nice place," he said.

"This old monster? Been in the family three generations. Damn, I'd love to get the money together to get it all brand-spanking-new again. Then it would be something. Sorry it's so ratty, but the taxes alone eat me alive, and I can barely keep my nostrils out of the brine. Come on in."

Marty led them into darkness and more of the same. The house had a mildewy quality, many of its rooms filled with ghost furniture under white sheeting, the smell of dust hanging in the air, and where slants of sunlight fell through shuttered windows, they revealed an ecosystem lively with debris.

Marty took them into what was his workroom and presumably had been a pater and a grandpater's study. It alone was populated by dead animals, all with intense glass eyes caught up in the taxidermist's high drama, shot by one generation or other of Adamses. The room was paneled and shelved with every book ever written on firearms, some of them by Marty. Behind the cluttered desk stood the glory wall, the young Marty in black-and-white slimness with this or that prosperous-looking older man of the gun world. Swagger saw a few he recognized, a few he knew.

"Say, isn't that Elmer Keith, the gun writer?"

"I knew Elmer. He was very old by then. You like the old gun writers? God, what men. Look, there's Jack O'Connor, and over there, Charlie Atkins, Border Patrol gunman and dangerous gent. This one is Bill Jordan. He was also Border Patrol. He had hands like hams, and I swear, I never saw a man so fast. Bill could put an aspirin on the back of his right hand, draw his Smith 19, and blast the falling pill before it hit the floor. He did it once on *Ed Sullivan*."

Swagger had some memory of most of these fellows. They'd been his heroes growing up, not ballplayers or fighter aces or disease-defeating doctors but gunmen, like his father. He could say nothing because those memories didn't belong in the head of Jack Brophy, retired mining engineer.

"When I was trying to learn more about all this," he said, "I think I read a batch of them. They all seemed to have good times."

"They sure did," said Marty. "Now look at this—" and he was off. The next half hour was spent observing his treasures strewn about on random shelves, and he did have many. He had the first serial number in the last six models of .22 target pistol his father had manufactured, pristine, in perfect, untattered cardboard boxes. He had Colt's experimental 9 mm double-action automatic, offered to the army in the early sixties for consideration in replacing the government model. He had the .300 H&H Winchester Bull gun that Art Haymon set twenty-seven national records with in the late thirties, before being nudged aside by the great Lon Scott. He had Henry rifle no. 15, the brass-framed gun that could be "loaded on Sunday and fired all week," which ultimately morphed into the 1873 Winchester, which won the West, though as frequently for red people as white. He had Colts, Smiths, Marlins, all exquisite, all virtually pristine, all glorious.

"Sell the guns, Marty," said Richard. "They'd buy your house a new paint job."

"Oh, no," said Marty. "You don't sell history. At least not this history. I hope—again, maybe it's more a dream than a hope—to display the collection coherently in its own museum. Maybe this place, all spruced up. That would be an Adams legacy."

"Marty, don't tell me you've lost that gun case?" asked Swagger, meaning it to be perceived as a joke. "And you're just softening the blow?"

"No, no, it's here," he said. "I can see I've kept you waiting long enough. You boys sit over there. Coffee?"

"Not now," said Bob. "Suppose I spill it on the thing."

More laughter.

"Okay," Marty said. He went to what seemed to be a wall and pulled on some lever or something, and the shelving, laden with books, floated outward on hinges, state-of-the-art 1932, to reveal a vault door, dead black, dead steel, dead heavy. He leaned and grabbed a knob beneath the rotary of the combination dial, pulled down, and a heavy steel clank reverberated through the room, loud enough to awaken the dead animals on the walls, stir dust from the books, and maybe make a buried Adams or two turn over.

The vault door swung out, and Marty dipped in.

He emerged in white gloves. He held in his hand a stoutly constructed pigskin-and-canvas case, maybe two feet wide, three long, one deep, of extremely elegant manufacture. He set it down on the bare coffee table before his two guests—before Swagger, really, as Richard's contributions at this time were negligible. Swagger leaned forward, hungry to apprehend its meanings.

It wore its age well, with scuffs and stains and obscure marks everywhere, but integrity vouchsafed and complete. The leather seemed richer in patina, as if the process of aging had turned it from the utilitarian to the exquisite. Bob didn't touch it. He put his nose two inches from it and scanned every detail. The locks were tarnished, but he'd noticed that there was no play between lid and case, so he presumed it was tight and nothing had loosened or worn within.

"You have no key?" he asked.

"No. Maybe if you went to the Arkansas state police and got Mr. Albright's possessions from his death in '93, it'd be on a key chain. But at this end, nothing."

"I'd hate to damage it when we open it," said Richard.

"We'll have a bonded locksmith open it," said Bob. "He can get it open without damaging it; he can attest to the age of the lock; he can date the lock and notarize it for us."

"See, those are the things I'd never think of," said Marty.

"Marty, do you have a magnifying glass? I'd like to look at the shipping tags."

"Of course," said Marty. He went to his desk, got the glass, and returned to give it to Bob. "I'd prefer to handle the tags with the gloves."

"You got it," said Bob.

Richard crowded next to him, and Marty hovered close on the other side, leaning to lift the tags for Bob's inspection.

In the circle of the glass, the red one floated in and out of focus until Bob found the right distance between eye, lens, and object for clarity. He examined every square inch. In black crayon clerk's scrawl against the stiff red paper under the company rubric BRANIFF AIRWAYS, INTO THE BRIGHT TOMORROW, he saw:

Date: 11-24-63

Flt: 344 DAL/RICH

Psnger: Scott, L.D.

The tag was looped over the double handles of the case, sealing them together. Since the handles were on different halves of the case, that meant it had not been opened since 11-24-63. The heavy paper appeared unrotted and, at least under Marty's gentle handling, didn't show any give-and-take when manipulated, suggesting that whatever adhesive unified the two ends of the loop, it held solid, itself without decay or much in the way of loosening. But it looked brittle, as if to bend it would send flakes of dead glue to the floor.

"Looks goddamn genuine to me," said Bob. "I guess we'd have to find an expert of some sort to verify that as the proper Braniff tag, in the proper time frame, and do some chemistry on the glue to make sure it's the same kind Braniff used."

"Where would we find such a guy?" said Marty. "That's pretty arcane knowledge."

"The FBI forensics people are good at document interp. And this is a piece of evidence in a crime, don't forget. I'm thinking we're going to have to bring in law enforcement."

"I'm not wild about that," said Marty. "Those guys might want to hog the spotlight. They'll sniff the gold. I hate to be mercenary, but I have a house to paint. This thing is pure gold."

"If it's got what we think it has. Let me look at the other tag."

Marty let the shipping tag fall and scooped up the other. It was less frail, a luggage ID locked in place by a leather case, its face spared the elements by a sheet of plastic.

LON DUNN SCOTT, it said in blue fountain pen, presumably in Lon's own handwriting. And below that, SCOTT'S RUN, RR 224, CLINTONSBURG, VA.

Bob said, "It's possible Lon's fingerprints are under the plastic. I'm assuming they're all over the locks and the stuff inside. The more, the better. Marty, could I see that X-ray again?"

"Sure," said Marty, disappearing to his desk, reappearing in seconds. He laid the heavy dark celluloid sheet over the case. Bob could see that it was a one-on-one ratio.

"Got any backlighting?" he asked.

"Yeah, I have a light table over there. I use it to go over contact sheets for the picture books."

Marty led them to the light table, a large metal frame supporting a square sheet of white-frosted glass. He turned a switch, and the fluorescent bulb inside blinked to life. Marty laid the X-ray out, and it displayed the case's contents in perfect outline, everything recognizable.

The incomparably graceful Monte Carlo stock, the ovoid trigger guard still on, bolt, action, containing receiver, bolt slot, barrel, with the scope—a long tubular construction belled at the muzzle end, maybe fourteen inches—held parallel above the action by the ancient Redfield mounts and rings of the time, and above them all, a long tube with a flange at one end that had to be the Maxim suppressor. In the corner were a collection of screws, what looked to be a folded gun cloth, and a small bottle, presumably cleaning fluid. In the other corner, the silhouettes of three cartridges.

Bob took something out of his pocket and laid it next to the three. It was a .264 Win Mag cartridge with a 140-grain spitzer hunting bullet. "Look at it," he said. "The shells are the same size. Two-sixty-four Win Mag. See how Lon's have a blunt tip compared to the point on the hunting bullet? That's because he's loaded a Carcano bullet into the .264 shell." He went on with a brief description of his newly revised theory on the ballistics deceit that lay at the heart of the issue. Possibly Marty understood, or at least took it on faith; Richard gave no sign of being awake.

"I think we've figured it out," said Marty.

"No," said Swagger. "There's the big issue of speed. We won't have anything till we have that. If the route wasn't chosen until late on November 19, they only had two and a half days to set it up. Impossible in that time. They couldn't have done it. But they did it."

"You'll figure it out," said Marty. "It'll be something stupid and obvious that everybody's missed."

"If it's stupid and I haven't figured it out," said Bob, "then I guess that makes me stupid."

"I think we're already there," said Richard. "You've got stuff nobody has gotten before. Believe me, I know this crap up and down, I—"

"What did you say?" said Bob.

"I said we're already there. You've got it. The rest is just details."

Already there.

"Already there," he said. "Goddamn, already there." The insight hit him blindside.

"What on God's earth are you talking about?" said Marty.

"It's the final piece of the puzzle," Swagger said, as much Swagger as Brophy in the flash of revelation. "I couldn't figure out how they could put it together so fast. They were already there on some other job. They had Oswald under discipline, they had the ballistics, they had Scott in town, ready to shoot. Then fate brought them Jack Kennedy, and they couldn't resist taking him down. It would have been so easy!"

"Does this call for champagne?" asked Marty. "Shall we toast? I don't need much of an excuse to pop a bottle."

"Nah. It's just something I've been working on."

"This is exciting," said Marty.

"Marty, please put the case away and lock it up tight," Bob said, pointing at the case.

"I will."

Marty did as requested, and the three returned to the couches around the coffee table. Under the raging glass eyes of animals dead nearly a century, they talked a little bit more business, mainly schedules. Swagger's job was to refine his theory and put it in writing, striving for clarity and simplicity. Marty thought photos would help, because both he and Bob knew that many Americans had no idea what "reloading" was and how plastic it made the medium of the cartridge. They'd have to be talked slowly through Bob's theory. Richard's job was to find the various experts that the project would require. Meanwhile, Marty would put together a proposal, forward it to the others for comment, and then, with their permission, send it to his agent. He thought Bob ought to be ready to come to New York to meet the agent, and then meet the publisher, the editor, and the team who would handle the book. Once that process was in shape, Marty would draw up an outline and they'd begin to deal with ancillary rights.

When no one could think of anything more, they ambled outside, and Bob took a deep breath of the pine-and-oak-scented air, enjoyed the pure blue of the sky, and felt the pleasant, persistent pressure of the breeze. It felt good to be out of that mausoleum.

"I think we've got something here," said Marty. "I can't tell you how pleased I am. In fact, now that you teetotalers are gone, I believe I will open a bottle of bubblelicious and drink that toast to Jack, to Richard, to our good fortune in coming together, and to our bright and shining future."

"I still can't believe this is happening," said Bob.

"It is. Pinch yourself, it hurts. You're awake."

"I guess I am."

The three walked to the car. Handshakes all around. Then Bob said, "Richard, do you mind if I drive?"

"Sure, no problem," said Richard.

"Great." He got in and slammed the door behind him as Richard eased into his seat.

Swagger pulled out, and Marty watched them go.

And so at last the mighty day had arrived.

My killers had infiltrated two days before and lay without moving over that long stretch of time in case any rogue surveillance had been put in place, as unlikely as that might seem. Besides movement discipline, they maintained radio silence throughout and simply lay in place, vectored on the kill zone while passing the time in isometric hell.

Meanwhile, at no time were the approaching Swagger and Richard monitored. Part of the plan was to place no human eye upon them. Besides Swagger's sensitivities, there were practical reasons: the supercautious Swagger might have hired or gotten from his pal Memphis at the Dallas FBI his own team of countersurveillors to stay with him from a discreet distance and look for signs of followers. We couldn't run that risk. But we did have Richard under control, though he had no idea for what purpose, and his constant e-mail updates by iPhone informed us that he and Swagger had flown the day before from Dallas to Hartford, secured a blue rental Ford Focus, license number given, spent the night at a Marriott in Hartford, and would leave early the next morning for the assignation. They were slated to arrive at the rural Adams estate at 9 a.m.

I was pleased, therefore, when I received, at approximately the appropriate time, the notification from Richard: "Everything cool. Leaving now."

In the car they would have privacy. No need to plant a bug that Swagger might pick up on. Also, I had decided not to electronically penetrate Marty's place. Swagger might have some kind of miniature

452 • STEPHEN HUNTER

scanner that would alert him to the possibility of electronic ears, which could give up the game; and there was the possibility that somehow, some way, whoever went in would leave a sign of his presence, and Marty might pick it up and divulge it to Swagger in casual conversation, alerting the man. Worse, he might decide not to divulge it, which would cause him to sustain a fiction over the meet, and Swagger would detect that easily enough and take compensatory measures, which could ruin everything. It was important that monitoring of Swagger, by whatever means, be kept to an absolute minimum. I didn't have him shadowed by air, though I had the helicopter on standby; he might notice an orbiting bird, catch a glimpse of reflected sunlight off the windscreen, hear the pitch of the rotor blades changing as the craft began to descend. All these tells could ruin us.

I settled into jittery anticipation. Two hours of travel time, then perhaps two hours of meet time. In four hours it would be finished. I watched *Double Indemnity* for about the six hundredth time; superb movie, with the great Fred MacMurray and that scheming little vixen Barbara Stanwyck. It ate up the time admirably, but I still had over an hour to kill. I summoned Shizuka. Finally, there was nothing left to do, or at least nothing I could do, except wait. Tick-tock, tick-tock. It was about time for Swagger to arrive at the estate.

I lay on my veranda dressed in expensive après-M'Bongo wardrobe—I was hunting, after all—of cargo pants, boots, and a heavy dark green cotton hunting shirt with epaulets and bellows pockets. I suppose I looked ridiculous: Francis Macomber's wardrobe lavished on a spry pink eighty-three-year-old who couldn't weigh 135 dripping wet. At least I didn't have one of those absurd hats with a leopard-skin band, as Preston had worn in the movie. My prescription Ray-Bans lessened the glare of the sun, but at this time of year, the day wouldn't turn hot.

I used my Bic and energetically updated this memoir, bringing it at last to the present, in which I now write in real time, and felt sadness. In truth, I've enjoyed the writing over the past few weeks. Recalling my life has been an invigorating experience, confronting my follies and misjudgments, recalling the men and women I loved, seeing them again in the middle distance of my memory. God, I've had a great life. Who has lived as hard and well as I, who has known such giants as I? Grand old Lon, the immensely gifted Jimmy with his nerves of steel and his bright laugh. Peggy. I miss you, old girl. You were the best. I'll see you all soon, my friends. Not quite yet, and you'll forgive me for not rushing, but soon enough, Hugh Meachum will join his wonderful colleagues, all of whom he was so lucky to serve with—

The buds in my ear were linked to the commo center, where a fleet of experts bounced signals between dishes and orbiting orbs so that I could eavesdrop on the drama as it played out. Now the buds crackled to life, and I picked up the initial confirm as my commandos registered the arrival of the Swagger vehicle at the compound with a brief break of radio silence.

"Blue Team, this is Three, I have a visual on road dust. They're on the property."

"Easy, Blue Team," said Blue Leader, "I will confirm on passage. I want all your eyes down, don't try to see anything, don't make visual contact."

"Roger, Leader."

There was a pause.

Then, "This is Blue Leader, I have a confirm on vehicle, two occupants, blue Ford Focus, Connecticut license plate checks as Romeo Victor Foxtrot 6-5-1, as per intel. Target confirmed on-site. Stand down for now, I will call a weapons check within the hour."

"Roger, out," came three crackly voices in simo, trying to out-abrupt one another.

They were there. So far, so good. I lay back and enjoyed all that I saw before me. The surrounding forest was lush, and the meadow that was open a mile to the river for some reason at this late-summer date blazed green. I'd never seen such a vibrant shade. It seemed almost to shimmer as the sun rolled across it, matted only by a few clouds, all of it given animation by the persistence of a low, friendly breeze.

There was nothing left to do, nothing left to write. I lie here, feeling the slow and easy slip of the seconds, and it seems to go by not in real time but in super-real time, and I don't dare check my watch, for that would somehow break the spell and I'd be back to the slow tick-tock, tick-tock, instead of being privileged to experience the heated rush of seconds.

"Blue Team, weapons check."

"Blue Leader, this is One, cocked and locked, sighted in."

"Roger, One."

"Blue Leader, this is Two, all samey-same."

"Blue Leader, Three, ditto on that."

"This is Blue Leader, all good."

More silence. It became time to add the last team member.

"This is Blue Leader to Blue Five, let's get airborne and to your hold."

"Blue Leader, this is Blue Five, I am lighting up and going airborne and will be monitoring the police channels and holding at point one for quick evac."

"Roger, Blue Five, notify when on point, good and out."

More time dragged by.

"Blue Leader, this is Airborne Blue Five, am on point, holding at about two angels, police channel open. The Smokies are all out at some accident on the interstate, and all local roads in or out are low-volume. You are cleared to operate."

"Roger, Blue Five, I have you so noted, and out."

Silence. Tick-tock, tick-tock. If a bird cried, I did not hear. If a cloud masked the sun's radiance, I did not notice. If the wind rose or fell, the temp rose or dropped, the shadows deepened or softened, I did not care.

"Blue Leader, I heard a car door slam."

"Good work, Two. Go to guns, fire on my fire. Stay ready, Blue Five."

Four simultaneous "Rogers" crackled out.

"Blue Team, I have road dust rising."

I could see him, Blue Team Leader, all cammied up like a beast from the bog with a ludicrous green-brown face and a full canteen, leaning in to the machine gun. I could see it all: the car suddenly visible in the trees, then it's there, in the bright sun of the kill zone on the straight-away, coming right at Blue Team Leader.

"Blue Team, on my fire," Blue Team Leader said, and the radio picked up the ripping sound of the one and then the three other light machine guns joining as they emptied their one-hundred-round belts into the automobile.

CHAPTER 23

As the green tunnel of trees absorbed them, Richard babbled away happily.

"Boy, that was great, really, this is going so well, we're contributing something, we will be adding something to our understanding of history, we will make some, maybe a lot, of money, it's all coming together, and the best thing is we get along, we like, we respect, each other, and it will continue to—"

Swagger hit him in the mouth with his elbow. Richard's head bolted back, his hands flew to his wound, and his body posture seemed to collapse as all strength left and he became instantly senile. The blow loosened some teeth and opened a two-inch gash that spurted blood down Richard's chin.

"Jesus Christ! What the hell are you doing? Oh, God, that hurt, you madman, what is—"

"Shut up, Richard," said Swagger, halting the car. "Now tell me. Who's behind this thing? What's his name, where is he, what's he get out of it?"

"I don't know what you're talking about," yelled Richard through a snaggle of loose teeth and two hands attempting to stanch the blood flow. "Why are you doing this, God, you hurt me so bad, I never—"

"Richard, about three hundred yards down the road, we pull into some sunlight, and about five or six guys with machine guns are going to shred this car and anybody inside it. I will clonk you again and let you stay here while they do their job. They will kill you dead as hell. Or you can scurry back to Marty's and hide in the basement with that fat blowhard. You got one second to decide."

Richard needed only half a second. "I don't know. No names. He's rich, powerful. He talks to me via satellite phone. I report, I get instructions. It's all professional, top-secret, well done. I have no idea who he is."

"Not enough, Richard."

"I don't know a thing about killing. It was represented to me as some kind of stock maneuver, some high-end Wall Street thing. They want to get a house to publish the book, then they'll expose it as a fraud, the stock of the house collapses, they buy in and use the leverage to pick up a whole cluster of related companies from a guy they've targeted. That's all I know, I swear."

"Give me the phone, Richard."

Richard reached into his breast pocket and came up with a satellite phone with its stubby, folded aerial and handed it over, fingers shaking wildly. "You push one; it's a direct line. He's running it himself, but I don't know anything except he knows everything and he pays very, very well."

"Okay, Richard, get out of here. Lock yourself in and don't come out until the state cops arrive and get you. Cooperate with them from the get-go, or you will spend the rest of your life as someone's boy toy in the Connecticut pen."

"Who are you?" Richard cried.

"I'm the man with the nails. And this is the day I nail all you guys. Now get the fuck out of here."

Richard hit the dirt running. He vanished in seconds, not that Swagger noticed. He got out himself, dipped into the looming woods, and came out in seconds with a dead branch about fourteen inches long.

He drove along at twenty, no rush, no hurry, controlled the whole way. The car followed the curve of the road, which followed the curve of the hill, and before him, he saw the darkness of the canopy give way to a blast of sunlight as the trees fell back from the road for a bit. About thirty yards out of that zone, he halted and took time to precisely regulate the wheel, checking to see that the front wheels were locked straight ahead.

He climbed from the car and hunched beside it. He wedged the branch against the seat, saw that it was a little long, pulled it out, and snapped four inches off. He re-wedged it, lowered the unsecured end to the gas pedal, took a last look, and pushed the branch down against the pedal, driving it forward perhaps two inches and holding it there. The car accelerated as he spun away, and *whack,* caught the rear of the door-well across the back of his right shoulder, knocking him to the ground.

He rolled, found his feet, and began to race down the road as the car hurtled forward.

He heard the firing, one and then three more guns, so loud that they drowned out any sound of metal shearing or glass shattering. The guns roared on for a good three seconds, then quit abruptly.

Swagger turned left and slid through an opening in the trees, but before him, he saw only more trees, all of them vertical against the slope of the hill. Up was the only way to go.

"The seven-six-two did great," said Blue Two, the first to reach the wreckage. "Unfortunately, there's nobody here."

"Shit," said Blue Leader. "Any blood?"

"Don't see any. Just blasted upholstery and a million pieces of glass. He set the accelerator with this." He displayed the branch.

"Okay," said Blue Leader. "The car couldn't run far like that, so he set it up fifty or so yards down the road. He got off the road, he's running hard; the question is up or down."

"We going after him?" someone asked.

"I don't know," said Blue Leader. He pulled up his throat mike. "Blue Five, this is Blue Leader."

"Roger, Blue Leader."

"We have a running target. I want you to vector to our kill zone, then look to the south, and I will pop smoke. Orient on the smoke, then deploy your FLIR. I have to know which way the bastard is running and if he's got a team in there waiting for us."

"Roger that, Blue Leader."

"Okay, dump the ghillies, this is high-speed stuff."

The team collectively shook itself free of the cumbersome branch-and-leaf constructions that had obliterated their human shapes. Now they were in digital cammo, sand-and-spinach-pattern, a weave of forest colors and shadows.

"I want intervals of thirty yards," Blue Leader barked, "and if Five gets him nailed and it's all clear, we will pursue. If there's heavy opposition, we'll bug out. This is a kill, not a war."

"Roger that," came the replies.

The four operators hustled down the road, fingers on triggers. Their equipment bounced as they ran, the MK48s dangling on slings, the M-6s light in hands, ready for return fire in an instant if ambush came, all red-dot optics on and set to ten, smoke canisters and shoulder holsters flopping on harnesses, body armor slopping up and down at each step.

"Fine here," said Blue Leader. "Deploy into intervals."

He pulled a smoker off his belt as the boys spread themselves out, went to knee, and began to eyeball at full intensity. Blue Leader pulled the pin and dumped the signal device on the ground. It fizzed, then began to produce copious volumes of roiling yellow smoke that drifted upward, and in an instant, the shadow cut into the sunlight as the helicopter swerved over them. The machine hovered there for seconds that seemed like minutes.

"Do you have anything in your green eye, Five?"

"Okay, okay, I have a fast mover uphill from you, maybe a hundred yards, he's pulling himself over rocks, he's twelve o'clock to your line, going straight up."

"Anything else hot?"

"I have no other targets, I repeat, no other targets. Only the one fast, hot one; man, he's moving for an old guy."

"Can you azimuth us to him?"

"Zero-zero degrees. Just go up, baby, he's dead on a line for the peak and not going much farther once he reaches it unless he finds a stairway to heaven."

"That's our job," someone said, breaking radio protocol.

Blue Leader stood, pointed upward to the three other members of the ground team, who, having heard the conversation, were rising too, and made the whirlybird hand gesture to give them the order they'd been waiting on, which was to pursue and kill.

Swagger climbed. Jesus Christ, he was too old for this. The incline fought him, the trees fought him, the slipperiness of the pine needles and leaves sheathing the ground fought him, the boulders fought him, his hip fought him, gravity fought him, age fought him, everything fought him.

Fuck! A slip and he went hard to ground, slamming his knee against the inevitable rock, sending a flare of pain up through leg to body and brain.

I am way too old for this, he thought.

The sweat loaded in his eyebrows, then dumped to his eyes, stinging them, turning the world to blur. He tried to blink them clear. A gut ache came, bearing the news that he'd been so immersed in this quest over the past weeks, he'd lost a lot of his conditioning. Tremors slithered through arms, dizziness through vision, and he sought handholds, anything to pull him upward. Now and then he'd find a bare spot where his New Balances would find traction and give him a boost, and he'd gain a second or two, but he knew that four young athletes in superb condition, superbly armed, guided by the chopper that floated just over the canopy of the trees, were closing on him.

The hip. He tried to concentrate on it, to accommodate his mind to the pain, which was now severe, but in its time on Earth, that joint had been shattered by a bullet, replaced with a steel ball, then cut deep and hard by a blade of legendary sharpness at full force, and finally, just recently, the whole mess had been shot again, though at a shallow angle, and was not fully healed.

It burned, it boiled, it seethed. It disrupted what coordination was left in his old limbs, and it eroded his will and stamina as he fought for gulps of dry air, wiped his soaking brow, ignored the dozens of raw abrasions his passage through bush and needle, over rock, and in thicket and copse, had inflicted upon him. How close were they? Should he zig? Should he zag? Was a red dot even now settling on his spine, about to sunder it and leave him flat and begging for the coup de grâce?

Suddenly, he broke into the light, and the slope lessened. He'd made it to the top.

Up here, the wind precluded the trees achieving any height, but the acre of hilltop was strewn with boulders, clumps of brush, patches of raw earth, and a few small, scabby trees that had managed, against all odds, to hang on.

Around him, the green state of Connecticut rolled away to far horizons, now and then throwing up a cluster of black roofs in trees to signify a town. Blue mountains blurred the edge of the Earth miles away.

Bob slipped, and at that moment a bullet came. Swagger's luck, the shooter missed by inches, and Swagger felt the push of the atmosphere as the bullet knifed through. He dropped and began to slither.

Too old for this shit.

"Did you get him, Three?"

"No, dammit, he went down just as I fired. I had a real good sight pic on him; goddamn, he is a lucky sonovabitch."

"Do you see him, Five?"

The chopper, hovering four hundred feet over the hilltop, floated this way and that. "I have a visual, Blue Leader. He's low-crawling among the boulders, maybe a hundred feet ahead of you. I don't know where he's going; there's no place to go. If I were armed, I'd have the shot. But he's stuck up here for sure."

"All right, any police activity?"

"Negative. No reports, no dispatches. It's all clear on that front, over."

"Good. I need you to retire to point one now. We don't need you hanging overhead, attracting attention."

"Check and commencing."

The chopper veered off, headed for an orbit a mile away, out of range.

"Blue Team, listen up, mates. You guys on the flanks, I want you to move laterally. Locate at each hard-ninety compass indicator and hold up. I want to come at him from four directions. I don't want any chance of him evading us and making it off this hill alive, do you read?"

Affirmatives came back at him.

"You are cleared to fire if you get a clean shot. But I think this is shaping up like fire and movement and then an up-top rat hunt."

"Got it, Blue Leader."

The three high-speed operators scurried away to their holding spots. Blue Leader crouched, did an equipment check, then took out a smoke and lit up. Always time for a butt. He'd been doing hilltops for about twenty years, sometimes trying to hold them, sometimes trying to take them. It was all the same. Old hand, lots of war behind him, presumably lots of war ahead.

He waited, enjoying the cigarette, an English Oval, a thick blunt fag unlike the scrawny filtered candy tubes the Yanks smoked. When he was done, years of military experience in rank and officers' mess demanded that he carefully peel the paper, rub the remaining tobacco and ash away between his fingers, crumple the paper, and put it in his pocket.

"Blue Leader, this is Blue Two, I am set at due east and ready to rock."

"Three?"

"Due west, holding."

"Visuals?"

"Got nothing but rock and brush. No movement. He's hunkered down solid."

"Ditto that."

"Ditto again."

"Okay. Let me try a thing." Blue Leader rose. "Swagger, mate," he shouted. "Make this easy, go out with dignity. No point in squealing like a pig in the bush as we hunt you down, shot a dozen times, bleeding out in pain. You're an old bastard, you've seen this game a thousand times, you knew your day would come. Dignity, chum. A cigarette, a laugh, a sip on the canteen, I've even got some damn fine Scotch aboard, and it's over clean and painless."

No response. Of course not. Swagger wouldn't give a location indicator. He'd play hard to get.

"All right." Blue Leader spoke to his team via the throat mike. "One and Three, move out. Two, with me on the cover fire, do it."

He rose, rocked a MK48 burst across his front, and watched the bullets blow lines of dust spasms and rock frags up where they hit. On the other side, Two put in his two cents' worth.

Then it was Blue Leader's turn to move, and he went low and hard, hearing the cover fire against the hilltop from the two other points on the compass, got to a nest of boulders, and slid in. He looked and, in the jumbled landscape ahead of him, saw nothing. There wasn't much area left unpenetrated. Swagger was running out of hilltop.

"Okay, nice and easy, Blue Team, one at a time, you move in twenty or so feet, scan, and hold. He may have an ankle piece on him or a knife. Use your corner discipline, be aware of blind spots. I'd go to M-6, for better movement; he's just a few feet ahead now."

Blue Leader let the heavier MK48 fall to sling support, pushed it around to his backside, and deployed the shorter M-6 carbine, stock locked in short, cocked and unlocked, Eotech on and turned to ten so a bright red circle displayed his aim point to either conscious or subconscious.

"One in."

"Two in."

"Three in."

He scurried in, movements smooth, fast, practiced, the gun locked to shoulder, scanning for threat, finger riding the light trigger, ready to put a burst into anything ahead.

He could feel them. They were so close. The shout from the leader, some Brit tough guy, Mick Jagger on steroids, followed by fusillades from all points on the compass that filled the universe with bad news and drove him down so he felt he could shrink into the earth, the cold blade of fear that maybe this time was the time. Then it passed; he had his war brain back and knew exactly how it would work. They'd close the circle, driving him back, and there'd be no place to go. Then it would be over.

He slithered around a rock, forced himself (tasting dust, feeling pain to knees, elbows, and skin) through the low tangle of brush, found a path between more low rocks that seemed to reach center, and scurried ahead.

He saw it.

A red-orange hunting vest, crumpled but vivid, the only primary color in a landscape that ran from dull to duller brown, even with the sun above. He scrambled to the signal, dug behind it until he encountered a canvas strap, and pulled. Fifteen pounds of canvas gun case emerged from hiding. A quick unzip.

It was the Thompson M1A1, thirty-round mag, like the gun with which his father had shot his way across the Pacific. Nick had gotten it here from Aptapton's widow just in time.

Thank you, Nick. Once again, you save the old man's bacon. Thank you, Aptapton, for your love of guns, especially the old tommys.

He slid the bolt back, locking it, admitting a .45 ACP to position to be swept up and fired as the first round in a burst. Six other loaded stick mags lay in pouches on a belt curled into the case, and he pulled the belt around him and cinched it tight.

At that moment, a young man—perfect commando, from Oakley tactical boots to green-brown face paint—enough firepower on him to take out a platoon, crept into the space between two boulders not twenty-five feet ahead. They felt each other in the autistic Zen of predators, made a flash eye contact, and got down to business. Swagger beat him on the action curve by a tenth of a second, jacking a ten-round burst into his legs, knocking him down and askew, tearing up limbs and hips but not spending bullets against the armor vest. The guy went down hard, and in a second his twisted lower extremities were wet and red to the world.

Swagger slipped back into the brush.

"Fuck, fuck, he has a tommy gun, a goddamn tommy gun!" screamed Blue Two.

"Are you hit?"

"He blew my goddamn legs off, oh, shit, I can't stop the bleeding."

"You hold, Two, don't panic, use your clotting agent and tie it down to stop the blood flow, we will be with you soon. Hold on, mate."

"Ah, fuck," said Two.

Blue Leader had recognized the sound of the .45s instantly and knew it was of the Thompson declension because the rate of fire was well above grease-gun speed. He was not surprised, disappointed, stunned, or breathless. The surprise of it did not occur to him; nor would it ever. The fact that he was hunted as much as hunter did not matter. His hard practical mind simply went through steps.

New situation.

Armed target.

Full auto, heavy bullets.

Savvy, experienced operator.

One man lost.

Need to triangulate, lay heavy fire (back to MK48s), and close to engage. He will be tricky, he will—

Another burst of Thompson fire roared through the atmosphere.

"Blue Three?"

"I'm good, I think he hit One, off to my left. Blue Leader, I am moving on the fire."

"Do not rush, Three—I will lay down cover on the sound of his gun, move under my cover."

"Roger."

He rose, readjusting weapons at speed as he came, got the MK48 up, and fired a hundred .30-caliber rounds into the rocks and brush where the Thompson fire had sounded, and saw and felt what he always saw and felt, the world being ripped to dust and supersonic grit, the blur of the ejection of the spent shells arching to the right, the urge of the muzzle to rise—after all these years, it was still so bloody cool!—while his sharp eyes scanned for movement or target indicators.

The Brit's gunfire whistled overhead, eating up the world that it struck, raising smeary clouds of fractured dust. Swagger knew the other operator would move under the fire, and he drew the Thompson hard to shoulder, waiting, waiting, as six inches above his head, fleets of supersonic FMJs flew by, seeking his destruction and—

The gun quit as round one hundred passed through it. Swagger jerked up hard and saw to the right the advancing operator in the hunch, not fast enough to get into cover before his time ran out. Swagger acquired and fired in almost the same instant and put a burst into him, watching the bullets lift a straightaway of dust eruptions, then went down fast and crawled, again just under the line of fire of the team chief, who'd gotten a quick new belt into his gun and used it up in the search.

Swagger thought he'd hit his guy, and when he had a chance, as the boulders grew oddly larger, he went to his feet and curled around, putting his target between him and the remaining shooter. In seconds he got around enough to see the downed man, rifle on the ground, wrapping a bandage tight around a bad thigh bleeder. Swagger screamed, "Hold!" But the man went for his weapon—stupid SEAL motherfucker, hard to the end!—and Swagger had to fire three into his only target other than the head, which was the root of the man's arm where it disappeared into the hole on his vest. He opened a hideous wound, shattering arm and clavicle, rendering the gunman maimed for life. Even still, the man stayed in the fight, shaking off the destruction, looking up in rage and betrayal, his teeth white against the green-brown jungle of his face, and reached awkwardly with his off hand to acquire the 1911 holstered diagonally across the front of his armored vest. Unfortunately, it was tilted to favor the dead hand and tightly Velcroed in, and by the time he got it, Swagger was on him and hit him a butt stroke in the head. He went down soggily, maybe dead, maybe with a concussion to render him eternally stupid.

Swagger noted that this one too had smokers on his web belt beneath the vest, and though the vest was a temptation, he knew he didn't have enough time to get it off the SEAL and on himself, so he pulled off three smokers, pulled the pins, and tossed them in the direction from which Team Leader's fire had come.

Smoke! Who would have thought of that? From three points just ahead of him, red, green, blue, catching in the wind, blowing mistily across the scrap of flat if rough ground that comprised the hilltop. It was like a screen of myth, impenetrable, masking all movement. Brilliant improvisation. This old bastard was too good!

Blue Leader dropped hard, feeling vulnerable. He knew he was alone, it was man on man. If he could get close enough to get to hand-to-hand, victory was his. He had about nine black belts and knew shit for which there wasn't a name and no books had been written. He unlinked the heavier MK48, first disconnecting the belt box and tossing it far, then opening the breech latch so this bad boy couldn't use it against him. He toyed with the idea of dumping the carbine and making it a pistol fight, which would give him much more maneuverability and let him get to full play on his superior toughness, speed, and stamina. But this old one was a trickster who knew a thing or two and might be circling around or might be, at the same time, two hundred yards downhill, racing like a demon, knowing that in distance lay survival.

He stood, eased forward as the smoke ceased from the two rightmost grenades, and tried to see a target. Nothing. Swagger was somewhere ahead. But Blue Leader saw nothing. This was room-clearing, really, two men squatting as they worked their way through a maze, guns at the ready. Who would see whom first, who would fire first, who would win?

He eased left, then right, feeling the whip of wind, feeling the warmth of the sun. He pushed off his watch cap, ripped off and tossed ears and throat mike for total concentration. He negotiated the avenues between the rocks and brush with care, in that commando crouch, and it happened that, as he edged around a boulder, something flashed in his peripheral and he was on it fast, to see a man withdrawing because he didn't have a shooting angle, but Blue Leader did and fired, knowing that he'd hit.

He waited.

Nothing.

"Swagger, give it up. I know I hit you. I saw the blood. It's no good going out like a rat."

No answer. Was he dead?

He squirmed ahead a few feet and was rewarded with a blood track. Got him!

Got him!

Got—

Swagger hit him hard with the crown of his head, a smash that skulled both of them into incomprehensibility, but Swagger, expecting it, got in his follow-up and clocked him harder with the inverted barrel of the old weapon.

Blue Leader went so still that he couldn't have been faking, but in the next second, he tried to fight his way out of the grog and Swagger was on him. He pressed the muzzle hard into the throat, and with his other hand, he ripped the man's fighting knife away, unlatched the Velcro on the Wilson and tossed it, pulled and threw the M-6 as hard as he could.

He leaned over the Brit, pressing the blunt Thompson muzzle into the neck. "What's your rank, troopie?"

"I— What, what are you—"

"Your rank and outfit, goddammit."

"Major, Royal Marines, 42 Commando."

"Major, get that bird in here fast. Pop your evac smoke and get these men out of here. One's dead for sure, maybe another, maybe not. Get them to goddamn emergency in Hartford fast, and save them. That's your last job as commanding officer."

"I shot you," said the major.

"In the fucking hip. I been shot there so many times I didn't even notice. It bounced off. Now get these guys out of here, save some lives."

"Why?" said the major. "I don't get it."

"I only want one more head on my wall. And it ain't yours."

I heard the fight. It was brief, violent, and as such things always are, ugly. Gunfire, shouts, bits of panicked radio-speak, screams, something that sounded like a physical tussle, and then the radio went dead. That silence that follows a disconnect. The airwaves located and destroyed, communication lost.

I shook my head.

He did it, I realized. He'd beaten them somehow.

I hated Swagger even as I loved him. God, was he an operator. Could he have prevailed again, against those odds? The man wouldn't die. Was he Achilles, dipped in the potion of immortality but for a heel that no archer had found?

A hit of vodka calmed me, and I had to appraise my situation realistically. He could know nothing else. He would be stopped by the firewall of the person I'd become. He'd have to set about finding me. Good luck on that, because Niles Gardner, long dead, had built a perfect identity, and it would withstand any attempt at penetration.

I lay back, watching the sun yield its hold on the day slowly. It stayed light so long now, which had the odd effect of elongating life. I felt like these extra hours were a gift to me; they stood for the fact that I would go on and on and on, that in the end, if through longevity as much as genius, I would prevail.

My phone rang.

What? I reached for it, noting that it was not my cell but my satellite. Richard! Maybe Richard had a report.

I pressed the talk button. "Richard?"

"No, he ain't here. He's hiding in the basement."

"Swagger!" I could tell by his laconic voice, its dryness, its ur-text of Southern cadence, its lack of need to dominate, its irony, its detachment.

"Yes sir. We meet at last," he said. "By the way, if you want to talk to your commando team, they ain't here neither. The survivors are in the emergency ward."

"Dammit, you are a resourceful man," I said. "Woe unto him who tries to outthink Bob Lee Swagger."

"I ain't no genius, Mr. Meachum. I just show up and pay attention."

"How? I have to know. Tell me my mistake, goddammit."

"It was that forgery in the Abercrombie files. Had me snookered completely. Then I realized, if Abercrombie sent your cousin a rifle in a new caliber and asked for a story, Lon would have written the story. He had to keep the bargain. Part of his noblesse oblige, or whatever you fancy donkeys call it. But he didn't write no piece on reloading the .264, and I ought to know, as I read every word he ever wrote."

Lon! It was Lon's decency reaching out of the grave to bring me down! I almost had to laugh. That is what I loved about Lon, and that is what betrayed me.

I was speechless. Finally, I realized I had only one question to ask. It was the only one that mattered.

"Why? Why does it matter to you, Swagger? Tell me. Did you love JFK, the myth? Do you wish you'd been a trusted knight of Camelot? Did you have a crush on Jackie? Did the brave little boy and girl at the funeral break your heart? Why, Swagger, why?"

"A young man in service to our country was murdered on November 22, 1963. He was handsome and beloved. Everyone who saw him admired him and trusted his judgment. In all eyes, he was a hero. He was slaughtered in the street without a chance. A bullet blew up his brain. He left a hole in society, children who weep today, everyone who knew him. Possibly you have heard of him."

"His name was John F. Kennedy."

"No, it wasn't. He was not the president of the United States, John F. Kennedy, about whom I give not a shit. The man I speak of was a Dallas police officer named J. D. Tippit, and like my father, he was doing his duty until someone killed him for it. So that is who I am. I am not a national avenger, I am not Captain America, I don't give a crap about Camelot. I am the dead policeman's son, and I did what I did to find out who really shot Officer Tippit. I am the dead policeman's boy."

"Swagger, you are a bastard. I know you think you've won. But you haven't. You have no idea where I am, who I am, what my circumstances are. Are you going to indict a dead man? Hugh Meachum is dust and ashes scattered across the countryside outside Hartford. He is a beloved hero, and if you try to bring him down, you will unleash unbelievable trouble on yourself. Meanwhile, I will keep going on and on and on, and you have no idea if I'm a mile from you right now or sitting at the North Pole under the nom de guerre S. Claus."

"Not so fast, Mr. Meachum. Maybe you ain't as tricky as you think. Your pal Niles Gardner shared your enthusiasm for this Nabokov, the Russian writer. Niles liked cross-language puns, wordplay, games, that sort of thing. He had one other thing in common. Like his hero, he suffered from a condition known as synesthesia. Because of some confusion in the brain pathways, he sees some numbers in color. He saw the number nine in color, red. That's why he had a pistol on his desk called a Mauser Red Nine. And when he came to cook up the last and best and deepest fake life for his pal and fellow Nabokov lover, Hugh Meachum, he paid a gamesman's tribute to his connection to Nabokov, to yours, and to Nabokov himself, by using synesthesia as the key. You were born from synesthesia. You're the child, the son, of the Red Nine, Mr. Meachum."

"Thin, Swagger. So thin. It tells you nothing."

"I ain't done yet. His smartest trick was the code that wasn't a code. It was what it was, in plain sight if you could see it. You don't even get it, do you?"

"This is nonsense," I said. "You've gone insane."

"He hung a name on you that gave it up if you could see it clearly. The name began with I-X, Mr. Meachum. Cross-lingual pun. I-X, from English into Latin. I-X, Mr. Meachum, meaning nine. You are the son of the Red Nine. Your new name is Dimitri Ixovich Spazny. Niles really loaded the Nabokov mayonnaise on this sandwich. The old butterfly catcher would be so impressed."

Niles! I thought. All these years later, tripping me up with his cleverness.

"When it came time for you to 'die,' you slipped into Russia and took up again as Dimitri Ixovich Spazny, of KGB, with all the contacts and the timing exactly right. You even own the gun company that manufactured the nine-millimeter I used in the fight in Moscow. As Yeltsin's pal and money guy, you also own, what, electricity, newspaper, taxicabs, the Izmaylovskaya mob, radio, the air, most of the water, half of Belgium, three quarters of Hong Kong, and what else?"

"By the time you move on me, I'll be someone else," I said, though my heart was hammering in my chest. "You're not fast enough. Brains are meaningless without speed."

"Then how come I know you're wearing tan cargo pants and a green shirt? How come I know you're resting on a chaise longue, in sunglasses, with a yellow tablet in your hand? How come I know you're drinking vodka? How come I know you're on your back porch, looking down across a mile of grass framed on either side by pine forest? How come I know there's a river a mile off?"

I swallowed—or should I say, I swallow. I had not seen that one coming. It hit me blindside. I suck for air, while in my stunned panic, I look for a spotter who is clearly, at this very second, eyeballing me through binoculars.

"You're lying on the chaise at your dacha down Ulysse Nardin Boulevard behind a thirty-foot green steel wall, in an area patrolled by an MVD special battalion. You're a mile from the Moscow River. The sun is setting there, Mr. Meachum, but the days are long, and it's light enough for a sniper."

Stronski! Stronski is out there somewhere.

"He's on the trigger now. A KSVK twelve-seven."

No understanding, no context, no empathy, no regret. Just the sniper's bullet. It was the ultimate application of the New Criticism.

"See you in hell, then, Sergeant."

"I'll be along soon," Swagger said, and hung up.

And so: yes, it's come to this. So be it. I've had a good life, maybe a great one. I loved my wife and never cheated on her, I loved my sons and saw them grow into fine men and fathers. I love my country and tried to serve it well. I fought its wars—

Never mind. With seconds left, it's time to face whatever's next with a clean breast. Talk about an unreliable narrator! Talk about a murderer with a fancy prose style! I killed Jimmy Costello. I blew his action and cover to the RCMP, and I knew he couldn't let himself be taken alive. I regret it and always will, but what if, in a few years, he— I just couldn't help myself.

And I killed Lon. I knew by the last move that Swagger was strong and my team was weak, and I bullied and forced Lon to go on that last, absurd mission, and he finally relented and died.

I regret both. Failures of nerve and character. I am so sorry. I deserve whatever it is I'm about to get and I hope

CHAPTER 24

Swagger threw the phone off into the trees somewhere.

Account closed, he thought.

He took a look around saw nothing but green. He tried to think of his next step but had some trouble concentrating. He looked at the wound in his battered hip. More blood than he'd expected. Maybe the bullet had ticked downward into the flesh instead of off into the air.

He didn't have any first aid or clotting agent. He peeled off his jacket and wadded it against the blood flow, but it quickly absorbed its limit, went magenta and heavy-damp, and proved useless.

Better get to the goddamn road so they can find me, he thought.

But downhill with a bad wound bleeding hard was not easy, particularly as he could feel the leg numbing out on him, and in time it ceased to work in coordination with the other leg, and there came a moment when he lost it, toppled forward, put a bruise into his spine, ripped the hell out of his arms rolling through brambles, felt his shirt rip, and hit a rock solid with his head, which was already concussed from the clout he'd delivered on the 42 Commando major.

He got himself up and put his hand on the wound. It wasn't gushing copiously, but he could feel the steady, warm liquefaction finding ways around his fingers. He got a little farther down and noticed that a sudden chill had come into the air, as well as a fog that eroded the edges of his vision.

He staggered over a hump and hit the road. He couldn't remember which way was which and realized it didn't matter. He'd never make it back to the house, and what was there except those two guys whose names he didn't remember and he knew they weren't worth a damn.

He began to shiver. Damn, so fucking cold.

He looked for a splash of sun to warm him up and saw an opening in the canopy a few yards ahead that admitted the light. He limped to it, falling once, then got to it and, of his own volition, decided to stop fighting gravity and let himself tumble into the dust.

It was warmer. In time, he saw someone approaching him. He tried to rise, but the man waved him back down as he rushed to him. Bob saw that it was his father, Earl.

"Dad!" he cried.

"Well, Bob Lee, damn, it's good to see you, boy."

Earl came to him and knelt down. Earl wore the uniform of the Arkansas state police, 1955, as he had on the last day of his life, and it was razor-sharp, in perfect duty condition, as it was always for Earl. He had the strong, kind, wise face of a hero, and he was everything a boy could love in a father.

"Dad, God, I've missed you, I missed you so much."

"Now there'll be plenty of time for a nice long visit, you'll tell me all the things you've seen."

"Dad, you—"

"Bob Lee, you just relax. I'm so proud of my son, you have made me so proud."

"I tried so hard, Dad, I didn't want to ever let you down and—"

"He's coming back, he's coming back."

Swagger blinked, and it wasn't his dad's face but some crew-cut young man's.

Bob coughed, realizing that the guy had just jacked a charge through him with an external defibrillator.

"Hit him again?" another medic asked.

"No, no, he's good, the lactate is going in fine, the adrenaline is taking effect, he's breathing again, his pulse is rising."

Swagger breathed, feeling clean air come into his lungs.

"Jesus Christ, you scared us," said Nick Memphis.

As Swagger's eyes cleared and the fog thinned, he lifted his head a bit and saw an ambulance, a batch of state police cars, a lot of police activity along the road, and above him, in the hands of another young man, a bottle of intravenous fluids feeding life through a brown tube into his arm. He lay on a stretcher; his hip was strongly bandaged and bound, but some numbing agent quelled the pain.

"Okay, STAT, let's move this man to the chopper and get him to Trauma. I'm staying on him to monitor vital signs."

"I'm riding too," said Nick, and he turned to Bob and said, "Baby, you were gone, you were in negative heartbeat, but we got you back, don't ask me how."

"I saw my dad, Nick," said Bob.

"And you will again," said Nick, "but I hope not for a long time."

A Note on Method

Readers should be assured that I've made a good-faith effort to play fair by the data established in *The Warren Commission Report*, *Case Closed* by Gerald Posner, and *Reclaiming History* by Vincent Bugliosi. Lee Harvey Oswald is always where those volumes say he was, and he always does what they say he did. All "conspiratorial business" takes place in times uncovered by any of the foregoing works. In my effort to construct a legitimate alternate narrative to the WC, I alter no known facts in order to make my argument tighter. I do reserve the novelist's right to reinterpret motive and reason.

For a demonstration of my method, take as an example the shooting from the Book Depository and Oswald's last run. I accept as factual the following: that he took three shots, that he cocked a last live cartridge into his chamber, that he walked across the ninety feet of the sixth floor, rifle in hand, that he hid the rifle at the head of the stairway down, that he escaped north up Elm and took a bus south down Elm, then a cab to his roominghouse on North Beckley in Oak Cliff, where he secured his revolver. Fifteen minutes later and a mile distant, he shot Officer Tippit, including a coup de grâce to the head. He was arrested in the Texas Theatre fifteen or so minutes after that. The Warren Commission, Posner, and Bugliosi agree on that.

To that historical record, I added motives and reasonable conjectures—that he planned to shoot when Kennedy was just below the sixth-floor window but somehow botched the opportunity; that he hurried all three shots at a diminishing target (exacerbating exponentially the likelihood of a miss on his last shot); that he was driven by a more pungent fear of his betrayers than he was of law enforcement, which drove him to an extremely foolhardy trip through the assassination zone to recover his .38; that he administered the final brain shot to Officer Tippit out of rage at his betrayal.

I should also add that all the firearms and reloading data in the book have been tested by myself and colleagues; it is possible to fire a Carcano bullet from the .264 Winchester Magnum case in a Model 70, with great velocity and accuracy. (NOTE: Firing a jacketed .267 Carcano bullet throught a .264 bore is not a recommended reloading practice, and the fact that we were able to do it without incident does not mean you will.) There are some tweaks I purposely left out to keep non–gun culture people from slipping into a coma, but in general, it is easily accomplished as I have described it.

I should add that I have deliberately avoided conspiracy books and have stayed out of assassination-community culture in hopes of not inadvertently picking up somebody else's intellectual property. If I have accidentally absorbed something by osmosis or random white noise, I do apologize. I mean to steal no one's bread.

I should also add that I made no inquiries into the state of the Abercrombie & Fitch firearms records and my account of their location and disposition is entirely fictitious.

Acknowledgments

Any book has a multitude of starting points. This one began on November 22, 1963, in the lunch hall of New Trier High School, in Winnetka, Illinois, where I got the news. I followed the events of the next three days with the concentration of any teenager whose world has just been rocked. And I followed the subsequent developments over time. It was the kind of thing that never went away.

I basically paused at each of the stations of the cross of assassination theory over the following forty-nine years. I believed the Warren Commission, then I believed Mark Lane and his compatriots (I never believed the secret surgery at Andrews Air Force Base, however; did anyone?), then I believed Posner and Bugliosi.

In my mind, it was pretty much settled history until John Carroll, the great editor of *The Baltimore Sun,* knowing I knew a thing or two about guns, asked me to cover Howard Donahue and the book *Mortal Error,* written about his theories, by Bonar Menninger. I met Howard, a Baltimorean through and through, I respected Howard, I liked Howard (who didn't?); however, like Swagger, I found his explanation of the third bullet convincing but thought he went off into the wild blue yonder by ascribing it to a Secret Service agent with an AR-15 in a following car. It was hard to believe such a thing could happen in front of two thousand witnesses and nobody would see it.

Later in the process, Howard invited me to lunch. By that time he'd been pretty well fried in the press and was looking for a new method to illustrate his idea; he asked me to write a novel expressing his theory. I politely declined. I guess my subconscious, however, took up the challenge, and in a way, this is the book that Howard wanted me to write. To do it, I had to come up with my own theory about the second-rifle/third-bullet mystery.

Somewhere in all this—I can't remember the exact chronology—I wrote a book called *Point of Impact*. It was inspired by the old *Sun* reporter Ralph Reppert's earlier account of Howard's theory in the *Sun* magazine. Howard had been one of the shooters in the tower at the H. P. White Ballistic lab in Maryland who took and hit the Oswald shots for CBS News's re-creation. That was what started Howard on his odyssey.

I picked up on the idea of a marksman in a tower solving a shooting problem against a time clock and later realizing from the angles and the speed that he'd just reenacted the JFK assassination. I had to come up with a shooter, and so, with the help of Carlos Hathcock, I invented Bob Lee Swagger.

The idea was that the actual assassins were using Swagger in another hit, casting him in the role of Lee Harvey Oswald, to their infinite regret. As I progressed, I lost faith in my ability to bring it off, and I lost faith in conspiracy theories (I think *Case Closed* came out around then), so I ultimately kept Swagger but ditched JFK. At one point, I went through the manuscript and got rid of all the JFK references. Alas, I am by nature sloppy, so I missed many, and those accidental survivors later became the joinery between *Point of Impact* and this book. That's how Hugh Meachum and Lon Scott came into it.

The most recent starting point was February 2011. I was writing a book called *Soft Target* and sitting around with my good pal Gary Goldberg in the living room. Somehow, the JFK assassination came up, and I performed my assassin-from-the-future routine, just as Richard does, and then I did riffs on the context of the Mannlicher-Carcano, the angles versus the proximity issue and several other subjects that I reuse in this book. We had a good old time, and I think there was hooch involved.

I said to Gary, "You know, maybe I ought to have Bob Lee Swagger solve the JFK conspiracy," and we got a hearty laugh out of that one, and one second later, I thought, You know what? That's a damn good idea. I *ought* to get Bob Lee Swagger to solve the JFK assassination.

The day after I finished *Soft Target,* I began *The Third Bullet.* It was a great ride, believe me. One of the best ever. Let me thank all those who pitched in.

First of all, Gary. He was with me from the start, and he became my researcher and contact with the world. He took care of all my computer glitches, dug up all the relevant WC testimony, found the new owners of Dal-Tex, and secured permission for me to go a-prowl in its mysterious (to me) insides. Gary even took over an eBay auction for me and got me the exact scope mount and Hollywood scope that LHO used. Gary was great.

Kathy Lally, who might be the basis of Kathy Reilly, put my wife and me up in Moscow and hauled us around with her husband, Will Englund. They are, jointly, the *Washington Post* correspondents in that most engaging city, as well as being old *Sun* alumni. In fact, Kathy invented my life back in 1982, when she prevailed on the debauched aristos who ran the *Sun* in those days to appoint me film critic. They probably wanted someone who would work for free.

My great friends and enthusiastic readers Lenne P. Miller, Bill Smart, Jay Carr, Jeff Weber, and Mike Hill were extremely supportive and enthusiastic. My editor at Simon & Schuster, Sarah Knight, was terrific and helped me reorganize the material into a more accessible form.

Barrett Tillman, the distinguished aviation and naval historian, was also an early reader and enthusiastic supporter. My good friend John Bainbridge returned to proofreading duties and, as usual, caught fifteen things I never would have.

Dave Emary, the brilliant technician at Hornady (he devised the 6.5 Creedmore) discussed Mannlicher-Carcano ballistics with me and revealed that he had come to a similar conclusion regarding the third bullet. He loaded a dummy .264 Win Mag/Carcano hybrid for me and sent it on with some other sample bullets doctored as we agreed the conspirators would have done them. I was introduced to Dave by Mark Keefe IV, the editor of *American Rifleman*.

My gun buddy Roger Troup also helped; it was under his auspices that we reloaded some .264 Win Mag/Carcano cartridges for real and tried them out in one of two pre-'64 Model 70s in that caliber I had bought for this project, by which we learned that not only was it feasible but the load produced excellent accuracy and velocity.

Through Roger, I met Bill Vanderpool, retired FBI Special Agent and firearms instructor. He patiently met with me and had many good ideas and contacts.

Dan Shea, the entrepreneur behind *Small Arms Review* and Long Mountain Outfitters of Henderson, Nevada, gave me counsel on suppressors circa 1963 and light machine guns circa 2012. I'm indebted to his wisdom and experience.

Also, Jeff Clemmer, of LWRC, the superb AR builder in Cambridge, Maryland, took me through the plant and coached me on the intricacies of the M-6s Blues 1–4 used in their unfortunate matchup with Swagger. I told him his guys were going to lose, but after all, they were up against Bob the Nailer! He was okay with that.

In Dallas, Scott W. Ehley, of International Capital, LLC, current owners of Dal-Tex, guided me through the building and answered my questions about its past. He was a very good guy to my enterprise, about which he knew nothing and which he took entirely on trust.

Dr. David Fowler, the chief medical examiner of Maryland and a good friend, gave me time and patience as he vetted my velocity-explosive theory of November 22, 1963. In the sci-fi tale that Richard tells Bob via Hugh's instructions, the time travel/location in space is a last gift from my late and wonderful friend Bob Lopez. *Vaya con Dios, amigo.*

And, of course, my wife, Jean Marbella. I have no doubt she would go out to Idaho and sit in a diner for a month to persuade Bob Lee Swagger to investigate *my* death, exactly as her doppelgänger does in this book. More to the point, she put up with my nutty enthusiasm, my purchase of four Mannlicher-Carcanos (it took that many to get one that would shoot!), my distraction, and my babbling on the subject of each new idea, and she made the coffee that got me going every single day, which may be why there's so much coffee in this book. She did all this while pursuing her own extraordinary career at the *Sun*.

Of course, no blame for errors should attach to any of these fine people; I and I alone am responsible.

About the Author

Stephen Hunter has written eighteen novels. The retired chief film critic for *The Washington Post,* where he won the 2003 Pulitzer Prize for Distinguished Criticism, he has also published two collections of film criticism and a nonfiction work. He lives in Maryland.